The Pirate Queen

The Pirate Queen

The Story of Grace O'Malley,
Irish Pirate

ALAN GOLD

NEW AMERICAN LIBRARY

New American Library
Published by New American Library, a division of
Penguin Group (USA) Inc., 375 Hudson Street,
New York, New York 10014, USA
Penguin Group (Canada), 90 Eglinton Avenue East, Suite 700, Toronto,
Ontario M4P 2Y3, Canada (a division of Pearson Penguin Canada Inc.)
Penguin Books Ltd., 80 Strand, London WC2R 0RL, England
Penguin Ireland, 25 St. Stephen's Green, Dublin 2,
Ireland (a division of Penguin Books Ltd.)
Penguin Group (Australia), 250 Camberwell Road, Camberwell,
Victoria 3124, Australia (a division of Pearson Australia Group Pty. Ltd.)
Penguin Books India Pvt. Ltd., 11 Community Centre,
Panchsheel Park, New Delhi - 110 017, India
Penguin Group (NZ), cnr Airborne and Rosedale Roads, Albany,
Auckland 1310, New Zealand (a division of Pearson New Zealand Ltd.)
Penguin Books (South Africa) (Pty.) Ltd., 24 Sturdee Avenue,
Rosebank, Johannesburg 2196, South Africa

Penguin Books Ltd., Registered Offices: 80 Strand, London WC2R 0RL, England

First published by New American Library,
a division of Penguin Group (USA) Inc.

First Printing, January 2006
10 9 8 7 6 5 4 3 2 1

NEW AMERICAN LIBRARY and logo are trademarks of Penguin Group (USA) Inc.

LIBRARY OF CONGRESS CATALOGING-IN-PUBLICATION DATA:

Gold, Alan.
The pirate queen : the story of Grace O'Malley, Irish pirate / Alan Gold
p. cm.
ISBN: 0-451-21744-6 (trade pbk.)
1. O'Malley, Grace, 1530?–1603?—Fiction. 2. Ireland—History—1558–1603—Fiction.
3. Women revolutionaries—Fiction. 4. Women pirates—Fiction. I. Title.
PR9619.4.G65P573 2006
823'.914—dc22   2005053424

Set in Centaur

Printed in the United States of America

Part the First

Chapter One

Dubhdara Castle, County Mayo, Ireland, 1544

"Granuaile!"

Silence, when the stone walls had finished reverberating with the boom of his voice.

"Damn you, madam! Granuaile, come here!"

He waited but there was no reply.

"Grainne of Umhaill, come here this minute or I'll thrash your backside."

Still insolent silence.

"Grace O'Malley!"

He used the hated English form of her name now, to show her how angry he was that she'd ignored his orders . . . and her only fourteen years old!

Still silence.

"GRACE!" he screamed in fury.

A darker silence followed, but this time it was an unnerving silence, as still as the air of a graveyard.

"Damn you, Grace O'Malley, obey the command of your father!"

Servants throughout the castle looked at each other and nodded in understanding. It was the clash they'd been expecting these seven years, the confrontation between daughter and father. It had been inevitable, ever since she'd stood in the center of the hall at the age of three, well past her bedtime, legs apart, hands on hips, telling the entire company of noblemen and women that she wouldn't go to bed when everybody else was having such a good time, she just wouldn't!

"Grace O'Malley, if you don't come here immediately, I shall set sail without kissing you farewell."

Again silence enveloped the stone castle as his demands evaporated like the mist. From the change in the timbre of his voice, the servants knew that the brave and invincible sea captain was about to surrender.

"I shan't bring you back the present I promised from Scotland."

The father held his breath. So did the entire castle, servants and all.

He realized then that he was beaten. He had to concede.

"Granuaile, darling, why won't you come down here and farewell your daddy? Come now, and I'll bring you two presents . . . two very special presents."

The servants dared not breathe, only prayed for a response.

"Very well, young lady, I'm going, but I shall bring you back nothing from Scotland."

Still silence. The servants barely restrained their grins. Another round to the daughter. By God, they thought, but she was a brave girl.

"Damn you, madam, come here immediately and kiss your father goodbye, or I'll spank your arse so hard you won't be able to sit for a month."

Now even the servants were beginning to think that Grace had played the game of brinkmanship for too long. Until they heard the father say, "Well, I shall be mounting my horse and leaving."

This last shot was more a plea than a statement.

And when the response came, it was barely audible.

"I shan't come."

"You will come. You'll come now, madam, or I'll scour the castle and drag you out by your ungrateful hair."

"I shan't! So there!"

Those who were brave enough to risk Owen Dubhdara's temper looked out of the windows of the butteries or the pantries or the bedchambers to see what was happening. He was standing within the bailey, holding the reins of his horse. There were four other men with him, though these were mounted. Each had a smile on his face. Each was like a father to Owen Dubhdara's willful daughter.

It was still early morning and Dubhdara the chieftain was anxious to ride the two miles to the hidden cove in Clew Bay where he'd moored his ship and there catch the outgoing tide.

"If you don't come immediately, madam, I'll thrash your bottom and no mistake."

"When Mother said I couldn't come to sea any more, you didn't fight for me. You remained silent, Owen Dubhdara, and you didn't come to the aid of your Granuaile. I shall not kiss the father goodbye when I should be going with him."

Owen Dubhdara shook his head. His other children weren't this stubborn; they accepted the will of their parents. They'd all lined up to kiss their father goodbye.

Only Granuaile had been absent.

Granuaile! She of the flaming red hair and the evil temper. Fourteen years old, and already ruling the castle as though it was her domain!

He looked at his men. They hid their smiles, held their horses still, reins taut, eager to be off, yet not wanting to miss a moment of their captain's certain defeat at the hands of an overwhelming enemy.

"Well, what should I do?" he asked.

Donnal Connaire, who had been sailing with the captain for thirty years, and with his father before him, shrugged his shoulders. "Take her with us. She's more boy than girl, and she loves the sea fiercely. How can you lock a spirit like hers up in pretty dresses? She's loved by the men. They'll be as downhearted as she if you leave her behind."

Owen breathed heavily in the cold morning mist. The night had been squally, and first light had brought heavy gray clouds which threatened more downpours; he was keen to be underway before the rain started up again and weighed down the sails.

From high in the castle Granuaile's mischievous voice came again. "Tell me, Father, if I was a boy, would you take me? Is it my sex that keeps me here?"

He remained silent.

"It is, isn't it?"

Owen didn't know what his daughter was planning, but knowing Grace O'Malley, it was something spectacular. Like the time he'd been entertaining a Spanish grandee and suddenly the music had started and she'd entered the room dancing like a trollop from Cordoba; the grandee had nearly fallen off his chair, he'd laughed so hard.

Or the time they'd only just managed to outrun an Algiers pirate ship with twice their cannon, and as his galleon was rowed furiously toward the horizon, Grace had climbed into the riggings, lifted her skirts and bared her arse at them.

But her true spirit had been demonstrated only last year when he had been returning from a trading trip to Spain and had been attacked by a seventy-five-foot English man-o'-war. Outgunned, and with a wind which favored the Englishman, they'd been boarded, and Owen had immediately sent Grace down into the hold for her protection.

He thought she'd gone, and suddenly he was faced with a cutlass-wielding sailor, skilled in the art of attack. Owen lost his sword and was about to be skewered, when from nowhere young Grace pounced on the Englishman's back, screaming like a demon. The other English sailors looked up, distracted, and the Irish crew gained courage; it turned the battle. They just managed to beat off the English, and to sail to safe waters off the southern Irish shore, where the O'Sullivans gave them shelter and patched up the wounded.

But it wasn't just her courage and determination that made the grizzled sailors love the child. She'd gained her sea legs almost before she was able to walk upon the land, and even though she was still a child, she knew as much about sailing as some of the hands. Yet while grown men had to learn the ropes and the ways of the sea, Grace seemed to have absorbed the knowledge as though it was her mother's milk. She could look up at a clean sky and declare that within two days there would be terrible storms; she could look down at an opaque sea and tell the men to drop nets for there were fish for the catching. More and more the men relied as much on Grace's skills as they did on her father's.

Yes, Grace was loved by the men, but now she had developed breasts and a woman's body, he had to be more careful of her. She herself knew this, because instinctively she was becoming more modest. And because she was becoming a woman, her mother, Margaret, had determined that she'd go to the convent and gain an education, that she'd learn the ways of older women, that she'd be married off in a year or two to a rich Irish nobleman and lead a life of ease and comfort. Some Irish girls married when they were thirteen or fourteen, but Owen had held Grace back—he wanted to strike a particularly favorable bargain, and the right union hadn't yet presented itself.

Moments later, Grace appeared. She was dressed in breeches and a tunic, and her head was covered by a scarf. She walked toward him, unflinching, staring him in the eye. He loved her with all his heart, this proud and beautiful and strong girl. Nothing cowed her, not her father's command, nor her mother's determination, nor the priest's authority. Nothing! By God, Owen thought, she'll be a handful for any husband.

"So, Father," she said, standing close to him, "is it because I'm a girl that you won't take me to sea any more?"

"Your mother has decided that the sea is no place for a girl who is soon to become a woman."

Grace smiled and Owen's heart sank.

"Then," she said defiantly, ripping off her scarf, "your troubles are at an end, because I've become a boy."

She'd shorn off her beautiful red hair. He looked in horror, for what little was left was to her collar. Where once it had cascaded like a burnished waterfall down her back, now it was a pitiful crop, a scrawny and boyish bush which made her look like . . . like . . . a lad.

And Owen Dubhdara burst into gales of laughter. The four men on horseback looked on in horror, caring little for their captain's amusement but knowing what would happen when the mistress saw what her daughter had done.

"Captain," Donnal Connaire said, knowing he'd feel the sharp edge of the mistress's tongue later, "now you *have* to take her. And we'll call her Grainne Mhaol."

Grace O'Malley looked up at her old friend, a man she loved as fiercely as she loved her daddy. "Grace the Bald," she said. "Yes, I like the name. Might I ride with you, Donnal?"

And without being invited, she grasped his arm and swung herself onto the back of his horse.

With a sigh the Baron of Murrisk mounted and kicked his horse in the flanks. "Quick," he said, "let's get out of here before Margaret sees the disaster her daughter has become. . . ."

More than life, she loved the sea. It was everything to her. Others of her age might play games or ride to hounds or knit and tat and embroider cushions and tapestries, but not Grace O'Malley.

She loved the smell of the salt air, the swell of the waves. She loved the rhythm of the ship, the fact that it was as close to nature as it was possible to be. She loved the foreign ports and the adventure of unknown seaways. She loved the camaraderie of the men, though hated their vicious quarrels and all-too-frequent knife fights. She loved the singing of the shantyman as he laid out the massive ropes, the way in which he made the song last till the last rope was pulled and the sheet was in place.

For Grace there was only one life and that was atop a heaving deck watching the white-topped waves far below carry her to some mystical port in the Indies or the western coast of Europe, or around the Pillars of Hercules into the Middle Sea where there were vast islands on which grew olives and oranges, limes and lemons, and other strange and sensuous fruits. Where the young men had the darkest of skin and flashing eyes and hair as black as pitch, and didn't mind baring their backsides when they swam; men whose penises were shorn of foreskins and whose backs were as hairy as their fronts, lovely hair about which Grace O'Malley fantasized night after night.

And it was the sea which made all this possible. It was the sea which fed her family and gave them great wealth, for her father was permitted by the Great

Council of Chieftains of Ireland to send his caravels and galleys to trade with Spain and Portugal and France and Scotland, though not with Galway, which the damnable English controlled.

They were now two days out to sea and Grace was keeping out of her father's sight, though it wasn't easy, even on a large, overcrowded ship. There were two hundred men aboard, most of them spending their day hunched over oars, the helmsman trying to catch the waves and ease their straining with the power of the sea.

She loved the overcrowding, the hustle and bustle, the sharing of food and drink and even space. But at times she craved to be alone, and just last night she'd taken a blanket and huddled in the crow's nest. Up there the movement of the ship was magnified. She rolled with the swell then lay down, her body bent around the mast, her eyes taking in the vast canopy of stars moving this way and then that way, this way and that, until she fell into a deep sleep. She awoke the next morning as night swill was thrown overboard and men complained loudly to each other as they hung their arses over the side, clasping the riggings and shitting into the sea.

She climbed down and mingled with the crew as they breakfasted on beef or lamb stew and bread and apples and ale from the galley.

"Grace, child," called her father who was standing beside the helmsman. "There's no point in avoiding me. I know where you've been, so tonight you might as well sleep in your bunk. And it's not me you should be fearing but your Ma, for when we get back to land she's going to be in a terrible temper; you'll go to convent school that very day, and you'll not come out until you walk down the aisle."

"I don't need to go to another school, Father. And I certainly don't need any more tutors. I already know Latin and Greek; I read and write perfect Gaelic; I know the Al Jabr of the Arabs, and I know the geometry and the mathematics of the Greeks, and much more besides."

Owen beamed. He loved to hear how clever his daughter was.

Grace had a precocious intelligence and often drove both her father and the crew mad asking question after question. When they were in foreign ports, she would insist on picking everybody's brains about the condition of the inhabitants, the economy of the country, its history and culture. What, Owen wondered, could monks and nuns teach a mind like hers?

He looked at his crew, who were listening in amusement, and shouted, "D'you hear that, you ignorant pack of thieves and brigands all? You hear what my little Grainne Mhaol knows? Things which you bastards could never begin to understand, reading and writing and mathematics and such. And she only fourteen years."

Defiantly, one of the men shouted back, "Jesus rot you, Captain. I can read."

Owen looked for the man, and saw who he was. It was Padraig Betagh from Meath, whose life Owen had saved countless times.

"So you can read, can you, Padraig? Well, I'd guess that the only word you can read is 'Whorehouse', and that in twenty languages."

The men burst out laughing, Padraig loudest of all. Grace climbed up the steps to the aft-castle and sat defiantly on the windlass beside her father. He put his hand on her head and ran his fingers through her shockingly short hair. "You've done a terrible thing, Missy. That hair was your mother's pride and joy. She sat for hours plaiting it and knotting it. Now her fingers are free, she'll find new things to do with them, and if I'm halfway to being right, it'll be my neck she'll knot for bringing you aboard."

"Father," she said softly, "my life is at sea, not as mistress of a castle."

"Darling girl, you can't be at sea as a grown woman. You know the rules of the sea; no man will sail with you. What will you be? A captain? Of what ship? And of which crew?"

"But the men know me, and like me," she said anxiously.

"Certainly they do. As a daughter. But order them, give them commands, lead them into battle, and they'll look for a captain and not a woman. I'm sorry, child, but you were born of the wrong sex. You're as brave a man as any I sail with, but you've got womanhood between your legs. You can cut off your hair, but you can't grow manhood."

Grace turned to her father. "They will follow me! You'll see! I shall be cap-

tain of this and other ships, and I'll sail the seas and fight galleons of the English fleet, and I'll sink caravels and capture their cargoes and we'll be the richest
people in all Ireland. And then Mother will say that you did the right thing in
taking me to sea."

Chapter Two

Bunowen Castle, County Connaught, May 1548

Margaret O'Malley was happy at last. For a year since the return to shore of her shorn daughter, whom the whole world seemed to be calling Grace the Bald, she had been in a state of fury. The moment the voyage ended and the child reappeared in the castle with her apprehensive father, the mother insisted that her youngest child be sent to a convent for three years, and then an abbey—where Grace had been for the past twelve months—in order to change her from a wild and unruly ship's trophy into a girl of marriageable prospect. And the result was pleasing.

Margaret O'Malley was fussing about her daughter as though this was a marriage of love and not a political union between the O'Malleys and the O'Flahertys. It was a good match: Donal O'Flaherty was next in line as the leader of the clan, and with the marriage came the castles of Bunowen and Ballinahinch. The O'Malley land gave the O'Flahertys security to the north, and the O'Flaherty land gave the O'Malleys security to the south; together the two clans would be a force against the increasingly strong English.

Certainly her soon-to-be-husband was older than Grace by some twenty years, and had a fearsome temper, but the young woman seemed tamed after a year of additional learning in the abbey. She would behave herself properly as a mistress of the O'Flaherty, and she would bear Donal sturdy children, for she had grown into a voluptuous woman of eighteen years with wide hips and a full bosom, and her hair had grown back to something of its once-flowing glory.

Standing back looking at her, Margaret was greatly pleased.

"My, but you're a beautiful girl, and no mistake," she said.

Grace curtsied as she'd been shown by the mother of Donal O'Flaherty. It had taken quite some persuasion, and a lot of screaming and shouting, before she had finally agreed to the marriage, but eventually it had dawned on Grace that a life with a man was better than a life in a convent, as her mother had threatened if Grace didn't obey her father's dictates.

All the other symbols of good luck and fortune for the wedding had been carefully attended to by the old women of the village of Bunowen. They'd scrutinized the color of her dress, which was a deep blue. Indeed, so important was the color that the maids of the village had been instructed to check carefully that there was no green in the stitching, because the green of Ireland was the most beautiful color of all the world and the fairies seeing green would get jealous and steal the bride away. A new horseshoe had been carefully forged by the blacksmith so that Grace could hold it pointing to her breast as she walked down the aisle and be certain in the knowledge that her luck would never run out.

The straw boys, lads from the village dressed up in straw, who would appear suddenly at the reception, dance and then disappear again, had been organized. Nobody, not even the old maids, could remember the origin of this good-luck custom, but no wedding in Ireland could be held without it, or the bride and groom would be in terrible trouble for the first two years of their married life.

And most importantly, the rings had been inspected by the priest and had been declared fit to be worn.

Even Grace, at first apprehensive about the wedding, was getting excited. It would be a change from the routine of the convent where she'd lived previously, and the abbey in which she'd studied. When her father had first told her of the union and explained how the joining of the lands would strengthen the clan, she had been overjoyed finally to be escaping the confines of her convent life.

But her mind had changed when she'd met Donal O'Flaherty. His reputation as a hard and mad man preceded him. In the towns and villages of northwest Ireland he was called Donal-an-Chogaidh, Donal of the Battles. He didn't just win victories over his enemies, he chased the very last man to ground, even though the day was his, and slaughtered entire armies, giving no quarter and showing no mercy. He had a disposition as fearsome as the scars on his cheek and a reputation as a demon in human form.

To assert his growing power over the neighboring chieftains, and to warn off the English who were looking at western Ireland with increasingly avaricious eyes, Donal had imported his own army of mercenaries—five hundred fierce fighting men from Scotland, known as Gallowglass—who promised to blacken the eye of anyone who coveted the O'Flaherty lands in a way which displeased their leader.

Owen O'Malley kept to himself his disappointment about the end of his daughter's sailing life, concerned about reigniting Margaret's fury. In some respects this was a sad day, for there was many a discontented bride of an unhappy marriage and he knew how Grace's heart yearned to be at sea. But a strong union between the two clans was far more important than her desire to sail. He'd tried to put his daughter's mind at rest, saying that because this was a political union, she would lead her own life and be mistress of her own court; that she would have little to do with her tempestuous husband, other than bear the occasional child and run his household; but this did little to assuage her fears in the face of her future husband's reputation.

"They're all nothing but stories, darling girl," he sneered contemptuously. "Mere stories. Would I marry you to a beast and a monster, you, my very precious bald Granuaile? Stories abound in Ireland, and you'll go crazy if you believe a quarter of them. Why, do you know what the O'Connors of Sligo say about me? That I'm the son of a Moorish prostitute and that I was suckled by a walrus."

Her father burst out laughing. "As if my father knew any Moorish women, let alone whores . . . though I'm not prepared to deny the story about me being suckled by a walrus is true."

His humor didn't appease Grace, who told him that if ever Donal was rude or crude or aggressive toward her, she'd slit him from ear to ear with a dagger. Owen beamed as he listened, pleased that the damned abbey and convent hadn't completely ruined his daughter's spunk, but stopped smiling when he looked at the face of his wife.

Margaret O'Malley listened to her daughter's threat, and rounded on her husband. "See, you idiot. Listen to her speak. Killing her husband, indeed. It's all your fault. You taking her to sea with those ruffians. She's less woman than sea louse, thanks to you. Look at the harm you've done . . ."

As the wedding neared, Grace became accustomed to the idea of marrying Donal—she had no alternative, for the contracts had been drawn up and signed and witnessed by the priest, and if she'd tried to refuse the marriage, there would have been war, and it would have caused the deaths of many of her parents' liegemen that she loved.

And so she determined that she would give Donal a couple of children, but would never retire to the life of a mistress of a castle. Instead she'd spend her days riding and exploring Ireland and going back to sea in her very own ship, for within the articles of the marriage contract she would possess her own fortune, so she could buy whatever it was she wanted, including a ship and a captain. She'd present Donal with heirs, then live her own life and to Hell with him.

Grace's family led her out of the bridal dressing chamber and onto a path strewn with petals. Servants and members of the O'Flaherty clan gathered and were standing like an honor guard along the path to the castle church to see what the new mistress looked like. A small pipe and drum band accompanied a harpist playing a jig.

As Grace appeared, the women threw petals over her, and two maids came forward, one placing on her head a crown of flowers intertwined with birch leaves and bound by strips of the bark of an ash, the other handing her an identical crown which she knew she had to place upon her husband's head moments after they kneeled before the altar of God.

They had almost reached the church when a tall man wearing the mask of the Devil suddenly jumped out and blocked their path.

"Are you Christians who enter here?" he demanded.

Mustering a strong voice for all to hear, Grace called out, "We are all Christians."

"And if your marriage is blessed with children, will they be baptized in the font of the church, or will you hand them to me to do with as I will?"

"My children will follow in the way of Christ," she shouted.

And with a cry of pain, the acolyte of the Devil stepped out of her path, to the applause of the onlookers. Owen looked at his daughter with pride. Many brides went to pieces and burst into tears when the Devilman appeared. But he knew that his Grace would give as good as she got.

And so they entered the dark enveloping world of the church, with its musty smell of candles and incense, the brilliance of the outside light suddenly transmuting to ochres and greens and blues as the sun shone through the painted and leaden windows. Adjusting to the gloom, Grace followed her father and mother down the aisle. Standing on either side were the villagers from the lands of the O'Malley, many of whom had journeyed all the previous day to attend the wedding of their Granuaile, whom they'd known from baby to woman. And with them, though distinct in their precedence in their own church, were the servants and friends of the O'Flahertys.

And sitting at the back of the church were Donnal Connaire and many of the friends she had known from her father's sailing ships, men she'd grown up with, who'd been like parents to her. She fought back tears as Donnal winked and blew her a kiss.

The wedding party walked up to the altar and smiled at the priest. He looked embarrassed, and immediately apologized for the absence of Donal, who had been unavoidably detained.

"Why weren't we told?" asked Owen disdainfully for all the congregation to hear.

Liam O'Flaherty, younger brother to the future clan leader, spoke up, annoyed with the presumption of these O'Malleys who, for the past three days, had been treating the castle as if it was their very own, ordering servants around and criticizing this and that. "Brother Donal was hunting this morning, as he hunts every morning. If he's hunting a big stag, then nothing so trivial and ordinary as a wedding is going to interrupt him . . . unless it's hare coursing," he said, a malicious grin on his face.

Owen was about to answer, when Grace turned on the young man and said, "Then like a good little brother, go find Donal and tell him that his bride is waiting. And that if he isn't here shortly, I shall be doing my own hunting."

A shudder spread through the ranks of the O'Flahertys, though those in the O'Malley gathering who knew her smiled and wondered if the other clan knew what they'd let themselves in for. Never had anyone heard a young woman speak in this way to the brother of the O'Flaherty. And this was no way to start a wedding. Liam's eyes flared in fury at the way this foal had just spoken to him, and in front of family and friends and servants. He was about to give vent to his anger, when there was a commotion from the west wing door of the church and Donal appeared, dressed for the hunt, shouting his apologies.

"Damn me if my horse didn't go lame on me," he said to nobody in particular. "Sorry for being late. Now, let's get on with it, shall we. There's a full day of hunting left ahead of us. Priest, begin . . ."

With an audible sigh of relief, the priest opened the missal to begin celebrating the wedding.

But before he could say even a few words, Grace looked at her future husband in annoyance and commanded the priest, "Wait, Father!"

He looked up at her in shock, but she paid him no attention. Instead, she addressed Donal softly and calmly, "Husband-to-be, do you not owe a few words of apology to the Lord Jesus for being late for the most sacred ceremony of marriage?"

The whole congregation held its breath. The clan leader O'Flaherty and his wife looked at the snip of a girl in astonishment. First she'd spoken to their son Liam in a disrespectful way. Then she'd spoken over the priest, and now, if you please, she had the temerity to address her future husband directly, and in front of everyone, as if she was already mistress of the castle. They looked at each other in horror.

Donal too was taken aback, and looked at her in surprise. He'd met her on a couple of occasions. She'd been quiet and compliant then, just as a wife should be. He'd been quite happy to marry her for the lands, but he'd also discovered she had a good body and sound teeth and her breath didn't stink, all of which was a bonus. However, to be spoken to in this manner by such a young woman, little more than a girl. . . . He looked at the congregation and the fury on the face of the O'Malleys and decided that an apology to Jesus was no big thing. Besides, he'd been wrong to delay, and saying sorry would do no harm.

He crossed himself and said softly, "Lord God and Blessed Jesus, I'm sorry I was late."

The priest smiled and turned again to his prayer book, but as he opened his mouth, Grace said, "And do you not also, husband-to-be, owe an apology to your own parents, who have been standing here waiting on your pleasure?"

Donal's mother let out a cry of surprise, but then remained silent, holding her breath for the onslaught.

The Master of the O'Flaherty looked first at his father, with whom he shared the title, and then at his future bride; he was in a state of fury which, in other circumstances, would have driven him to draw his sword and run the offender through. But the O'Flaherty needed this marriage and, despite his fury, he knew to keep his mouth shut. Donal's mouth was little more than a thin scar as he hissed, "I'm sorry, Mother and Father."

The priest, sweating like a pig, didn't even have time to look down at his missal before Grace again spoke. "And husband-to-be, my parents were also kept waiting by your tardiness."

Her mother hissed, "Granuaile, enough!"

"Well," said Grace, waiting.

Now Donal's eyes were narrow slits of hate. "I'm sorry to the Clan O'Malley," he shouted. "I'm sorry to every fuchking man, woman and child in the whole fuchking world. Now can we get on with the damn wedding before the English come and kill all the deer!"

Smiling, Grace turned to the priest and said, "Father, I think my husband-to-be is now ready to marry me."

Grace could still hear the noise of carousing seeping in through the cracks in the stone and wafting through the wooden floorboards.

She had been waiting for over two hours. The candle had burned down two markers, increasing her fury every time it guttered in the chill wind which blew through the window. She had prayed, sung herself songs of the sea and the Isles to amuse herself, called for a maid, who never showed up, and even thrown a chamber-pot downstairs to remind her new husband that there was also life up-stairs and a duty to be performed.

But he'd ignored her from the moment she placed the crown on his head and the ring on his finger. Yes, he'd kissed her on the cheek and the congrega-tion had cheered and thrown oak leaves, but she was sure he'd shown more pas-sion for his horse than for her.

Her parents and the villagers had ridden to the couple's new home and wished everybody health and happiness, then had begun their long journey home, leaving Grace without a friend or a member of her family, or even a ser-vant of her own.

Alone, she had retreated inside her new castle and begun the job of look-ing around, even though she was still dressed in the silks of her blue wedding gown. But when she entered the great hall and approached the head of the table where her husband was dining and drinking with his friends and family, he com-pletely ignored her. Others turned their backs in payment for the insult she'd done to him in church.

Their laughter increased in volume, their drinking became more frantic, their eating more urgent. She looked at them with disdain, then slowly walked around the hall and positioned herself in front of the roaring fire. And there she stood, silent and accusing. And stood. And stood.

One by one, the men and women in the room stopped laughing and drinking, until all eyes were on the proud and imposing figure, waiting for her to speak. But she didn't. She remained silent, merely standing there, surveying all the faces.

Some began to feel embarrassed; others looked down at their wooden platters to avoid her piercing gaze. But her husband Donal was not to be tricked again by this nothing of a girl.

"Well, Mistress of the Castle," he boomed, intent on demeaning her in public, "do you interrupt to castigate us again? Are you here to correct my manners a second time? Why are you standing there?"

"Because it's time for my husband to retire to his bed and satisfy both his marriage vows and his new wife."

All the men and women in the room burst into laughter. But not Donal, who took the remark as another insult.

"Madam, I'll come to you when I'm ready."

She nodded silently, turning to a servant and telling him, "So that I shall know in the future, inform me of how much ale your master must drink before he's ready and able to bed a young woman."

Despite themselves, the entire room again erupted in gales of laughter, but it quickly ceased when they turned to Donal and saw that his face was as black as a thundercloud.

"Do you think I need ale to bed a woman?"

"I don't know, husband. You haven't attempted to bed me yet."

Even Donal's mother laughed at this. She was beginning to warm to this spirited girl, whose sharp tongue was a good match for her son's wicked temper.

Donal realized that he was losing this match of word skills. He'd never been good with words. Fighting, yes! Hunting, certainly! But he couldn't match learning with learning.

"I shall bed you in my own time, madam. I need no ale to give me courage, nor do I need your tongue to goad me to my duties."

"Good, for if you've had sufficient ale to give you courage, then I'd like to show you that there are other uses to which I intend to put my tongue once we're alone. So, husband, once you've stopped drinking with your friends, come to bed and I'll teach you much that you don't know."

If there was any restraint before now, this last remark made everybody howl with laughter; some cheered, some clapped, and some even stood on chairs and tables and threw food at her as they did with skillful entertainers.

His eyes glazed in fury, and not knowing properly how to respond, Donal turned to one of his kinsmen, the brother of his mother, and said, "Seamus, I'm busy. Why don't you take my young wife to bed and deflower her? She's obviously in need of the company of men, and I can't be bothered with one so skinny and unappealing."

Many of the men burst out laughing. But only the men, for the women suddenly bristled at this particular insult. His Uncle Seamus, drunk and barely capable of standing, struggled up from his chair, suffused with sudden sexual excitement at the thought of having such a young and pretty girl. The room grew silent as he staggered toward Grace.

As he stood before her, she snatched a knife from a nearby table, grabbed the old drunken man by his hair, and spun him suddenly and viciously around. The room gasped in shock.

"How dare you insult me, Donal O'Flaherty," she shouted, close to tears, as she dug the knife's point into the old man's throat. "I come to you as your bride and this is what you offer me!"

The servants stood around the hall, looking on in horrified amazement.

"Donal!" screamed Seamus. "Donal, for God's sake, she'll kill me."

Men of the family stood up and drew their weapons.

Softly, Grace said, "If it's a slaughter you want, then this old bastard will be the first to die. Then the rest of you, for be assured that my family will descend on this castle like Joshua descended on Jericho, and nothing will be left standing. Now put up your weapons, for I'm off to my bed."

Grace pushed Seamus roughly away from her. He fell against the table and then to the floor. Grace forced herself to smile, turned, and walked slowly to the door. Breathing a sigh of relief when she realized no one was going to challenge her, she ascended the stairs to her bedchamber to await the consequences of her actions.

She'd lain awake since then, alternating between indignation and fear. She might have been forced by her drunken husband to stand up for herself, but she realized now that she'd never be forgiven by the family. Never.

The door was flung open violently. Grace's eyes snapped open and she saw him standing in the doorway, encased in light from the torches in the outer hall. She glanced over to the candle and saw that another two hours had burned down. God, she thought, it must be near sunrise. She looked back at him, his face full of fury, and knew that she was going to get the beating of her life.

He weaved around, patently too drunk to stand, his state attested to by a couple of servants who had obviously carried him up to bed.

Staggering, he almost fell into their bedchamber, though he managed to totter and pitch forward onto the bed. And he lay there, face down, snoring loudly. His servants stood watching, grinning like two mischievous dogs.

Grace sat up in bed and ordered them, "Come here and carry your master to another bedroom."

The older man stepped forward, though still not inside the bedchamber, and said, "The master ordered us to take him to your bed."

"And I'm ordering you to take him elsewhere."

The servant shook his head, and started to say, "I can't do that, because—"

"Listen to me, and listen carefully, for it's the very last time I'll say this. I'm mistress of Ballinahinch. You'll obey my orders or I'll dismiss you from my service, and I'll ensure that no castle or house nor even piggery in Ireland will give you work. Now, remove your mistress's husband by the time I've counted to five, or pack your belongings and see how warm the outside world feels."

The two servants stared at her, trying to determine the lesser of the two evil choices with which they were faced. They'd seen her with old Seamus and weren't prepared to take the risk. They hurried into the bedchamber, picked up their master by his armpits and dragged him mumbling and snoring into the hall. They closed the door, and Grace, overwhelmed by the first few hours of her marriage, burst into tears of fear and loneliness.

✦　　✦　　✦

The following morning nobody appeared at her chamber, so Grace dressed herself and went downstairs. The castellan was there, organizing the clearing away of the remnants of last night's wedding feast.

"Where are my maids?" Grace asked.

Without bothering to look up, he said curtly, "After your treatment of the Lord Seamus last night, I suppose they're too frightened to attend to your needs."

"Then, Castellan, I order you summarily to dismiss all my maids and servants. Send them packing immediately. Give them no pay except for what they are due. Allow them no notes of approval or reference."

He was looking at her now—in astonishment. "But . . ."

"It will be done today. They're of no use to me; they didn't arrive at my chamber to dress me, nor to give me fresh washing water. I'm better off without them, and their dismissal will save my husband money. See to it immediately," she ordered, and then walked to the kitchen.

Horrified, the castellan shouted, "Not without my master's permission."

"I am your mistress, and you'll do it or suffer the same fate."

He looked at her coldly. He was not afraid of this young spit of a thing. But as new mistress of the castle, the servants were her responsibility.

"Madam, they've served in this castle for many years."

"No longer," Grace said from across the room. "If they don't serve me, then they're not servants. See that my orders are carried out immediately."

"I shall have to confer with my master."

"You can confer with the Devil if you want, but they go. And while you're about it, bring me the castle records. I wish to ensure that you're serving my husband well and aren't lining your own pockets with kickbacks from the merchants of the village."

He blanched. "But the records are in Latin, my lady, not Gaelic."

She smiled. "That's excellent, because I speak Latin fluently, and Greek, and I'm very good with arithmetic and geometry."

Grace was gratified to see that the supercilious little man was starting to look most uncomfortable. "Now, bring me the records for I wish to check every purchase made and how many pounds have been paid out for them. If the receipts and the payments don't tally to the farthing, and any of my husband's money has found its way into your pocket, then it'll be the scaffold for you."

The castellan stood speechless. His master was drunk and useless upstairs, and this whippet of a girl was dealing with him as though she was the mistress of the castle. And then he remembered that she was the new mistress of the castle, and the precariousness of his position quickly dawned on him. He remained silent.

Grace knew by the sudden grayness of his face that he fully comprehended her power.

"Perhaps, mistress, if your maids were to come to you now, they could dress you and tend to your needs."

"No, tomorrow morning will be time enough. And I'll have my breakfast now. Tell the cooks that I like oatmeal with a raw egg mixed in, and a glass of ale to wash it down."

With that she turned and walked out into the inner courtyard to explore her new domain. She smiled to herself. It was a good victory. It would spread her reputation throughout the castle in a matter of moments. All would now be wary of the new mistress . . . all except her new husband.

God, but how would she deal with him when he woke with a head like a turnip?

Hertfordshire, England, 1549

Elizabeth sat demurely beside the window which overlooked the long and narrow ribbon of road that disappeared over the hill and into nowhere. For beyond the hills of the house in which she'd lived these past years was a world which Elizabeth had almost forgotten. Since she'd been taken in at Hatfield and protected as stepdaughter to the late Queen Dowager, dear Catherine Parr, she had spent her life confined to the house and its grounds, and was allowed only occasional visits to the nearby village.

For being the daughter of Anne Boleyn, beheaded as a witch and a seducer and a treasonous whore, Elizabeth had been regarded with deep suspicion by those in Henry's court. And while her father had been alive she had been prey to his moods and his hatred for her dead mother; with each new wife's lips whispering in his ear, her survival had been due to luck more than guile.

Death had been a constant threat for Elizabeth as she grew up, and only in her short time with her father's last wife, the beloved Catherine, had her life been free of fear.

Then, when her dear brother Edward had assumed the throne, Elizabeth had begun to look forward to a life of increased security. However, it seemed she was again in danger of being thrown to the wolves.

The news had come yesterday from London that a party of men from the Royal Council was coming to see her, to interrogate her! She hadn't slept last night. She had lain awake, pondering her answers, and the almost certainty of her demise. And now the moment had arrived. Elizabeth watched in trepidation as the horsemen appeared over the hill. At first they were mere specks on the horizon, little more than dark interruptions to the green velvet lawn of grass and the surrounding copses of oaks; but they grew larger and larger as they neared her home, and with their size came the threat they posed.

She had dressed modestly in black with white lace. Her long red hair was tied in a bun and encased in a black lace mesh. She was freshly washed and her cheeks were free of the rouge she had often put on when Catherine had entertained in the house. For this interview she had to be the epitome of modesty and decorum and godliness. Every move, every attitude would be reported to the court, and those who had Edward's ear would magnify everything untoward that Elizabeth did or said.

She watched the four men, capes billowing in the strong breeze, gallop through the massive wrought-iron gates and ride through a scampering flock of sheep, scattering them hither and thither through the grounds. Imperiously, they reined in their horses and called for additional stableboys to tether, wipe down and feed their mounts. From her bedroom window, three flights up, she could hear their booming voices reverberating through the oaken walls, demanding the servants bring them mulled wine, refreshments, and fetch the Princess Elizabeth to them immediately.

Without waiting for the demeaning summons, the young princess walked alone and in fear to the door, her heart pounding and her throat dry.

She met her maids on the way up to fetch her, and gave them an encouraging smile, for they looked gray with worry. She looked for Kat Ashley, her governess, and Thomas Parry, her treasurer, but they were nowhere to be seen.

When she entered the withdrawing room, the men were gathered around the fire to warm their arms and legs after the coldness of their ride.

"Gentlemen, good morning. Welcome to you all," she said pleasantly, though her heart was beating so hard she could barely hear even her own words. She walked forward as though she was stepping onto the scaffold of Traitor's Gate for her execution.

The four potent and gaunt men scrutinized her. None had seen her in many years. She had grown into a tall, thin girl, redheaded like her father, though without his enormous bulk.

The first to speak was Sir Anthony Denny. "I'll be plain, madam. Your stepfather, Thomas Seymour, husband to the late Queen Dowager, has been arrested and is in the Tower."

Though she was pale by nature, her face turned white with shock. "The Lord High Admiral?" she whispered. Elizabeth grasped for a chair to prevent herself from falling. "But he . . . I . . ."

Somerset was in no mood for girlish emotions. There were matters of state to be dealt with. "Last night he attempted to abduct His Majesty the King. He tried to gain control over all of Henry's children, and for all we know is attempting to usurp the throne as well as the offices of the Lord High Protector, his very brother Edward Seymour."

Elizabeth's legs threatened to give way and she felt the room weaving around her.

Sir Anthony looked harshly at her. "Your swoon belies your feelings, girl. It is said that you and Thomas Seymour were lovers, even while he was married to the Queen Dowager, in whose house you were living, under whose roof you received sanctuary. Is this true?"

"No!" cried Elizabeth, forcing herself to recover quickly from the shock. "No, it isn't true. How dare you."

"I dare, madam, because I am charged by His Majesty's Protector, Edward Seymour, to determine what dangers lie to the Crown. The Lord Protector knows much of his brother's ambition. He believes that his nefarious brother's control over you and King Edward and the Lady Jane Grey is his pathway to the throne of England. Marriage to you would suit this purpose well. Now, madam, answer my question, and answer it plainly if you want to escape the sharpness of the axe. Were you the lover of the traitor Thomas Seymour while he was married to Catherine Parr?"

"Again, sir, no. I am a virgin. You may instruct any doctor to examine my womanhood and you will find it as intact as the day I was born."

"Do you deny that you and he engaged in unnatural acts between a married man and his stepdaughter?"

"Yes, I deny it."

"Did you not kiss, did he not come into your bedchamber while you were in a state of undress and cavort with you, did he not spank you on the bottom?"

"I was a young girl! Do you kiss and play with your daughter, Sir Anthony?"

"Don't bandy words with me," Denny shouted. "I'm the interrogator and you are in mortal danger."

"Then why are you come here," she asked, "if not to bandy words?"

In exasperation, Denny was about to abuse her, but the Earl of Nottingham sensed that this was no way to conduct an interview with a girl known for her keenness of wit and learning. He stepped forward from the fireplace and offered the Princess Elizabeth a place at the table. She sat, but did not return his smile.

"Highness," he said, "we are merely here to determine whether there is an understanding of marriage between yourself and Sir Thomas Seymour."

"Marriage, Nottingham? You look at me and ask whether I wish to marry? Do you have any comprehension of my disgust at the institution of marriage?"

"God's institution, madam," shouted Lord Hunsdon, who had, till this point, remained silent.

"Aye, God's blessed institution, yet corrupted by the venality of mankind. Marriage is purgatory, my lords. Childbirth is death. I have no love of purgatory or of death. I would no more marry than I would take an asp to my bosom. And as for birth, having seen the results of bearing children and the torturous pain of Eve's sins, why would I contemplate such an act?"

Nottingham continued, "But you are an attractive and high-placed woman and such a match would be important for England."

"Marriage! Fie on marriage. Catherine from Aragon was beloved for two decades but in the end it was her marriage which made her a miserable woman, divorced, abandoned, ending her life unloved and ridiculed by all England. I can barely remember my own mother, Anne Boleyn, for she was beheaded when I was a child of three. She, gentlemen, was married, and it cost her the life she loved and the head with which she was born; my mother wasn't even stiff in her grave when stiffness came again over Henry. Just one day after my mother's head was separated from her body, he was betrothed to poor Jane Seymour, whom he married shortly thereafter, and whose brother you so cruelly slander and imprison. Queen Jane died giving birth so that this country could have a prince on the throne. God save His Majesty Edward, my brother."

Her cheeks flushed in the heat of the room, and in her anger at the interview. Others tried to interrupt, but Princess Elizabeth continued, "Marriage? No, gentlemen, give me none of it. Remember ugly Anne from Cleves, whom my father called 'the Flanders mare'—unlovely yes, but a noble woman who was married but was soon given short shrift. And who here doesn't cry with the shame by which Katherine Howard was executed on the merest whimsy of evidence of adultery with her own cousin? Yes, fortune smiled on dear Catherine Parr who outlived my father, and yet she herself married four times, each marriage bar that to good Thomas Seymour ending in unhappiness; yet even she, as good and decent a woman who ever walked the earth, died giving birth to my Lord High Admiral's child.

"And after all these nightmares, after seeing so many good women beheaded or deeply unhappy, you expect me to marry? If I am to die at your hands, then bring down the death sentence on me if you must, gentlemen. But let the sentence of the court be carried out quickly with the executioner's sword, and not be the long-drawn death which begins with the ceremony of marriage and ends in childbirth."

The four councillors reeled from the vehemence of her onslaught. "Be that as it may, madam," said Sir Anthony, the first to recover, "Thomas Seymour is arrested on a Bill of Attainder, signed by his brother the Lord Protector of the King, and is charged with treason against the Majesty of the Crown. We need to know of his desire to marry you, madam, and hence place himself in line to the throne."

"But why is this important?" Elizabeth asked. "England has its king. I will never be monarch. Edward is a young and good king who will live these many years and—"

"And who has dropsy and scrofula."

Princess Elizabeth looked at him in horror.

"And that means that Mary, Catherine of Aragon's daughter, will ascend the throne if God fails to save the King. She's a damn Catholic, and there'll be bloodshed throughout the realm. But it also puts you, madam, despite your protestations, one step nearer the throne."

"Me?" she said in a gasp. "Elizabeth? But surely you don't believe that I could ever be in line for the succession?"

"Who knows, madam? Who knows what will happen in the Tudor line? Henry tried for twenty years to have a son, and although he sired King Edward, God bless him, he is a weak and sickly youth. He may live to marry the young Mary, Queen of Scotland, but she's only seven years old and won't be of child-bearing age for another six years at least. And if, God forbid, illness takes King Edward from us, then Mary Tudor will come to the throne, and all Protestants will hide beneath their beds. Which makes the question of succession even more important than in the days of your father. Now, damn you, answer my question. Have you or have you not agreed to marry Thomas Seymour?"

Chapter Three

It was after the birth of her first child that Grace O'Malley decided to return to the sea.

Owen was born to her when she was nineteen. In the short period between her marriage and the birth of her son, she hardly ever saw her husband, who spent much time aboard ship, trading and pirating; and much more on land, whoring and drinking and fighting with whichever clan happened to oppose his mood at the time. When he surprised everybody by returning home, he paid Grace no courtesy of acknowledgment at all, but hurried to his own chambers, visiting her in her bedchamber only during the dead quiet of the night to force himself upon her, entering her with such force that she was sore for days afterward.

While he was in the castle, he took every opportunity to undermine her role as mistress of the domain by screaming at the servants for changing the way in which things had always been done. And when the poor servants tried to justify the changes by attributing them to the mistress, they were scolded at best and severely beaten at worst.

Grace had brought about the changes to make the house run more efficiently, less expensively, but Donal was infuriated when he found his ale served from barrels instead of flagons, and when the bread he tore at was risen and tasted of ale, instead of being flat as it had always been.

But during the months of peace and quietude during which he was away, Grace gradually took charge of the running of first Ballinahinch and then Bunowen castles. She enlisted her mother's help and between them they managed to create a system of payments in which food, wine, ale, cloth, plows, knives, spoons and all other goods used by the household or the crofters who owed their living to the castle were purchased from local merchants in common for the two castles; and because they were bought in bulk, she demanded a considerably greater discount than the merchants were used to offering. Many withdrew their business, but quickly sought the right to continue trading—at Grace's price—when they saw goods arriving at her castles from Galway and Dublin.

By now Grace had gained the assistance of the castellan, who found working with his mistress made his life easier. The rest of the castle staff also appreciated Grace's knowledge and competence in running a household, and although she was strict when it came to money and budgets, they appreciated her compliments on good food and housekeeping. Wherever Grace walked around the castles, she was gladly welcomed by staff. This wasn't the case, however, with Donal's family, who still treated her with deep misgivings and suspicion, some even with hatred.

It was a lonely life without the love and support of a husband or a family. She'd grown up in a household where, despite Margaret's occasional fury and Owen's prolonged absences, there had been much love and comfort between husband and wife. And the love had increased with their adoration of their children. But Grace was living a loveless and solitary existence in a marriage that wasn't a marriage at all. She had only hard work to keep her company. She longed for the sea, for the freedom she'd known as a child, and promised herself that when she'd fulfilled her duty and produced an heir, she would return to the ocean.

Baby Owen was just four and a half months old and already his brown hair was turning auburn, when Grace stepped back onto a ship. It was one of her husband's merchantmen, a two-masted caravel, which had put in to Killary Harbour for repairs to its sails.

Donal was not around, and hadn't been for two months. Last word she'd had of him was that he and his Gallowglass mercenaries were in some protracted and interminable battle with the chieftain of the clans of Sligo.

This meant that the estimate for fixing the sails had been sent to Grace for approval. She had viewed it in horror, snorted that it was a king's ransom for what had to be done. She'd shown it to her castellan, who shrugged his shoulders. "These things cost money, my lady. It's what we normally pay."

"And how much is the cost of thread to repair a tear? Dear God, we're not making new sails, just repairing the old ones."

"Madam, the men who repair that tear have to come all the way from—" but she didn't allow him to finish, saying that she'd go there in the morning to examine the matter herself.

It took her much of the following morning to ride to Killary, but when she got there, her heart lifted with joy at the sight of the merchantman. It was a small caravel, built on the Spanish model, with a high prow and the quarterdeck and aft-castle loftily elevated to give the captain a good view of the horizon. Grace was a child again, her home a ship's deck rather than a grand castle.

She walked to the water's edge and hailed the captain to send over a rowboat so that she could come on board. A short time later she was being helped up the rope ladder and over the railings by a bemused midshipman, who hadn't seen a woman on board a ship before and didn't know whether to salute or forbid her entry. As she climbed over the railings, a tall and elegant man walked over, saluting.

"Captain Ferrick, ma'am. Welcome aboard."

She smiled as she recognized the part of Ireland from which his name derived. "Ah, a man from County Mayo. My own lands. And from which part, Captain?"

"From Bonnyconlon," he said tersely.

"Near the border of Sligo county. Now that's a dangerous place to be born," she said wryly.

"I had no choice in the matter, ma'am. Now, may I ask to what we owe the privilege of a visit from the wife of the Master of the O'Flaherty?"

Grace stepped away from the railings and grasped the riggings to steady herself. "Why, Captain Ferrick, I'm not here as the wife of the master, but as the Mistress of the O'Flaherty. For that is what I am, Captain, and while my husband is away on business, I authorize payment of the bills. And I'm shocked to see how much we're paying for the repair of sail."

Captain Ferrick had heard of Granuaile O'Flaherty's reputation for frugality, and he knew, too, that the master and his brothers were in a constant state of anger about everything the mistress did. There were some who talked about the mistress as though she was some interfering harridan. Looking now at the bright-eyed girl, the captain decided he would determine in his own mind whether or not the reputation was deserved.

"Ma'am, we're in the hands of the sailmakers. They have had to come from Galway and live on board for four days. The whole journey has cost them a week's work, and so they must be recompensed."

"Galway! But ships of the O'Flaherty and the O'Malley are not permitted to trade with Galway. The damned English who sit there on their fat arses see to that," she said.

"Indeed we're not, but there are no sailmakers in these parts who have the skill to knit canvas."

"Nonsense, Captain. My father's ships in Clew Bay are regularly repaired by people who live on the bay. Whose idea was it to send to Galway?"

"It's the way your husband has always done it, ma'am. And his father before him."

"Then it's about time things changed. Call the sailmakers on deck. I wish to speak to them."

The captain turned and nodded to the midshipman. A few moments later the two bemused sailmakers from Galway stood before the tall redheaded young woman, blinking in the unaccustomed light of day.

"I've decided that you're far too costly to repair the sails. Kindly pack up your belongings and give me your account, and it'll be settled within a week."

The two men looked at each other blankly. "But we haven't finished yet," one of them said.

"Yes, you have. My own father is captain and owner of six merchantmen, and his sails are repaired by local people for a half the fuchking price my husband is paying. For the money we're handing to you, my husband could have bought a complete new set, not just have them repaired."

"We're charging higher prices because of the danger of Galway men aiding the O'Flaherty."

"Then we'll get the men of Mayo to do the job. Good day to you both." She turned away and began walking toward the prow.

"What say we lower the price of the repair?" blurted one of the men. "We're here now, and to move ourselves back to Galway is a terrible shame, especially as we've no work to return to."

Still with her back turned, Grace said, "How much will you reduce the price?"

"By a pound."

"By five," she said.

"Five pounds! We'll be ruined!" he shouted at her back.

"Rather be ruined by the Irish of Mayo than the fuchking English in Galway."

"By two pound," the man said after a few moments.

"By five, and I won't bargain any further with men who are treacherous in their dealings with their own city fathers, even if their fathers are lying in bed with the English."

She continued to walk slowly down the length of the ship. If they packed their bags and departed, it would be a month before the ship would be under sail again, and that would cause a great loss on trading.

"Alright," the sailmaker said. "Five pounds it is, but we'll hurry and finish tomorrow so that we can be back in Galway and earning a living where there are no pirates."

She smiled at the insult. It was the least she expected.

The captain began setting up a table on deck so that the mistress could eat in the freshness of the open air. When she saw what he was doing, Grace stopped him. "My father took me aboard his boats when I was a child of three, and I didn't get off them until I was fourteen, and that was only because my Ma caused such a stench about my being more man than woman that she locked me away in a convent. But despite what the nuns tried to teach to me about womanhood, I'm more used to wearing breeches and eating belowdecks with the men than I am to eating in style on the fo'c'sle deck like an English gentlewoman."

And so she went below and sat at the galley table with ten of the crew. She introduced herself, and asked after each man, his town or village of origin, whether or not he was married or single, how long he'd been in her husband's employ.

The men barely answered, looking at Grace with suspicion, even contempt, for being a woman on a ship. So she said, "Who's been serving at sea the longest?"

Nobody answered.

"Who here has been to the land of the Ottomans? To Greece? To the south of Spain?"

Again there was silence.

"Perhaps I'll take you there one day," Grace mused. "I know those parts well, having sailed with the O'Malley fleet for nigh on fifteen years."

She drank a draft of ale. Softly, one of the men at the far end of the table said, "I've been to Greece."

"Have you seen the Parthenon?" Grace asked.

The man nodded.

"Wondrous, isn't it? Did you know that it was built for the goddess Athena, from which the city of Athens takes its name?" she asked.

The men looked at her with renewed interest. She knew she was winning them over.

When they had eaten their fill, the men rose, doffed their caps to the wife of the Master of the O'Flaherty, and departed. Grace turned to Captain Ferrick and asked, "Why so few crew, Captain?"

"Ma'am, the majority of the crew have taken leave while the ship is at anchor, as they were told it would be a week before they were able to sail again."

Grace could hear the diffidence in his voice—her powers of negotiation had meant they were now able to sail on the following day's tide, but he didn't have the manpower. It would be he who would get into trouble with the Master of the O'Flaherty when the log books were examined and the cost of three days laying idle worked out.

"How are you going to man the ship to sail tomorrow, Captain?" she asked.

He shrugged. "I can round up some who live nearby, and with those we'll have not far short of a complement, though I need at least another couple of able-bodied men to help in the riggings. I'm afraid that without a shantyman and a couple of others, I'll be too short-handed to sail."

"I can be your shantyman, and set your sails, Captain Ferrick," she said softly.

He looked at her in amazement. "I can't take a woman on the sea! Even the wife of the master of the line. This is a merchant ship, not for passengers. The men would never tolerate it."

"They'll tolerate what they're told, if you order them," she said.

"Ma'am, they won't sail with a woman. And even if I did order them, the master would have to give his permission first."

"He's a hundred miles away, engaged in the business of battle. Do you really think he cares about me?"

"But your baby, ma'am."

"I have a wet nurse. And little Owen is far too young to miss his mother. Now, Captain Ferrick, I think I've answered all your objections. This is my husband's boat, and hence I have a strong vested interest in its capacity to trade. It's five years since I last put to sea, and things have changed. I want to visit the harbors of Portugal and Spain and see if we're being charged too much for the port wine and the sherry we trade in Scotland. I want to put in at France and find out the true price of the French wine we sell to the English. I know you're a good seaman, Captain, but as to how good you are at negotiating with the French and the Spaniards, well, that's something I'd like to examine myself."

Captain Ferrick stared into his goblet of ale as he listened to Mistress O'Flaherty. What should he do? A woman on board ship was unheard of, but a woman trading on shore in a port full of footpads, cutthroats and men jabbering in all kinds of indecipherable tongues was . . . well, it was downright improper. Yet she was the Mistress of the O'Flaherty and the master's wife, and she'd dealt with the sailmakers as would any man.

"Ma'am, I feel bound to ask my master's permission before—"

"Captain, like it or not, your master sits before you. And anyway, my husband is not here; I, your mistress, am! My permission is all you require. And how many mistresses do you know who can scale a rigging in a gale, or furl a sail when the weather's blowing a storm? How many women can down a glass of ale in heavy seas without spewing all over the galley? Answer me that, Captain."

He remained silent.

"Good, then we sail tomorrow on the evening tide. I'll return at midday with my breeches and my vests and a scarf to tie up my hair."

It was her first sight of Lisbon in many years, yet she remembered it clearly. She remembered the dry burning heat of the southern sun, the feeling of warmth which pervaded her entire body, the sensuousness the sun engendered in her arms and legs and those parts of her body which remembered the gentle and tender fingers of the first boy she had ever allowed to kiss her. She remembered him with pleasure; he was fifteen and she was only twelve, so she'd had to wait until her father was engaged in buying cargo before she'd managed to sneak off with him. They kissed forever behind one of the warehouse sheds, until the stentorian voice of her father demanded to know where she was. But from that day to this, she still remembered the taste of the boy's lips, his eager hands, his nearly overwhelming desire.

She'd carried the memory of the city with her too, its white houses and their red terracotta roofs, the ancient Alfama quarter with its Moorish architecture, its alleyways and cul-de-sacs, its crumbling arches and overhanging porticos, its stairways that disappeared into anonymity. The houses here were so close together, so very different from the houses in an Irish town, that all she had to do was to stretch her hands across a street to touch either side. Above her head were streamers full of lazy washing and limp laundry hung like ship's message flags, some dry in the broiling sun, some wringing wet and dripping on unsuspecting passers-by.

But it was the markets of the Alfama which most captivated her imagination. Elderly men and women sat cross-legged on rugs, in front of them baskets full of exotic and multicolored fruits and vegetables which the weak sun would not allow to grow in Ireland—yellow and red and green peppers, bananas from the Indies, lush green cucumbers, large purple eggplant, rice, sugarcane, juicy grapes, the most luscious and succulent of oranges.

When she first landed here with her father, she'd been too young to understand how the sun and such fruit as was displayed in the markets could have lent themselves to erotic dreams . . . but when she revisited as a girl of fourteen, she became an Arabian princess, a Portuguese Infanta, a French whore, a Spanish Marquessa, a black African slave woman sold into a life of bondage to a lecher who kept her locked up all day, and in the evening had his way with her in every manner that her young mind could conceive. And most pleasant of all in her juvenile fantasies was imagining herself hidden in some Moorish turret, an olive-skinned Jewess from Spain, left over from the expulsions of Ferdinand and Isabella a half a century earlier, secretly intoning Hebraic prayers beneath her breath lest she was overheard by some harsh Catholic cardinal who would imprison her and torture her on the rack, threatening with the *auto da fe* unless she confessed her beliefs; and would she confess? Never! She'd die on the rack or in the cleansing flames before she gave him the pleasure of confession.

The noise of a gull circling the stern of the boat startled Grace out of her daydream, and she realized they had entered Lisbon Harbor. Soon they were moored in the Tagus River, which rose in the highlands of central Spain and flowed westward all the way to Lisbon and then into the Atlantic Sea.

The sunny quayside was alive with strange animals in cages, and wooden carts sagging beneath the weight of sacks of corn or ironstone or marble. Emaciated donkeys, wearing ridiculous straw hats with their ears sticking through like little old men, pulled wagons ten times their puny weight. Men shouted in a dozen different languages; fisherwomen in heavy black woollen dresses with black scarves on their heads sat on low stools on the dockside, before them multicolored cloths on which were laid out the fruits of the sea—lobster, cuttlefish, crayfish, mackerel, oysters, octopus, tunnyfish and many more that Grace had never before seen.

The sky was a deep blue, so much livelier and more animated than the dull leaden skies, clotted with gray clouds, which perpetually overhung the northwest of Ireland. Still, it was a trade-off between the hues of the grasses and leaves of the trees of Portugal, which were a dull green, as lackluster as the skin of the olive, and the shining emerald green of Ireland after the rain had stopped and the clouds parted, tiny beads of water coruscating in the sudden bath of sunshine.

The first day in Lisbon passed quickly, paying landing fees to the harbormaster and finding out what cargoes were available. Two-thirds of the crew was permitted to take shore leave, having to return and relieve the ship's watch after thirty-six hours. They disappeared into the void which was the life of a foreign sailor on a foreign shore, and Captain Ferrick hoped and prayed that they wouldn't become so inebriated and whore-bound that they would forget their duty.

Grace spent the second day buying crates of pepper spices and salted fish and cloth from Andalusia which they could trade in Scotland and, if they were sufficiently daring, in Liverpool and perhaps even Bristol, provided they didn't meet any English gunships.

They would sail on the morning tide, but for now they had to content themselves with another night in port. It meant more port charges but it also enabled those members of the crew who hadn't managed yet to enjoy the entertainments the port had to offer, to come ashore and gorge themselves in one of the dozens of quayside inns.

The men drew straws to determine which ten of the crew would stay behind to protect the ship and its rich cargo. Grace O'Malley insisted that she, too, would take her chances, but as luck would have it, she and Captain Ferrick both drew long straws; he looked at her with great misgiving, but she gave him a smile and a little wink and joined the other fifteen men who clambered down the gangplank to partake again of the pleasures of Lisbon. She walked boldly through the queues of people to the nearest inn.

But before she could enter, Captain Ferrick grasped her arm and whispered in her ear, "Ma'am, you must not go in there."

She looked at him in surprise. "And whyever not?"

"Mistress O'Flaherty, I've witnessed your seamanship which is as good as an old dog's, and I've seen you treat with these merchants in tongues I don't understand, and I've admitted the mistake I made back in Ireland when I didn't think you could do the work of a man, yet you've done more work than any sailor on board; but if I take you into an inn, where the other women are serving wenches or whores or both, the master will have my guts. I can't do it, ma'am. I must ask you to wait here with me while the men go inside and have fun. We'll sip port in the quayside and you can tell me about the foreign mathematics you love so much, but I'll not take you into this bawdy house."

Grace smiled at him, for in the two weeks since they'd set sail, she'd grown to both like and respect him. She knew he wished to protect her reputation as much as his own. And she knew that her acceptance by the crew was due as much to Ferrick's public approval of her as to the sailing skills she had proved along the way.

"Captain. When I was a lass of five, my father would take me into the inns and public houses of Spain and Morocco and Piraeus and to other places of which you've only heard speak.

"Now you may think that he was sullying my reputation, or endangering me, but my presence seemed to calm these places down somewhat. What that taught me from an early age was that women can and should go anywhere that men go, and that when they do, men behave themselves differently. They're less bold and audacious and blustering. Women calm down their natural instincts for bad behavior.

"Be assured, Captain, I can hold as good as my own in drink; I can match any man with a cutlass or dagger or flintlock; and no man is a match for me when it comes to the use of my tongue—he might swear, but I'll tie him up in knots with curses so complex it'll be morning before he's worked them out.

"Now let's go in and drink, Captain Ferrick. And in case you're worried about my husband's reaction, let me calm your mind on that score. In the two years I've been his wife, he hasn't asked after my health once, nor is he interested in what I do. If he hears about my innocent escapades in a Lisbon bawdy house, he'll laugh his fuchking guts out."

The following morning a freshening nor'easterly wind blew up and carried them beyond the breakwater and out into the open seas. They sailed north northwest to clear the observation posts on land before tacking in a northeasterly direction on a course to take them parallel with the French coast.

The men who had stayed on board to watch over the safety of the ship and its cargo were tired from lack of sleep; the men who had drunk all night in the inn were bleary-eyed and mumbling, though the spray of water in their faces woke them up sufficiently to follow orders.

Grace, who had drunk as much as the rest, laughed at the coarse remarks and ignored the gloating of four of the men who had gone upstairs with serving girls, was given charge of the helm. She felt totally alive, more alert and energetic than she'd felt in years. The sea did well for her, and seemed to fill her body and soul with the food she needed to live life to the full.

When they'd put enough latitude between themselves and Portugal, Captain Ferrick set course to sail inshore within sight of the coast.

"When are we putting out to deeper water, Captain?" Grace asked.

"We're not, ma'am. We're plying a course close to land."

"Whyever are we doing that, Mr Ferrick?"

"We have a full cargo now. Many in Lisbon saw us load and have taken note of our country of origin. We're rich pickings for a pirate or a Spanish galleon, and there were plenty of those in port."

"Then why stay close to land where we can be spotted from any one of a hundred lookouts and our position reported? At twenty leagues to sea, we're beyond the horizon of even the tallest hill on the coast, and we'll be lost in the vastness of the ocean."

He shook his head. "You don't understand. If we're sixty miles to sea and we're attacked by a passing ship, we'll stand no chance. We've only got enough guns on us to make a loud noise, not to sink a man-o'-war. If we're set upon close to shore, we can hug the coast like it was our best friend, and being high-drafted, we can sail in waters far shallower than any other ship. That means that we can make good an escape."

"Why in God's name aren't we carrying more cannon? How are we expected to protect ourselves?"

"It was your husband's decision, ma'am. He removed thirty cannon in the name of weight. That means that we can carry more cargo and make more profit on the journey."

She looked at him in horror. "I knew nothing about this, Captain Ferrick. Nothing whatsoever, or I'd never have allowed it. How could my husband risk his ship and crew in the name of profit? When I get back, I'll have words to say."

Donal O'Flaherty's face was a mask of hatred; even the vivid scars on his cheeks seemed to glow in the anticipation of violence.

"You will remain confined to this fuchking castle!" he screamed. "You will never venture out of doors again! For the rest of your life you'll stay in the kitchens! Do you understand me, madam? If ever I'm told that you've interfered with my fuchking business or my fuchking ships or my lands again, I'll have you chained and tethered like a fuchking bitch dog."

His shouting echoed throughout the hall. His family and their attendant servants remained like statues, too terrified to breathe. Even his elderly father was unwilling to intervene.

Donal stomped over to the banqueting table and drank down a mug of beer, then stormed back to the fire to face his young wife. The family watched his movements anxiously. They'd seen all this before, and they knew that with his foul and evil temper, it spelled violence. They feared that his drunkenness would make him forget himself and he'd use his fists to flay her. Then there'd be war with the O'Malley and that would cost a lot of money, and money wasn't something in such supply that it could be squandered in a war between two clans which were supposed to be united.

The fact that Grace stood and refused to be bowed by his facing off, that she didn't cower under the onslaught, made her husband even more furious. Indeed, he was almost incapable of speaking, he was so enraged. The fact that she looked at him with a face devoid of fear, eyes alive with self-righteousness, mouth set impudently, brought him perilously close to striking her.

He'd killed men, and some women, for less. Yet despite his drunkenness, he was all too well aware of the consequences if he gave his wife a serious beating. Yes, he'd struck her many times, but that was expected. She'd ended up on the floor, crying in pain, but he'd been restrained. Even in his drunken state, he knew his ire was so wild that he could very well kill her, and that would be serious trouble for him and his family.

But how to punish her insolence? Although he'd threatened it, he knew the consequences of imprisoning her. She'd contrived to send a personal letter every week to her father in case of such an eventuality, and if no letter arrived, O'Malley would come looking for her with a hundred kinsfolk, and once there was war between the counties, it would quickly run down the O'Flaherty treasury so badly that he'd be prey to other lords, and then he and the O'Flahertys would be finished.

None of this helped cool the fearful temper he was in because of what the interfering harridan had said to him. Him! Master, along with his father, of the Clan O'Flaherty; and in his own castle in front of his brothers and sisters and his mother and father and the servants.

He slumped in the chair beside the fire, spent of the ability to form speech. For the first time all evening, he was silent.

It was then that Grace spoke. Quietly at first to show the entire room that she, at least, had control of her temper.

"Husband. Perhaps you didn't listen to what it was I told you, but by removing cannon from our merchant ships you're endangering—"

"My merchant ships," he screamed. "My fuchking merchant ships, Jesus curse you, you bitch a whore!"

Again with infuriating control, she continued softly, "Removing cannon from *our* fleet of merchantmen—*ours*—Donal, because under our marriage contract and until the day you die, the conjunction of my lands with yours entitles my family to part ownership of your property—removal of cannon endangers our profit. If you think that additional cargo-carrying capacity is equivalent to the dangers of potential loss of ship, crew and cargo, then you're a poor judge of business."

"Oh, and you're a good judge of business, I suppose. You in your breeches and headscarf like . . . like . . ." He was again lost for words.

"Yes, husband. I believe I've a good head for business. I've studied my father's methods as merchantman and pirate since I was a child, and I've picked up a dog trick or two. Wasn't it me who brought you home a profit of £3000, and also saved you a fortune in the repair of the sails and the cost of the ship weighing at anchor? Wasn't it me who—"

"It was Captain Ferrick, damn you. Do you take credit from him?" Donal shouted.

Suddenly an unexpected voice arose from the end of the table. "No, sir. You're wrong. Forgive me, but the mistress is correct."

If the hall was hushed before, then it descended into the silence of the grave when all eyes turned to Captain Ferrick. Even Donal O'Flaherty was too surprised to speak against the audacity of the sudden interruption.

Captain Ferrick stood and said, "You'll forgive me, Master O'Flaherty, but it was the mistress who bargained the prices. She speaks the language of the merchants in the ports and was able to understand what they were saying. Not only that, sir, but I've seen no man better than the mistress for being able to barter with such style that she left the merchant thinking he'd done a good deal, while being undercut so viciously."

Donal was about to shout him down, when the captain continued, "And more than that, sir, the Mistress O'Flaherty was as good a seaman as any hand on board when called upon, she was a shantyman as well as a deckhand and she took the wheel like she was born to steer a ship. And that meant, sir, that the profits of the voyage didn't have to be shared out with so many."

He nodded and sat down, knowing that he had just invoked the master's fury. But to his surprise, Donal didn't round on him but instead looked contemptuously at Grace, and said, "So, madam, you have champions in my court.

Then let's have a contest. You and the good captain think you're so skilled, let's put it to the test. We'll both sail on the same day. Me to Cadiz on the Spanish coast, and you to Tangier on the African coast. They're only a day's sail apart, and you should have no trouble with your seamanship in making good wind. Whoever comes back with a richer profit can run the entire fleet."

Grace fought to remain calm, trying to grasp the intent behind this unexpected challenge. She'd never been to Tangier. Her father hadn't permitted any of his ships to go to the northern Barbary Coast, a place known as a haven for its pirates, the most evil and dangerous in all the world.

Just then, another voice arose in the room. This time it was the other head of the Clan O'Flaherty, Donal's father.

"Donal, not Tangier. Another port. Algeciras, perhaps; Piraeus maybe; but not Tangier. It's certain death. This is the mother of your son. And would you endanger the value of a ship by putting in to such a port?"

"This is a challenge, Father. I'm told by the good Captain Ferrick that my wife, the mother of my son, is a cunning merchant and a valued hand at sea. So she will prove her worth—"

"If I accept the challenge, then what are the rules?" Grace interrupted.

"We each sail with five hundred pounds. Whoever returns first and with the greatest profit is the winner."

"And the reward for me and my crew?"

The room breathed a sigh of relief. The anger seemed to be dissipating.

"Your crew will be paid in the normal way, or would you have each man given a silken purse just for the privilege of sailing with you?"

"My reward then?" she demanded, ignoring his sarcasm.

"Assuming you win, madam, your reward will be to run the affairs of the O'Flahertys at sea. I've never liked being on the waves. It upsets the sense of balance I need when I'm bedding servants or other ladies."

His brother Liam burst out laughing, but nobody else was amused by the gratuitous insult, least of all Grace.

"I'm sorry for you then, Husband Donal, for the men I take to my bed don't have a problem with balance."

Donal shot to his feet, but realized that the entire room was laughing. To have struck her at this point would have brought the roof down on his head. And would have made him look like a cuckold and a ninny.

"Well, madam, I hope the men you take to your bed have more pleasure there than I've enjoyed."

"They've all had more pleasure, and given more. Indeed, husband, you might have been the first man to enter me, but I have found the world you come from to be a very puny and little place indeed; thankfully I've had the pleasure of learning from other men how big the world can be."

Again the room erupted into gales of laughter. Donal felt ridiculed. She'd done it again! She had a tongue on her which hurt more than a whip and was trickier than that of a Dublin whore, and he had no way of controlling what she said.

"Are you avoiding the challenge, madam? So far I haven't heard whether or not you're game to take me on."

"You, sir, and a dozen ships of your line. Not only will I sail to Tangier, not only will I return with a cargo of twenty times the outlay of five hundred pounds, but I'll be waiting in harbor for your return like a good and dutiful wife."

"Then the challenge is on. Good! I'll have the papers drawn."

Grace turned to the end of the table. "Captain Ferrick. Will you sail with me, sir?"

He stood again, and said boldly, "Gladly, ma'am. It'll be a privilege and a pleasure. And the crew will follow you wherever you put to."

Grace turned to her husband, smiling in triumph.

"Smile as much as you want, madam," Donal's face was a thundercloud, "but you have to contend with Tangier, and you still have to win."

In two and a half days of hard and determined sailing and favorable winds, they'd cleared the southern coast of Ireland and the coast of northern France, and were well on their way to Portugal. They'd lost sight of Donal's ship many hours earlier, Donal having decided to sail far to the west into the deep ocean,

Grace and Captain Ferrick having chosen not to risk the prospect of inclement weather by staying close to the shore. It meant they had lost the good gusty winds of the open sea, but they had safe harbors to pull into if the waves became mountainous, as they often did at this time of year.

The hours they'd spent in preparing the ship, and finally securing the stores and rations, had kept Grace and the captain apart until this moment, and so she only now broached a subject which should by rights have been asked much earlier.

They were alone at the prow of the boat, looking down into the waves and as far ahead as possible to spy approaching ships. "Captain Ferrick," Grace asked tentatively, "tell me truly, how do you feel about putting into Tangier?"

"If I was to be honest, ma'am, I'd have to say I was somewhat uncomfortable. Algerian and Moroccan pirates have no sense of fairness. They'll slaughter men, women and children just to get their hands on a cargo. Pirates such as the master and, I'm sure, your own father, do it as a profession, but they don't set out to kill. They see no sense in that, whereas your North African Arab now, he's a very different kettle of fish. A Barbary pirate will slit your guts just to see the pain when you bleed to death. You asked me honestly, ma'am, and I'm telling you truly that I'm not all that easy at the prospect."

"Nor me," Grace said quietly. "My father wouldn't have put in there even if he was sinking in the middle of the Mediterranean. From everything I've heard, it's a stinking and festering place, with the plague and the pox and every other malevolent fuchking spirit all concentrated in the *shuks* and the other marketplaces. I've heard the wine is thin and acidic and the food gives your stomach the rots and the women all wear veils because they're so ugly."

Captain Ferrick burst out laughing. He was growing increasingly delighted to be in the company of this willful, talented and, he had to admit, beautiful girl with her flowing red hair and her glorious Irish green eyes. It had been an act of bravura to offer to follow her, but so incensed was he by O'Flaherty's treatment of such an able and decent young woman that he'd decided to shame his very own master, even at his own peril. If he had to look for another command when he returned, then so be it; he'd rather work hard for a decent man than rob blind a devil like O'Flaherty.

"Then are you regretting putting to sea with me in this contest with my husband?"

"Not at all," he said immediately. "I'd rather not go to Tangier, but I'd love to beat the O'Flaherty at his own game . . . and his treatment of you, ma'am."

"It was a rough night, wasn't it? I thought he was going to lay me out with the back of his hand. God help him if he had. And when he boasted of his conquests and all the women he'd bedded . . ."

Ferrick looked down at the boards of the ship.

Sensing his unease, Grace said, "I'm sorry, Captain. I shouldn't be so vocal about our private lives. . . . But in fairness it wasn't so private, when he abused me so violently in front of all his friends and family . . . and you."

"I felt you showed great dignity in your restraint, madam. Great dignity and composure."

She turned and smiled at him. He was a charming and attractive man, tall and lean and muscular beneath his jacket and shirt. And he had long legs, which she always found attractive.

"I was wrong in responding to his crude remarks, though. I shouldn't have insulted myself by saying those things about my having bedded many men."

"Then they weren't true?"

Grace looked back to the sea and remained silent. But Captain Ferrick wasn't willing to leave it there.

"I'm glad." He shifted uncomfortably beside her. She felt his body's heat, as though he was flushing with embarrassment. "Ma'am . . ."

"Oh! For the sake of Jesus and all the Saints, Captain Ferrick, enough of the *ma'am*'s if you please. My friends call me Grace."

"Grace, I know he was goading you mercilessly, but I'm pleased your claim to have bedded so many men isn't true. That's not how I like to think of you . . ." His words trailed off in the freshening wind.

She turned back to him and smiled. "Tell me, Captain, or do I yet know you well enough to call you by your forename?"

He said that he would consider it an honor.

"Then tell me, Rogan Ferrick, why am I admitting things to you which in ordinary times would be the intimate secrets between a young woman and her priest in the confessional?"

He didn't know how to answer. After twenty-three years at sea, he had neither the wit nor the skill to deal with women, especially one as adept with words and ideas as this potent beauty.

"I've embarrassed you, Rogan. My, but you embarrass easily."

"Not at all, Grace," he said, trying to recover his composure.

"Then tell me, Rogan, why you'd rather I hadn't bedded men other than my husband? Girls my age are rarely virgins when they walk to the altar. Today's women are adventurous, not like they were a hundred years ago when they wore chastity belts. We live in a world where chastity isn't prized highly, except by a few. So are you one of those few, my dear Rogan?"

"I . . . I . . ."

She put him out of his misery. "My husband is the first man to have entered my body . . . and the last. Though God knows, it wasn't what I expected. All he seems interested in is forcing himself upon me and getting his part of the performance over as quickly as possible so he can return to his drinking and his friends."

Grace was surprised by her frankness—she'd never been this personal with a man before, certainly not with a man of a lower social order than she.

And just as embarrassed by the intimacy was Captain Ferrick; he flushed deeply at such openness from the wife of his master.

"Do you treat your wife in the way my husband treats me, Rogan?" Grace asked quietly.

"I have no wife. I've never married. I put to sea at thirteen and have never had a proper home or family. Now I'm thirty-six, it seems too late to start."

"But you've surely had mistresses, as bold and handsome a man as you."

"I've known the gentle touch of a number of women in my day."

She smiled and turned back to look at the swelling ocean.

Softly, she said, "Well, dear Rogan, maybe that day will soon dawn again, and perhaps even extend into the night."

But she didn't know whether he heard her words, snatched by the wind which rose to fill the sails.

CHAPTER FOUR

It was because of the pirate trade in Tangier that Grace and Captain Ferrick had ordered the replacement of the thirty cannon, fifteen added to both port and starboard, which Donal O'Flaherty had removed.

Although the complement of cannon undoubtedly increased the deadweight of the ship by nearly eighty ton, or fifteen percent of the weight of the ship, and lowered her keel in the water, they were vital to her protection.

Grace had also insisted on putting aboard two ten-year-old lads to serve as powder monkeys in case the ship was rounded on by pirates; for the last thing the crew needed when they were under attack was the distraction of going below and fetching up barrels of gunpowder and shot when they should be spending their time aiming and firing their artillery. She'd chosen the boys carefully herself, as they had to be strong enough to carry the powder, yet short enough to run beneath the low overhangs below decks and not trip over the snakes of ropes which made the gundeck so very treacherous.

She knew the moment the men began firing practice that her powder monkeys would prove their worth. When they'd put England two hundred leagues behind them and were far enough out to sea off the coast of France so as not to attract attention, she insisted that Captain Ferrick put the men through their paces in case they were attacked. He objected on two grounds. The most compelling was that they were in a race with the Master of the O'Flaherty and every moment of seamanship was precious; the other reason was that he was sure the men were ready, for they'd fired cannon many times. Yet when he was pressed, he had to admit that never had they fired cannon when under sea-borne attack, but only against emplacements and battery on land.

Grace, however, had been many times aboard a pirate vessel, and she knew the altered conditions a sea battle caused. She wanted the men to be prepared, and to understand the different requirements of firing against a moving target, understanding how to maintain aim when the helmsman was changing course, and most especially how to cripple a ship by shooting the decking and rigging and not the superstructure.

She insisted on firing nine-pound shot, larger than the ship had ever fired before, but necessary if they were to inflict damage at a distance when a pirate ship was bearing down on them. She also cleared space in the upper hold for thirty barrels of gunpowder and ten barrels of wadding. A pyramid of twenty-four nine-pounder balls was built beside each of the cannon, eight at the base to give it stability in rough seas, boxed in by wooden staves.

They were fifteen leagues off the Burgundy coast on their way to Tangier when Grace suddenly pointed off the starboard bow and screamed out, "Pirates!"

The men rushed to the side, but could see nothing other than open ocean and gentle swelling waves.

"Quick!" she yelled. "Bring up powder and wadding. Prepare to load your cannon on my command."

Captain Ferrick looked at her, trying to hide his admiration and amusement. She was a magnificent girl, eyes bright with excitement, standing tall and gallant on the aft-castle, taking over command of the ship.

The men at first looked at their captain to see what they should do; but when he yelled at them, "Well? Get to it! Do what you're damn well told!" they ran around like frantic hens, bumping into each other, cursing and swearing, tripping over rope, some of them laughing at the performance, others checking to ensure that there really wasn't a pirate ship bearing down on them.

Grace and Rogan Ferrick smiled at each other, but both realized the deadly earnest of the game they were playing.

Grace turned to the helmsman and ordered, "East by northeast, Mr Helm. Broadside on and not too close, if you please."

The helmsman turned the wheel to swing the ship around so that the starboard cannon were facing the imaginary oncoming enemy.

"As soon as the shot is depleted from starboard, I'll give you the signal, and then you turn west by southwest so that the portside cannon can do their work," she shouted. "Powder monkeys, as soon as shot is fired, go below and replace it."

Then she turned to the sailors who were beginning their job of loading the starboard cannon. "Now listen carefully to me. The pirate ship is bearing down on us at ten knots in a moderate swell. He's got the wind behind him so he has the advantage of speed and maneuverability. It means that he can close on us as fast as a cantering horse. But we also have an advantage, because he's closing prow first, and he's only got two puny guns to fire when he's head-on, whereas we're now broadside on and our entire starboard cannon can attack him. However, he makes a smaller target in the water, so you have to be very accurate in your firing. Again fortune is with us, because his sail and rigging is facing to us, and if we can hole his mainsail and take off his mast, he'll be crippled in the water, and then we're halfway home to safety.

"Now, aim high to take down his rigging and disable him in the water. Knock away his mainsail, and he'll be ours by rights. He'll be dead in the water, and won't be able to navigate. Then all we have to do is to stay clear of his port or starboard by maneuvering around him, hole him at the waterline and watch him sink. Load your cannon . . . and an extra noggin of rum to the cannon crew which fires first and most accurately!"

Grace and Rogan watched the men begin their feeble attempts to traipse over the breech ropes. They leaned over the gunwale as the sea heaved and threatened to pitch them overboard; then, legs wrapped around capstans, hoists and bollards to stop themselves from falling, ran the worm down the gun barrel to remove pieces of dead wadding still remaining from the last time the cannon was fired, and pushed the wet swab down the barrel to put out any embers which might cause the gunpowder to explode prematurely. When all the muck from the inside of the cannon had fallen down into the water, they pulled the guns back to the gun ropes, and the powder monkeys handed them a flannel cartridge filled with four and a half pounds of gunpowder, half the weight of the shot, and then one of them compressed it down hard with the rammer. The nine-pound ball was put in, the cannon elevated, and the wick lit. Moments later, the ship shuddered as a series of thunderous explosions from the starboard bow rent the quiet of the ocean; and moments after that, Grace and Rogan watched in dismay as waterspouts erupted over a huge area of sea, not a twentieth of a league from the ship.

The men all cheered and turned to Grace and their captain, smiling expectantly.

When the noise of the cannon had quietened and the cheering ceased, Grace stepped forward and returned their smiles, asking them simply, "Are any of you married?"

Most put up their hands.

"I suggest you write to your wives wishing them farewell, because with cannon fire as slow and woefully inaccurate as that, you'll be fuchking fish food within the week. Now, gentlemen, let Captain Ferrick and me show you how to load a cannon, fire it and be deadly accurate, all in a quarter of the time you've just taken."

By the time they reached Tangier, the men were sufficiently skilled to repel all but the most accomplished of pirate ships, though everyone knew that if they were approached by a Spanish galleon, they'd stand no chance. But such was the risk of sailing these waters in a merchantman.

After all the hullaballoo of the journey, it was delightful to sight land again. And what a stunning shoreline it was, to make no mistake. The sand was burning white in the blisteringly hot sun, and beyond rose tall and mysterious mountains. Near to the shoreline Grace could see swathes of palm trees and other exotic plants. From time to time she saw herds of camel and flocks of the most exotic birds imaginable, with plumages like the very rainbow itself, and massive birds with long pointed beaks which waded in the shallow water, digging their beaks into the sand, presumably fishing for the little crabs and shellfish which lived there.

As they sailed along the North African coast, Grace saw encampments aplenty, as well as the ubiquitous mosques with their crescent symbols and minarets and dome-like roofs. Once she fancied, when it was particularly quiet, she heard the strange call of a muezzin, his voice seeming to command and beg the very earth itself to listen to his song, a paean of hope and pain. And as he called, tiny black-coated figures from throughout the landscape seemed to stop whatever they were doing and walk toward the mosque.

As they sailed further eastward, the sand dunes and fringes of palm and date trees began to give way to human occupation. Fields of crops sprang up everywhere, dry and dusty compared to the lushness of Ireland's emerald greens, but nonetheless watered by some sort of irrigation system, probably from the rivers which Grace saw occasionally as they flowed from the parched land into the sea. And as the land became increasingly etched with the presence of humanity, there were more and more buildings, not the scattered huts or mosques which had been present in the west of the land further toward the mouth of the Middle Sea, but substantial encampments with forts and roads and buildings which stood imposingly on the seashore. They were reaching Tangier.

And then suddenly they rounded a headland and the city appeared before them. Even from a distance, it looked mysterious and menacing. There were many different ships of strange shapes and with sails she'd never seen before. Even Captain Ferrick, normally busy with navigation at this crucial prelude to docking, came to the prow to see the strangeness of the land for himself. Some of the ships were single-sailed, the sails being oddly shaped triangles; some were little more than barges with a sail at the very prow to pull the ship along; and still others were large-hulled ocean-going vessels, though the structure was set so high in the water that they looked in danger of capsizing at the sight of the first wave. They were strange boats indeed.

And stranger still was the port. Here there were none of the squat and dusty warehouses for the storage of goods, nor the officious buildings which housed the masters of the port and the numerous tally clerks who kept count of the dues and fees payable to the master of the harbor. No, instead, there was a mass of humanity and pack animals, jumbled together on the port's edge without order or reason. And as the ship drew nearer, Grace heard a cacophony of shouting and screaming and laughter and jabbering which was so loud it could have been heard all the way to Dublin.

As they were putting into the dock, Grace stood by the railings and viewed each ship already moored there as a potential enemy. Their flags showed them as hailing from all over the world. Tangier was a Portuguese city and the local laws offered protection to ships from any country, provided they weren't at war with Lisbon. Nonetheless, a half-day out of port and all ships were fair game to the cutthroats and pirate captains.

They were guided into a berth at the eastern bay of the port by the rowboat of the harbormaster, and while the men were preparing to tie up, Grace was joined once more by Rogan Ferrick.

While they'd been traveling up the coast, they stood side by side as mariners. Now, they were readying to go ashore and she'd changed her clothes—she was wearing a dress flounced outward by the latest farthingale hoops which were so fashionable in Spain—she noticed him watching her closely. She felt his eyes upon the nape of her neck and her creamy shoulders, upon the swell of her breasts and her slender waist.

There was a charged silence between them, broken by a shout as the ship's hawsers were pulled by landing gangs to secure her to the dockside.

"Do you know much about Tangier?" the captain asked.

Grace shook her head.

"It was originally a Roman city called Tingis, but then it was captured by the wild men from the east until the Arabs took it. They held it till seventy years ago, and now its sovereignty seems to shift between the Spaniards and the Portuguese. They've converted the heathen mosques to churches, but the Arabic influence is still visible in the buildings, and the people of the land still pray to their Arab God."

"How do you know," she asked, "if you've never been here?"

"When captain meets captain in foreign ports, they talk of where they've been and what they've done. They pass on knowledge of the danger of the sea, of submerged rock and where wrecks cause a hazard to shipping."

Grace nodded, studying the way in which the dusky men, some in filthy breeches and pantaloons, others in striped *jellabas*, were straining to pull the hawsers against the outgoing tide. If they lost the battle, the ship would have to down anchor and wait for the tide to turn before they tried again.

"This is a strange land," Grace said. She felt like a little girl again, full of the enthusiasms she remembered so clearly from when she'd sailed with her father to the distant ports of Europe. "I've been to the Baltics and the Azores and far within the Mediterranean, but never the coast of Africa. These domes on the buildings and the colors of the houses are very strange to me. I've seen similar in southern Spain, but somehow not like this. There's so much color here, so much excitement. It isn't like the ports of Scotland or Germany or France where things seem to be done properly. Look down there, Rogan," she said, pointing to a group of black-frocked women, their faces and bodies completely covered by cloth and veils. "What do you make of that? And listen to the sound they're making."

"They're Moorish women," he explained, "probably from the Atlas Mountains far yonder. The noise they're making I've not heard before, but I've been told of it. They make that sound with their tongue and their throats and they do it when they're celebrating some victory or farewelling a man of valor. See, that must be him there." He pointed to a magnificent-looking Arabic man dressed in robes and a headdress. "He must be going on a pilgrimage to the city of Mecca. It's the season."

"Mecca?"

"It's the holy place of the Moslems. Like Jerusalem is the holy city of Christians. They go there every year on a pilgrimage called a *hadj*, in order to celebrate the birthday of their prophet, Mohammed, or so I've heard."

She glanced at him in admiration. For the entire journey she'd happily taken a secondary position to him, deferential to his knowledge and learning much from his treatment of the men and the way he handled the ship. Now she was discovering he knew a lot more besides.

"You're a knowledgeable man, Rogan Ferrick," she said.

He shrugged modestly.

"So tell me, why is there so much talk of war these days?" she asked. "In Ireland, we're the last people on earth to hear about what's going on in the rest of the world. What do you hear?"

"What do you want to know?"

"For one thing, why is there always so much trouble with the Spanish? Why can't England and Spain stop their constant squabbling?"

"Because the father of England's boy king, Edward VI, was a man of great power and determination. Henry VIII turned England against the Church of Rome and created his own religion, but it was only in order to marry a witch called Anne Boleyn. The Pope had told him that marriage was forever, and so King Henry told the Pope to go to Hell and back."

"I know that much. And he had a daughter called Elizabeth who is locked up in a castle, and another older daughter called Mary who is his daughter with the Spanish queen, Catherine from Aragon. So if there are these close links between them, why do Spain and England hate each other?"

"Because the ruler of Spain is Charles I, but he's also known as Charles V and called the Holy Roman Emperor. He's got a desire to join England to Spain and have the whole world Catholic, but England refuses to return to the Church of the Pope in Rome. They say that Charles is looking toward marrying his son Philip to Mary. Mary will become queen if Edward dies, and there's a good chance of that, for they say that there are some days that the boy can hardly walk he's so weak."

"But how can Mary become queen in her own right? She's a woman," Grace asked in surprise.

"Apart from Edward, there are no men sired by Henry to rule the land. Plenty of bastard children, or so I've heard tell, but only Edward born in wedlock. So there's only Mary left if Edward dies, and then following her, if she dies without issue, Elizabeth might become queen."

Grace laughed. "I can't see a woman ever becoming Queen of England."

Rogan shrugged and said softly, more to himself than to Grace, "I never thought I'd see a woman take command of a merchant ship."

The port of Tangier smelled of spices and sunshine and shit. Even the air itself was dusty; the vivid shafts of sunlight which slanted between the buildings appeared diffused and dimmed, dulling passageways and making crowded alleys look as though they were in the midst of a sandstorm.

Grace took a walk around the city, accompanied by several sailors for protection. She loved the open spaces of the place, where the air was bright and vivid. Green and blue and yellow parrots glided overhead, screaming and squawking and fighting for a scrap of food; monkeys clambered up and down the palm trees like miniscule beggars, running up to satchels and bags to steal whatever food was inside, before the owners realized what they were doing and chased them away, screaming in some guttural language which was harsh and coarse and foreign to her ears, not unlike the language of monkeys themselves.

It was a place of magic and spirit, but also of diseases and dispirits, a place which excited her but which she'd be glad to see retreating into the distance as the cleansing wind in her face and the smell of sea spray in her nostrils dispelled the stench of rotting meats and pungent spices.

But while she was here she was determined to learn and enjoy as much as she could. It was the colors of the people and their clothes which transfixed her; she caught her breath in amazement every time a tall and magnificent African woman or a sailor from Araby walked past. They were dressed in the colors of the parrots which flew overhead, brilliant raiment as multihued as the skins of the people in the port. Olive skins from Italy or Greece, dark brown from Arabia, earthy colors from India, and the deepest of blacks from the dark and mysterious continent of Africa.

This was a colorful place alright, but colorful like a desert snake—beautiful to look at, but deadly to the unwary. For here were mercenaries who would sell themselves to the French one day, the Spaniards the next, and be Gallowglass for the Scottish the day after. Here were whores who slept with captains to gain both money and information which they'd pass on to their paymasters, who would then know which ship carried what cargo. Here were pirates who paid handsomely for this information and who followed a ship out to sea, blasting her sails off and crippling her, even within sight of the shore. Here was a land which was rich and plentiful by the shore of the sea, yet which ten miles inland was a deadly desert which could kill the unwary in a day and bleach his bones in a week.

Yes, it was a treacherous and treasonous place, a beautiful and dangerous landscape, breathtaking even as it caused one's final breath.

Grace and the captain had parted company for the afternoon, he to pay the landing and mooring fees; she to continue searching for cargo they could purchase with the agreed five hundred pounds and make a profit of ten times that by selling it to the French and the Scots.

She ordered ten cases of pepper spice, two of saffron, dozens of carpets of every shape and size and hue imaginable, bales of the finest wool she'd ever felt, as well as sandalwood from the orient, scented candles, golden crucifixes and silver necklaces. There was also a bale of the finest Moroccan lace she'd ever seen, and even though it took her beyond what she could afford, she hoped that the dealer would throw it in as a courtesy.

The dealers were instructed to have the stock delivered by noon, when they would be paid. The ship would then sail on the evening tide. She returned to the merchantman, well pleased with herself.

Though she didn't want to interfere with Captain Ferrick's command of the ship, she knew that when he returned he would be anxious to sail as soon as possible. The more time they spent on shore with people knowing they'd just paid a fortune for cargo, the greater the danger of their being robbed. So Grace gave orders to prepare the ship for immediate sailing. The ropes were uncoiled, made ready for immediate unfurling when the ship was poled away from the shore; the galley was stocked with adequate provisions for the return journey; water barrels were rolled and wheeled aboard; boxes of fruits were lofted up from the quayside on slung panniers, along with plentiful supplies of rum. Though all the traders wanted immediate payment, Grace told them to return when Captain Ferrick was on board, for he held the ship's treasury.

As the sun rose high in the sky, and the noises and smells of the port intensified, Grace began to grow anxious. Everything had been made ready to slip the hawsers from the quayside bollards and glide out of port on the evening tide. She and Captain Ferrick had already planned their course to avoid being followed by pirates. Instead of sailing nor'west out of Tangier to skirt the coast of Spain, they'd sail eastward into the Mediterranean for twenty leagues, as though sailing for Araby, before striking out for deep water and the Spanish coast. Then, when lost to the sight of land, they'd turn on a course due west which would take them past Gibraltar and the Pillars of Hercules and far into the Atlantic Ocean.

It was a good plan, and would confound the pirates and Spaniards who no doubt were planning to follow immediately into the deep and clandestine waters of the Atlantic, where they could pillage the cargo and scuttle the ship with impunity. By sailing a false course, they'd be over the horizon and lost to sight before any pirate ship could catch them.

Grace looked up at the setting sun in the sky in concern. Just then she heard a carriage clattering along the quayside. She rushed to the side, expecting to see her captain, but when three Portuguese, one a grandee, all feathers and ruffs and perfume, stepped out and ascended the gangplank, her heart filled with dread.

"Who is in charge of this ship in the absence of the captain?" the grandee asked in heavily accented English.

Grace stepped forward ahead of the small party of sailors who had gathered on the deck to see what was afoot.

"I believe I'm in charge," she said.

He looked at her strangely.

"I am the wife of the owner. I am also one of the ship's crew," she told him.

He looked at his colleagues, who shrugged. "Madam, I have discomforting news. The captain of this merchantman, Mr. Ferrick, was attacked on his way to the harbormaster's offices. He and the two men accompanying him were attacked by robbers and cutthroats. They were all killed. We attempted to assist them as soon as we heard, but by the time we reached their bodies the villains had disappeared with the contents of the captain's money pouch. I'm deeply sorry. Naturally we will not expect you to pay port charges because of this outrage."

Captain Ferrick . . . dead? Rogan Ferrick? Her gentle friend? Grace's mind was reeling. It didn't make any sense. He had been so alive when he'd left the ship, she thought, so full of vigor, so full of the excitement of the return voyage and beating the O'Flaherty at his own game. He'd taken two strong men to protect him in the port; they'd all been armed with pistols, cutlasses and daggers.

"What happened?" Grace asked hoarsely. In the background she could hear the news being spread like the plague among the other members of the crew.

"It was a common trick, often played on strangers. His route to our offices was blocked by a deliberately overturned cart, which meant that he and his protectors had to divert to a narrow and less-used laneway. Once they were deeply into the lane, a group of thugs appeared at one end, blocking off their exit; then another group appeared at the other. The captain and his men had no chance. They were outmanned. The governor of the city sends to you his deepest commiserations and hopes that you won't think too poorly of Tangier in the future. These things happen, even in the best-regulated port.

"Now, if you'll forgive me, I must depart as I have much work to do. Their bodies will be returned to your ship shortly."

He turned and walked down the gangplank, followed by his small entourage, leaving Grace standing in shock. She felt her legs begin to buckle and her resolve disappear. She wanted to burst into tears of anguish and rage, to collapse on the deck and shout her misery and fear to the sky. But the crew were on deck now, watching her and waiting in silence.

For reasons which she never quite understood, her mind cleared and all emotion, all fear evaporated.

She turned to the men and saw their shock and dismay. They had loved their captain; he was acknowledged as one of the most skillful and considerate in all of Ireland. She knew the next few moments were of the greatest importance in her short life if she and the crew were to get out of Tangier alive.

"You've all heard," she said in a voice which was loud and confident, taking the men by surprise. "Rogan Ferrick is dead, as are Mr. Corcoran and Mr. Monaghan. This is a tragedy, but we must think of the protection of the living before we have time to mourn the dead. We are the living. We must now protect ourselves against the fuchking murderers and bastards of this fuchking hellhole.

"We have provisions to last us the return journey. We haven't yet paid for them, and we don't have any more money for such niceties now that our treasury has been robbed. Yet these provisions are on board, and it would be the cause of our deaths at sea if we were to return them, and an especially nasty death it would be from thirst and ravenous hunger."

The men looked at each other, not sure where the young woman was going with her talk.

"Yes, I may only have the body of a weak and feeble woman, but I have the heart and mind of a sea captain; yes, I may be young, but I've been sailing longer than many of you, having suckled at the breast of the sea since I was a child in my father's arms. This isn't the time or the place for you to decide whether or not to follow me. You will follow me, for you have no choice. For if you jump ship in Tangier, you'll be dead before morning, killed by that mob of cutthroats and villains out there.

"Now, will you follow me out of the heads of Tangier, or do you entertain your forthcoming deaths by staying in port?"

They didn't answer. They just nodded.

Then one of them, the senior man on board in the absence of the captain, Mr. Tiernan, said, "Forgive me, ma'am, but how do you propose to pay for the cargo when we've got no money? And the providores who loaded the supplies will be back shortly for their payment."

"I can't pay for the cargo, and so I'll turn it back. I'm tempted to take the damn stuff from the dockside, but we don't have the time to load it. Anyway, the ship will be lighter and faster when we make a run for it on the evening tide. Those to whom we owe money for supplies might like to present their accounts to the bastards who killed our captain."

Again, the men nodded.

"Right, gentlemen, let's get to it. Mr. Tiernan, could you kindly supervise the setting of the mainsail and ensure that the rigging is made good for light winds. Mr. Bourke, would you and three men secure the supplies in the galley as well as ensure that the portside cannon are primed and loaded in case we're fired upon from the castle. Meantime, I'll go and tell the merchants that I've changed my mind and they can take their fuchking merchandise back from the dock, for I shan't be purchasing any of their damnable goods."

She turned and descended the gangplank, her head and heart in turmoil. She wanted to wail for the death of so honest and lovely a man as Ferrick, but she'd have plenty of time for that once they were out of harbor. For now she had to show herself as a man with the body of a woman. Her crew knew they had no alternative but to follow her out of Tangier. However, once they were safe and in deep waters, she'd have to prove her ability to captain the vessel. And girlish tears were the one thing that the men didn't want to see.

When she returned from the amazed merchants, who'd anticipated substantial profits even though the young woman had bargained harder than they'd expected, Grace O'Malley forced a smile onto her face so that her mood wouldn't show to the men. She could see they were morose and despondent. They'd obviously been talking among themselves, and nervousness had set in. Leadership was what was wanted, strength of purpose and courage, so that the men had someone to rally around.

"Mr. Tiernan, come here if you please, and bring two men with you."

Grace walked to the middle mast and gestured for the three men to huddle close to her. She sensed that they wanted to say something to her about the crew's unwillingness to follow her, about her lack of experience, but out of deference to the wife of the owner, they were holding their peace . . . for now.

"Mr. Tiernan. We're going to need a diversion when we sail out of port, so that our leaving isn't noticed. I want you and these two men to take a barrel of gunpowder and a fuse into the middle of the *shuk* and hide it there. Then, when I hoist the Irish flag, I want you to set light to the fuse and run like rabbits back to the ship. It'll explode and cause mayhem; hopefully it'll kill some of the bastards who killed our captain and his crew. And in the confusion, nobody will notice us slipping away. If the tide is a strong one, it'll take less than half an hour to clear the heads and be out of reach of the castle's cannon. Then we'll be on our way home, light and high in the water, and a match for even the fastest pirate ship."

Tiernan looked at the other two men, who nodded. "Alright, ma'am. We'll do it. And we'll take as many of these filthy Arabs with us as God will permit."

Shortly afterward, when Tiernan and his men had left the ship, Grace looked down at the water and saw that the debris which floated on top was starting to move westward toward the harbor mouth with the change to the evening tide.

Any moment now traders would be arriving for payment for the supplies now safely stored below deck. The bodies of poor Captain Ferrick and his men hadn't yet been returned, but she wasn't as much concerned with their mortal remains as the danger the ship was in now.

She reckoned that Tiernan had been gone long enough to have found a suitable place to put the powder. She ordered two men to go and release the forward and midship ropes, so that the only rope securing the ship was astern. Another order was given to raise the Irish flag. She saw it run up, and instructed another man to stand by the hawser astern and to release it from the bollard the moment Tiernan and the others were seen running back, like bats out of Hell.

Moments later, Grace was stunned by a most hideous explosion, a boom which shattered even the frenetic music of all the voices of the quay. So violent was the explosion that she felt the heat and rush of wind on her face, even though its source was in the middle of the marketplace. Then a huge plume of smoke and fire erupted, looking like a black and malevolent octopus, its tentacles weaving up into the air. Suddenly the far side of the *shuk* was enveloped in a plume of fire as the cloth awnings of the stalls caught fire, and the bales of hay and even the underside of the palm trees burst into flame. Smoke and flame roiled together in the maelstrom and quickly rose to the rooftops, flattening out over the buildings until it became a cloud, blocking out the light.

And then came screams. Men, women and children cried out in pain and fear and horror. The screams rose in agony, joined by the screeching of monkeys and the howling of dogs; a flock of birds rose skywards in noisy panic, flapping and flying hither and thither to escape the turmoil.

If there was a vision of Hell, then this was it. Grace was caught up in the horrifying spectacle, and for just the briefest of moments thought of running off the ship to aid the victims; but then she saw Tiernan and the two others running like crazed men toward the ship and suddenly she remembered where she was and the purpose of causing the inferno.

Her mind reeled as she stared at the hideous cloud of black smoke and heard the screams of innocents horribly injured by the explosion she'd caused. She wanted to beg their forgiveness, to give aid, to bind their wounds and explain to mothers and fathers, husbands and wives, the reason for their grief. But as Tiernan and the others shouted to her to cast off, she instantly remembered the danger she and her men were in.

It catapulted her into action.

"Release the stern hawser!" she shouted. She turned to the crew who were standing at the railings, riveted by the scene of devastation. "Prepare to take in the gangplank the moment Tiernan's back on ship. Man the poles and push us off the quay the instant the gangplank is up. Prepare to set mainsail. Helmsman, set to for the middle of the channel."

Nobody moved, all stood staring at the ferment.

Grace withdrew her pistol and fired a shot into the air. All the men turned in shock to look at her. "NOW, you artless bat-fouling lewdsters!" she screamed.

The men instantly turned and rushed to their duties. Tiernan and the other two raced up the gangplank, sweating and panting after their deadly race to the ship. The gangplank was raised, polemen pushed the aft, then the midship, then the stern off the jetty clear of nearby ships, and the merchantman slowly gathered speed as the current, grudgingly at first, but soon with increasing certainty, carried her westward.

The ship struck center channel quickly, and the helmsman set his course for the harbor heads. The mainsail picked up the following westerly wind and gave them a good speed, but they would soon be sailing past the Castle of Tangier which guarded the entryway to the harbor, and without the proper clearance from the harbormaster, they were likely to be shot at.

Grace ordered her men to stand by their cannon, though against the formidable firepower of the castle, there was little the merchantman could do.

Shielding her eyes from the glare of the sun descending into the west, Grace saw that there were three or four soldiers posted as lookouts on the walkway. But to her amazement, none of them was looking to sea. All, as she'd hoped and prayed, were looking at the billowing smoke from the explosion in the distant *shuk*. She thanked her Christian God that the garrison commander was obviously out of the castle and in the city, for nobody had given orders to ensure the harbor exit.

It was with luck and bravado that they sailed beyond the castle and out of range of the castle guns; then through the heads so that they could see the stretch of the coastline on either side of them.

"Mr. Helmsman, set a course for the western Spanish coast," Grace ordered.

Tiernan looked at her strangely. "But the captain said we were going to sail eastward, because—"

"Mr. Tiernan, my orders are clear. We sail north by northwest to the Spanish coast, and then head sixty leagues due west before bearing due north. We have no cargo; we'll not be of interest to pirates. Of more danger to us will be the ships of the Governor of Tangier, and I want to be far away and in deep water before they come after us."

Mr. Tiernan nodded, and the helmsman followed the course set by the young woman.

It was her first true command; the first time she'd been in absolute control of a ship. Other times the men had jokingly taken orders from the spirited daughter of the Captain O'Malley; or when she'd sailed with Captain Ferrick, the crew had obeyed because they knew the captain was truly in charge. But now they only had her command, and they weren't happy.

Grace knew that she had to gain their respect as captain within hours of sailing or there would be mutiny. It wasn't too much to suppose that in their cur-rent mood, the crew might pitch her overboard in the dark of a night, and who would ever know?

And so, gently yet firmly she began to give the men orders. Simple orders at first—which sails to hoist to take advantage of a breeze, which lines and nets to cast for fish, which direction to sail to take advantage of unexpected and un-seen currents. They were orders which could have been given by any experi-enced captain, but they created a sense of normality following their escape from Tangiers, and most importantly, established Grace as the undisputed cap-tain of the ship.

It was one thing to use guile and deception to escape from the harbor, yet another to navigate them all safely home.

The skepticism of the men, their anxiety at following the real commands of a woman, rather than just playing around with her instruction on the can-non, had frightened them at first. By right, the first mate, Mr. Tiernan, should have taken command in the absence of the captain, but Mistress Grace's deter-mination to command the ship was so great, and she the wife of the owner, that even he didn't have the gall to stand up and face her. And so far, she was doing alright.

They'd been at sea for a night, and by dead reckoning, they were in the Gulf of Cadiz, soon having to bear northwest if they were to avoid the shallows close to landfall.

It was a bright morning, and the crew felt a growing confidence in their new and unusual captain, though nobody was happy returning to Ireland without the profits of a cargo to divide up. So dire was this prospect, that unless things turned round quickly, some of the men and their families would be hungry this winter.

Just then the lookout in the crow's nest shouted down, "Sail to starboard."

Grace walked over to the railings. She saw the ship in the distance, though it was too low on the horizon to determine anything about it. She called up to the lookout, "What flag is she flying?"

"Dutch," he shouted down.

Mr. Tiernan scowled. "You'll address the Mistress as Captain, you poltroon!"

"Dutch, Captain," came the hasty response.

Grace smiled and nodded her appreciation to Mr. Tiernan. She was pleased that it was a Dutchman, for she disliked the Dutch for being cold and mean-spirited.

"Is she sailing low in the water?" she shouted.

"Too far to say, Captain, though she's certainly not high in the bow. Yes, ma'am, I'd say she was fat and slow. We're doing twice her speed."

Mr. Tiernan came over and stood by her. None of the crew had enjoyed much sleep, but the sadness of the previous day's loss was not weighing them down as she'd feared. Indeed, their spirits weren't nearly as distressed as they might have been, for they'd killed many Arabs in revenge and stolen their victuals, and that was enough to ensure satisfaction, if not happiness.

Grace's own distress and grief at losing Rogan Ferrick and the other men was held very privately. She'd retired to her cabin to cry and mourn the loss of a man whom she knew she could have grown close to. She also knew that if God ever permitted her to see Ireland again, she'd compare a man such as Rogan with her own husband, and mourn the dead captain afresh.

"A Dutchman, Mr. Tiernan."

"Yes, Captain."

"What do you think, Mr. Tiernan? A nice fat prize?"

He looked at her in astonishment.

"You're surely not thinking . . ."

"I certainly am. We've ample shot and powder, and it'll make the men feel better about the loss of Mr. Ferrick if we come home with a fat fuchking cargo. We're in deep ocean, and so nobody will know she's been attacked until she fails to dock."

Her logic was good, but he was skeptical. "What will she be carrying, do you think?"

"A Dutch merchantman heading from the Balearics, and then beyond, possibly just put sail from Genoa or Venice. My guess is that she'll be carrying cargo from the east for the Hanseatic League. Silks, maybe, or other Asian textiles, or jewelry or gold or spices. Who can say? But one thing's certain. If they're a merchantman, we'll have double the guns they've got. What say, Mr. Tiernan, are you game?"

"But don't the ships of the Hanseatic League often travel with an armed escort? What if there's a galleon hugging closer to the shoreline and she comes upon us when we're loading the cargo? What if . . . ?"

"What if there's a gale and we're sunk? What if Captain Ferrick hadn't been killed? What if . . . What if . . . For God's sake, Mr. Tiernan, life's full of "what-if's." Let's get in there and make up for our losses from Tangier."

He nodded. She was right. A good prize would set him up for the rest of the year and would reward the other men for the dangers of putting into the North African coast.

Grace turned to the helmsman and shouted, "Put to alongside the Dutchman." Then she shouted to the flagman, "Put out a flag of distress. The square one with the ball beneath."

Tiernan again turned on her in astonishment. "But that says our ship's disabled. You can't put up that flag, not even in disguise."

"Mr. Tiernan, I'm rewriting the articles of piracy. We're fooled into thinking that pirates are gentlemen. Today's pirates are Algerian and Moroccan and Arab. They're evil and give no quarter. Do you expect me to be ladylike when Captain Ferrick has just been killed?"

"But the sailors have done no harm to us, Captain," he continued to protest, pointing to the Dutchman, which was growing in size by the minute.

"They mightn't have, Mr. Tiernan, but the crew of this ship has been badly damaged by bastards in Tangier and I'm in no mood for propriety. I'm of a mind to get my ship and my crew safely back to our home, with a tidy profit to make up for our loss."

Tiernan shook his head in disquiet. "If word gets back that we've flown a false flag, our name will be—"

"Do you think I care a jot about our name in the mouths of such as sail these waters? The only reputation we need for sailing this sea is of strength and cunning. Gentlemen pirates die from having their guts skewered just as surely as the scum in Tangier. No, Mr. Tiernan, we'll take the cargo from the Dutchman and send her on her way. And if it becomes known that Grace O'Malley breaks the rules of the sea, then so be it. Like I said, I'm rewriting the very name of piracy itself."

Mr. Tiernan shrugged his shoulders and wondered if he'd ever manage to come to terms with the changes taking place around him.

The captain of the Dutchman had seen their flag of distress and was changing course to make for her.

"Lower the mainsail," she ordered. She saw Mr. Tiernan's look of concern. "If we're slow in the water, we'll have greater stability to fire at her when she approaches. It's a technique I learned from my father."

Tiernan had been with Donal O'Flaherty when he'd been pirating off the Tenerife and Santa Cruz, but on those occasions the master had gone at the booty ship like a hound out of Hell, bearing down with guns blazing and then men in the rigging screaming and shouting like demons. Logically, what the mistress was suggesting was more intelligent—let the ship sail toward them, and control when and how they demast her—but the way she was doing it didn't sit right with him, and he worried about the rest of the crew and how they would react to such a devious device.

As soon as the ship was in range, the helmsman was ordered to turn broadside on, and fifteen cannon rang out in a volley of shot which holed the side of the Dutchman, tore through the rigging and caused mayhem on deck. From the distance the Irish crew heard screams and crying and shouts of rage.

At first musket shot rang out, and then the helmsman of the Dutch trader tried to turn broadside so that his captain could engage cannon, but her masts were broken, and the rigging so badly damaged that the turn of the rudder was too sluggish, and the ship wouldn't obey the helmsman's command. The ship was virtually dead in the water.

Unscathed, Grace's ship turned and soon she was starboard on, and more cannon fire rang out, until there was no further opposition from the Dutchman.

Another volley of shot into the rigging to ensure the Dutchman was totally crippled, and then Grace walked to the side of the ship and shouted across, "I wish to speak to your captain."

There was no answer, so she repeated herself in French.

A man's voice called from the distance, "I am the captain. You are a devil woman. Let me speak to your captain and ask him how he dares to fly a flag of distress, and we come to your aid, and you attack us. Let me speak to your captain immediately."

"I'm the captain."

There was a long silence, punctuated by shouts of pain and despair from the Dutch ship, and noisy attempts to put out the fire in the rigging.

Eventually the captain shouted over, "But you're a woman!"

"Yes, and you'll hand over your cargo."

She turned to her men, who were looking at her in admiration. "Cutlasses at the ready, lads, in case we encounter resistance. Prepare to board. Any show of force and cut them dead."

"Aye, Captain," her men shouted.

She turned to the Dutchman. "I'm coming aboard, Captain. My name is Grace O'Malley. I'm an Irish pirate."

CHAPTER FIVE

D onal O'Flaherty looked at the ten large purses of gold pound coins with a mixture of avarice and abhorrence. It was as though the money, seductive and captivating as it was, was somehow tainted.

His father, old Muireadach, the Lord of the Name and an old sea captain himself, had no such misgivings, however. He walked over to the purses, which were displayed on the table in the center of the great hall, and picked up a flagon of wine. Holding it close to his lips, he stroked one of the purses and shouted to the assembly, "All men of the O'Flaherty, stand before the Mistress of the Good Name, the wife of my son and drink to her health and wealth and fortune."

Everyone in the room stood and drank, many of the spouts from the flagons missing mouths and spilling wine down the front of tunics.

Together, they banged the flagons down on the table to a raucous racket, and shouted out, "Grace O'Flaherty, Grace O'Flaherty!"

Then Muireadach O'Flaherty held up his hand for silence. He turned to his daughter-in-law, and said, "When I first met you, when you had already walked down the aisle of the church and before you would allow the poor fuchking priest to let my son marry you," he burst out laughing as he remembered the fiery young thing who'd withstood the tempest which was Donal, "I was very afraid that your mouth was going to be your downfall. We O'Flahertys have always paid respect to our women, but it's been the men who run the clan and its estates and businesses. I was afraid that your mouth would get in the way of your duties, and that you wouldn't settle into our ways.

"But I was wrong, for you, my girl, are a lady out of the ordinary. Whoever heard tell of a woman who was both a sea captain and a pirate and who beat men at their own game?"

All the men and women cheered. Grace was flushed from wine and from the admiration she was receiving.

"And to have downed a Hanseatic League merchantman, why, that'll cause all sorts of problems for the English, for nobody will believe that a woman did it, and an Irish woman at that." Again, he burst out laughing, and once more raised the flagon over his shoulder to toast Grace, twisting his head so that he'd catch the stream as it emerged from the neck of the bottle. But much of the thin spout which arced over his shoulder and into his mouth missed and spilled over the table and down the front of his jerkin, causing him to laugh even harder.

"Stand, you bastard sons and daughters of whores, and toast the woman who is my daughter-in-law, and the wife of my heir Donal and the mother of my grandchild. Stand and toast Grace O'Flaherty."

Again they stood, and Grace bowed in joy to all parts of the room.

"So," Muireadach shouted, "tell me again how much the cargo from the Dutchman fetched when you traded in France and Scotland. Let me hear how our treasury is suddenly so hale and hearty."

"We lost £500 in Tangier, but gained £8915 from my little adventure. From that has to be taken £600 as payment to the crew for sailing, as well as a bonus dividend of £400 which I've ordered for the bravery which my crew showed following the loss of their beloved Rogan Ferrick. That makes a fraction over £7500. Not quite the £10 000 I promised, but nonetheless a good profit."

"Aye," shouted her husband, who hadn't stood once to toast his wife, "but you lost a fuchking good captain and two of my crew."

"It wasn't her who lost them, Donal," his father snapped, "but the bastards in Tangier. Sons of whores for Arabs, they all are. Didn't I tell you not to send her to Tangier with the Barbary pirates and all! And tell me, which sea-farer here hasn't lost a man to a foreign brothel or some cutthroat in a foreign port? It's the risk of being a sailor. Don't go blaming your wife for the death of poor Rogan Ferrick, for he knew the risks and he was well paid for those he took."

The room lapsed into silence, for Captain Ferrick had sailed with many of the men in the great hall and had been liked and admired by them all. His loss would be felt, but now wasn't the time to mourn. Now was the time to celebrate.

"And with the two thousand which Donal earned from trading out of Cadiz, we've over nine thousand new and lovely gold pounds. That'll pay for many a journey, and will fund the fights you seem to get into, Donal."

His son looked at him in anger. Muireadach knew that something had to be done, or it would go badly for Grace later in the night when the festivities were over and she was alone with her husband.

"And this brings me to the other cause for my inviting you tribal leaders of the Clan O'Flaherty to the castle. For now that my son has a suitable wife, it's time for me to hand over all the estates and fortunes to him. I'm in my sixtieth year, and God has granted me twenty years more than most men are permitted. Until Donal had a wife who would stand by him, I've been loath to grant him full access to the title which by rights should have been his on my death. For these past five years I've made him joint chieftain because of my need to share the workload and because of the pains I get from my joints, but now is the time for him to become the leader in name and in property.

"Now he has Mistress Grace O'Flaherty to share his burden, just as I've had my wife to share mine, he is fully equipped to be the chieftain. And like my wife, Grace is as powerful and prevailing a woman as any who stands by her lord and master, and I'm certain that the Clan O'Flaherty is in good and safe custody in the stewardship of my son and his young wife."

Grace looked at Muireadach in astonishment. She had returned from Tangier as a heroine, and now suddenly she was fully the Mistress of the O'Flahertys. Not just wife to the master, but mistress in her own right. Her word, in much the same way as her husband's, would be law, always assuming that he didn't countermine her instructions. She looked at Donal, whose face had brightened with the news.

"Father. I didn't expect . . ." he stammered.

"No, you didn't expect the title, but it's up to you to earn it. I confer it, but now every man on O'Flaherty land has to recognize you as their leader. And that means you can no longer fight unnecessary battles with neighboring lands. It means you have to call your castellans to account for every farthing and halfpenny. It means that you have to dispense justice to your serfs and servants and those in bond to you. Justice from the head, Donal, and not just from the sword." He looked at Grace. "And it means that you have to honor the promise you made to your wife when you set her the challenge. For she has, by all accounts, won the challenge, Donal. She didn't beat you back, but she raised far more capital than you, and is respected by her crew to the same extent as any captain in men's breeches. Grace O'Flaherty will be the master of our fleet of ships."

Donal's younger brother, Liam, jumped to his feet and shouted out, "No! No, that's not the way it'll be. Donal promised those fuchking ships to me."

The entire banqueting hall turned and looked at the young man who had interrupted the proceedings. Everybody knew Liam as a puny young man, a lad who lived in Donal's shadow, who did Donal's bidding and was the butt of every servant's joke. And most especially, everyone knew the hatred he felt toward Grace, who had seen through all his lies and prevarications and had uncovered many of the thefts he had committed against his parents and even his brother Donal.

"Donal said that as he was first back, I'd be made master, that she was a woman and would never . . ." Liam stammered, withering under the gaze of so many eyes.

Grace looked at the young man coldly. Ever since she'd first married Donal, Liam O'Flaherty had done everything in his power to affront and diminish her. She knew that he was more than just young and silly and offensive; she knew him to be cruel to the servants and vindictive of those he thought disliked him; she knew that he'd forced himself on many of the servant wenches, and when one found herself pregnant, she was sent packing with neither food nor money nor a word of commendation for a new employer.

Before Muireadach could intervene, Grace said menacingly, "So Liam wants to be master of the line? Tell me, Liam, have you been to sea?"

"Yes!" he said defensively.

"Have you captained a boat?"

"You know I haven't. But Donal said you had it easy, for all you had to do was order your men to do whatever was needed, and he said that you were certain to lose the challenge and he promised the line of ships to me."

"But I didn't lose, Liam. I won. And not only did I win at the trade of being a merchant, but I also captained a crew halfway around Europe. What equivalent can you offer the O'Flaherty clan, except for speaking shite from your mouth and enough bluster and wind to fill a mainsail?"

The young man looked at her in contempt. "I'm a man. Sailing is men's work. Not women's!"

The room descended into a deathly silence. The young man hadn't seen the trap he'd foolishly fallen into. Like a dog rounding on a hare, Grace stepped away from the table and slowly walked into the center of the room.

Theatrically she drew herself to her full height and said loudly, "So it's a man you have to be to captain a ship, is it, Liam? A man, indeed. Well, my man, let me tell you a thing or two about the other men you'll be commanding. They've seen men aplenty commanding them, and if the man who has command of the ship is hated and despised for stupidity or arrogance or cruelty or making mistakes, if the man who commands the ship takes it into dangerous waters because of his lack of experience or ineptitude, if the man who is captain can't do all the things the crew is asked to do, and far better, well, Liam, that man will find himself mysteriously hoisted overboard in the dark of one lonely night.

"You have much to learn about the sea, Liam, before I will allow you to take command of more than a rowboat. For men won't follow you just because you call yourself. "Captain," or shout orders at them. No, Liam, not just because you're a man.

"You see, Liam, you have to prove your manhood to your crew each and every hour of the day. And not just by bedding serving girls who are too terrified to say no, or by paying for the services of foreign whores. You have to prove your skills before a crew of hardened sailors who've already sailed ten thousand leagues while you were still drinking milk from your mammy's tit; you have to show them that you're a real man when things get rough, when you're in the midst of a gale and you're alone in the black of night and the crew's too terrified to bale out the flooding hull for fear of drowning and you have to make certain your commands are followed, even when you know that some of your men will be lost to the deep; for it's then, Liam, that you can't just shout out, 'I'm in command because I'm a man,' but you have to show you're a true man in front of the entire crew.

"Do you follow what I'm telling you, Liam? You can stand before your mammy and pappy and shout out loud that you're a real man, but if you want to captain a ship, it'll take more than the balls you were born with. Every man here has balls, Liam, but it's a real man who'll put them on the chopping block when faced with the horrible challenges the sea throws up."

She looked at him and her face showed her contempt. Liam flushed in embarrassment. He looked for guidance to Donal, then to his father Muireadach. But neither would come to his assistance, for he'd dug himself into the pit and it was up to him to get himself out.

Everyone was looking at him, waiting for his response. As was Grace, who could have let it go at that and earned his permanent hatred. But she decided instead to give him a way out.

"Perhaps, Liam, you would accept the offer of sailing with me and learning what I and the other sailors of your family's line already know. In a couple of years you'll have sufficient skills to captain your own craft. What say you? Will you let me teach you the craft of the sea?"

He said nothing. Instead, to the horror of everyone present, he spat at her and stormed out of the great hall to his chamber.

The room fell into total silence.

Softly Grace looked at her mother- and father-in-law, their faces downcast in shame, and said in consolation, "Well, at least he'll keep his balls for a while longer."

She was alone in her bed and fast asleep, enjoying the comfort of clean linen and a soft straw mattress, when the door to her chamber suddenly burst open.

Donal stood there. Grace was quickly awake and alert; she knew she had to find an escape out of the room before he began to beat her. If he was sufficiently drunk, she could reach the door quickly and then escape into the night. She'd done it four times previously, and on each occasion he hadn't managed to lay a hand on her.

But this time he didn't stagger around, but stood straight and in control within the frame of the door.

"Donal?" Grace said tentatively.

Softly, he said, "Grace, I'd like to apologize for what Liam said to you. It's true I offered him the ships, but it was on the assumption that you'd fail the challenge. I never thought you'd better me."

She was stunned into silence. Not only wasn't he drunk and shouting, but he was talking to her. And being deferential.

"Donal, I—"

"No, let me finish, for these things should have been said to you long ago. I'm not your match when it comes to learning, for I'm a man of action and, in many cases, violence. And I know that I've treated you with contempt since you became my wife. Yet you've proven yourself as a captain, a merchant and a pirate, and by accounts I'm getting from my castellans, you've made considerable savings and the estates are now running in profit. Grace, I want you to know that as the new Chieftain of the Clan O'Flaherty, I'm grateful. I'm proud to have you as my mistress.

"We'll share the running of the estates between us. I'll take the castles and the crofts and the revenue from the merchants who trade and the tolls from our roads; you take our ships to sea and command the fleet. Naturally, in dealings with the other clan chieftains of Ireland, I'll be in command, for they'll never accept a woman as leader, and Brehon Laws prevent a woman from taking the chieftainship; but between the people of the O'Flaherty, it's both of us, you and me, in command!"

He looked down at his feet in diffidence. It was the longest speech he'd ever made to her, and the strangest. For this was a Donal O'Flaherty who was gentler and kinder and more reasonable than any she'd previously encountered.

"I bid you goodnight, madam, and I look forward to seeing you in the morning," he said, turning to leave.

"Donal?"

He looked round at her quizzically.

"Where are you going?"

"I'm leaving you to sleep. It's the early hours of the morning."

"But this is your bed, husband. God knows you haven't seen much of it, but this is where you should be sleeping at night."

He remained silent for an awkward moment. "You would welcome me into your bed?" he asked in amazement. "After all I've done to you . . ."

"I was under the impression that you were my husband."

"But I've treated you evilly. When I've come to your bed, it has been to satisfy my lusts."

"Ah, but that was before I was Mistress of the O'Flaherty. Now that I am who I am, you'll have to treat me with dignity and consideration. Anyway, there's much that I crave, and as you're the only man I've ever been with, it's my right as your wife to satisfy those cravings. Now come in, close the door, and get into your bed with your wife."

During the year in which their relationship improved, Grace gladly welcomed Donal into her bed. When they weren't enjoying the privacy of their marital life, Grace spent her time modernizing her fleet of ships, plotting and planning routes and trading missions from the Baltics to the Balearics. She designed a new flag for the O'Flaherty clan, and a separate one for when she felt like attacking a merchant ship and relieving the captain of his cargo. She sold the clan's smaller ships and purchased larger galleys with rows of oars to give them speed when there was no wind. The calculation of the cost of extra men, versus their speed to port when sailing ships were becalmed, gave Grace confidence that she'd done the right thing, and she would be proven correct over the next year or two.

However, she couldn't participate in the calculation from the beginning, for during the year she fell pregnant with her second child, whom she named Murrough. When the lad was two months old, she gave him into the custody of a wet nurse in order to return to sea.

Her firstborn, young Owen, was now a toddler, and loved to go to sea with his mother on short voyages. These were moments of great joy for Grace, who delighted in giving him the same indulgence as she herself had enjoyed at this age from his grandfather, after whom he was named. If only Owen had lived long enough to see his grandchild. In her first unhappy year of marriage, when her father was still alive, he'd often talked in anticipation of taking his grandson aboard and reliving his joy at seeing young legs struggling to balance on a heaving deck. But her father had died in his bed eighteen months past, and his hoped-for joy was not to be.

As Grace's trading expertise was honed by visits to France and Portugal and Spain, and then the goods she bought were traded with the north of England and Scotland, the coffers of the family began to swell. Indeed, the O'Flahertys had never been richer. For the first time in their history, they had more money than expenses. Donal was fighting less, and saving a small fortune on the importation of Gallowglass. Liam was out of the county, learning how to run the estate of an O'Flaherty friend in Dublin in preparation for running his own estates. Even the weather seemed to have tempered, with a relatively mild winter, no ice to bind the ships to their coves and harbors, and then a warm spring for a good planting and harvest in the summer.

But soon tension began to grow again between Grace and Donal, because as quickly as she returned with chests full of gold ducats and florins and escudas and pounds, Donal demanded half the contents to equip his expanding army. He claimed to have an innate sense that there would soon be a major dispute with the Joyces, eternal enemy of the O'Flahertys, who lived beyond the Maumturk Mountains to the east.

When she was twenty-four, and already spoken of with respect by the Great

Council of Chieftains of Ireland, Grace's flagship, the *Uachtarach*, landed at Bal-lyconneely Bay. Her journey of two months had taken her from the port of Pireaus in the land of the Greeks to Venice where she'd traded bales of fine goat hair for glass, and then to Rotterdam where she'd sold the Venetian glass for a huge profit and purchased a consignment of salted meats and German wine, which she'd sold on the coast of Scotland in the city of Edinburgh to the seneschal of the Palace of Holyrood.

When she returned, exhausted but satisfied both with the profits and the way in which her men were acting as a crew, she expected a loving welcome. But Donal was nowhere to be found. Concerned for his welfare, but mainly furious that she and her ships weren't being accorded the respect they were due, Grace asked the castellan where her husband was.

"At war with the Joyces, madam. A month back, one of the Joyces, the youngest one named Cullen, killed one of our crofters who he claimed had stolen a lamb from over the border. The master ordered the march of the mili-tia and now he's engaged in battle. The Joyces sent for Gallowglass from Scot-land, and there's a barney of a fight brewing. But the master is acquitting himself well, for we've had word back last week that he won a good victory at Maum Bridge and that he's riding north to Leenane where the Joyces are gathering."

"And how many men has he taken with him?"

"Five hundred."

"Five hundred!" she screamed. "Jesus Christ and the Mother of God, five hundred! And while he's out gallivanting and fighting with the neighbors, who's looking after the lands? There's crops to gather, sheep to be sheered, land to be plowed for next year's crop . . ."

"But the master said that unless the dispute was settled, the Joyces would attack us, and—"

"And what?" she shouted. "And the slaughter continues. One of ours dies and then we kill one of theirs."

She was too tired to think. She needed to rest and feel the stability of God's earth instead of a rolling deck beneath her feet. She longed to wash in clean cold river water instead of the saltwater she was forced to bathe in on board. But she also knew that something had to be done immediately or the feud between the clans would wipe out all the profit she'd made.

"Saddle a horse for me," she ordered.

Grace was only able to spend two hours with her young baby, Murrough, before she rode eastward toward the Maumturk Mountains and over into Joyce country. By the time night was beginning to fall, she'd arrived at Cloughburn Castle.

Grace nearly fell off her horse, she was so tired, and the stablehand had to grasp the reins from her hands to steady her as she stepped onto the ground in the castle keep. Unlike the castles in her county, tall towers which could be defended against a year-long siege, this castle was built in the English style and looked like some large stone manor house, defended by turrets and elevated walkways.

She just wanted to sleep, to fall into a bunk or a cot on a mattress of fresh sweet straw and curl up underneath a blanket; but she knew that no matter how she felt, she mustn't show any sign of weakness, for she was here on vital business.

The seneschal came out and spoke to her. "Yes?"

"My name is Grace O'Malley. I wish to speak to the Head of the Clan Joyce." So angry was she with Donal that she used her maiden name instead of her married name.

"And why does Mistress O'Malley wish to speak to the master?"

"For matters which concern the Mistress of the Clan O'Flaherty and the Master of the Clan Joyce."

The moment the name O'Flaherty was mentioned, the seneschal's face changed to stone.

"Wait here," he said icily. He turned to the stableboy. "Instruct the guards to close the gates and keep a close eye on this woman."

"But it's not night," the boy said.

"Do as you're told. Stay with the Mistress O'Flaherty until I return." And he disappeared through the portico of the castle entrance.

Grace waited and waited, desperate to sit down and to have a drink of something warm, like mead or wine infused with cloves, a new spice which traders were now beginning to bring from the far east. But she knew that she had to concentrate her mind on matters at hand.

The seneschal returned and said to her, "The master is away, at war with your husband. The Mistress of the Joyce will interview the Mistress of the O'Flaherty in the antechamber."

He led her up the steps to the portico and in through the entrance hall, where a large gray-haired woman was waiting.

Without any formality, she said, "So you're Grace O'Flaherty. You're younger than I expected. What is it you want in my house?"

"I bid you greetings, Mistress Joyce."

"I'm not interested in your greetings, madam. Only why you've come here when your husband is out in the wilds fighting against mine."

"I'm here to stop the fighting."

Mistress Joyce burst out laughing. "And how do you propose to do that? Your husband's a madman and a drunkard and of a hideous and truculent disposition. He'd kill all of us if he had his way."

"You're right."

Mistress Joyce looked at her in astonishment. She studied the young woman for a long moment. She'd heard much about this young bride, about her captaincy at sea and her exploits as a pirate. She'd assumed that much of the story was tales told by those with an interest in blackening her name, but now she could see for herself, she recognized great courage and audacity in her.

"You look exhausted. Come inside and have a glass of wine," she said.

Grace smiled. "I am exhausted. I've just this morning returned from two months at sea."

"Dear God, and you came straight here!"

"I came to save lives and property from the madness around us."

"The madness of your husband," snapped Mistress Joyce.

"Yes," said Grace, "though it's odd how often madmen find the company of other madmen."

"And what does that mean?"

"Simply, ma'am, that if my husband is provoked to madness by your clan, he'll retaliate, and vice versa, and the fighting becomes a cycle which won't stop until all of us are dead . . . or worse, until the English send in their armies because they can see how weak we have all become from fighting one another. Madness of this kind can't be cured by fighting, only by reason and understanding."

The Mistress of the Joyce looked at the young woman, nodded, and said softly, "We have much to talk about, Mistress O'Flaherty. And I think that a mulled wine will cheer your stomach and my heart. And you'll stay the night of course."

Grace followed her into one of the anterooms, where women of the household gathered after a feast to allow the men to continue drinking. As she sat down by the fireside she noticed that the arms of the chairs were made from the horns and antlers of deer. The room was small and warm from the fire, and Grace saw that it had been decorated with shields and swords, different from the furnishings and tapestries with which she'd ordered her rooms at Ballinahinch to be decorated.

Mistress Joyce poured a glass of wine, then took the hot iron from the fire. She plunged it into the wine, which hissed and sizzled and steamed. Then she handed it to Grace and offered her cake from Madeira, heated and steeped with honey. Grace ate and drank greedily—this was the first meal she'd had since the ship had docked in the harbor.

"So what do you plan to do about stopping the fighting, Grace O'Flaherty?" Mistress Joyce asked.

"I have no idea, but if between us two strong and determined women, we can't get our husbands to put away their swords and muskets and act like men instead of children, then there's something wrong with us."

Mistress Joyce looked at her sternly, for if Grace O'Flaherty wasn't willing to defend her husband's reputation, then Mistress Joyce, if she was to have any purchase in these discussions, would have to shield the name of her husband. But when she saw the openness and lack of dissembling in the young woman's eyes, she realized that this wasn't some trick or quickness of tongue, but a genuine and heartfelt statement.

"Why do you think that my husband is at fault?"

Grace smiled. "I don't say he's at fault. Neither do I say that my Donal is at fault. But between the two faultless and guiltless men to whom we're married, all Hell has broken loose."

Mistress Joyce burst out into laughter. "I like you, Grace O'Malley, never mind that your name is O'Flaherty. You're smart as a horsewhip and honest as a child. So you want to stop these stupid disputes between our clans. As do I. It's costing us a fortune and wasting our time and our manhood. It's the English who are our enemies, and yet we fight each other. I can just imagine the nobility in London laughing into their roasted beef at the way we're killing ourselves and saving them the trouble of sending in more troops to join their conquering army."

Grace nodded and munched on another cake. "You're right, of course, Mistress Joyce. It's the English who are the victors every time my husband fights yours, and that goes for all the other clan leaders and lords of Ireland. Every time an Irishman dies at the hands of another Irishman, the boy king of England and all the fuchking English lords and ladies smile to themselves."

"Damn them to Hell, all Englishmen. Coming across here to Ireland and offering us pretty-sounding titles, and we have to pay them tithes and taxes. And for what, I ask you, Mistress O'Flaherty?"

"For the loss of our country and our pride. And since old King Henry died, the young and sickly Edward seems to be going Protestant mad. Have you heard tell that Mary of Scotland landed in France to wed Francis II?"

Mistress Joyce shook her head in astonishment. "But that will mean . . ."

"It will mean that England is surrounded by Catholic enemies in the north and in Ireland and in France and Spain and everywhere. By God, it was a sorry day when Henry told the Pope to go to Hell. I'll wager that the fat old bastard himself is rotting in Hell right now."

Mistress Joyce raised her cup and said, "I'll drink to that." Then she asked,

"So, Grace O'Malley, how do we stop our men from fighting? And let me say immediately that it's your Donal who is the cause of most of it."

Grace sipped her wine and pondered the matter. "I shall charge you for going to war against my husband. Ten pounds a day for every day your husband causes mine to be away from his work. Plus one pound per day for every man my husband is forced to take with him to defend his property."

Mistress Joyce looked at her in amazement.

"Naturally," Grace said, smiling at the simplicity of this devious plan, "that money will be paid directly to me from your coffers. And it goes without saying, Mistress Joyce, that you'll issue a charge against me in precisely the same terms, which I will pay to you for every day my husband forces yours to be away from his responsibilities, plus the men he is forced to take with him in order to fend off my husband's attacks. The money I pay you will go into your hands, to do with as you will."

Mistress Joyce shook her head, failing to understand what was being said.

"It's really quite simple. Deprive the men of their money and the battles come to an end. How long will your husband be able to wage war against mine without money to buy food and drink, to replenish arms and pay his men for their service? A week? A month? I'll tell you honestly, Mistress Joyce, that if you charge me those rates I've just mentioned, my husband will be forced to return home within days, because his part of the household treasury will become depleted that quickly. Then what will my Donal do? He'll have no money to pay men, or to fight. He'll have to stay at home and dream about his battles instead of fighting them."

Mistress Joyce still didn't understand. "How do you expect me to pay you, Grace O'Malley? I have no access to my husband's treasury. He'll not honor a debt he hasn't incurred, especially one to the O'Flaherty."

"But he'll have to, because under Brehon Laws, if you and I as mistresses of our husband's clans enter into a contract and agreement, then it's binding upon our husbands. Now if we threaten our husbands that we're going to get this agreement witnessed, signed and sealed by the Great Council of Chiefs in Galway, they'll have no alternative. They'll lay up arms and turn them into plow shears, as Christ wanted all men to do . . ."

"That's rich, coming from a pirate," she scoffed.

"I'm a pirate because there are so many freebooters and privateers plying the coastline of Ireland and England and France that unless I rob and pillage, there'll be too little cargo left to make a profit. Half the ships which set sail from Genoa and Venice and other such ports are seen as fat prizes for any captain with a boat and cannon. If my flag wasn't known and feared on the high seas, then all the ships of our line would be fair booty for them. I've worked hard these last few years in becoming known as a pirate whose ships can only be raided at great peril, for it's known far and wide that I'll run to ground any master who fires on my men. It's a reputation of which I'm proud."

Mistress Joyce burst out laughing. "Dear God in Heaven, you make it sound as though you're not breaking the law. You kill and steal and plunder, Grace O'Malley! On land you'd be a highwayman and you'd be hunted down by the King's men and shot on sight; there'd be a reward of ten pounds on your head. Just because you're at sea, doesn't mean that what you do is right."

"But that's where you're wrong, Mistress Joyce. For there's no law on the sea. It's every man for himself. Look at the English, if you don't believe me. Since their boy king has ruled, there's not a merchantman which is safe entering or leaving their port. The English navy is useless, despite their guns and sail; they've no resolve. And truth to tell, I'm sure that King Edward's protector, the Duke of Northumberland, is encouraging English merchantmen to become pirates and go out against the Spanish galleons."

Mistress Joyce shook her head. "Enough of all this talk, Grace. Let me hear more about how we're going to stop our menfolk from killing each other, and instead kill Englishmen and bring peace to our lands."

"Grace!"

The name rang throughout the castle. Those servants whom she had taken into her confidence had already hidden lest the master's fury erupt and strike them dead.

"Grace! Grace O'Flaherty! Come here this instant, you damnable woman!"

Still no answer.

"Grace!"

Servants found reasons to avoid the entry hall and the great hall, sensing that trouble was brewing.

"GRACE!" Donal screamed at the very top of his lungs. "Come to your lord and master and explain yourself, madam. Come now, or by God, I'll hang, draw and quarter you this very night. Come here when your husband commands. NOW!"

Grace was sitting in her bedchamber. She'd planned for this moment since leaving the Joyce household, and now it had arrived. The most recent skirmish had ended. Both sides had withdrawn to their castles. A few men had died, a lot of animals had been stolen. But as always in the battles between the O'Flahertys and the Joyces, nothing much had been gained or lost.

"GRACE!"

Her mind flitted back to when she was a little girl in her home and her father's stentorian voice had resounded throughout the castle. But she mused on happier times for only the briefest of moments, because she was pursuing a strategy which could prove deadly against someone like Donal.

She stood and went to the door of her bedchamber. Looking over the balcony down into the great hall, she saw her husband standing there, alone, still dressed in his battle gear.

The moment she appeared, his fury increased. "Why is there no money to pay for my victory celebration? There was £1000 when I left here two weeks ago, and now Caleb tells me there's not a farthing left. He says that you've spent it all. On what? And how am I going to pay for the banquet, pray?"

Calmly, although still concerned that her men, hidden yet ready to restrain their lord should he try to kill her, might not obey her commands, Grace said, "Donal, I've sent the money to Mistress Joyce in payment for the lost production she has suffered as a result of your going to war against her husband."

All the steam and bluster evaporated from Donal O'Flaherty. It was as though he'd suddenly been struck through the guts by a pikestaff. His mouth opened but no sound came out. Despite the danger to her, Grace fought to prevent herself from laughing at the look on his astonished face.

While he remained in stunned silence, she explained the arrangement she'd come to with Mistress Joyce. She told Donal of the fortune which was now in her treasury and which would remain there while ever he went to war and destroyed the family finances. And she told him that Mistress Joyce would be having precisely the same conversation with the Chieftain of the Clan Joyce right at this very moment.

When she'd finished her brief explanation, Grace began to descend from the balcony down the staircase. Donal remained silent, looking at her, his eyes fixed and narrowing like a dog about to attack. Nearing him, smelling the stench of blood and guts and the decaying flesh of battle on his clothes, she suddenly became very nervous. If he assaulted her could she survive long enough for her men to pounce out from where they were hiding and restrain him?

But he didn't move. Instead he allowed her to come close to him, before he said calmly, "You will return my money or I'll imprison you in the dungeon and you'll starve to death."

"I don't think so, Donal. I've written to my family, telling them to expect a letter every day. If one doesn't arrive, they'll be here with five hundred men and will take this castle apart, stone by stone."

"Then I'll kill you now, and suffer the consequences," he said. "If it's a war with the O'Malleys and a war with the Joyces, then so be it."

She shook her head. "Again, I don't think so, husband. For it's at the victory banquet tonight that you'll be paying your Gallowglass and your army. And without money to pay for the banquet or their wages, who will remain and stand at your back to fight with you?"

Cornered like a rat, he became angry. "Give me my money, Grace. Give it to me now, or there'll be Hell for you to pay. I'm not making light of this matter, woman. Give me money to pay my army and to celebrate, or I'll make you regret every day you live from this moment onward."

"Donal, understand this clearly. Mistress Joyce and I have agreed that there will be no more fighting between our clans. She has been true to her word, and

I shall be true to mine. Now, I shall pay off your Gallowglass from the money Mistress Joyce has given to me, money which is hidden so securely that it'll take till kingdom come for you to find it if you dare to offend me. I shall pay the wages of our menfolk, for they cannot be blamed for the squander of their master. But there will be no banquet. There will be no more wars between the Joyces and us. Our fight is with the English and their avarice over our lands. Our fields must be plowed, our ships must be victualed, our animals tended. These things can't be done when you're off making unnecessary wars."

As a leader of men, he knew when he was beaten, and this was the time for him to cede the battle if he was to fight again in a war.

Donal nodded slowly. "Very well, madam. You will pay our men and send them off. But don't think that this is the end of the matter. You've crossed me in ways which are against the laws of the Almighty. You have trespassed on the affairs of men. And that, madam, is something for which you will answer, both to me and to God. By Jesus, Grace, you will answer for this day."

And he turned and stormed out of the castle.

Grace O'Flaherty stood for long moments looking at the door. She shook her head sadly. Marriage, she thought. Why in God's holy name did women ever marry?

CHAPTER SIX

The Road to London, 17 November 1558

Those who had not previously seen her were struck, not by her tall and proud bearing, nor by her youth and beauty, but by her vivid red hair. Those in the crowd who were old enough to claim that they could remember her father as a young man swore that his hair was of precisely the same color, but others argued vehemently that her father's hair was brown, while hers was as red as a rosy Kent apple.

She did not hear their comments, for her mind was ablaze with the prospects before her. In the twenty-five years the Almighty had granted her, this moment was the first when she could truly and honestly say that she could look forward to a future, that she was finally free.

Since she had been imprisoned in the Tower nine years ago, she had been under constant threat of execution. When Edward had died, his successor, Mary Tudor, had seen treason to the Catholic cause under every stone. Elizabeth's Protestant life had been lived as though on the edge of an axe blade.

But now it was all over! The danger, the nightmares, the whispers behind her back, the dark doings late at night when she was locked in her apartments and could hear conspiratorial voices talking about her in some nearby room, the sudden appearance of a lord of the Privy Council with thunder on his face.

Now she was to be monarch, to be crowned Queen of England, and not one person could touch Her Majesty. Now she had the power to conspire and talk about other people's futures, she held the power of life and death, the power to be good or evil. A power granted to her by God and the fates.

It was all over, and yet it was all beginning. This was the first time in her entire life when she could look out at the trees and the sun and the clouds and know with absolute certainty that she would see them again tomorrow, when she could look at people and rejoice that they weren't potential executioners sent by an English monarch fearful of usurpation, when she could look at a house without wondering what plans for her assassination were being plotted inside.

She was England, queen and mistress of all that remained of her father's once-great realm. She was Elizabeth, the first of her name to be queen in the annals of royal English history. She was Queen Elizabeth, now that poor Queen Mary Tudor had swelled up like a barrel of lard and died in terrible agony from dropsy. Catholic agony, for she was hated by the Pope in Rome and despised by her husband Philip of Spain for failing to produce an heir.

Unforgiving Mary! She could have been loved by all England if she'd only allowed her people to find their own way to God; yet in her Heaven there was only room for Catholics, and she had ensured that anyone who protested against the Pope was branded as a heretic.

Careless Mary, for she had lost Calais, and now poor England had no more possessions in France, but was a lonely and impoverished island nation, surrounded by enemies. England was endangered, for France and Spain and Portugal and so many other nations who had quaked at the knee for fear of England's expansion into their territories were starting to cast their eyes in her direction and wondering whether she could withstand a war or two.

Poor Mary, for she'd bloated up like a suet pudding and only two years ago had told the world that even though she was forty, God and the Pope and her young husband had granted her a Catholic heir, and that it would be a boy, and that she'd restore the holy realm which her mother Catherine from Aragon had so wanted. The Catholic suet pudding had grown and grown until it threatened to burst, but there was no sign of life, and it was soon known that she had only pools of evil-smelling liquids in her belly. At the end she could neither sit nor stand nor do anything but call for her maids and beg them to fetch her husband . . . not that he cared. He was a man, yes, a Catholic man ten years her junior, and when his wife was dying in agony, he was out playing and prettying himself and planting the Spanish seed in the maiden soils of France or Portugal or the Netherlands.

Evil and cruel Mary, for in trying to turn all England Catholic, she'd burned Latimer the Bishop of Worcester and Ridley the Bishop of London and even poor old mild and gentle Cranmer the Archbishop of Canterbury, as well as three hundred other true and stout-hearted Protestant Englishmen.

Spendthrift Mary, for she'd paid out the entire contents of England's treasury on supporting Philip of Spain's adventures to reclaim the northern lands of Europe and bring them back into the fold of the Catholic Church. England was now bankrupt, and it was to Elizabeth that the whole of the country looked to rebuild its fortunes.

The news of Mary's death had been brought to Elizabeth at Hatfield, yet she already knew because the bells had begun ringing all over England and men and women were kissing each other, celebrating that the reign of terror was over. All England rejoiced even more when they heard the news that Protestant Elizabeth had been hailed as queen.

As her transport clattered along the rough and gouged roads toward London, Elizabeth sat back on her cushioned seat and gloried in the moment. She was queen. Ruler of all England. Monarch. Safe.

What a day yesterday had been! It had begun with the frightening arrival of the Great Council, come from London on urgent business; yes, they were expected, but maybe to arrest her and have her shipped to the Tower. For until they paid obeisance, they were still the most powerful men in the realm and could dispose of her as they wished. Had they come to make her queen, or for her final march to the executioner's block?

Wanting to show modesty in case she should be questioned about her intentions, Elizabeth dressed herself in black and whitened her olive complexion with a lotion of poppy seeds, borax, alum, egg whites and shells. Then she descended the staircase, intent upon asking the gathering her first and only question: "Is it to be the Tower?"

But when she appeared and saw that three of the councillors had come forward from the crowd and that one of them was William Cecil, she knew in her heart that everything was going to be alright. Dear, sweet Cecil. He had been her closest ally throughout the evil times, and he was smiling . . . no, beaming.

He was the first to remove his cap, sweep the floor in a majestic bow, and say, "Long live the Queen."

She stood there for long moments as they bowed, waiting for her to release them. But a great and enduring sadness welled up within her bosom, and she knew that she was going to cry, so she excused herself and retired quickly to her room.

When the door was closed, Elizabeth looked at her governess and dearest friend, Kat Ashley, and nodded. She mouthed the words, "I'm the Queen."

Kat smiled. Then they both burst into paroxysms of tears and hugged each other, jumping up and down in their triumph, in their relief.

Kat stroked Elizabeth's head, and kept saying, "My pet, my pet."

And Elizabeth cried time and again, "I'm safe, Kat, I'm safe."

Encouraged by Kat to go down to her subjects and release them from their anxiety, Elizabeth Tudor returned to the withdrawing room. Regally, as befitted her rank, she walked in silence to the window and looked out at the gathering crowd in the park. Already the road to Hatfield was filling with suitors from London. Before the old Queen's body was cold, they were arriving on horses and in litters, eager to secure an interview with the new monarch, desperate to kneel before her and swear their eternal loyalty and love and devotion, to assure her that they had never truly been Catholic in their hearts, nor had they loved any other than Elizabeth. All this to gain the enormous gifts which were now in her power.

But even though she knew that her subjects would now be preening themselves in hope of advancement and its handmaiden, avarice, Elizabeth vowed to remain modest in all things. Unlike previous monarchs, she would not spend the money of her people in building palaces nor stately homes. She would not squander her treasury on unnecessary wars.

Elizabeth roused herself from such thoughts of the future and sat down at the head of the table. The councillors stared at her, as though she was not a real person, but a vision in a church. Sir William Cecil was the first to speak, both because he was the most senior and because his relationship with Elizabeth was the closest.

"Your Royal Highness, we are come to advise you formally that the Queen is dead, and that may God grant long life to the Queen. God save Her Majesty, Elizabeth, Queen of England."

Everyone cheered and applauded. She smiled and acknowledged them, and thought about her last encounter with the members of the Great Council, when she'd been accused of treason in plotting to marry Thomas Seymour. Were any of those present here now, she wondered, culpable in the crimes perpetrated against her?

"My lords," she said, "much has been done against my person in my journey to the throne. With a new reign comes new hope, and now is not the time for recriminations or the settling of old scores; rather, may old scores be ended. So may I thank you for your good wishes and ask you now what is the nature of the throne I am to sit upon?"

Elizabeth listened to them as they discussed the arrangements for her journey to London, her accession, the coronation and the revival of the True Faith of her father Henry. She was shocked when she heard the truth about Philip and his assumption of the role of leader of the Counter Reformation of Europe; she was concerned when she heard the extent of Henry II of France's meddling in the affairs of Scotland. But when they told her how parlous was the state of the exchequer, which was in debt to the extent of £266 000—a fortune—she shouted out in horror. "Why was I not told these things?"

"On the orders of her late Majesty Queen Mary," replied Cecil. "She was always of the assumption that you would lead a revolt against her, and so when you were released from the Tower, she ordered the restriction of information to you."

"But you, Cecil! You should have told me!"

He nodded slowly. Although he was thirty-eight, his hair was already graying, and he looked as burdened as an old man. "Yes, Majesty. I should have, but I was warned that if I uttered one word of politics to you, my own dear Mildred would have been . . ." His voice drifted into a deep silence, the silence bred of fear and subjugation.

Elizabeth breathed deeply and stood. She walked over to Cecil, and put her arms around his neck; she kissed him on the head and said, "Friend, spirit, I bleed that you have been so wronged by the throne of England. I swear this to all you gentlemen. Although I am a woman, I will govern like a king; although I wear a dress, I will clothe myself in the mantle of a prince; and although I am a queen, I will have the courage of a man and shall be ruled by God and His commandments as much as I rule by the laws of England. This is not the body of a tyrant, nor someone who is timid in the face of an enemy. And at this moment, the people of England deserve a ruler who loves them, so that they can love her in return. May my people only fear me for my retribution of their own wrongdoing, and not for mine.

"I will rebuild our fortunes, recapture our lands and rededicate our realms to the glory of God and not of Rome. All men who look upon Elizabeth as their queen will know that I am friend and not foe, that I care for their liberty as much as for their stomachs, and that as they serve their monarch, their monarch will serve them. This, gentlemen, I swear to you, as I will swear to God on the day of my coronation."

And as one, the councillors applauded.

The litter carrying her closer and closer to her new palace reached the outskirts of London, and the crowds grew thicker and thicker. Elizabeth pulled aside the curtains and looked out of the window. At first she thought she saw love in the eyes of her people, but soon she realized that it was relief—relief that the evil times were over, that the murderous reign of Bloody Mary was at an end.

Relief, however, was not settling on the heads of Catholics, for they must have woken in their beds, quaking at the thought of a Protestant queen, wondering what the future held in store for them. Elizabeth closed her eyes and pondered this delicious thought. Perhaps the Catholics, like Protestants in the reign of Bloody Mary, were terrified of being dragged from their beds and accused of witchcraft, terrified that their own children would confess that they conducted Mass in secret. Perhaps, Elizabeth thought, she should embark on a crusade against the Pope who had uttered a Bull of Excommunication on all England in the year she was born. Yet, her soul had not been damned or torn asunder from her body, despite Rome's fulminations. Indeed, England seemed not to have sunk into the sea, despite the withdrawal of the annates which her father had refused to pay to Rome. If the English still lived and breathed despite Rome's curses, what price the Pope? If Elizabeth hadn't felt the sharpness of God's Catholic axe, what value Catholic prayers and redemption? Christ, it seemed, was as much Protestant as He was Catholic.

Elizabeth pulled wider the curtain of the carriage window to see where they were. She had so rarely traveled to London, save to be taken as a prisoner to the Tower. How many times had she been in that damnable prison? Too many! The last time was four years ago when she'd spent three months in the accursed place, accused by Bloody Mary of conspiring in Sir Thomas Wyatt's rebellion. Her love, Robert Dudley, had also been imprisoned within the grim, dank walls, but they had never been allowed to see each other. She consoled herself now with the fact that her first act as queen would be to reward the lovely Robert Dudley for his loyalty and love and make him Master of the Horse, so they would see each other every day.

As she passed the cheering crowds, she looked at those she would now be ruling. God, but they were a dirty lot, and the closer she came to London, the dirtier they seemed to be. The stench of the city seemed to seep into the surrounding countryside. Elizabeth was wondering about the cost of cleaning the roads when she saw a sight which shocked and angered her.

Frowning at the effrontery, she looked again to ensure she hadn't made a mistake, fixing her eyes upon a man whose back was turned to her carriage. It was an insult, a Catholic insult, which could not go unchallenged, otherwise word would spread through London's narrow streets like a plague. She would deal with it as a queen.

She stooped to the floor of the carriage and picked up her rod to bang on the floor of the coach for the horseman to stop. The coach shuddered to a halt, and the cheering crowd suddenly became hushed. Elizabeth opened the door before the postillion had a chance to jump down and open it for her.

She stepped out onto the muddy and rutted road. Her eyes sought the man in the crowd. His back was still to her, and she walked the twenty paces toward him.

"Why do you turn your back on your queen?" she demanded.

In shock, the old man turned around to face her, and Elizabeth saw tears in his eyes.

"Why are you crying?" she asked more gently.

He struggled for words, shaking his head as though he was a mute.

"Tell me your trouble," Elizabeth said, the crowd now pressing forward, listening for the response.

"It's over," he whispered.

"What's over?"

"The nightmare. The blood. You're one of the faith. For twenty years I've been loyal to the English Church and then Mary made me turn my back on my English God. Now you're here, they say you'll allow me back into my church and I shall be able to be an Englishman again and not have to go to Mass. Now I'll not have to bow to Rome but I can worship my English God."

"Is that why you cry?" she asked.

The old man nodded.

Elizabeth turned to the others who had gathered around her. "And you," she said to a young woman whose face was blistered by cankers, "will you worship an English God in an English church?"

"Yes, Your Majesty," she said hesitantly.

"And you?" she asked a boy of not more than six, who had matted hair and the marks of green snot caked onto his nose.

He shrugged. "I dunno. Who are you?"

Elizabeth burst out laughing. "I am Elizabeth, by the grace of God—the English God—Queen of England. And what is your name?"

"Tom."

"Well, Tom, now you look upon your queen, what do you have to say?"

"You're very white."

Again Elizabeth laughed. She'd been locked away from the people of England for so long, she'd forgotten what it was like to be free. Tom looked at her searchingly and asked, "Are you the queen who kills Protestants or the one who was locked up in the Tower?"

"I was in the Tower. But now I'm free, as is every man and woman here."

She opened her purse, full of pennies and halfpennies and farthings, which she'd wanted to distribute to people who lined the streets on the way but had been prevented from doing by the speed of the carriage and the urgency of her getting to Westminster.

"What if I gave you a new penny, Tom?"

"Yes please," said the boy eagerly. "My dad has to work a full day for a penny."

"Good," Elizabeth said, giving him the coin of the realm with her father's head on it. "Take this and buy your family a goose for dinner tonight. And the rest of you, use this to celebrate the God-given accession of Elizabeth, your queen."

She poured the rest of the money from her purse into her hand and threw it up into the air and over the heads of the crowd. They scrambled for it, cheering her as it landed on the muddy road.

Elizabeth stepped back into her carriage and continued her progress into London.

"Philip!" she screamed.

She looked at her councillors in utter horror. Some looked down at the table. Some braved her withering stare.

"Philip!"

Lord Kersham nodded reluctantly, in fear of the Queen's temper.

"Philip? Philip of Spain?"

Kersham gulped, and was about to expound on the advantages when he realized that silence was by far the safer course.

"Are you mad? Are you insane? Marry Philip the Catholic of Spain? God's blood, when my sister Mary Tudor was on her deathbed, screaming in the agony of dropsy, he was too busy plowing the virgin fields of Spain and Portugal to visit the poor woman. And you expect me to marry the man?"

"Majesty," Lord Kersham began, but to his relief, William Cecil intervened.

"Your Highness, the Spanish ambassador has asked merely that you consider the match. It will strengthen our nation against the danger constantly posed to us by France, and . . ." He hesitated, but determined to continue, "And Your Majesty must find a husband, the people demand it, and you need an heir, and—"

"Even you, Cecil? Even you are complicit in this match. You are my guide through the course of kingship, yet even you'd have me marry that . . . that man!" She turned on all of the men advising her and shook her head sadly. She'd been queen for only seven days and already they were telling her whom to marry to ensure that England had a king. But marriage was the very last thing she was contemplating. "Does no man here have any understanding of the meaning of a marriage to one such as me, one whose very father jumped from bed to bed in order to produce a male heir?"

The company of men looked down at the table to avoid the Queen's eyes.

"Marriage! I detest the institution. If marriage is ordained by God Himself, then why did my very father decapitate so many worthy women to satisfy his lusts? Oh, he was a great king, and we all bow our heads to his memory. But what of the women who were his queens?"

Still the men stared at the table, listening to a litany of sins that Elizabeth had repeated in one form or another, night after night, since coming up to London.

In her indignant fury the Queen was flushing under the cake of white make-up she wore. Cecil was desperate not to enrage her further and to bring the discussion about her marriage back to the table.

"We're all married men, Your Majesty. And I dare say that many of us have known of husbands who have strayed. Your father was but one of many. But that has no bearing on your need to marry and secure the continuity of the Tudors. You must marry, Majesty. You must do as your father did and secure England. And it must be before your womb dries up and you are no longer capable of bearing a child. Your Majesty is twenty-five years of age, and England demands an heir to carry the Tudor dynasty forward, or else."

Elizabeth looked at William Cecil sternly. She wasn't yet crowned and they were already talking about her marrying and giving birth. "Or else what, Master Cecil?"

He looked at his colleagues on the Privy Council and they signaled their agreement for him to continue. "Or else, Majesty, with your death will come the accession of the Catholic Mary Queen of Scotland, the granddaughter of your father's sister, your late aunt Margaret, who carries Tudor blood and whom the Catholics of England are already demanding replace you as the rightful heir to the throne. And now that she's married to the Frenchman, Francis—"

"Enough of Mary!" Elizabeth shouted. "My life is dominated by Marys. Francis is a sickly boy, and with the pox raging through Paris, I dare say he won't last the year. And as to Scotland becoming master of England, well, I didn't spend so long imprisoned in the Tower to give England away just as it fell into my grasp.

"I have no great love of Scotland, gentlemen, and Scotland has no great love of me. That true minister of Christ, that true child of reformation and goodness, the evil and terrible Mr. Knox, made it quite clear that he feels I and all other women are unsuited to govern."

She went to her desk and picked up a file of papers. "See here," she said. "This was written by Mr. Knox last year when Mary was already at death's door. Listen to this, gentlemen, for true Christian compassion and spirit."

She glanced at the title, and said contemptuously, "'The First Blast of the Trumpet Against the Monstrous Regiment of Women.'"

"Do you hear that, gentlemen?" she cried. "Monstrous Regiment of Women! As though we're all whores selling ourselves at Billingsgate for a penny.

He calls it a monster of nature that women should reign above men. Why, at this very moment, my own Crown's lawyers inform me that they are writing a pretty fable about my body, saying that the moment I am crowned, my debased womanly body will be of no more use, and somehow and miraculously it will be joined forever to the mind and spirit of a king. That I shall somehow be composed of two halves of the whole, in which there will be the 'body natural' of a puny and weak woman and of no consequence, and a 'body politic,' which is immutable and the body of a king.

"By God, cousins, I find no joy in the prospect of marrying—I've seen more marriage in my life than other families in ten generations—but if I must do so for my country, then find me a proper suitor and I'll marry and give all England an heir. Many heirs. For unlike my father, I don't concern myself with the gender of my children. The good burghers of England are not so silly as to believe that women are temperamentally and morally unfit for any duty outside the bedroom and the pantry. England might have a queen's bottom on her throne but she has a king's head for its government."

"Madam?"

No word. The corridors echoed. Not even a giggle from her ladies-in-waiting. So he shouted again, "Madam? Highness? Elizabeth?"

And then he heard the faintest of breaths, a rustle in the air, an indication that she was hiding and holding her breath. He looked down the length of the corridor, but could not see her feet beneath an arras, nor her form behind a tapestry.

"Come to me, my queen. I know you're hiding."

Sir Robert Dudley, tall, darkly bearded and with glistening curly hair, played with his earrings and quietly tiptoed along the oaken corridor. His position was given away by the creaking floorboards, but that was for the good, because from his past experience at hide and go seek, the closer he got, the more she giggled. This time he thought of a variation to their game, which would be exquisite in its torment of her.

"Elizabeth . . ."

Still no sound. And so he *harrumphed*, and said loudly, "Because my queen isn't here, I shall return to the audience hall."

He turned, and walked noisily away from the Queen's apartments. But before he came to the end of the corridor, an angry voice shouted, "Robin! Come back!"

Robert Dudley turned in surprise, and said, "Your Majesty, but I thought . . ."

"What did you think, my lord? You thought that your queen would leap out at your approach and surrender to you like a little girl? Then you thought wrongly, Sir Robert."

"I couldn't find you, and so I was returning—"

"So soon, dear Robin? Giving up on me so soon? Am I not worthy of somewhat more of a chase? Like a fox or a deer, am I not a beautiful prey, worthy of the sweat of your brow as you ride me down and I stumble at your feet, helpless and in your thrall?"

"Ye Gods, but what a prey you make, Elizabeth. How I'd like to take you up in my arms, and do those things which you talk about, yet which you never permit."

"But you turned and ran, my lord. Is that the mark of a hunter?"

"I couldn't find you, so I was going to look elsewhere."

"You were going to give up the chase, Sir Robert. You were happily going to return to the audience hall and seek your pleasures elsewhere, leaving me alone and unloved."

"Majesty?"

Dudley carefully noted the subtle change in her voice, the slightly higher pitch which seduced sensible men to speak more freely than they ought, the enticing tone which he and her other advisors had so recently learned at their cost to be so very dangerous. Her voice told him that she was about to bare her fangs. She sounded like an ingénue, innocently goading and seeking, yet suddenly and without warning she would skewer men with the lance of her tongue. Elizabeth's seductive tone had only recently sent a number of gallant men, once loyal to Mary, to the Tower.

"Surely you know what I'm talking about, dearest Robin. You think that your covert attentions to other ladies of my court—*my* court, Sir Robert—are unnoticed by me. You arrange assignations with ladies and swear them to secrecy. You use your time as *my* Master of the Horse in riding other women, thinking that your pursuits are hidden from me."

"Majesty!"

"Oh please, Robin, don't compound your faithlessness by playing me for the cuckold. You think that I am blind to what you do? You profess your love to me, you crave my hand in marriage, you beg to be let out of the marriage to your wife, yet all the time you're eyeing the cunny and boobies of some other woman of my court."

Dudley was trapped by his own indiscretions. "Highness, these are common rumors, silly tattles of maids . . ."

The Queen stamped her foot, the noise reverberating along the corridor. "Don't play games with me, Sir Robert. You've been prodding your manhood between every open and willing pair of legs."

"You are my only love, Majesty," he protested, "and if you ever once allowed me to stay in your bedchamber and show you the delights of coupling, then my eyes would only be for you. Elizabeth, why do you deny me?"

"How dare you speak to your queen like that?" she cried. By now, she was halfway down the corridor, her skirts rustling in the still air. Dudley knew that he was in great and real danger, indeed, something must have happened in the court of which he was unaware, for she was more dangerous than he'd seen her in many weeks.

"Kneel, you craven dog-hearted coxcomb, you goatish fen-sucked flirt-gill, or I'll have you in the Tower by morning."

Robert Dudley stiffened in fury. He stood there, transfixed. Yes, he was terrified of the Queen's rage. But kneel after such insults? Before his lifelong friend? In private?

"KNEEL!" she screamed.

Sir Robert fell to his knees just as the Queen arrived at his side. She lifted her leg and pushed him violently so that he sprawled on the floor, banging his head against a plinth on which was a bronze bust of King Henry VII. It teetered and fell, hitting Robert Dudley hard on the shoulder.

The Queen stood silent in horror as Dudley cried out in pain. But when he rubbed his shoulder and looked up at her with the eyes of a mournful dog, Elizabeth burst into laughter. But the solid bronze bust had hurt Dudley badly, and now it was he who became furious. Never in all his life had he been kicked and injured and ridiculed.

He stood, rubbing his neck and shoulder to relieve the pain, and said sharply to Elizabeth, "I leave immediately for the countryside, ma'am. I will not stay in court and be made a mocking jay."

He turned, and began to walk away.

"Stay!" she commanded.

But he kept walking.

"STAY!" He continued to walk.

"Stay, you slime-drenched poltroon, or I'll have your manged carcass sold to the knackers and your balls hung from my door. Guards!" The doors at the end of the corridor were flung open, and two of the Queen's men stood at the ready, halberds in hand.

"If Sir Robert attempts to leave my presence, arrest him and convey him to the Tower."

Immediately the two men blocked the exit. Knowing it was death to take another step, Robert Dudley stopped. Silence descended on the corridor.

"Would Your Majesty prevent a husband from returning home to his ailing wife? Mistress Amy Dudley lies sick in her bed. Is Your Majesty intent on depriving this worthy lady of the husband she so needs?"

Even though he had his back to her, Dudley could hear the Queen breathing deeply. She must have made some signal, because suddenly the guards bowed and left, leaving the two of them alone.

Softly, she said, "Your wife?"

"Yes, she is ill. Again! The lump in her breast has grown larger, and she is losing weight. She has no strength and is incapable of attending to the service of the house. I am afraid that the servants are mocking her and thieving."

"Then you must return to her," said the Queen. He heard her approach, and turned. This was a different woman, no longer the coquette, nor the stern and authoritarian prince, but a friend and a concerned queen. "Shall I send my physician to accompany you?"

"No, Beth, but I really must return. I should have left days ago."

"Why didn't you tell me this, Robin? How your . . . Amy must have suffered because of your service to me. She is too good and noble a lady to suffer at my expense. I will not permit you to tarry. Go! Go to your wife and comfort her."

"Majesty, I stayed because of my love for you. I have no love for Amy. Yes, once I loved her, but now my eyes are blinded to all others by your glory. I wish to divorce Amy and marry you. Why won't you marry me, Beth?"

"Because God ordained marriage, Robin, and despite what my father did, I am of the belief that the commitment between husband and wife isn't some petty thing."

She walked over and threw her arms round him.

"Did the bust of Henry hurt you very much?" she asked, changing the subject.

"Yes, it was very heavy, and fell onto the bone of my shoulder."

"My grandfather hurt many men when he was alive, though God knows, I would have thought his reign of terror would have come to an end now that he's dead!" She rubbed his shoulder. "Perhaps you should take off your doublet and I'll massage some unguent into your shoulder."

Dudley smiled, and kissed the Queen on her neck. He grasped her hand and placed it between his legs. "The bust also fell onto my manhood and hurt me there. Perhaps Your Majesty would apply liniment there too."

Elizabeth snorted and laughed out loud. She continued to hold him close, and he stole another kiss. She put up her lips and kissed him fully and passionately. But when he put his hand onto her bodice and tried to feel her breasts, she shook her head. "No! That is too far, my lord."

She withdrew from him and straightened her gown. She looked down at his codpiece and saw that it was bulging provocatively.

"Aren't the ladies of the court satisfying your manhood well enough, Sir Robert?"

"You, Beth, are the only woman who can satisfy me."

"Then, my lord, you'll have to return to your wife greatly unsatisfied."

And she turned with a giggle and walked back to her apartment.

CHAPTER SEVEN

Off the Western Coast of Ireland, August 1561

How long had she been married? A year? Ten years? Twenty perhaps? What did it matter? Time was not an issue when there was so much pain in her life. All she wanted was to be with her wondrous children and to be freed from the misery of the man who was her husband.

Her marriage was a blur; some moments were calm and happy, some were close, some even tended toward understanding; but these islands of calm were drowned by the turbulent sea of years of anger and fear and pain which threatened to drown her.

Was it really only thirteen years ago she'd married Donal? Thirteen years of battle. Twelve years of fear. It was at night that she feared him the most; then, her personal guards, in whose care she had entrusted her personal safety against assaults by Donal, were asleep, and might not respond quickly enough to her screams for assistance.

If her marriage had been terrible in the first years, then since the agreement with Mistress Joyce, it had been doubly so—no, ten times so.

After she'd informed him that he had no more money to fight his battles, he'd stayed away from her for three entire months. She heard stories of how he'd ride from village to village on their estates and would drink himself into a stupor, then sleep in a roadside ditch till morning. He'd force himself upon some serving girl or the daughter of one of the farmers, before riding on to do more mischief. For food he'd demand whatever was on some poor man's table, or he'd visit the castle of a nearby clan chieftain and demand his rights under Brehon Laws to house and hearth.

Grace received deputations from farmers and villagers and even nearby chieftains. But what could she do? He was the lord and master, and even though she had equal rights with Donal, she could not in law prevent him from doing what he was doing.

And then early one morning he returned. It came as a shock, for she hadn't heard of his whereabouts for some time. Grace was in the great hall beginning the orders for the day, when Donal suddenly burst in, stinking of the fields, his hair long and unadorned, his clothes like rags, and announced, "Grace, order me food from my kitchens."

She looked at him in astonishment, as did the serving staff, until he roared, "I demand food!" He sat himself down in the chair before the fire and kicked off his boots, waiting for his servants to carry out his order.

After he'd eaten and drunk, Grace approached him and said gently, "I'm pleased that you've returned, Donal. There's a lot to be done."

He looked up at her and gave a smile which told her that her troubles were just beginning.

"Is there, madam? Is there a lot to be done? Well, then I suggest you do it. I suggest that you gather yourself all the menfolk around you and do what needs to be done. Oh, and when you've done it, might I suggest that you also arm your men, because the Joyces are going to attack this fuchking castle within the week, for the Master of the Joyce clan has, it appears, convinced his mistress that as the great Grace O'Flaherty has now weakened the O'Flahertys so grievously, we are vulnerable to an assault, and he's going to capture all of our lands and put me and you and all of our clan to death."

Grace looked at him in amazement.

The smile transmuted into a sneer. "Well, madam, what do you think of that? That's what you get for interfering in the affairs of men."

He stood and turned his back to her, facing the fire. "Soon we'll all pay with our lives for your mistakes, but so be it."

Of course, no assault had taken place. He had managed to fool her, and she had returned to him his treasury and he'd gone off to war.

Looking out over the clear and sparkling sea in the early morning, Grace still remembered her fury when she realized that Donal had tricked her. But now all she wanted was to put the agony of the past behind her so that she could look out to the purity of the sea.

As she stood on the fo'c'sle, lulled by the gentle swell of the waves, she mused about the way in which her life had turned out. Although she despised Donal now, she had gained much wealth from her years of marriage. Although her husband was considered a violent drunkard, she was known far and wide as a woman of stature, respected in her home, her county and her nation; she had two beautiful and proud children; she ran a significant fleet of ships to rival anything the English merchants could sail against her, and was running rings around the traitorous scum of Galway who were pissing into the pockets of their English overlords.

Grace turned as she heard the sound of footsteps behind her. Grace assumed it would be her cabin boy, but she was surprised to see that it was her first mate, Mr. Laffey.

"Carrig, good morning to you."

"Fair morning, Captain. How are you? Did you rest in the night after yesterday's excitement?"

The previous day had seen an engagement with a merchantman who had fired volleys of shot at them, but it had only taken half of an hour to overcome his resistance.

She took the cup of mead he offered. She loved the taste of warm honey in spirited hot wine in the early morning. "I slept like an angel. After yesterday's battle, it was a much-needed rest. How are the injured?"

"One of them will have to go ashore, I'm afeared. Tady Flynn. His arm's cut real bad, and the bandages aren't holding the blood."

"Aren't the stitches I put in stemming the flow?"

"Somewhat, Captain. But if it starts again, he'll be for gangrene, and then he'll lose the arm."

"God forbid. If it gets bad again, we'll put in for Limerick. That's the nearest port with a good surgeon, and one of the few places my husband hasn't caused trouble for my name. If not, we'll make for Galway."

The first mate nodded, and went to tell the ship's crew of their plans.

Grace neither felt like an O'Flaherty nor allowed herself to be called by that debased name. She had reverted to the name O'Malley a year after the birth of her second child. As Mr. Laffey disappeared, she contemplated how she was going to deal with her husband.

He was not only damaging the reputation she was building for herself, but he was also draining the family of the wealth she earned. She'd thought that her little ploy with Mistress Joyce had worked, but since Donal had tricked her and he'd attacked the Joyce once more, any possibility of a treaty or an end to his warmongering had been out of the question.

She had to prevent him fighting with everyone around. His drinking these days was so excessive that there were times his servants truly believed him to be dead. It was only the surgeon pricking him with needles and causing him to groan that attested to life.

Every man on board her many boats knew of the problems which Donal was causing Grace. For every ducat or pound or doubloon she earned by pirating and trading, he would have spent half on his evil ways if she'd allowed it. Not that there was much that she could do to prevent it, for by Brehon Laws he was entitled to run his half of the estates as he saw fit. They shared the income and the outgoings of the estates, but most of their profits now came from her sea trading and piracy, and most of that was supposed to go into the family treasury. Of course, that was the way it was while ever he was alive, but the moment he died and she became his widow, she and her children would lose almost everything.

So latterly she'd taken to lying to him about the success of her ventures and giving him one-fifth of the earnings, taking the remainder and hiding it on O'Malley property for safekeeping.

Grace now ran a fleet of twenty-two galleys and caravels which traded and pirated the Irish and British coastlines. Most were powered by sail and oarsmen, which cost far more but enabled speed over sail and greater security when she was being chased. She'd lost only two of her ships in the years she'd been sailing the O'Flaherty fleet. She was thirty years of age and enjoyed a reputation of men twenty years her senior; and not all of her fame was due to the fact that she was a woman in a man's world. She was acknowledged far and wide as a brilliant sailor and a merciless fighter, a woman who was a skilled tactician and a valiant adversary.

She already had over six hundred sailors and far more oarsmen accountable to her; she was held in apprehension by those who failed in their duty, and adored by those she rewarded more handsomely than any other pirate or merchant commander in the generosity with which she divided booty and profits. Yet her generosity wasn't altruism, because she knew better than most that her sailors would fight more valiantly if they were fighting for their own pockets as well as for hers.

She was strict when it came to timetables, navigation and most especially valiance in battle—she detested cowardice. In the past ten years, she'd judged, tried and sent eight men to their watery graves because they'd cowered in their bunks when their ship was under attack by gunboats or other pirates. It was behavior she wouldn't tolerate, for the cowardice of one man put the lives of all others at greater risk.

Despite this, she was understanding of human emotions. She wouldn't allow a captain to sail more than eight months of the year without spending the remaining four months with his family, at one half pay; she wouldn't allow senior members of the crew to be away from wives who were pregnant, and paid them a quarter of their stipend when they were on shore.

And best of all, Grace O'Malley gave all her twenty-two captains complete autonomy. It was a device she'd learned from her late father Owen O'Malley, who said that if you couldn't trust a captain at sea, then he shouldn't be a captain at sea. The only thing she demanded of them was fifty percent of the booty they captured on the high seas, and seventy percent of the trading profits they made when sailing as merchantmen. The rest was divided between captain and crew.

She allowed her captains to sail the laneways of the Spanish islands, the Scottish islands, the coasts of northwest and northeast England and all of France. But for herself and the two ships in her direct command, she retained the entire coast of Ireland, and the southern English coast.

Her special love was pirating the waters of the central western Irish coast, and making the burghers of Galway Bay hate her intensely. For during the past four years she'd cost them dearly—hundreds of thousands off pounds in lost revenue—by sailing the north and south sound of the entryways to Galway Bay, off the islands of Aran and Inishmaan and Inisheer, and waylaying merchantmen who were intent on entering Galway.

It was sweet revenge for what the men of Galway had done to her father, and to those Gaelic sea merchants before him. Those ports on the western coast of Ireland traded with England and had long considered themselves more English than Irish. And Galway was the very worst of them all. Because of their wealth and their petty English titles and their pretty houses, the burghers of Galway disdained the peasant Irishmen from other parts of the land. In their arrogance, they had enacted a series of laws which prevented anyone who wasn't a resident of the city, especially those who were members of the Gaelic clans, from trading there. There were fines for Galway citizens who entertained their Gaelic neighbors within the city walls without the express permission of the mayor and the council on holy feast days, and it had been written that "neither O' ne Mac shall strutted ne swagger thru the streets of Galway," as if Owen O'Malley and his family were no better than dogs or sheep or rats.

The arrogance of the men of Galway had cost Owen O'Malley dearly; Grace took great pleasure in making them pay handsomely.

When she came across a merchantman bound for Galway, a fat and slow galley burdened down by its cargo, Grace would offer the captain a simple alternative—pay her a vast entry fee to visit Galway, or be relieved of his freight. Only occasionally would some foolhardy captain, full of braggadocio, see fit to go up against her. If he was particularly full of spit, he'd angrily tell his men that no woman would take his cargo, then he'd attempt to put some shots into Grace's rigging and stand on the railings and rattle his cutlass.

Grace would order a cannonade to be loosed and the waters all around his ship would explode white with anger for fully fifteen minutes as the captain and his terrified men stood impotent at the ship's railings. Not one shot would land on the uncooperative captain's ship, but he'd wallow like a duck on a pond, sitting pretty, knowing that at any moment Grace could order her men to aim for the deck or the hull or the masts and then there'd be blood on the decks and the ship would be dead in the water.

Then Grace would order the sounding of the ceasefire and an unnatural quiet would settle on the sea. She'd sail close up to the merchantman and shout across the gulf of water between them, in such a polite and ladylike voice, "So, Captain, what's it to be? Entry fee or your cargo?" They usually settled on an entry fee of half the value of the consignment, which Grace preferred, for it meant that she wasn't forced into the necessity of sailing to Spain or somewhere else to trade. And she'd charge them an additional margin of cash for the pyrotechnic display she'd just put on to cower them into submission.

Oh, but the city fathers of Galway hated her with a vengeance. They sent out their own gunboats, but the sea swallowed her up and they could never find her; they sent to Elizabeth in England, but the reply came back that all Her Majesty's navy could spare was a couple of caravels, and besides, Galway should clean up its own mess.

So the fathers of Galway Bay spent a king's ransom on two corsairs out of Ottoman Turkey, men and ships who promised that they'd clear up the waters within a month. Of course the burghers realized that once the corsairs had put an end to Grace O'Malley, they'd have the Devil's own job of getting rid of them, but it was a risk they were willing to take. The corsairs set sail one June morning, full of high hopes, following an official reception by the fathers. After much wining and dining and congratulations in advance of killing the evil Grace, the corsairs sailed with 2000 gold pieces as part payment, a further 3000 if they brought back proof of Grace's death.

Then the city fathers waited and waited. And waited.

On a morning a month later, Galway town awoke to the hideous sight of the heads of the captains of the corsairs stuck on poles on the quayside.

It was then that the fathers of Galway realized that Grace was more than a match for the entire county. They tried the art of negotiation, offered her ten percent of every ship's cargo without having to fight, asked her to join them in their global trade. But she'd let them know in no uncertain terms that their insult of closing off trade to her father Owen O'Malley many years earlier, was an insult to all Irishmen which couldn't be erased, not even if she was given free rights to use Galway as her own port at any time she wished.

Captain O'Malley gripped the railing as the wind began to freshen and she felt the ship's sails stiffen with wind. Soon they would be on their way westward of Croaghnakeela Island, where she liked to wait ready to ambush some merchantman heading toward Galway. That was her secret, for the fools of Galway patrolled the waters of the sounds, but she was always northward out of reach of them, too far away to be spotted but close enough, with the help of her oarsmen, to waylay her quarry.

Of course, this hiding place was only one of Grace's secrets of success; the other was a cooperative clerk who worked as a secretary to the Master of the Port of Galway. The man was amassing a tidy fortune informing Grace of every coming and going of the ships visiting the port, so that she knew precisely which ships to attack, and which held cargo not worth the trouble.

Just then, Carrig Laffey approached her and said, "Wind's up, Captain. Time to sail. Do we make for Galway, or to Limerick and put Tady Flynn ashore?"

"How is he now? Still bleeding?"

Mr. Laffey shook his head. "The bleeding has ceased. I'd say it's safe to wait if there's a cargo to be had. I know Tady, and he'll be alright with half a bottle of whiskey inside of him and a good day's sleep while we're working hard on deck."

"Good. Then let's try to gain a cargo before we return to our homes, for this has been a most unfortunate trip and no mistake. After we've found ourselves a cargo, I'll put to in Limerick, and make sure that Tady is taken care of."

She gave orders for them to weigh anchor, hoist the main sail, and steer due south so that they'd arrive off the Mal Bay to the south of Galway in time to intercept an Ottoman merchant which she'd been told by her tame clerk was carrying spices, gold and carpets.

As the sun was climbing to its zenith in the middle of the morning the wind suddenly changed direction and Grace was forced into a tacking maneuver if she was going to make her rendezvous. The rowers in the galleys below deck were straining against the strength of the current, but they had strong backs and she knew that they'd try their best. Thankfully good fortune was with her, because after only an hour of difficult sailing, the lookout shouted, "Ship ahoy!"

The Ottoman merchantman was five miles off the starboard bow. She would have to sail south, and then come up behind him, which wasn't her preferred manner of attack.

The crew looked at her, waiting instructions. They were all still wary, she could tell. Yesterday's skirmish had gone some way to restoring their confidence, but they were still ginger after last week's disastrous encounter.

Standing at the railings, she remembered the incident and shuddered. She'd been so close to losing her ship and her men and her own life. They'd lain in wait for a caravel from Bristol sailing to Galway for provisioning to make the journey to the New World. Rumor had it that the ship was carrying a fortune in bullion for the purchase of animal pelts from Boston Harbor. They'd attacked her head-on, and she'd put up only the most minimal of resistance. It had surprised the entire crew, for they'd expected a fight from such a valuable ship and cargo.

What they hadn't realized was that five miles behind her, sailing out of Galway, was an English naval galleon of war which had sailed into the harbor on the previous day in total secrecy. It was armed with fifty oarsmen, and carried with it two rows of twenty cannon on either side.

Just as Grace and her crew were about to step on board the defeated merchantman, the English gunboat had suddenly appeared like a wolf dog over the horizon, growling and barking and blasting its cannon at Grace's ship.

The moment Grace ordered her men to turn and defend themselves from the rapidly closing English navy vessel, the crew of the merchantman let out blood-curdling screams and were joined on deck by fifty musketmen from an infantry corps of the English army.

It was an ambush, and Grace had fallen blindly into it. She cursed herself for being so vain and arrogant she'd failed to foresee it and take better precautions. She'd become complacent, overly confident, and now her entire crew and her ship were at risk.

Caught in the crossfire of musket shot from the army on board the merchantman and cannon fire from the navy, she had one option only, and that was to run.

Somehow fortune was on her side, because as she gave orders to sail for deep waters, one of her cannon shot disabled the merchantman's wheel and rendered it rudderless in the water. Grace was then able to put the merchantman between herself and the naval vessel, ensuring that the gunship's cannon couldn't be fired for fear of hitting the cargo ship. By the time the gunship had tacked to have her again in its line of sight, she'd been far enough away to escape much harm. Still, it had been a nasty fright, and one which had made Grace uncharacteristically cautious.

She knew that the crew was demoralized, she needed a successful engagement quickly to restore their confidence. Yesterday she'd attacked a fat and lazy merchantman, an easy conquest; her men needed something they could get their teeth into. The Ottoman merchant was perfect.

She sailed closer and brought her biggest cannon to bear on the starboard bow, and let off a volley of shot to tell the captain that he'd sink if he didn't hove to.

In reply, he fired fifty round of cannon, all of which landed harmlessly in the water between them.

"Bring Donal around, and blast his mainmast," she said, referring to the Greek cannon she'd acquired two years previously, which took twelve-pound shot and which had a greater range than any other gun sailing the Irish waters. She'd named it after her husband because it was all fury and bombast. On the occasions it was fired, the entire ship shuddered with its report.

They wheeled the massive cannon to the starboard center position, and two men primed and loaded her. At Grace's orders, the men aimed for the midship position, and suddenly the ship trembled as the massive cannonball roared through the sky between the two vessels. With pinpoint accuracy it struck the rigging just aft of the mainmast and set it ablaze. Grace's men let out a roar of approval as they watched the captain of the Ottoman give the orders to lower the sail and dowse the fire. She was effectively disabled with just one shot.

But Grace didn't sail straight toward her, instead waiting for the fire to be put out and for the captain to appear to see what bargain he could strike with the pirate ship. Grace wasn't going to fall into the trap again of being confronted by stern resistance.

The two ships lay apart by a quarter of a mile, Grace's crew calm but watchful, the Ottoman's crew wildly trying to stop the fire from spreading.

When the fire had been brought under control, Grace was able to see the captain clearly. He was a tall and striking man, black as a dark night, wearing a white turban and the most colorful robes she'd seen on anything other than a bird.

He came to the port side and called out in heavily accented English, "Who is it that attacks my ship? What is the name of the pirate who steals from me?"

Grace picked up the instrument she'd purchased three years earlier in Greece. It was a marvelous and magical device, with two curved pieces of glass within a tube, which enabled her to see things far off with a clarity that astounded even her most sharp-eyed crew member. In Greece, it was called an opticometer, and it was her secret weapon, enabling her to see miles further than the naked eye.

Through her opticometer she could see the captain of the Ottoman quite clearly. He stood tall and proud. She liked the look of him.

"Captain," she shouted. "My name is Grace O'Malley, and it is my privilege to have conquered your ship today. Will you please climb into a rowboat and join me on board for a meal while your men ferry your merchandise over to my ship."

He seemed mystified. "You want me aboard your ship? Are you going to kill me?"

"No, Captain. But I want no surprises, and so to prevent me from blasting you and your men into a hundred fathoms of Irish sea, may I ask you to row over here with two of your crew and enjoy my hospitality, then we'll all be at peace with ourselves. Should your men attempt anything which upsets me in the slightest, then you'll have a long way to swim before you get to Galway. Now kindly do as I order . . ."

It was an uneven match from the start, and that's what made it all the more intriguing. As a strict Moslem, Osman Abdul Mehmet, called Man of Men, or the Beylebey, formerly a senior ship's captain in the Imperial Navy of Süleymân the Magnificent, and now a captain in the merchant fleet of Grand Vizier Kemalpasazade, refused all offers of wine.

He wouldn't eat the salted pork she offered him, and neither would he touch the freshly cut bacon rind which was a favorite among naval people.

He told her it was forbidden, and was quite happy to eat some of her bread, fruits and a morsel of fish.

Grace enjoyed their conversation from the very beginning. At first he was all huff and puff when he came aboard, telling her that no Beylebey had ever before been taken prisoner by a woman, and her barbarous and ungallant act must lead him to commit suicide. But when she sat with him at a table groaning with food which her cabin boy had set up in her private apartments at the rear of the ship, and told him of her exploits, he listened in fascination, eventually deciding that it was a privilege to have fallen into the grace and beauty of her arms.

Osman had a deep and mellifluous voice, and his black skin was smooth and beautiful. His teeth were white, his lips full and red and his eyes flashed when he laughed, which was delightfully often. Yet he was more than just a man who enjoyed life, for he knew a lot about the world and had read many of the Greek writers from antiquity and knew as much about Al Jabr and geometry and the science of numbers and astronomy as did she.

She was well into her fifth glass of wine when the desperation to have him came over her. Sometimes when she lay awake in her bunk at night, she could have screamed in loneliness for her desire of a man's body. Donal paid more attention to the serving girls than he did to her, showing her no affection or love or gentleness. When her men were ashore visiting the brothels of foreign ports, she slept alone in her cold, unwelcoming bed. When she did business with a merchant and he entertained her in his home, it was always in the presence of his wife and family. Rarely, if ever, was she alone with a man; never since the day she'd married Donal had she enjoyed a man's lips on hers, nor the scented breath of his desire on her neck or breasts.

So having this black naval man, this enemy sea captain on her ship, in her control, was intoxicating. Her head swayed with her power over him. At first she toyed with him, but when he refused to play her games, preferring instead to sit looking at her as though she was some intriguing creature, she became even more aroused.

Seemingly oblivious to the heat that was suffusing her body, Osman talked about his home in Egypt and how he came to be a part of the Ottoman navy. During her next glass of wine he told her that he had four wives, as befitted his rank, and more children than he could count. And then Grace made the unexpected comment that to satisfy so many women, he must have the equipment of a bull.

He looked at her in astonishment, which caused her to drink yet another glass of wine. By the time she'd drained it, she found it difficult to remember why he was aboard her vessel in the first place.

"So tell me, my dear Osman, do Egyptian men make love in the same way as Irishmen?" She realized what she had said and burst out laughing.

The Egyptian looked at her strangely. She was, indeed, a most peculiar woman.

"Captain O'Malley, madam, are you playing with my sensitivities?"

"I don't know what you mean, Osman."

He stretched, and she admired the way in which his colorful clothes seemed to flow with his body, so different from the tight and constricting clothes Irishmen wore, with their belts and buttons and fixtures and fittings. And as the Egyptian stretched, his robe opened at the top and she could see his chest. It was smooth and completely hairless, so very different from Donal, whose body looked as if it was encased in the skin of an aging black bear.

Grace stared at the folds of the caftan and caught her breath as she saw the taut yet gentle muscles of his neck, the precisely outlined shoulders glowing with health and youth and strength. Yet this was a man in his middle thirties, a man who had fought in wars and had bedded many wives; a man who should have been far, far less beautiful than he was.

"You stare at me. Have you not seen a man with black skin before? As a pirate, haven't you been to the North African coast, the Barbary seaboard?"

She found speaking hard. She merely nodded, finding it difficult to take her eyes from his beautiful face, his bedazzling body.

There was a knock on the door of her cabin. It took her moments to realize that there was another world out there.

"Captain?" came the hesitant voice.

"Yes," she hissed.

The door opened a crack and Mr. Laffey poked his head through. "Forgive me, ma'am, but the crew from the Ottoman ship have brought over all the carpets and the spices. They say there's no gold aboard, so with your permission, I'll take ten men and search their vessel."

Grace looked at Osman, and thought she saw a fleeting look of dejection. She said to Mr. Laffey, "Wait an hour, Mr. Mate, and I'll investigate the matter further. Leave me now."

Osman frowned as the first mate closed the cabin door behind him.

"Between you and me, Captain, how much gold do you have on board?"

"None, madam. That I promise you."

"And if I send a search party over, what will we find?"

He shook his head in innocence. "Nothing. We carried spices from the Indies and Persia, silks from the looms of Cathay, as well as carpets from the mountains of Cush and the land of the Turks. Apart from that, my holds are empty. You have everything I am carrying."

They left the table and sat on the cushions of her bunk. She played with the rim of her wine goblet. "And if I demand proof? If I command you to open your dark and hidden recesses up to me, what treasures will I find deep in the blackness of your holds? What gold do you have that I can grasp in my hands and play with, that I can touch and feel and kiss? What is there in those mysterious places you command that I shall remember for the rest of my life, that will fill me with joy and make me truly rich, not rich with wealth, but with the richness which is every woman's just deserts?"

She started to giggle like a little girl. She knew she'd slurred her words, and could hardly remember what she'd just said.

Osman Abdul Mehmet, the Man of Men, the Beylebey of the Ottoman Empire, fought to resist smiling. Instead, he stood and slowly, seductively unwrapped himself from his caftan, letting it fall to the floor. He was tall and slim and perfectly black. The only whiteness was in the loincloth which was wrapped around his waist and through his legs. But with a flick of his fingers he'd loosened that, and it too fell silently to the floor, leaving him standing naked before her.

Grace's eyes nearly popped out of her head in amazement when she saw him tall and erect and naked. She wanted to undress immediately, to remove herself from the shackles of her garments and let him kiss her breasts and run his hands over her stomach and her thighs. But she was immobile. It was as though her body was tethered to the bunk by rope, or weighed down by one of the huge balls which exploded from the massive cannon she sarcastically called Donal.

And as her eyes became the size of penny pieces, Osman's manhood continued to grow and grow until it stood at a severe angle, massive and proud. She lifted her hand and grasped it in her palm, feeling its strength and solidity and vigor.

Grace opened her mouth to speak, but words wouldn't come. Instead, the Egyptian said gently, "Here, Captain O'Malley, is all the gold you've been seeking."

They lay together in each other's arms, black Egyptian skin touching the fairest skin of Ireland, hair the color of jet intermingled with hair which was defiantly red.

"Tell me again of this place," she murmured.

He was close to sleep. He'd been called upon to satisfy her four times that night, and even an Egyptian carried only a certain amount of gold in his saddlebags. But he roused himself nevertheless, and as he began to speak, the story grew in the telling.

"Lomb is a wondrous land, somewhere on the coast of far-off India. Many have been to India overland by way of Arabia and Persia and Afghanistan and over the mountains into that land of peacocks and elephants and the richest of spices.

"As for me, I prefer to travel to the south of my lord's Ottoman Empire and captain a boat in the Red Sea. I sail around the Horn of Africa and across the Sea of Araby into the Western Coast. There, I am met by mysterious men whose noses are pierced with diamonds the size of your fingernail and whose ears have been cut off so that they can hear no dissent. I pay them a golden coin and they take me to the Land of Lomb. First they blindfold me, then they place me on a camel, and we ride for three days into the densest jungle which exists on the face of the earth. It is so dense that many of the men who ride through it are hanged by their necks, caught up in impenetrable vines."

Grace reached up to stroke the sinews of his neck, kissing him as he continued his tale.

"Eventually we reach the Land of Lomb. I know that we're there because there is a constant hissing in the air, the voices of snakes. In fact, there are so many snakes in Lomb that the inhabitants anoint their hands and feet with the juice of snails mixed with pepper, for no snake will bite so disgusting a combination.

"In Lomb, my dear Captain Grace O'Malley, they grow pepper which is so strong that many of the citizens are blind from its sting. There are said to be two main cities in this wondrous land, one is called Fladrine and the other Zinglantz, and each has an equal population of Christians and Jews, who have been there since they were expelled by the madness of the Roman emperor, Nero.

"On my last visit, I managed to escape the eyes of the Grand Vizier's spies, and stole away into the hinterland. There I came across the city of Polombe, which no outside visitor has seen in two thousand years. In the middle of Polombe is the well of the same name, to which the residents come each hour of the day and night to drink. At first, I was horrified by the smell and taste of the waters of this well, but then I was entranced, because the smell and the taste and the color of the water changes every hour. I was told that drinking from this well three times cures any sickness and enables a man to live forever. The man who told me this said that he had argued his expulsion from Rome with Nero himself."

Osman paused and listened to Grace's rhythmic breathing—she was finally asleep. He considered himself lucky, because it wouldn't be until sunrise the next day that he would once again be able to perform the act of lovemaking which she'd told him was his duty as her captive and her slave.

He looked at her. She was a remarkable woman. Middle-aged certainly, but with a beauty which was both of her nature and her body. He would be happy to count her as one of his wives. . . . The thought of taking her back to his world, of making her subservient to him and his other wives, was ridiculous. This was not a woman who could exist as part of the world of a man; this was a woman who created worlds of her own.

The two ships held fast to each other throughout the rest of the day, the entire night and the following day.

The only thing which was allowed to disturb the cabin-bound captain and her captive was the need for refreshment, which was supplied at regular intervals by bemused servants who left the plates of food and mugs of wine at the foot of the steps to the captain's cabin.

And as the sun descended into the west on the second night, the door to Grace O'Malley's cabin opened and out strode the Egyptian, tall, colorful and completely unbowed by his exertions of the past thirty hours.

He sniffed the air, and the amazed crew, standing on the deck or high in the rigging, looked intently at this man who had captured their pirate queen. He stared back at them silently, his face and manner betraying no hint of embarrassment or excuse; rather it was one of pride in having done a good job.

The Egyptian shook his head in bemusement. He'd just spent the better part of two days locked in the company and embrace of one of the most amazing and outstanding lionesses he'd ever encountered—in body and mind—yet she was surrounded by such a crew! A colorless lot, looking somehow deflated, as though their lack of a leader during the past day or so had turned them into a group of widowers, moping around the ship in search of direction.

As he stood there, Grace joined him. There was a blush in her cheeks which the men hadn't seen before, a sparkle in her eyes, yet an exhaustion in the way she carried her body. The men smiled to see her return to them so hale and hearty, and spent!

Grace could feel her entire crew stifling their mirth at her very public antics. Well, she thought, there was only one way to handle this situation.

Grace moved amidships and yelled out to the entire company, "By God, but it's a privilege to be shafted by such a man. He puts every white-skinned Irishman to shame. I hope that when you men are ashore you give your wives as good a service as Captain Osman has given me these past two days. Now, gentlemen, our ships are going to separate and we'll both of us get on with our lives, so let's spend the next hour pulling strange faces and making rude comments about your captain, and after that, let's all put our sniggers and grins away and begin our work, shall we?"

Immediately her crew began to run across the deck, gathering sail and unhitching rope and battening down for the journey.

Grace accompanied Osman to the side of the ship. "By Jesus," she whispered, "so this is what it's like to be properly married."

Osman smiled. "Perhaps you and your husband should do the things more often which we've just done."

"Him!" she snorted. "He wouldn't know that the places you explored existed on any woman's body, and especially not mine. All he's interested in is burying his wick, emptying his sacks and getting on with his drinking."

"I'm sad for you, Grace, for you deserve more than marriage has given you.

Still, perhaps now you have explored your womanhood outside of marriage, your journey through life will not be as lonely."

"Oh, I'm not convinced of that. How many men like you are there around the world?"

Osman climbed over the rail and down into the rope chair suspended between the two ships. Clinging onto the carrier ropes, he said, "Grace. I will remember you for the rest of my days. Who knows in which port we'll meet again? But be assured, our paths will cross, and when they do, the seas will boil again with our passion. Meantime, I thank you for setting me free from the silken threads in which you've bound me, and for leaving me with my dignity intact."

He pushed off from her railings, and his men hoisted the chair from one ship to the other, carrying him away from her. They untied the ropes which had tethered the two vessels together, pulled in the canvas fenders and parted company.

Grace didn't wave, but she and Osman looked at each other as their ships separated, their first mates taking command while their respective captain's thoughts were elsewhere.

Eventually Grace turned and saw her crew looking at her.

Mr. Laffey came over and said, "So, Captain, you've had a rare time, and no mistake. God, but we thought you'd been murdered in there."

She nodded. "I'm a thirty-year-old woman, Carrig. Thirty years. And I've been married for half my life. And in all that time, I've never once known the gentle touch of a man. It's about time I had some fun. Now," she said, ignoring her first mate's embarrassment, "let's not spend the remains of the day talking about these matters. We've a distance to put between us and Galway, for as soon as Captain Mehmet reaches port and the burghers find out what's happened, they're going to send their gunships after us."

"Shall we make for northern waters, Captain?" he asked.

Grace thought for a while, looking at the Ottoman ship disappearing toward the horizon. She sighed. Vainly, desperately, she wanted to get away from Ireland and follow Osman to sunnier climes. For in Ireland lurked her husband, like some monstrous spider which tethered her in its web whenever she was at home, and sucked the very lifeforce from her being. How she wished for that curragh to appear over the horizon, frantically rowed by a sailor desperate to catch her; how she yearned for him to yell out, "Bad news, Grace, for your husband Donal is dead."

But no curragh ever appeared, tiny though it would be in the enormity of the ocean. And God only knew when He would gather up Donal into His bosom. So for the time being at least, she was free to roam the world, without thought to her husband and his ways.

"North? I think not. No, this time, Carrig, I fancy warmer climes. My body urges me to seek out the sun and bid farewell to these dark and drear Irish mists of ours. What say we set sail for the Mediterranean? We'll trade this cargo in France and then sail further south. I fancy swimming in the blue waters of Spain for a while."

Chapter Eight

Hampton Court, Near London, 10 September 1560

Elizabeth looked urgently around the room, trying to determine from the expressions of her courtiers precisely how they had reacted to the shocking news. Everyone, especially she, knew of the consequences of this turn of events, both in England and abroad. But all her courtiers looked to the floor, their eyes hidden from her.

Only the wily and uncompromising Spanish ambassador stared at her, as if looking into her very soul.

Alvaro de Quadra, Bishop of Aquila, was a thorn in the side of the English queen, and had been since he began his embassy from the Spanish king. His spies were everywhere, and it was even maliciously rumored that her own Robert Dudley was in his thrall. She didn't believe it; she suspected that the rumors had been started by those on Sir William Cecil's staff for their master hated Robin Dudley for his hubris.

The messenger, Mr. Bowes, remained kneeling, waiting to be released. But the Queen was so shocked by the news from the home of Robert Dudley, the news of Amy's death, that she remained speechless.

"I . . ."

People looked up in anticipation of Her Majesty's words, but they saw a woman in too great a state of distress to say anything.

"I . . . it is . . ."

Elizabeth lapsed into silence. She looked around for Sir Robert Dudley to support her, but he was absent from the court. She saw Cecil, but his face was black with the consequences.

"I am grieved. This is a bad day for England. One of its rarest and brightest jewels has been plucked by Almighty God from His English diadem and has been taken back into the Heavens for His crown. Mistress Amy Robsart, beloved wife of our dearest Master of the Horse, Lord Robert Dudley, has died."

The Queen lapsed into silence.

There was a murmuring in the court, indeed the entire long gallery would have erupted into a thousand gossiping conversations had not the Queen been sitting on the throne.

"Amy Dudley was a sickly woman, confined to bed by . . ." She paused as though to think. "Even though she died from this tragic fall, she was still very sick, and her sickness must have . . . She couldn't have . . ." Her voice trailed off.

The Queen began again and did her best to continue, but was unable. Instead she stood abruptly and, to the surprise of her ladies-in-waiting, walked off the thronal plinth without bringing the audience to an end, and hurried through the doors at the back of the audience hall to her privy chambers.

Sir William Cecil immediately followed in her wake, indicating to the other councillors not to follow—this was a private matter, for he and the Queen alone.

Inside the Queen's private sanctuary, the one place in the palace where courtiers and ambassadors and emissaries couldn't reach her, Cecil found his monarch crumpled upon the floor like a sack of grain.

"Majesty?"

She made no response.

"Your Highness, can I help you?"

"They'll think I did it," she whispered.

Slowly, eyes brimming with tears, the Queen turned to her most loyal subject and looked up at him for consolation. "They'll all say that I conspired to kill her. She didn't die in her bed, William, but died from a broken neck . . . from a fall down one step . . . one step!

"William, they'll say that the Queen of England was party to the killing of the wife of her lover, that I'm a murderess, not fit to wear the crown."

"No, Majesty. My dear Elizabeth! Nobody would dare accuse you—"

"Scots Mary would! I can feel her now, wallowing in her station as a young widow in France, eyes downcast at the tragedy of losing her husband. Beautiful and eighteen and already having been married. How long, dear Sir William, before she's sitting in her dank palace in Scotland, rubbing her hands in glee at my misfortune? I can hear her now, rejoicing that Elizabeth Regina has joined the damnable company of those women whom she most abhors."

"Highness, Mary is a young woman of virtue, and—"

"And how long will her virtue last, now that she's a widow? I know her, she's a woman whose lusts are only held in check by her love of the Catholic Christ."

"Majesty . . ."

"I tell you I know her, Cecil! She will gloat that Elizabeth has fallen to her knees and allowed her horse master to ride her. Scots Mary gloats that she was so virtuous, but she is so like me, William. She needs the company of men. She's a woman who can't live without a man at her side. She'll return to Scotland as queen, once that evil mother of hers, Mary of Guise, departs this earth, and then she'll become prey to any Catholic man who offers to protect her; and now that the whisperers and conspirators will say that Amy Robsart's death must be attributed to me, she'll lay claim to my throne, Cecil."

"But Your Highness—"

"I can feel all the Catholics of England muttering beneath their breaths. They'll say that my claim to the throne is suspect, that Mary of Scotland has greater claim than I. They will say that I have allowed the holy Crown of kingship to become desecrated, that the Crown of Henry is debased, and as soon as Protestant Lizzie is replaced by Catholic Mary, all wives will again be able to sleep soundly in their beds."

"No, Highness."

"Yes, Cecil! Do you think I didn't see merriment in the audience hall when the news was announced? My loyal subjects will believe any gossip about me, even that I would kill poor Amy, a gentle and loving and goodly soul, wife of my closest friend. They're quick to think that Robert Dudley and I are lovers, to spread the news throughout the palaces of Europe."

"Nobody believes that you and Dudley—"

"You do, Cecil," she said harshly.

Sir William Cecil fell silent. He had no desire to confess his doubts, especially when the Queen was at her lowest ebb, but how could he deny to her what was in his heart?

"Majesty, your close friendship and harmony with . . ." How far should he go? The Queen was distraught, yet he was as much protector of all England as she was. "Highness, your behavior with Sir Robert naturally gives your court reason to believe that you and he are more than intimate friends."

"I swear to you, William, as my dearest friend and councillor, that although Dudley and I have been intimate on many occasions, it has been the intimacy of dearest friends. I was born a virgin and I remain to this day a virgin. I love Robert Dudley as his queen and as his boon companion, but my duty was made clear to me when I became ruler of this commonwealth of England. My Crown and my God are of greater moment than any other device of mankind, and both Crown and God to me are more precious than any affair I might enjoy on this earth."

His long-time disgust with the way Dudley conducted his affairs with the Queen, his blatant ambition to be consort, welled up inside Cecil's normally politic breast and caused him to be bolder than he'd ever been before. "Then why has Your Majesty given Dudley a bedchamber near to yours? Why does Your Majesty permit him such public liberties? Why do you use him for horseriding, for archery, for dancing, for all such triflings, forsaking all others in the court?"

"Because I'm a woman, William. Because I love an Englishman who excels as a horseman and a dancer and an archer and a gallant—"

"And who was, until now, a husband?"

The Queen was silent, knowing the full import behind Cecil's words. She gave her arm to him so he could help her up from the floor. Together they walked into her bedchamber apartments. For their complete privacy, he ushered away the attendants who waited upon her in her room.

When they were alone, Elizabeth said softly, "You're wrong, Cecil. Not a husband. I will never marry sweet Robin, no matter how much he desires it. For how can a queen marry one whom she rules, who is so far beneath her?"

There was an immense sadness in her face, the sadness of an old woman, not one who was only twenty-seven.

"Yet you give him hope, Highness. You encourage him to believe that one day the Crown of England might rest upon his head."

She nodded. "Yes, I give him hope, for if not, he would find reasons not to appear in court. Then I would have to command him, and he would no longer be my friend, but my subject. For without him, where is my smile, my laughter, the lightness in my step? Where is the one to ease the cares of my duties as queen? You, William? I think not, for you carry the burdens of your high office even while you sleep. I am young, my lord. I must have relief from the weight of this land upon my shoulders. Do I give him hope? Yes. And I will continue to give him hope in order to keep alive his ambitions in me, and those ambitions of other princes who will fight harder for me knowing that a commoner stands in their way. I know my duty, Sir William."

Cecil's face lit with relief, which not even a lifetime of the intrigues in the Tudor courts could mask. "While it may bear heavily on Your Majesty not to marry your lifelong friend because of that role which God has ordained for you, this nonetheless is good news for England. However, Amy Dudley's suspicious death means that Your Majesty must now put all relationships with her husband aside.

"Any contact Your Majesty has with the Master of the Horse will be spoken of with great discredit to your person. You are right in thinking that Mistress Robsart's death will be viewed as murder. Dudley was absent from his household while she lay at death's door. All would have been well had she but died of natural causes, yet she died of a broken neck falling down a single step, and almost completely alone in a house when all her servants had been dismissed to attend a fair. Without witnesses to his innocence, the walls of Dudley's very own house cry out his name for bloody murder.

"Truly, madam, whatever innocence you proclaim will be howled down by the dogs of England should you ever again be intimate with Robert Dudley."

Elizabeth turned to him in fury. "How dare you speak to your queen like this? By what right do you broach matters which are mine and mine alone?"

Despite her flushed and enraged face, she didn't intimidate him. He said quietly, "I dare, madam, because I am the voice of England. A monarch has no right to allow even the whiff of scandal to corrupt the throne."

"My father's life was a scandal from start to finish. Yet he was loved by every English man and child."

"And feared by every wife and maid in the realm. Elizabeth, I speak to you like the father you never had. You said to me that you trusted me because you knew that I would never give you an answer which would be contrary to the interests of England. You know that I am speaking the truth. Dudley has asked you time and again for your hand in marriage. You have always told him to wait, that your decision would be soon. Madam, you must give him no hope that one day he might marry the Crown. Even the thought of such preferment, and the way he acts upon it, elevates him to too high a standing. He is unfit to be a consort. The lords, the Church, the people, will never stand for his naked ambition. It will diminish you in God's eyes, and those of your subjects. It will pave the way for the return of the Catholics.

"England's interests will be best served by you marrying Spain or France, Sweden or Holland. Then England will enjoy all the benefits that flow from a union of two great peoples. Dudley, on the other hand, is neither suitable nor wise, no matter how well you think his legs are shaped."

Elizabeth looked at him in amazement, and then was overwhelmed by embarrassment. He was repeating a private remark she'd made in jest to a lady-in-waiting some days earlier; yet it had already reached the ears of her principal advisor.

She remained quiet for some time, allowing her fury to abate. She wanted no quarrel with William Cecil. Of all her advisors, he was the most skilled, the most intelligent, and the one whose guidance was always the wisest. Yet surely she had the right to enjoy herself, to be like other women, to feel a man's breath on her breasts? After twenty-five years of feeling the sharpness of an axe on her neck, and after two years of the burdens of kingship, surely she was entitled to a few years of happiness?

Sighing, almost in defeat by the circumstances of the day, she asked, "What would you have me do, Cecil? Give my life to my country or to my husband?"

"Both, lady. But give your country an heir. Give England a lusty boy who will grow to be a Tudor man who can sit on the throne when we are dust, and on whom we can look down from Heaven, knowing that all's well with England."

She nodded. "An heir? A son? Then all will be well?"

"Then all will be well."

The first mate and the ship's cook held Grace O'Malley's legs firmly apart, staring into the depths of her womanhood. She struggled against their strength, swearing at them, fighting to release her hands and arms so that she could tear the hair from their scalps.

"By God, I'll kill you all!" she screamed.

She lay back on the bunk, exhausted from the struggle, but the two men wouldn't let go of her legs. Indeed, the more she fought, the firmer and wider they held her legs, her skirts falling back to expose more of her body.

"Let me go, you malignant bastards, or I'll cut your balls off and hurl them into the sea!" she yelled. And she screamed louder as her arms were pinioned even firmer to the bunkhead by others recently on deck who had heard the commotion and come down to join in the event.

Doused in sweat, her legs and arms aching from fighting off her crew, her body racked by upheavals and pains, she looked in hatred at her first mate. "I'll have you, Carrig Laffey. I'll keelhaul you, so help me."

But the first mate merely smiled, and said, "Yes Cap'n."

Then a contraction came more urgently, her body feeling one moment as though it was on fire, the next as though it was being rammed by the stock of a musket. She lay back exhausted when the contraction passed, and the crew eased up on their strangleholds.

Grace breathed deeply, the perspiration pouring from her brows. Carrig Laffey got some cold water on a cloth and mopped her face.

Softly she said, "Jesus, but I'm in pain, Carrig. The babe's head is so big that it won't come out. You'd think after two lusty boys I'd be used to this by now, but this is bigger than anything I've ever known. Jesus Christ and all the Saints but it's so huge, I don't think I can birth it."

"The pains of childbirth are the punishment for the sins of Eve," said the first mate amiably.

She'd tried squatting, bending, lying on her side and her back, but nothing she did seemed to encourage the baby to be born. So Carrig ordered the men to hold her legs wide open in the hope that the birth canal could be sufficiently expanded to allow the head to come through.

Another contraction began, and the crew again held the captain's arms and legs tightly so that she wouldn't injure herself. Again she screamed blue and bloody murder, threatening the entire crew with death; but this time the contraction didn't go away, and Carrig Laffey shouted out in utter joy, "Thank God, for I can see the babe's head."

The other crew dropped Grace's arms and legs and crowded round her to stare.

"For God's sake," she yelled, "what am I, a pregnant cow? Allow me my modesty. Oh Jesus fuchking Christ but it hurts."

Her words trailed off as she screamed with a sudden inexpressibly evil pain, and then Carrig let go of her legs and grasped the babe's head and gently eased its shoulders out of the birth canal, twisting tenderly, coaxing, until a baby daughter slipped almost effortlessly out of Grace's body. The crew burst into a loud cheer. Carrig held the child upside down while the ship's cook tied the cord into a tight knot and eased out the afterbirth. Then, after quickly washing the mite's face and clearing her mouth with fresh water and spices, Carrig Laffey gave the babe a good tap on her backside. The baby struggled, and then let out

an almighty scream, at which the crew all cheered again and shouted their congratulations.

Beaming now, Grace fell back onto the bunk and began whimpering quietly
in joy at the relief she felt from the searing pains and that her baby had been
delivered safely, without the presence of a midwife. Carrig ordered the cook to
wash the captain's face with cold water. As soon as she was well enough recov-
ered, he'd send one of the boys for a fresh bucket of sea water to wash her insides thoroughly.

Carrig had ensured that the babe's head was washed carefully with a soft
flannel and her nostrils and mouth cleaned out properly. Then, like a proud and
beaming father, he placed the babe in her mother's arms.

The Pirate Queen—for that was what Grace was now called in the corridors of London whenever the Lord High Admiral was informed that another
English ship had been lost to the Irish woman—beamed a smile and looked
closely at her baby for the first time. "Well," she whispered hoarsely, "she certainly doesn't look like my husband."

The men gathered around Grace's bunk burst out laughing.

"She has the look of a Turk, Captain," said the cook.

"She certainly looks like a particular Ottoman. Maybe she's an Otto-
woman," said Carrig Laffey.

Again the crew burst into laughter. Grace joined in.

"What's your husband going to say when he sees the color of the babe's
skin?"

Grace stroked the mewling child's head, helping her mouth toward her
breast. "I'll simply tell Donal that she's the product of our last union, not a year
back. And that I stayed out in the sun too long while I was carrying her."

Carrig laughed, and then went to sit down beside Grace, staring at the newborn baby as though she was his own. "What'll you call her, Cap'n?"

The baby began nuzzling her mother's breast, and Grace tried to fit the
child's tiny mouth onto her large nipple. The crew watched in amazement and,
for those who had children, amusement.

"Her name will be Margaret, after my mother's mother," said Grace when the baby's mouth was almost over the nipple.

Grace glanced at her first mate, who'd fussed over her for the past four months since she'd begun to show, and ensured that she did no strenuous duties. He was a darling, and she loved him dearly.

"Carrig," she said to him gently, "I have decided not to carry out the threat I made against you when I was in the midst of God's worst pains."

He looked up in surprise. "What threat was that?"

"To have you keelhauled."

He grinned.

"Would you honor me and be my baby's godfather?" she asked.

Carrig looked at his captain in shock. "But . . ."

"It would be a great and admirable service you'd do to me and my Margaret if you'd consent."

"Margaret," he muttered as he stroked the baby's head. "My sister, God rest her soul, was Margaret. I'll be the best godfather that walked the earth since the Almighty became godfather to Adam and Eve. Bless you, mistress, for making an old man so proud."

And a tear formed in his eyes.

Grace slept most of the rest of the day, waking up when Margaret cried to be fed. There were no napkins on board, and so a piece of sailcloth was torn and boiled in water to soften it. Then they made it into a square and tied it gently around the babe's waist and through her legs. But soon they needed another piece of sailcloth, and then another, and the cabin boy was given the grave responsibility of washing the soiled napkins in sea water until the stains of feces and urine were rinsed out by the speedy flow of water rushing past the ship's hull.

Exhausted from the birth, Grace was happy to give over the management of her child to its surrogate fathers, and sleep long and sound. Grace woke from her slumber with a start, dreaming that she'd fallen asleep on top of her baby, only to find that the child was gone. She cried out in distress, and one of the crew crept into the darkened cabin to see what was wrong. But when he walked softly into the room, he carried the sleeping Margaret cosseted in his arms, stroking her head and singing a lullaby, and Grace knew that she'd lost her babe to the crew. She closed her eyes in gratitude and fell back asleep.

She woke the morning following the birth to a screaming and a shouting from the crew on the upper foredecks. Grace listened for a moment to the tone of the men's voices. She detected panic. Gone were the traditional orders of the day to scrub decks or hoist a sail or swab the shite of seabirds off rigging. They were replaced by barked orders, some rising in hysteria, given by men who were unused to the voice of command.

Grace struggled to get out of bed, but her exhaustion was too great and she collapsed back onto the straw mattress. Moments later she was asleep once again.

How long she'd been asleep she didn't know, but she was rudely awakened by the shot of a cannon and the yelling of men.

The ship reverberated as fusillade after fusillade of cannon shot was fired from the port side, making Grace's bunk dance a mad jig.

"Mr. Laffey," Grace screamed. "Mr. Laffey, what in the name of Jesus is happening out there?"

No response.

"Somebody come here and tell me what's going on!"

"Damn you all, you spongy iron-witted puttocks, come here and tell your captain what's happening at sea!"

Still no response.

"Damn it, I'll stick firebrands up your arses if somebody doesn't come down below and tell me immediately what's happening to my ship," she bellowed.

But there was still no response. The roar of cannon and the bark of musket fire on deck continued, as did the shouts of men and the sound of feet running hither and thither through the ship.

Grace attempted to haul herself off the bunk, but Margaret had been a big girl and had caused her birthing skin to rupture and bleed, and it was an agony to move, let alone to stand on her two feet.

Beside herself with anger and fear for her men and her ship, she lay silent, listening to the noises to determine who they were fighting and who was getting the better of the battle.

When she'd been confined to bed to give birth, they had been thirty or so leagues off the northern coast of France, bound for Portugal. Mr. Laffey had ordered the sail to be reduced so that the ship would be more stable in the water to comfort the captain's lying-in. So, Grace calculated, they couldn't be too much further south, down the French coast, maybe at the latitude of the entrance to the Loire River.

And then a thought struck her with the force of a bullet. Her ship was in real danger. It might be a Spanish galleon or a French galleas, or even an Algerian pirate ship that her men were fighting. She'd heard tell that the Algerians were now venturing this far north in search of the spoils of the coast. But it was more likely to be a fat and sluggish Spanish treasure ship, weighed down with gold from the New World, which had been blown too far north by adverse winds, and away from the protection of the Spanish navy, and her men were trying after booty. But if so, why were they running and shouting so? No, it must be a man' o'war.

Jesus and all the Saints, she thought, if the ship was Algerian, the men had better put up a good show, because the Moors were merciless fighters, and brilliant tactical seafarers. They'd run rings around most crews.

She held her breath and listened for the rapidity of cannon fire to see how well her men were acquitting themselves. Grace cursed after a couple of moments, because there seemed to be no rhythm to the salvoes. The shots seemed to be sporadic, as though nobody up top was giving direction as to what to fire, when and at whom. The fore cannon should be fired first and then give way to midships and then aft cannon so that the enemy boat would be strafed in the forward movement and the damage be so much greater, and her ship would provide a more difficult target to hit. And when the last of the aft cannon had been fired, the ship should be turned in the opposite direction so that the fore cannon would be readied and reaimed, and thus the salvo would continue until the enemy was devastated above and below the sea line.

But as Grace listened to the cannon firing from her own ship, she knew instinctively that it wasn't happening as it should. Volleys seemed to be coming from either end of the ship at once and only from the portside, and that meant that no directions were being given to the helmsman and there was wasted shot and greater opportunity for the Algerians, if it was those Moorish heathens.

"You grizzled earth-vexing louts, you!" she roared. "Haven't I told you to keep up a rhythm when you're attacking? Don't you sons of whores and bastards know anything at all?"

Again, she struggled to get out of bed, but then stopped when she heard frantic steps descending toward her cabin. The door burst open without knocking and Mr. Laffey ran in, his face defining the perilous nature of their circumstances.

"Moors, Cap'n. Algerians. They came riding high on the water, and they're giving us their best."

"We can beat Moors, Mr. Laffey. We've done so in the past!"

"Ay, but that was when you were on deck, Cap'n. Under me, the men have turned to mush. I can't get them to dance in the way you can. I'm sorry, ma'am, I gave them orders for the firing sequence, but they became scared and fired at will, and we're losing and now I think this time we're dead in the water."

"Not when I still have breath in my body," she shouted. "Now help me up, Carrig. Together, we'll blast these stinking sons of Hell back to the blackness from where they came."

The first mate left the cabin and returned moments later with three men who carried Grace up to the gangway on deck, where she could survey the damage. Two of her crew were putting out a fire which had erupted from a shot which hit one of the sails; more were fetching up ball and powder from the store below decks; others were firing at the Algerian pirate; others still were loading cannon and trying to aim at the weaving boat which was undoubtedly getting the better of Grace's crew. All in all it was a scene of panic and despair.

"Put the ship around, Mr. Helmsman. Hard to starboard! Raise the aft sail; we're going in, straight at her. We'll ram her amidships."

The men all turned from the urgency of their duties, and stared in astonishment at their captain, whom they'd assumed was out of commission.

"NOW!" Grace screamed. "Turn this ship hard to starboard immediately.
Carrig. Give me a pistol, carry me to the railings."

They did as she ordered. Seeing their captain at the railings, firing off her
pistol at the Algerian, the men gave a great cheer.

Slowly, Grace's boat turned so that she was heading directly for the Algerian. Because she was no longer side-on, most of her cannon were inoperative, except for two in the prow, and one further back on an elevated platform, which
she ordered her men to load and fire at will.

Morale returned to the crew. On board the Algerian galley, however, there
was a sense of amazement. One moment, the other ship and her crew had been
floundering, their shot ineffective and their battle strategy fruitless. Yet suddenly, instead of fighting or running, she was turning and heading prow-first directly at their beam. The captain of the Algerian came portside to see what was
going on. When he realized that the madman captaining the other boat was
going to ram him and send them both down to the bottom, he gave orders to
fire all portside cannon immediately.

But Grace ordered her helmsman to tack, and so even though some cannon
fire landed and damaged her superstructure, most fell harmlessly into the sea.
Now the Irishmen were cheering and whooping as Grace ordered her helmsman
to tack this way and that; they were rapidly closing in on the Algerian, whose
captain watched in horror as the Irish ship closed swiftly on him. He barked an
instruction to his helmsman to tack north by northwest and so present his stern
to Grace's ship.

But the Pirate Queen had anticipated what he'd do, and the moment she saw
his ship about to turn, she ordered her own helmsman to turn hard starboard;
while the Algerian crew was busy changing course, Grace ordered every available
man to the starboard cannon. As soon as she was starboard on, presenting herself to the Algerian's rapidly turning bow, she gave the order to fire cannon se-
quentially, first those forward, then amidships, then aft.

Ball after ball flew through the air as the Algerian, now virtually defenseless with no cannon able to be presented, took hit after hit in his rigging, his sail, his superstructure. Fires began to erupt in his rope, his sailcloth and his forecastle. Instead of concerning themselves with navigation or attack, all men on the Algerian concentrated their efforts on saving their ship, and their own lives.

Grace ordered the helmsman to turn hard to port, and as the ship slowly responded and began to present, she ordered the cannon to be loaded and fired. Then all Hell descended on the Algerians.

Satisfied as she looked at the scene of fire and smoke and panic on the Algerian ship, Grace ordered her crew to turn upwind and sail away from the stricken Algerian. Rather than finish her off and let her sink with the loss of all crew, she gave the crippled Algerian pirate the chance to make it to shore. For she knew that the word would spread along the Barbary Coast that Irish ships were too dangerous for the taking.

When the black smudge of smoke in the pristine air had diminished, the men let out an almighty holler for their captain. But she was white with exhaustion and loss of blood after the birth. Carrig Laffey gave orders for a chair to be brought on deck for her.

When she was comfortable and a bandage had staunched the bleeding, Carrig came to her.

Diffidently, he said, "The men are overjoyed. But I'm not. I let you down; I let myself and the men down. I tried to be Grace O'Malley, but I failed. I'm sorry, Captain."

"And so you should be, Carrig!" she said, a rare sternness in her voice. "As first mate, you had command while I was indisposed. You nearly cost me my ship, and my crew their lives or liberty. How could you have failed so badly, Mr. Laffey?"

"As I said, I'm no Grace O'Malley."

"Then thank your God that I am, for without me, we'd be drinking sea water instead of ale."

Carrig looked hurt at the rebuke. Grace, still flushed from the heat of the battle, felt sorry she'd embarrassed him.

"Mr. Laffey," she said, "I think it's about time we introduced your god-daughter to the dangers of the sea. Perhaps you'd be kind enough to go down to my cabin. You'll find Margaret safely in her bed in the antechamber. Bring her up on deck so that I can feed the poor mite, and show her the sight of our foe retreating with fire coming from its arse."

Carrig smiled and went below.

Grace looked at her poor damaged ship. Still, there was nothing that couldn't be repaired once the fires were extinguished. And that was a whole lot better than drowning in a thousand fathoms.

Chapter Nine

The Palace of Whitehall

It came to her in a moment of insight as she sat upon the throne in the presence chamber and watched the elderly Sir Ranald Ffolkes, her late father's master of the bedchamber, bent with arthritis and racked with gout, walk painfully down the long red carpet and bow stiffly at her feet. He had come to present a petition for an annuity which had never been paid by the Crown treasury, and now this elderly gentleman, crooked and stiff, had spent three precious weeks of his life in traveling from the north of England to London in order to beg for money to pay his debts, money which he had been rightly owed since the time of Henry, yet which the boy King Edward and the hated Queen Mary had refused to countenance.

Why, she wondered, should he and other knights and lords of the nobility—indeed all the common folk of her realm—be forced to journey to the palaces and courts of Whitehall, or Hampton or Windsor or Richmond to see their queen, when the Queen was a young and vigorous woman who could just as easily get out and visit them?

Certainly, since becoming queen, she had regularly progressed from palace to palace, and it was important for all Europe that they know of the splendor of the seat of her government. She always kept Christmas at Whitehall or Hampton Court, but during the rest of the year, she was constrained to remain in London or its environs.

Or was she? Why shouldn't the Queen of England see the entirety of her realm? Why should she know only those lands and peoples who were within a few days progress of the Thames as it snaked its way through London?

"Tell me," she asked Robert Dudley one morning as they were riding in Windsor Great Park, "I have been their queen for five years, yet do my people know me?"

He reined in his horse, and she rode on further, slowing, and returning to face him. They both sat high in the saddle, breathing deeply through the exertion of their gallop; the horses, glad of the rest, bowed their heads to eat the long lush grass beneath the oak.

"Know you, Beth? In what way should the people know you?" Dudley asked.

"As their queen, Robin, as their queen! Do they know that I have red hair, that I enjoy my father's height, that I wear beautiful gowns, that I sing and dance like Terpsichore. Do they know me?"

"God's bowels, Elizabeth, who cares what the people think? Surely what I think is what should matter to you. I'd give my fortune to know you like a husband. Forget the people; they're foul and pestilential and awful. Now that I am a widower, get to know me like a man, and I'll make your body sing with delight."

"Sing like a virginal?" she quipped.

"Don't toy with me, ma'am. I'm your lover in all but body. Forget the people, and think of my love. Beth, I throw myself at your feet in love, yet you tread on my good nature in derision. Why are you so cruel to me, Elizabeth? Why dash my hopes of being your husband when I know you love me as much as I love you?"

"Husband? But Robin dearest, I already have a husband. I am wed to England. And now I wish to visit my husband, my many husbands and wives. For they know of me, and some may have seen my portrait, but who of England knows me? Should not I be as visible to my people as my people are to me?

Bloody Mary was cloistered for all her reign; poor Edward was too sick to leave his bed, let alone his palace; and my very own father's court was more imperious than regal. Is it not right and fitting that my people should see their queen?"

"Yes," he snapped. "But how? Will you pull down Windsor and transport it brick by brick to the wilds of the north? How will you eat? Dance? Hold court?"

"As do all the lords and ladies of the north. And the east and west and south."

He fell silent. He knew to trespass no further, for she wasn't asking his opinion but merely asking him to confirm a decision already made. So Dudley pulled on the reins and kicked his horse in the flanks, spurring it away from his queen.

When she and Dudley returned to Windsor Castle after their ride, her mind was already set upon a course. She would spend a few months in the summer of every other year traveling from one place in the country to another. This year, she would travel to the south; in two years' time to the further castles and great houses of the east, and after that, well, she would go where she pleased.

"And it will save me a fortune," she confided to Throckmorton.

"How so, ma'am?" he asked.

"For the two months I am away from here, the months when the pox is rife in London and the air pestilential, I will not have to pay for the upkeep of my court. I will visit all those whom my ancestors, ancient and recent, have ennobled, require them to open up their houses to me and mine, and be their guest. I will stay in each great house for two or three days, and then move myself on. In that way I won't impose too much of a financial burden on my host, yet the cost to me will be minimal."

"The cost, Majesty, will be a paltry sum for the honor of entertaining Your Majesty and her council," he said.

"Council? No, Throckmorton, you misunderstand. I will take my entire court."

He looked at her in astonishment. "But Majesty, that's . . . ."

"A lot of people," said the Queen, a devious glint in her eyes.

In August of that year, after four months of preparations, negotiations, investigations, security and travel considerations, the Queen mounted her horse and left the keep of Windsor Castle to travel to Kenilworth Castle near to Coventry, which she had given the previous year to Robert Dudley. Since the death four years earlier of his wife, Amy Robsart, he had been accused by the courts of Europe and many of her own Council of State of the murder of his wife; he had been excoriated by the followers of the Catholic Church as an anti-Christ; Mary Stuart had made disparaging remarks about his being the Queen of England's deadly stableboy; and he had been abused by the people of England for the pursuit of his ambition in his pursuit of the Queen. Yet an independent coronial inquiry had cleared him of the charge of assisting in his wife's murder, and Elizabeth hoped that soon the matter would be put to rest, and poor Amy, remembered more in death than ever she was in life, would be forgotten.

Now, because she loved him so dearly, Elizabeth wanted to rehabilitate him. For it was important that all England should know that by her visit to his home, their queen did not hold him responsible for his wife's death.

On Cecil's advice, Elizabeth had distanced herself from Dudley these past years. Time had helped England to forget poor Amy, and any suspicion that Elizabeth might have had some hand in her death.

As she left the castle keep, guards on the ramparts called out, "God save Your Majesty."

She smiled and waved to them. Behind her were pulled two empty litters in case of an accident, or in case one of the ladies-in-waiting should fall ill. And behind these stretched her entire court. The retinue consisted of five hundred people, over two thousand horses, six hundred carts weighed down with one hundred of the Queen's three thousand gowns, jewelry, food, those effects of her household which she might not find in a country estate, all the papers she required to govern the nation, her treasury—guarded by an entire troop of sentries and yeomen—tents and washing utensils for those servants who could not be accommodated indoors, and finally footmen who walked behind the retinue to ensure that the needs of the court—in terms of refreshment and items of personal hygiene and sanitation—were met, even during the progress on horseback.

The length and pace of her journey had been planned and mapped out by Sir William Cecil, who had sent horsemen scouts to determine how far the court could travel in a day, what was the state of repair of the roads, which houses were a day's journey apart, which of the great houses could afford to accommodate such a large party of people, and whether there were known brigands who might cause difficulty for so noble a gathering.

Their coming to Kenilworth was planned for the early afternoon of the fifth day, so that Elizabeth could rest before the evening festivities which Robert Dudley had planned. However, because the road from London toward Coventry had been washed away by recent heavy rain, the court's progress had to divert through the nearby forest to the west of Leicestershire, and so they arrived just as the sun was setting. The castle still had the look and feel of the ancient fortresses of Norman times, but since she'd given it to Dudley last year, he had drawn up plans for its rebuilding into a modern and exciting home in the style Elizabeth preferred.

Twilight fell as Elizabeth gently encouraged her horse to turn off the main Coventry road and onto the approach to Kenilworth Castle. As she rode slowly past the oaks and elms, the beeches and ashes, the willows and the poplars of the entryway, she saw in the far distance that the castle, standing upon a hilltop, was blazing with light like a vast signal brazier on top of a mound.

Suddenly, a young woman, dressed as a Sybil, walked out of a copse of trees to the left of the driveway, and welcomed the Queen and her court with verses, praying for a long and continuing reign of peace and prosperity. The Queen reined in her horse to listen. Sir William Cecil and Sir Nicholas Throckmorton and others closed in behind her. The majority of the vast trail which was the court were forced to halt on the Coventry road, not knowing the reason for the delay.

The Sybil called out:

The rage of War bound fast in chains
Shall never stir nor move,
But peace shall govern all your days
Increasing subjects' love.
You shall be called the Prince of Peace
Peace shall be your shield
So that your eyes shall never see
The broils of bloody field

Elizabeth laughed and clapped, and called down from her mount, "Good Sybil, I thank you for your wishes, which were shouted for all England to hear, and not whispered in sibilance."

The drawbridge to the castle opened, revealing pillars which were replete with symbols of Elizabeth's reign, symbols of luxury and opulence and plenty—fruits and flowers and paper painted gold and silver, money and exquisite jewels strewn over the ground to symbolize the earthly paradise into which Elizabeth was transforming England. Interwoven with this cornucopia were branches full of apples and cherries and rare oranges and exotic fruits brought from the south of Spain; and all these delights struggled to compete with cages of live birds, salvers of fresh and smoked fishes, pendulous bunches of lucious white and red grapes, platters of oysters and molluscs and sea urchins, and silver goblets full of wines. And on the next of the pillars musical instruments of all kinds which signified man controlling the abundance of nature which had appeared before. The very last pillars before the wooden drawbridge gave way to the paved entryway into the castle were two massive staves of silver to represent the staffs of the Dudley coat of arms, hung with armor as an allegory announcing that Robert, her Robert, would give his very life for Her Majesty Elizabeth Tudor, Queen of England.

Beside herself with joy, Elizabeth dug her spurs into her horse's flank, and rode swiftly, eagerly, into the castle. And there, dressed in a gleaming silver doublet, a feathered cap proffered before him, bowing low in abasement for the grace and favor Her Majesty was doing him by deigning to visit his home, was Robert Dudley.

"Robin!" she called out.

"Gloriana!" he shouted back as he straightened up to receive his queen.

The happiness of their meeting didn't last long. Affairs of state quickly pressed themselves on the Queen. On the first morning of her visit, Elizabeth received a gaunt-faced Admiral of the Fleet, who gave her the ill news.

Elizabeth read and then reread the scroll handed to her. She shook her head, and again reread the first dozen or so lines.

"A woman?"

"Yes, Majesty," said the Admiral of the Fleet, who at last had found the courage to ride from London to inform Elizabeth of the identity of this scourge of English shipping.

"A woman did this?"

"Yes, Majesty."

The Queen burst out laughing. The court also laughed. Not Throckmorton, nor Kersham nor Cecil nor Dudley; no, they knew how great was the damage done to the economy of a sea-faring realm such as England by Grace O'Malley and other pirates.

"Tell the court what this—" she glanced down at the paper "—this Grace O'Malley has done." She was serious now, understanding why her councillors were so grim.

"Majesty," said the admiral, "she has attacked two of the ships of the King of France's navy, and sunk them—but not before relieving their captains of their cargoes of gold, money borrowed from the Venetians. When the piracy was reported to Paris, other ships of His French Majesty's navy set sail and chased her into the English Channel, where she disappeared. The French navy confronted the English navy and many insults were hurled. The French accused your navy of plotting the sinking of their ships by allowing a privateer to undertake their assault. Thankfully, reason prevailed when our captains explained that privateers and freebooters did not attack the ships of foreign navies, just merchant shipping, and the parties withdrew before any damage was done to the peace of the realm."

The court listened in rapt silence. Elizabeth fought to keep her anger under control. For years she'd played cat and mouse with the French king and now this pirate woman might bring the countries to the brink of war. She hawked a gob of spit into the bowl.

"Tell me about her, this Grace O'Malley, pirate woman," the Queen demanded. "What sort of a woman is this? Is she tall, short, strong? Does she have the horns, tail and wings of a demon that she can evade every attempt to entrap her, that she can make such ninnies of the Frenchman's navy? And how long, I wonder, before my own navy becomes prey to her attention?"

"She has been seen only at a distance by our navies, Highness. But those of Your Majesty's subjects in Galway and other parts of Ireland say that she is more man than woman, that she is strong and robust and of rude health. She has red hair, and—"

"Red hair? Like mine?"

"Yes, Majesty."

"Then she cannot be all bad!"

Again, those in the court who believed this to be a lighthearted inquisition burst out laughing.

The admiral continued, "She is more of a sea dog than most captains of the merchant navy. She is reputed to be an excellent sailor and navigator, and they say that she can find her way from an unmarked bay on the Barbary Coast to an undiscovered island in Scotland without being seen by any other ship. They also say that she has the morals of a bawdy house mistress."

"But, Admiral, isn't it often said that a canny woman is often more cunny than canny?" Again, the court burst into laughter. Elizabeth's reputation for quips was widespread.

The admiral, a man with little sense of humor, continued gravely. "She is a stern master who keeps discipline on her ships by regular whippings and keelhaulings; they say that any man who looks her direct in the eye must bow down and kiss her feet."

The Queen nodded. "A queen of the seas!" Again, the court laughed, but there was no humor in what this queen said.

"My lords," said the Queen, turning to her council of privy advisors, "what is our progress in Ireland? How many Irish chieftains have bowed their knees to my father's policy of surrender and re-grant?"

"Many, Your Majesty, give over their chieftainship for the honor of English ennoblement, though there are those in the north and west of the country who still refuse to recognize your rights over the land and refuse our offers of title," said Sir William Cecil. "We are in the process of increasing the presence of your army in Galway, as well as appointing a strong governor in the province to ensure Your Majesty's rights and privileges."

"And this Grace O'Malley, is she from the north or the west?"

"From the northwest, Highness. From the county of Connaught. She is the daughter of an Irish baron named Black Oak O'Malley and her family owns much coastal land. It is from this coast that her father ran his ships—galleys, galleons and lesser craft—and plied his trade in wines and skins and bales of wool and other such cargoes. His daughter is married to one Donal O'Flaherty, another chieftain. He, too, has substantial holdings of land and runs a fleet of trading and pirating ships. It is now thought that she runs not only the fleet of her husband, but also that of her dead father."

Dudley snorted, "A woman in command of a merchant fleet!"

The Queen looked at him sternly. "Any less than a woman in command of a nation, Sir Robert?"

Immediately realizing the danger of what he'd so thoughtlessly said, Dudley stammered, "Ma'am, I didn't mean . . . you are ordained by God Himself."

Cecil came to his rescue. "Be she man or woman, Highness, she is expanding her fleet, and will soon expand her range. She has to be stopped, as do all Irish pirates and brigands."

"My lords," Elizabeth agreed, "I will not have a pirate acting in my waters without my permission. Those privateers and freebooters who do so act on my authority and pay me their levies. This Grace of Connaught is a menace and a deadly threat to our sovereign rights. I hereby command that Grace O'Malley is to be caught and given over to my custody, and is not to be allowed to practice her piratical trade any longer. And when she is caught, Admiral, she shall be brought to England and hanged from Traitors Gate, so that all may see the fate of those who act against the interests of Elizabeth.

"This is my command!"

Chapter Ten

Ballinahinch Castle, County Connaught,
Ireland 15 September 1564

When Grace arrived home, she had lost weight and was physically and mentally exhausted. The birth of Margaret, the fighting, and the long voyages of trading had taken their toll. She needed time to recuperate, to spend with her boys and her new baby.

But as she cuddled Margaret in her arms she was worried. She'd never thought that a baby's skin could change, but change it had. When first born, Margaret had been almost pink-skinned, but as the days and weeks had passed, her skin had grown darker and darker, until now she looked as dusky as a Spaniard. Fool though he was, Donal would know that Margaret was the child of another man; and then all Hell would break loose over her head.

Her castle castellan was informed of her arrival by a runner from the shore, and he was there to greet her. She could tell by his expression that he was shocked by the exhaustion in her eyes and the way her normally robust body seemed to slump over the horse. Indeed, so concerned was he that he didn't even mention the babe in her arms.

"Good morning to you, mistress," he said as he took the bridle of her horse, which had been left by the ship's moorings last night when the distant flares lit the far hills to signal her return to land.

"Good morning, Flynn," she replied, without the customary excitement in her voice.

He asked how her trip was. She told him that it had been financially very successful, though two of the crew had died, one elderly man whose heart had given out as he struggled to pull on the oars while they were escaping an English navy boat out of the Solent; the other killed by a lucky ball from a musket fired from land in France while they'd been too close to the shore. Both men, she'd told him, had been buried at sea. As she was relating their deaths, she made a mental note to send the widows the men's share of the voyage, as well as the collection which had been taken up by their colleagues.

"And the babe?" Flynn asked, suddenly realizing what Grace had in her arms.

"My youngest child, sister to my sons, may the Almighty bless all my children," she told him.

But when he tried to look, she told him not to, because the babe was asleep.

"Is the master at home, or out whoring or fighting or drinking?" she asked.

Flynn averted his face so she couldn't see his expression. It was wrong for a castellan to side with either master or mistress, though anyone who sided with the Master O'Flaherty was either a drunken sot or a blood relation. It was the Mistress O'Flaherty whom everyone admired and respected.

"The master isn't home, ma'am. He was at war with the Joyces at their Cock's Castle—"

"Dear God," she shouted, "why can't he stop his fighting with them? What is it this time?" she asked as she dismounted her horse, handing Flynn the reins. "Money? Stolen sheep? What?"

A stablelad came and took the horse as Grace and Flynn walked through the keep into the castle. A fire had been lit in the great hall, for even though it was September, it was still cool in the early morning. Grace gave Margaret into the custody of a maid and told her to put the child in a cot in her bedroom.

Grace turned to her castellan in concern. He still hadn't answered her question. "Well?" she demanded. "Why is your master fighting the Joyces?"

"Why not rest and rescue your spirits, ma'am, and I'll tell you everything when you've eaten and slept in a soft bed. You've a new babe, and now's not the time to concern yourself with fighting."

"You'll tell me now, Flynn. What's happened while I've been away? Has that mad bastard of a husband of mine lost our land? Has he lost our fortune gambling on dice? What? Tell me now. Don't think to protect me."

"Sit down, mistress, for this will come as a shock."

She did as he suggested, finding a carver chair close to the inglenook of the fire.

"There was a war, ma'am," Flynn began, summoning all his courage to tell her. "While you were at sea, your husband attacked the Joyces' castle, Caislan-an-Circa, on the island in Lough Corrib. They were furious and they retaliated mercilessly. It all started in such a mild and unexpected way. It was the theft of grass, nothing more, mistress. For what caused the master to ride out was because the Joyces had trespassed over the border and agisted their flock of sheep without paying compensation. So the master took seventy men and rode over there to have it out with them.

"He was beside himself with fury, and rode out unprepared. But he had the sense to send to the O'Connors of Roscommon to beg for the use of their Scottish Gallowglass, and fifty came over to join him. The one hundred and twenty men besieged the Joyces' castle for two weeks, thinking to starve out the evil bastard. I was so concerned at the cost that I even considered sending to Galway and the English to beg them to come and knock some sense into the master and the Joyce. But then in desperation, the Master O'Flaherty made a suicidal attack on the north wall of the Joyces' stronghold. Ma'am, he fought so hard that even the Joyces are now calling him Donal the Cock for his bravery. But . . ."

She looked up at him. "But?" she demanded.

"But they poured boiling oil over the parapet." He lapsed into silence.

"Well?" said Grace, holding her breath.

"The Master O'Flaherty is dead, ma'am. He died of his wounds. He was returned on a litter, and was buried by the priest in the O'Flaherty chapel not three weeks hence."

The castellan looked at Grace in anticipation of the emotion which he assumed would pour out of her. It was a terrible thing to return home and find your husband dead. More terrible still, for the war and the payment to the Gallowglass had used up all the money in the treasury, and the castle was in debt to the merchants. As castellan, Flynn told many servants of the unfortunate deaths of their husbands or wives, and was well used to the shock. So he stood ready to bury the mistress's head in his chest when she burst into uncontrollable wailing.

He waited and waited. Grace merely sat still, staring into the shapes of the flames from the crackling oak logs in the fire.

Slowly, she crossed herself and said a silent prayer. Then she stood up, life seeming to return to her body. "So the evil bastard's gone, has he? The whore-monger is no more, dead and buried, rotting in his grave, no doubt pickled in all the whiskey and ale he—"

"Mistress," the castellan interrupted in shock. "Your husband Donal is dead. Have you understood what that means?"

"I understand right enough, Flynn. I understand that I won't be raped tonight in his drunken rage, that no longer will my legs be forced apart to satisfy his jealousy and hatred of my success, that I won't be beaten black and blue or forced to hide in the fear he'll beat me to death. And the children will no longer have to cower in the darkness now that the worms of Hell are consuming him and his evil rages and his violence.

"Yes, I understand well enough what it means to be a widow of the O'Flaherty. And I also know what it means to be a widow in Ireland, Master Castellan. I understand that because of our country's laws, I can only inherit a pittance; that despite my slaving my fingers to the bone these past ten years, braving the elements and risking life and limb, despite building up the O'Flaherty treasury to the biggest it's ever been, all the money and properties except for a piffling sum goes to his brothers and not me and my own children. But who's to look after Grace O'Malley? Who's to say that I won't be kicked out of my own castle by that bastard Liam who'll take everything for himself, the greedy fuchking pig?"

Flynn stepped back at the vehemence of her outburst. This was not a widow talking. He had no idea what to say or do.

"It's what I've been fearing these last five years and more. Since trading is going so nicely, there's more avaricious eyes on my possessions than ever . . . even his distant cousins have been sniffing around and licking the shite from his arse in the hopes of tickling some money out of his bones. But who will give a fuchk for poor Grace?"

She sighed, and turned to face Flynn, her back to the warmth of the fire.

"Well, Master Castellan, I guess you'd better prepare my armor and send word to the clan that there's another battle to be fought."

"Battle?"

"Of course," Grace said, rubbing the warmth into her backside. "I have to avenge my husband's death. No Joyce can kill an O'Flaherty without suffering the consequences."

"You would go to war?" whispered the astounded man.

"And why not? In a week's time, when I'm properly rested, I'm going to avenge the death of my Donal."

"A mistress at war?"

"This mistress will defend her husband's name and honor, even if he spent his entire life doing everything possible to disgrace that name and honor."

She strode from his company and walked across the room into the banqueting hall. In a booming voice Grace called out, "The mistress of the castle has returned and wants her breakfast. Oatcakes and beer and a good wine and then more beer to celebrate her changed fortune of being a widow woman. Now!"

Grace's spirit had returned now that she was Mistress of the O'Flaherty both on land and sea, though that was unlikely to last. She was particularly pleased that her children had taken so kindly to Margaret, and what also delighted her was the way that Liam looked at her dark-skinned babe. He was too stupid to comprehend that such a dusky child might not be his brother's, but in time, no doubt, words would be whispered into his ear and he would come to that conclusion. That was something she would have to deal with later.

Now that Donal's father was dead, Liam, the next brother in line, had already demanded his rights as master of the O'Flaherty name. She'd seen him off at the point of a pikestaff, but she knew he'd be back, and with the backing of the Brehon Laws.

For the time being she would play the part of the poor widow woman, for she was certain Liam and his family would lobby the Great Council of Chiefs and that they would be given most, if not all, of the O'Flaherty wealth. If ever they got to know of how much she'd stowed away on O'Malley land of the wealth she'd earned from her voyages, they'd be after that too. No, she would cry poor, maybe even write to Queen Elizabeth of England about the terrible injustice done to Irish widow women.

But for now she had a war to fight. The Joyces had to be made to pay for the insult to the O'Flaherty. To kill a clansman was bad enough, but to kill the head of the clan, the master of the family name . . . well, that was an issue which demanded blood satisfaction. And she would get it from them.

She rode out ahead of two hundred and forty men; two hundred of the O'Flaherty clan and its farmers, shepherds, crofters and landholders, all armed with swords and crossbows and shields; and forty Gallowglass, armed with flintlocks and muskets and vicious daggers to which they gave the name Sgian Dubh. These Gallowglass had been leased to her by neighboring clans who were eager to see the Joyces put in their place.

And these Scottish mercenaries were the fiercest-looking men she'd ever seen, with their wild and unkempt beards and their long hair in pigtails beneath clan berets. Their tartans identified which clan they belonged to and which man was a relation to another. But as warriors fighting for money in Ireland, there was no rivalry between them, as there would have been in Scotland, where the clans battled against each other as viciously and senselessly as did the Irish chieftains.

The men formed up behind her as she rode high on her white horse toward the Joyces' land. From time to time, she looked backward at the procession, feeling a sense of pride that all these men were following her into battle. Did any of them know that she'd never fought a land battle before? She hoped not, for she had to show leadership or else they would begin to desert. And that was the difference between fighting on land and on the water, because on a ship far out at sea, nobody could desert.

She was determined to gain as fearsome a reputation on land as she had on the sea, but to do that she had to plan a clever and convincing strategy and defeat the rotten Joyces, or she and the O'Flahertys—and the O'Malleys—would be shamed in the eyes of all Irish forever.

She remained silent, plotting the siege in her mind as she rode. She was concerned that Donal, despite all his experience of fighting and all his troops, had failed miserably. Since the army of the O'Flaherty had withdrawn weeks earlier, the Joyces would have had time to replenish their food and wine stocks, and probably had more men in the castle in anticipation of a revenge assault.

They would be armed, provisioned, rested and ready. Which meant that she had to determine a tactic which would bring them down in the quickest possible time. But what? At sea, the decision had to be made in the moment. If the wind was against her, she had to sail away and then tack back. She could fire a broadside from starboard and then turn on a gnat's arse and fire a broadside from the port railings before her enemy had time to load his cannon. But on land, what advantage did she have?

How the Hell she was going to capture a stronghold which had defied her own husband, as wild and fanatical a bastard as ever lived, she was damned if she knew.

Two days later, Grace O'Malley and her army stood at the base of the Joyces' castle, still pondering how to conquer the place. Several times, the Gallowglass leaders had asked her what she wanted them to do—frontal attack, rear attack, murder local people one by one in front of the castle in the hope of shaming the Joyces into surrender—but to each suggestion, Grace had politely said that she had her own plan, which she would not reveal to anyone for the sake of security.

And now she had to tell everyone present what was her idea, or else admit that she was an excellent commander of the waves but useless by land.

On her horse, which had panicked and nearly drowned as it was being rowed across Lough Corrib, she rode around the castle grounds. She looked up and saw the Master of the Joyce clan looking down and doffing his cap in mock politeness. And as she rounded another corner, there on the ramparts was the Mistress Joyce, the woman with whom she'd hatched a plan to stop their menfolk from fighting, but which, through Donal's lies and conniving, had come to nothing.

All throughout the building, on its walls and doors, she could see the signs of Donal's recent battle. The walls were scarred with gunshot and arrow wounds. There were still heads of arrows in the wooden doors; and the bases of the doors were still smeared with the stain of ashes and burning where he'd tried to set fire to the entryway but had been beaten off by the arrows and gunshot raining down.

She rode all the way around the castle, and it appeared impregnable. Dear God in Heaven, she thought, how am I going to capture this place?

As she rounded the fourth wall and came again in sight of her army, she was no nearer to the answer. She could see their faces from the distance, looking at her in anticipation. She couldn't let them down, or she would be finished in Ireland forever.

Slowly, deliberately, she drew her horse to a halt and dismounted. The leader of the Gallowglass looked at her expectantly. He was a huge man, standing two heads above her even though she was tall for a woman. There was little of him visible between his beard and moustache and his hairy brows and head, just narrow and quizzical eyes, pondering whether this Irish woman with a fearful reputation as a pirate and merchant was just a bag of wind or had the balls of a man.

"Well?" he asked simply, his deep voice resonating in the sudden quiet.

"Well?" she responded.

"How do we take the place?"

"How? You ask how? It amazes me that my dead and incompetent husband was unable. And you men, you Gallowglass with a reputation which puts fear in the heart of your enemies, you couldn't take it either."

"We tried," the leader said defensively. "But they attacked us with murderous arrows as we tried to break down the door. We lost dozens and dozens of good men; their bodies were piled high. It was a slaughter. So we tried other entryways, but it was the same. And the stones of the castle are too thick to be hacked by axes. So how do you propose that we enter?"

She gathered up her horse's bridle and walked down to the lake shore where her men were unpacking the rowboats with all their equipment and supplies. She was desperately trying to think of a plan. She knew that she only had moments before everyone realized that she had no idea at all.

Grace looked out at the placid lake, waves gently lapping against the stony shore. What would she do if she were in command of a ship and were attacking a naval vessel armed with guns on both bows? How would she get in under cover of their fire? What trickery would she use to put the enemy captain off his guard? How would . . . and then the answer came to her and she smiled.

She turned and faced her men. "We attack from all sides at once. We attack them so that their defenses are spread thin."

There was silence as the men pondered her words. And in their silence, she was also thinking through the scenario.

The leader of the Gallowglass spoke out, "Aye, but then we'd be spread thin as well. We haven't got the manpower to do what you're suggesting. We have to concentrate our power and—"

"Like my husband concentrated his? No, we'll attack to the front, then at the same time to the rear so they won't know which side is the major thrust of our assault. That'll mean that they'll have to divide their forces between front and back, and dilute their strength. And when their men are split front and back, we'll attack from the east and west, so that they'll be even more spread out."

The Gallowglass scratched his head. "Aye, but we haven't enough men to sustain a concerted attack . . ."

She shook her head in amazement at his stupidity. "Do you not understand?"

"But if they're spread out up top, we'll be spread out down on the ground. We'll not have the manpower to—"

"Jesus and all the Saints! Isn't it obvious? We keep twenty men in reserve at the rear of the castle, hidden behind the trees while the rest of us are fighting. We're assaulting their castle from all sides. They're up there in confusion, trying to keep up their supply of arrows and spears and musket balls. They can see no concentration of manpower, and so cannot tell where the real assault is coming from."

"Yes?" said the leader of the Gallowglass, unsure where she was going with this military maneuver. He was used to fighting in the open valleys and hillsides, where lines of soldiers faced each other, man to man, and where strength and valor won the day.

She looked at the rest of her men—kinsmen, servants, serfs—all were looking at her in wonder, waiting for her to reveal the secret of her plan.

"And then we withdraw," she said.

She looked in their eyes, and saw amazement.

"Withdraw?" said the leader of the Gallowglass. "Scottish fighting men don't—"

"We withdraw. We gather at the front of the castle and withdraw out of harm's way to the lakeside."

She nearly laughed as all the men looked at her open-mouthed.

"Think of the confusion above," she continued. "Think of the scene. They're in the midst of fighting a battle on all sides of their castle. Their defenses are stretched to the point of snapping, like a frayed rope. They're boiling oil but don't know which side to pour it; their runners are scrambling like rabbits all over the upper battlements, replacing spent arrows and spears from the storehouses below, but instead of the front or rear, they're trying to keep up supplies to front, to rear and to both sides. They've never had to do this before. They've always had to fight off a force on one, or at most two, sides. They don't know how to deal with this new method of fighting. They're beginning to panic. Then suddenly we withdraw. They look down and wonder what's going on. They see our men, unbowed and undefeated, laughing and slapping each other on the back, walking away just when things are going well for us, just when they're in the middle of confusion and at their weakest point."

The Gallowglass leader shouted, "Withdraw! What in the name of—"

"Silence!" she commanded. "Don't interrupt your commander."

In surprise, he withdrew.

"But remember, we have twenty men hidden in the trees at the rear of the castle. Twenty men, who are rested, anxious, keen for the fray. Twenty archers with flaming brands which can be lit at a moment's notice. And as our men withdraw, watched by a bemused and confused Master and Mistress of the Joyce, as those on the battlements sit and rest from their exertions, as they begin to think they may have won an unexpected victory. At this moment a rain of fire descends on the battlements from the woods at the rear. Men atop are pierced by the fire arrows and scream in agony. Panic and misery and death; smoke and flames erupt at the top of the tower. Suddenly the men atop are spurred into action. They all gather from the other three sides of the castle and look down at the woods to the rear where they see our archers showering them with death. Master and Mistress Joyce command all assault weapons to be brought to the rear, where the real attack is taking place."

The men's eyes were agog with wonder.

Grace continued, "Our archers pour arrow after flaming arrow into the castle, and hide behind the trees as the archers and musketeers above fire back at them. But unseen, around the other side, in the front of the castle, we have lit logs which have been soaked in pitch, and while the attention of the Joyces is distracted by defending their rear, our logs are rolled forward against the front door of the castle like a fireship at sea, where they'll burn merrily. Who knows, they may weaken it sufficiently so that a good strong gust of wind will transform it from solid oak into lightest ash and it'll fall to the gentlest push of our battering ram. But I doubt it, for it'll need something special. And that something, gentlemen, will go off with a bang. Because onto this inferno, when the men up top on the castle ramparts look down and order water to be poured on the flames, we'll toss a barrel of gunpowder and blow out the door, sending a plume of flame to singe the eyebrows of those looking down.

"And once the door is flattened, we'll fill the place with smoke from peat and bog and continue smoking them out and kill them as they leave. Or we might want to storm the castle and kill the Joyces in a mighty battle which will be the stuff of songsters for years to come. I haven't decided."

There was a silence which descended over her army as her final words were carried away by the wind. Not a word was spoken by any of the men; not one of them moved; they merely looked at her in awe.

Finally, the leader of the Gallowglass walked forward solemnly and kneeled before her as his ancestor had done before King Robert the Bruce of Scotland; the rest of his men, as tradition demanded, all fell to their knees in respect for their commander, as did the rest of the army.

Grace O'Malley looked at their bowed heads, and was suffused with a pride which she'd never in her life felt before. And then she prayed to Lord God Almighty that her plan would work!

Grace decided not to kill the Mistress Joyce. Her husband and two sons had been killed in the fighting, as had forty or so of their clan, some slain in the battle, some burned in the conflagration and some by choking on the smoke of the peat.

Grace O'Malley had lost only eight of her own men and two Scottish Gallowglass, who were now being floated on hastily made reed boats and sent on fire into the center of the lake.

Seated on a carver brought from the flaming castle, her back to the lake, Grace sat like the Queen of England as Mistress Joyce, tethered with rope by the neck and the arms, stood waiting with certainty for the judgment of death.

Grace looked up at the older woman and remembered their earlier meeting. Then Grace had been exhausted and desperate to retain the family's fortunes by stopping the fighting. She had initially, she remembered, been treated with disdain by the Mistress of the Joyce but subsequently with respect. Grace had mixed feelings now the boot was on the other foot.

Mistress Joyce stood there, proud and arrogant, but with a look of fear in her eyes.

"If it's killing me you're going to do, I'd appreciate it quickly, for I don't relish a slow and painful death. As one woman to another, you'll do me that honor, I hope."

But Grace shook her head. "No, ma'am. It's not killing I'm thinking of. Indeed, I had you brought here to apologize to you."

Mistress Joyce and the two O'Flaherty clansmen tethering her looked at Grace in astonishment. With a nod of her head, she ordered the ropes to be removed. Rubbing her arms and neck, Mistress Joyce looked quizzically at the younger woman.

"Ma'am, I came to you some years ago with a scheme to end all fighting between our families and our clans. My husband, God rot him in the Hell he deserves, lied to me and made me look like a fool to you. I recognize that it was he who did most damage to your family, for he was a terrible and violent and dangerous drunkard. And because of him, many good men are dead."

"Then why in God's name attack our castle, Grace O'Malley? Why kill my husband and my sons and my kith and kin? If your dead husband is the source of all our ills, why?" She lapsed into silence.

Grace looked at the bereft woman and nodded.

"You're an Irish woman, and a clan chieftain. You know the answer to that."

Grace stood and walked over to the Mistress Joyce and asked quietly, "Will the Brehon Laws ruin you now that you're a widow?"

"I'll be as poor as you, Grace O'Malley," Mistress Joyce replied.

"Then God help us both," Grace said, looking out over the lake at the setting sun.

Chapter Eleven

The Tiltyard of Whitehall Palace, 22 June 1566

The young knights, fifty of them, wore their hoses stuffed with silks to pad them out and add bulk to their manhood. They stood before the Queen of England, their doublets cut short in the latest Italian fashion, exposing so much of their stomach that married ladies should avert their eyes, though most of them didn't. The fifty young swains stood and bowed stiffly before Gloriana. Each, as though on cue from the Master of the Revels, removed and doffed his feathered cap, and one shouted up, "Gloriana, we fight and prepare to die for you."

Elizabeth, dressed as Diana the Virgin Huntress in a flowing white robe of purity, her hair adorned with flowers, stood and threw carnations at the feet of the young men. She had chosen the type of flower carefully, for people spoke of its name deriving from the word *corona*, the Latin for crown; yet others said that it derived from *carne*, the Latin for flesh, and that its color symbolized the divinity of the monarch as God made human. So she threw a carnation to each of the braves, and each jumped in an attempt to impress Her Majesty with his athleticism.

The ulcer on her leg ached and she wanted to reach down and massage it, but the Ambassador of France was seated in the enclosure below hers, and it was important that she show herself to be healthy and without ailment.

There were rumors about her all over the nation, flying like malevolent birds through the air. Rumors that she and Robert Dudley were lovers and that he was king in all but name; rumors that she was prepared to reintroduce the Catholic mass in order to accede to Sir William Cecil's demands and marry a prince of France or Spain; rumors that she had become pregnant to pretty boys in the palace; rumors that she was no longer the Virgin Queen.

More than anything, Elizabeth hated rumors which she hadn't started herself. And the one she hated most was that she and Dudley were lovers. She loved him, yes, and she allowed him liberties with her body which she would allow nobody else. He often touched her breast; and sometimes when she sat at banquets with him beside her, he would put his hand beneath the table, struggling to lift up the voluminous folds of fabric, so that he could feel her stockinged legs inside her gown. Sometimes her own hands wandered to his hose, for she loved to feel the smooth and silken, yet firm, shape of his wondrous legs. And sometimes, when she was pleasured by wine, her hands might wander from his knee, higher and higher until she could feel his muscles stiffening with the thought that she would go further than propriety decreed and touch his member.

But her hand never strayed that far, for it was at that moment she remembered the silly flirtations of Mary of Scotland and she became angry at Dudley's presumption and her own weaknesses. And then she became angry with Mary, and her breathlessness disappeared and a change came over her and she became Queen of England and no longer a flirtatious girl.

Silly Mary Stuart, whose head was full of love and romance and not queenship. Well, now that she had accepted England's royal gift and was wedded to Henry Stuart, Lord Darnley, all was well, for there was no longer any challenge from a foreign prince marrying Scotland and leading an assault on England from the north. At first, Elizabeth and the Privy Council had been concerned that the union would be dangerous to the common amity between the two nations, but Darnley was such a silly boy that little harm could come from him and the equally silly Queen of Scotland could let her eyes wander over her new husband's body, rather than covetously over the countryside of England.

Elizabeth was distracted by the sudden appearance at the back of the royal enclosure of the beautiful Christopher Hatton, the dear boy she had discovered when he was studying at Oxford and then at the Inner Temple. He was a young man of most excellent physique, like a statue of a Grecian god.

She'd first seen him dancing in the masque *Gorboduc* and his dancing was so stylish and elegant that she'd appointed him one of her gentlemen pensioners. Tall and strikingly handsome, with a wonderful knowledge of Latin and Greek, a manly man, he made poor Robin Dudley furious with jealousy, and that gave Elizabeth great fun. She loved to see Robin skulk off as she flirted with young Christopher; sometimes he'd disappear from court for two or three days at a time, refusing to come out of his suite. But after three days of his sulking, she'd command his presence, then she'd make a womanly fuss over him before the entire court, and he'd preen himself and puff up like a cockbird and feel potent and manly again. Poor, dear Robin, she thought. How delicious it was to be cruel and kind to him.

"Kit, dear boy, come over and sit by your queen," she called out.

The young man bowed, doffed his cap, and walked down the steps toward Elizabeth. But before he could reach her, she called out, "Before you approach, fill a plate with food for yourself and me, and we'll eat together."

She turned to one of her ladies-in-waiting and said, "Alice, bring me a glass of ale. It's a hot day, and I wish to refresh myself."

Lady Alice Eaves stood, bowed and retreated to the rear of the enclosure. Shortly afterward, Christopher Hatton stood behind Elizabeth and deferentially asked permission to sit. They sat side by side as the knights on the field prepared for the nod from the Master of the Revels to begin the jousting. The knights picked up their lances, donned their helmets, shut down their visors, and sat squarely in their saddles. Elizabeth picked up a piece of ham on the tines of her fork and ate it. Then she nodded to the Master of the Revels, and within moments, the silence of the tiltyard was replaced by the thunder of horses' hooves as two knights rode toward each other, the audience roaring them on.

They met in the middle of the field, and both their lances glanced off their opponent's shields to a cascade of sparks. The riders, still mounted, passed each other and rode to the ends of their rows, where they would turn and prepare to charge again. The crowd loved it when their entertainment wasn't truncated immediately by one knight falling off his horse.

"You know, after this tourney, the Master of the Revels has organized some bear-baiting. Two large brown bears, monsters of beasts, have been brought here from Windsor especially for the fight. There are a pack of hounds ready and waiting. It should be fun," she said to the young man.

He nodded but didn't seem to be very interested.

"Kit, what's the matter?" asked the Queen.

When he turned and faced her, she knew that it was bad news. His eyes were the outward expression of his innermost emotions, which was why she loved him so very much.

He remained silent.

"Well?" demanded the Queen.

"Majesty," he began, but hesitated.

"Come, boy, out with it. The quicker the better."

"I have been sent by Sir Anthony Waldron from the Tower of London. He has tried to speak with Sir William Cecil, but the gentleman, as with many of your other councillors, is at his home. And so he has asked me whether I would come and see Your Majesty."

"On what business?" she asked shortly.

"Highness, one of Sir Anthony's agents has returned just this morning from Scotland, where he was three days ago. Sir Anthony begged me to report some news to you."

"News."

Again the young man fell silent.

"News?" the Queen said, this time louder so that her ladies-in-waiting turned in surprise.

"Mary of Scotland, Queen Mary, Mary Stuart."

"I know who Mary is. What of Mary?"

"She has had a child. A male child, an heir. It will be named James."

An awful silence descended on the royal enclosure.

Christopher Hatton hardly dared breathe, let alone look at the Queen. The ladies-in-waiting, terrified, looked down at the floor.

At first the Queen did nothing, said nothing, seemed to the young man to be in a trance of death.

Then she screamed out, "WHAT?"

"Three days?"

"Three days!"

"But . . ."

"My lord, Her Majesty has been in her chambers seeing nobody for three days. Strange sounds are heard from the corridors, like the wailing of a wolf on a new moon, but not a sighting of Her Highness."

"And her ladies-in-waiting?"

"Only two are with her, and they haven't left her chambers. Food and drink are left at the end of the corridor, but there is no gusto to their consumption. Sometimes the food is untouched."

Sir Robert Dudley nodded gravely as he listened to Sir William Cecil's explanation of why he'd been sent for so urgently.

"And you require me to enter Her Majesty's chambers?"

The older man nodded, showing obvious signs of embarrassment that he was forced to beg such a thing from a man he considered completely unworthy of his place in court.

"You wish me—no, you beg me to accommodate your desire?" said Sir Robert, relishing Sir William's discomfort.

"Because of your intimacy with Her Highness, you are the most appropriate candidate. For the sake of the realm, I beg of you to see how Her Majesty is, to find out and report on her condition to her council." His gout, painful at the best of times, was throbbing in his foot. This was a bad moment for him. He'd often and publicly critized Sir Robert for his ambitions to marry the Queen, and now, because Elizabeth had locked herself in her chambers after hearing the news of Queen Mary of Scotland and was refusing to deal with the problems of government, he was forced to grovel to a popinjay.

Sir Robert nodded and stroked his beard. Softly, so that none could hear this part of their conversation, Sir Robert whispered, "Did I hear you say please, Sir William?"

The secretary of state looked at the Master of the Queen's Horse in utter contempt. "Please, Sir Robert, for the sake of the realm," he whispered back.

Loudly, for the benefit of the court, Sir Robert replied, "I shall attend on Her Majesty immediately, and beg her emergence as our body and soul."

The court applauded. Even Sir William smiled in relief.

Sir Robert bowed theatrically to the court, then turned and left the presence chamber to walk the long corridor of the palace to the Queen's privy apartments. Guards who lined the corridor recognized him immediately and fixed halberds.

But when he came to the entryway to her inner sanctum, he saw that it was protected by two guards who stood not at the side, but in front of the door, obviously intent on blocking the path of anybody who tried to enter.

"Stand aside," he ordered.

The guards didn't move, didn't even look at each other to decide whether they should disobey one of the most important men in England, for their orders came directly from the Queen herself.

Robert Dudley knew immediately that neither force nor threat would move these English oaks. Only subterfuge.

"Good morning, gentlemen," he said.

Both men nodded, their faces unsmiling.

"How is the Queen?"

A frown appeared on their foreheads.

"How does the Queen fare?" he repeated.

Again they remained silent, unaware of how to answer.

"How was Her Majesty this morning?"

Softly, one of them said, "We haven't seen Her Majesty this morning, sir."

"Yesterday, then? The day before? How was Her Majesty when you last saw her?"

They remained silent.

"Is the Queen dead?" he asked in shock.

"No, sir!" exclaimed one of the yeomen.

"How do you know? You haven't seen her since she entered her chambers. Perhaps she's ill."

"Then her ladies-in-waiting would have sent for a doctor," said the other, though there was no confidence in his voice.

"But if one of them had poisoned Her Majesty."

Their eyes widened in horror.

"But . . ."

"But what, gentlemen? What if your queen lies sick or poisoned or even dead, unseen by England for three days, three days in which she could have been helped or rescued by the yeomen who are there to protect her? How would Spain or France react if they found that the guards and soldiers of England couldn't even protect their most important person? They'd mount an assault and we'd be at war within a fortnight."

The tactic was working, because the men shifted uncomfortably.

Dudley drove home his advantage. "I am Her Majesty's closest and most intimate friend. She seeks me out. I have apartments next to hers. I have been absent from the court on royal business for three weeks, buying horses in Ireland, or she would have sent for me to protect her. I beg you, good yeomen, to admit me to her presence, for the sake of the safety of the Majesty of England."

Slowly, nervously, they looked at each other.

"But the Queen gave instructions that under no circumstances—"

"What if an assassin had a knife to her back? What if Her Majesty was under threat? No, gentlemen, I think that for the sake of your employment, or worse, your heads on a spike on Traitor's Gate at the Tower, you will let me through."

The guards looked at each other and, as one, turned to open the door. Dudley walked cautiously into the Queen's apartments which he knew so well.

The rooms, usually so light and gay, were dark and somber; drapes had been placed across the windows, from mullion to mullion. As his eyes adjusted to the gloom, Dudley saw seated in the gloomy antechamber the Queen's ladies of the bedchamber. They were looking up at him in shock and astonishment.

Lady Isabel de Vere stood to usher the intruder out, but when she saw that it was Robert Dudley, relief suffused her face.

"Dear Sir Robert, how good to see you. Her Majesty is in her bedchamber. We are only permitted inside to feed and wash her. Other than that, she commands us to leave her alone."

"Why?" he asked.

"The Scottish whore has had a male heir," she replied.

"Ah," he nodded, suddenly understanding everything. Why Sir William Cecil couldn't have told him was a mystery, but who could fathom such a mind!

He walked past Lady de Vere and picked up a tray of food and drink which was on a table outside the closed door of the Queen's bedroom.

"Lady de Vere, when I am in Her Majesty's bedchamber, you will probably hear her calling for the guards and for my execution. I need to draw the bile from her temper before she returns to normal. Please do not allow any interruption, no matter what you hear."

Lady de Vere nodded gravely. Sir Robert opened the door and entered without knocking or begging permission.

The room was dark, and had he not known its features, he would have been lost. However, he walked swiftly over to the bed where he could just make out the shape of a woman lying bereft. "Food, Elizabeth," he said jovially. "Food and drink. Sustenance for Her Majesty."

The Queen sat up in bed, amazed by the peremptory disturbance.

"How dare you . . ." she began to shout.

"I dare because you dare," he shouted back.

"What!"

"You dare withdraw from your people!" he said sternly. "You dare refuse them their sunlight, their vigor, their strength and potency, their majesty. You dare put your own silly and petty fortunes before those of your beloved people, who would die at your command, who would lie down and give their all for you, their queen. You dare lie in bed in a cold and dark room on a hot

English day, instead of galloping over the fields with your Master of the Horse."

Furious beyond measure, the Queen sat up and hurled a pillow at Dudley. She stood up in her nightgown, walked across the bed, and flung herself upon him, pummelling him with her fists.

"How dare you enter my bedchamber without my permission, you Master of Nothing. Guards!" she screamed. "Arrest this man! I'll have you hung, drawn and quartered by morning for your treason. I'll have you arrested, you peaked-up poltroon, you . . . you . . ."

She banged him with clenched fists, kicked him, screamed the worst of insults at him. "You son of a drunken whoremonger, you foul and leprous ninny, you wayward elf-skinned pumpion, you reeky pottle-deep whipster. How dare you presume to address the Queen of England like this!"

Dudley merely stood there, not lifting a finger to defend himself, not trying to prevent her blows, her kicks, her spitting, her screaming.

Eventually her anger and fury spent itself and she seemed to deflate like an empty waterskin. She looked at him and tears began to brim in her eyes. Then she began to sob, quietly at first, but then loudly, trying to speak, but her emotions preventing her.

Robert Dudley put his arms around her and drew her into him, so that he enfolded her body. He kissed her forehead, her hair, her cheeks, her neck.

"Darling lady," he whispered into her ear, feeling her paroxysms of distress.

"She has an heir, Robin," she sobbed. "She has a child, and a husband and a kingdom. She's a ninny and a fool, and would lose her kingdom to any man with a shapely leg in fine hose, yet she has a husband and an heir. And I have nothing."

She wailed as he gently picked up her frail body and carried her back to her bed. He laid her down and lay down beside her. She hugged him as she cried, and again he encased her in his arms.

"She's a silly waggish common-kissing malt-worm and yet she has an heir. All Scotland is rejoicing because the succession is assured, and all England is still waiting, pregnant in anticipation, for me to decide whether I'll marry. Oh, Robin, what shall I do?"

"Marry me, ninny."

She shook her head. "I can't marry a commoner, you know that."

"Make me an earl."

Again, she shook her head.

"A duke? A baron? A bishop?"

She smiled for the first time in days, and said softly, "Your rank is only a small issue, as you well know. I have desired an heir to Scotland for some time, but I thought that by now I would have married and had an heir myself. It was me who introduced Lord Darnley to Queen Mary—me!—thinking I would be made safer by her marrying an English oak rather than a Spanish olive. Yet instead of earning her friendship and loyalty, still she colludes with Spain, still she seeks to make all England Catholic. And still she claims that she has greater rights to the throne of England than I have."

"Then why are you so sad that she's had a baby? Its birth has made England safer. It's what you most desired."

"Because I'm barren, Robin. I'm fast approaching the age when my womb will be as dusty and dry as a desert, and there is no issue."

"But many men want to marry you, not just me. Why do you vacillate so? Why can't you marry one, at least, or two or three if the desire takes you. Your father set the example."

She punched him good-naturedly. "You know my fear of marriage."

"I'll help you overcome your fears, Gracious Majesty."

She sighed, and held him closer. Then she hugged him, and kissed his lips, then his neck, then his cheeks. She nestled into him, as though they were already married, and put her hand inside his doublet to play with the hairs on his chest. Her body ached for him. She wanted to stroke him and feel him smother her with kisses, to feel him pull aside her nightshirt and then feel the shocking but blissful pain and pleasure that her ladies-in-waiting often whispered about when they thought that she couldn't hear.

She moved her hand lower to his stomach and felt him stir; he pulled her closer to him so that he was almost squeezing the air from her body. Overcome by desire to feel him, she put her hand inside his codpiece and felt his stiff and earnest manhood. But she withdrew her hand, and became again the Queen of England.

"I have to have a marriage for the safety of my nation, and marrying you would be the sweetest gift of all, but a naïve gift. No, dear Robin, I have to marry France. Catherine de Medici wants one of her three pimply boys to be my husband. Me, a thirty-two-year-old matron should marry a seventeen-year-old pimply-skinned boy just because he's King of France. Yet . . ."

"Yet?"

"Yet for the protection of the realm from Spain's intrigues and Mary's Catholic tendencies, I may have no alternative."

"But France, Highness? France? For all of history, France has been England's enemy."

"I have no alternative, Robin," she said firmly.

"I am your alternative, Highness. With me by your side, we'll build the strongest army and navy in the world. We'll invade France and regain Calais, and even march on to Paris. Then we'll sail down to Portugal and get drunk on port wine. Then we'll sail on and tweak the beard of Philip of Spain. We'll—"

"You would make your queen into a pirate?" she said, thumping him in the chest as she burst out laughing.

Chapter Twelve

County Connaught, Ireland, July 1566

She was no longer just the Pirate Queen, now they were calling her the Widow Hen. Donal, her dead husband, had been named the Cock for the bravery he showed in trying to take the Joyce's castle, and because of her skill and bravery in defending her husband's name and finishing the fight, she was now the Hen.

Sure enough she was proud, but her status as a widow meant that all she had won would be the property of the O'Flahertys, and Grace would have to throw herself on the mercy of her brother-in-law, Liam. She'd rather hand over all Ireland to the English than do that, so she decided to return home to the estates of the O'Malley. For months she pretended to be organizing property on behalf of her sisters and brothers, using O'Malley money, but in fact using the money she'd earned from pirating and trading to purchase land from neighboring landholders. She bought cattle and sheep, traded those cargoes she'd kept for herself for things she needed in Ireland, and established herself, slowly and surely and without any undue fuss, as the leader of the O'Malleys.

Stories came to her ears of the way in which Liam O'Flaherty was quickly running down his family estates. He was dismissing people from service in drunken rages, forcing servant wenches into his bedroom, threatening with death anyone who dared to question his decisions. In some ways he was a replica of his brother, except that for all his evil ways, Donal was at least a real man; Liam, on the other hand, had a strain of weakness which he hid with bullying and savagery. The more the stories came to her, the more Grace realized that soon, by default, she would be mistress again of the O'Flaherty lands.

In the meantime, she enjoyed her relationship with her two boys and her daughter. She loved the lads with a fierceness which only a mother can know. She was proud of their skill as sailors and as farmers and she gave them increasing responsibility in the affairs of the family. But secretly it was Margaret, her glorious dark-skinned daughter who held that special place in her heart. For Meg's smile and happy disposition reminded her of the Mediterranean, and of a certain Ottoman sea captain who had lit up the darkest recesses of her life. She'd met Osman a few times since they and their ships had coupled off the coast of Galway; and each time she met him, it renewed her spirits and made her remember she was a woman.

But it was Margaret's disposition which brightened up her life as a widow and made the face she showed to the world able to be borne. Her sons were wondrous strong and vibrant young men, the backbone of her existence, yet her love for Margaret knew no bounds. For in her eyes and face Grace saw the gentleness and determination of the black Turk who had been her lover, a man who knew more about a woman's body and needs than all the hairy men of Ireland put together.

Margaret was loved and adored by all in the castle and by all those outside who knew her. She was a gentle child, though willful when she wanted her way. She would stamp her foot, but if that didn't work, she'd flash her black eyes and beam a seductive smile. Oh, but Grace loved her fiercely. And nobody said a word about the child's dark skin.

While Grace was at her castle attending to the O'Malley family's fortunes, word came to her of the O'Flaherty clan, and the new conditions which prevailed there. It was worrying news, for although she detested the O'Flaherty with a passion, there were many who worked in the fields, or in the great houses, whom she liked.

It took a mere six months for a delegation of O'Flaherty clansmen and women to arrive on Grace's doorstep. The members were known to her—twenty men and eight women, each representing a different village or hamlet of the O'Flaherty. Sean Dunlavey was the elected spokesman.

"Mistress O'Flaherty—" he began.

"Mistress of the O'Malley, Sean. Not Mistress of the O'Flaherty. I'm sure you're here to importune me, but—"

"Mistress!" he insisted. "We're in terrible trouble. You'll have heard that the Master Liam is a thousand times worse than the Master Donal, even on the dead master's worst of all days. He's—"

"I know what he does, Sean. I've heard tell often enough."

"With respect, ma'am, you don't know the half of it. Only a week last Tuesday, the master was riding through the Sheefrey Hills, hunting boar, when he came across two children, not more than twelve years old if they were a day, lying in the ditch in fear of the horses. They were the children of a farmer who's farmed those hills for generations. The master mistook their crying for laughter and thought that they were making fun of him, so he set the dogs on them. They were ripped to pieces, mistress. Both children died of terrible wounds." He stopped speaking, fury taking control of his reason.

Grace stiffened in disgust. "And did you report this to the Great Council of Chiefs?"

"Ma'am, we can only approach the Great Council with the permission of the master, and he'll never give his consent. I've myself been over to Dublin to beg the English Council to intercede, but I was told that Queen Elizabeth of England's eyes are turned south to France and Spain, and not west to Ireland, and she had no interest in the petty squabbles of this land of bogs."

Grace hawked a gob of spit onto the ground. "God damn the fuchking English," she cursed. "Where does it all get us, this giving over of our land to the English in return for pretty titles? Does it deal with the murderous masters who drink and whore? Not a bit of it. Well so much for English law, I say."

Many of the delegates hawked gobs of spit and cursed Elizabeth and England.

"So what is it that you want me to do?" she asked.

"Retake O'Flaherty land. Reconquer that which once was rightfully yours. Save us—"

She shook her head sadly. "Should I do that, Sean, I'd have the Great Council in Dublin, and in Galway too, mobilizing Fitzgerald and MacMurrough and O'Byrne and all the other chieftains to ride in with righteous zeal to take back what I'd wrongfully taken. No, I'm sorry, Sean, but the O'Malley can't be seen to be fighting with the O'Flaherty for the wrong reasons, not until the O'Flaherty do something to wrong the O'Malley."

She looked at them hard, hoping that they understood what she was saying.

"So we're lost," said Sean Dunlavey in dejection.

"Not unless the O'Flaherty do something to wrong the O'Malley," she stressed.

Sean frowned and shook his head, as did the others.

"Did you not understand what I said to you, you spongy iron-wit, I said that I can't do anything against the O'Flaherty until he does something against me!"

There was silence as they looked imploringly at her.

"Are you deaf, man?" she shouted in irritation.

But he continued to look at her in bemusement. Then he turned round to the other people in the delegation and shrugged helplessly.

"Liam has to do something to harm me or my estates first!" she insisted.

"But why should he do that?" asked Sean.

"Oh for God's sake, you ninny. Can't you see what I'm telling you?" She lowered her voice and in a conspiratorial whisper, said quietly, "It would be a tragedy if some of my sheep were stolen from the border of my lands with the O'Flaherty and I found his personal sword had been carelessly dropped in my fields. Then I might jump to the conclusion that Liam O'Flaherty had stolen from me. And knowing that, I'd inform the Great Council that I was going to retaliate, and then I'd storm down to Ballinahinch and confront him. He might be killed when I demanded vengeance for the terrible wrong done to my lands, or he might find himself stranded far out to sea in a leaky rowing boat. Now do you understand, you cloth-eared poltroon?"

And then slowly it dawned on Sean what it was that he was being told. He smiled. The others in the delegation smiled with him. And they left the Mistress of the O'Malley to contemplate the growth of her estate and the recapture of her fortune.

CHAPTER THIRTEEN

St. Brigid's Day, the Isle of Clair, 1568

Now that Grace was a widow and the mother of three children, for the first time since she'd left the convent, God and the Church began to play a part in her life. Since the death of Donal, Grace had thought more and more about questions of life and death, the killing and pirating she'd done, the life she'd led, and had decided that the occasional visit to a church, or a pilgrimage, might count well in the afterlife. Indeed, she had come to enjoy and look forward to these annual pilgrimages to the island of Clair, just off the coast of Connaught where she lived.

The two hundred and forty-five men who accompanied Grace on the pilgrimage fell in behind her as she ascended the steps to the abbey where legend had it that the Mother of Christ had appeared floating above the sea and had floated ghostlike over the land until she had reached the well which was high up on the hills and disappeared. People said that she was in the well, and the water was considered so holy that it was used for washing the wounds of the sick and injured.

Grace, now undisputed mistress of the lands of the O'Malley and the O'Flaherty, and one of the most highly respected chieftains in all of Ireland, insisted that as many as possible join her on her yearly pilgrimage to Clair Island to thank the Almighty for all the benefits He had given them.

The walk from the shore to the heights of Clair Island was steep and rocky, and although she was thirty-eight years old, and should by rights have been celebrating her middle life with a glass of ale, sitting at a fireplace, looking at her grandchildren's antics, Grace was a leader of men, and proud of it.

They arrived at the holy well outside the walls of the monastery, puffing and panting, and began their vigil of prayer, just as the wind was beginning to blow strong and the black clouds were rolling in from the Atlantic. Being one of the few sea dogs in her army, Grace recognized a bad storm when she saw one, and this was a mighty storm. Each of the clouds had a dark base and the blackness continued right up into the very heavens themselves.

But Grace was determined to tend to her men's souls first, and if it meant giving them a good wetting—well, no harm done. And as the wind roared higher and higher and the rain began to sweep across the sea and onto the land, it looked as though God Himself was bidding them a good afternoon.

Suddenly there was a disturbance at the back of the assembly. Grace looked around and through the curtain of rain saw that twenty or so of her men were huddling around a woman, wet as a ship's rat, who had run up the steep hill of Clair to inform the army of something.

A man from the back walked forward, struggling against the vicious bite of the wind, and shouted to Grace, "Shipwreck, ma'am. Shipwreck on the other side of the island across the water at Achill Head. Terrible crossing, ma'am. There could be casualties."

Grace nodded. "And salvage to be had. Come, lads, enough praying. We have men's bodies to save, and a cargo to rescue for ourselves."

They raced down the hill, some slipping and sliding over the sodden grass, and jumped into their boats. By now it was getting dark, and it was a perilous stretch of water which divided Clair Island from Achill. Their boats, little more than large rowboats with sail, were tossed by the growing violence of the sea. They couldn't use coracles or curraghs, which they would normally sail in inland waters, for they would have been deathtraps in such a crossing.

From the crests of mountainous waves, their rowboats sank like stones into the awesomely silent troughs, until they were picked up again like children's toys to ride the crest again, able to see momentarily onto the far land before being flung down into the depths of the water. Accompanying them like some demon from the depths of Hell was a howling wind which sounded like a million tortured souls screaming their agony. Their path through the water was illuminated by flashes of lightning which intensified as the storm reached its zenith, turning the inky night into day as the sheets of white flashed through the sky.

Some of the men, unused to the vigor of the sea, began to pray, thinking that this would be their last moment alive, but Grace steered them along the coast, standing on the stern, clutching the rudder and holding onto the mast, shouting encouragement and laughing at their fears. Finally, she put into a bay inside Achill Head and the wind appeared to drop down from its frightening intensity to the growl of a dog.

They rounded the headland until they came to the westward side, where they'd been informed that the ship had foundered on the rocks. Grace presumed it had been heading to or from Scotland, and had tried to run the westerly rather than the inner easterly route and hence escape the attention of pirates.

Somehow, despite the huge waves which crashed in fury against the shore, they managed to land, and Grace struggled up to stand on the shoreline as her crew painfully dragged their boats up the sand. With the ferocious wind howling around them, the bolts of sheet lightning and the roar of thunder, it seemed as though they were experiencing the end of the world.

Her sodden clothes flapped drunkenly in the wind, as Grace screamed her orders to form up and prepare to ascend the hill to find out where the wreckage lay. She was ahead of the men when she breasted a rain-swept windy cliff, and there below, smashed like a giant's plaything against the rocks, looking like some worthless bauble tossed around by vast unseen fingers, was the wrecked ship. The mast and rigging were pulled this way and that by the suction of the waves; the sail floated sluggishly in the water like a dishrag; the skeleton of the ship was creaking and groaning, splintering at the behest of the waves and the wind.

Men were calling in panic from the water, their frantic voices barely heard above the waves; some had managed to struggle to shore, and stood on the water's edge, bent from exhaustion and looking like limp children's dolls; and others were lying exhausted on the grassy hillside, too spent from their exertions to move.

Grace turned to her men and screamed, "Quick, down to the water now! Form eight lines of thirty men, each line close to the other. Find some rope so that you can link your bodies. Don't lose sight of each other under any circumstances. Don't go into the water more than waist deep or you'll get sucked out, and then we'll have to rescue you. Grasp man or cargo, and then hand it backward. Four men from each line are to stand on shore and ferry men or cargo up out of the reach of the waves . . . NOW MOVE!"

They ran downward like a band of brigands swooping on an unsuspecting village. Finding sodden rope washed up from the wreck, they lashed themselves into line. The men from the wreck looked at them in surprise and then seemed to go limp, now that help had arrived. They nodded their thanks, too exhausted to say anything.

Grace's army waded into the water, and it was only once they were knee deep that the leading men understood how wise their commander was, for the suction of the undertow was vicious, threatening to drag them down. As the huge waves broke ten feet or less out to sea, the very ground on which they stood seemed to be sucked from under them and would have pulled them horizontal had they not been lashed to the man behind.

The earsplitting winds and the roar of the waves made for a nightmare cacophony, and Grace could only just make herself heard as she ran up and down the seashore, commanding her men to rescue first this man, then that, then to bring this box up onto shore, then that chest . . .

Eventually, after nearly an hour of struggle against a furious sea, all the men who were still alive had been hauled out of the clutches of the waves and were on land, drenched, shivering, bruised and bloodied, but they were alive! Many men had died in the shipwreck, and their bodies were being washed up on shore, white and ghostlike in the illumination of the lightning.

Now Grace began to order the wholesale salvage of the boxes of cargo which were still floating. It appeared from cursory examination that it was a cargo of weaponry, crates of guns, knives, swords, shields and flintlock pistols. These would fetch a very fair price when they were sold to the other lords of Ireland and would be used in the fight against the English.

Grace looked up to survey the scene. The storm was still overwhelming, presaging the Day of Destruction, but the lines of her men were starting to retreat from the water, because the rest of the floating objects seemed to be planks from the broken ship, or sail or railing. She looked up and down the shore; her men were tending as best they could to those whom they'd rescued from the sea. She looked out to the wreck of the boat, which was now a useless hulk, rhythmically moving up and down, side to side at the behest of the swell of the waves.

And then she saw him.

He was a hundred yards further up the shore, away from the main body of men. He was lying half in and half out of the water. And knowing the pull of the waves and the precariousness of the undertow, he might very well be sucked back in if he wasn't pulled immediately up the shore.

Grace looked around for help, but she was too distant from her men to be heard, and so she raced the one hundred yards, slipping twice from the force of the wind, to where he lay. He was young, his fair hair sodden and sandy, his face cut from the rocks, his bodice ripped. But he was alive and his eyes lit upon hers as she grasped him under the armpits and hauled him from the greedy fingers of the sea.

Too exhausted to assist her, he lay inert, trying to mouth words against the roar of the wind.

She looked down at him. He was a man, perhaps in his twenties, but he had the looks of a boy. He had a beautiful face, gentle and tender; yet there was a strength about the jaw which prevented him from looking unmanly.

Grace fell to her knees and opened her whiskey flask, lifting the youth's head and gently pouring some of the fiery liquid between his lips. He swallowed, and began to cough. And out came a bucket of sea water.

In shock, Grace said, "My God, I never realized that you were drowning!"

She hadn't thought that he'd taken in such a lot of water. He must have been close to death when she hauled him out of the water and up onto the shore.

Grace thumped his back, encouraging more of the water to erupt from his lungs. When he'd stopped coughing and gasping, she again gave him whiskey; this time he drank it gratefully, for it fought the awful taste of salt and vomit.

He was such a beautiful youth that she held him close to her bosom, letting him feel as much of the warmth of her that would pass through her sodden clothes. She stroked his hair, trying to scrape the sand from his matted locks.

"Who are you?" the youth gasped, his voice rasping from the salt and vomit.

"Grace," she replied. "Grace O'Malley. I and my men were on Clair Island over the bay yonder when we heard of your wreck. We've saved many of your men, but you'll have to do a roll call to determine how many of you have died."

"Grace," he whispered, barely audible above the wind. "Pirate Grace? Jesus God and Mother of Christ, I'm supposed to fear you. Yet you've saved my life. Ma'am, my father warned me." Then he fell silent.

She held him closer to her and gave him more whiskey. "Are you strong enough to get up onto your feet, sir?" she asked. "What's your name?"

"Hugh," he replied. "Hugh de Lacy. This was my cargo. My ship. My first voyage as merchant. Ruined."

"de Lacy? Not the son of Wexford de Lacy? The merchant who's as rich as Croesus?"

He remained silent.

"Oh, don't worry, Hugh. I'm not after anything but your cargo."

She helped him to his feet. He was tall, a head taller than her, with a strong body. She supported him under his arms, and he grasped her shoulders as they trudged against wind and rain up the hill to where the grass began to grow. But the exhaustion from his struggles against the waves, the battle to get to the shore, and the swallowing of the sea water, had robbed him of all his energy, and he collapsed again onto the ground.

Grace smoothed his cheek. "Poor boy," she said. "I'll get wagons from the nearby village and take you and your men back to safety."

. . .

It took Hugh de Lacy three days to recover from his near drowning. Three days in which he was fed and washed and fussed over by the servants in the castle.

Every day, she herself took the handsome young man a tray containing oatmeal and beer, fresh bread and smoked herring, and griddle scones and honey from the castle's apiary. She'd wait till he was finished, and then she'd tell him more of the history of the island or the castle, or more tales of her exploits as a pirate in foreign parts. Whatever the tale, she could barely be away from him for more than an hour before she found an excuse to return to his room.

She knew that her behavior was silly, demeaning, girlish.

"I'm behaving like a lovesick girl, rather than a woman almost twice his age, old enough to be his mother," she admitted to her castellan.

"Ma'am, how long is it since you've had a man between your legs? Do yourself the honor of allowing him to repay some of your kindness."

Grace thumped the castellan in the belly, laughing out aloud, "Dear God in Heaven, you make me sound like a two-penny Dublin whore."

She left the castellan rubbing his stomach and walked up the two flights of stone stairs to Hugh's room. She opened the door for the third time that morning and tentatively poked her head around.

"How is it now, Hugh?" she asked, trying not to sound diffident.

"I have a sudden cramp in my thigh," he said, his voice agonized, his jaw clenched.

She threw open the door and walked quickly over to the bed.

"Where?" she asked.

He forced the words out of his mouth, gasping in pain. "My thigh. It hurts so bad."

She threw back the blanket. He was naked below the waist. Shocked, she looked up and saw that he was beaming.

"You'll need to massage me or I'll never be able to walk again," he told her.

"You young bastard!" she shouted. "I thought you were in pain."

"Oh come on, Grace! For three days you've been fussing like a mother hen, finding every excuse to feel my brow, soothe my chest, rub my back. Well, now I'm so much better, it's time you worked on the lower half of my body, which is in sore need of attention."

"You . . ." she stuttered.

But he pulled her down and she fell on top of him. He clasped her tightly, and although she struggled and could probably have overpowered him, it was the very last thing she wanted to do. She melted into his arms and he kissed her on the forehead, then the cheeks, and then full on the lips.

She responded softly at first, then more passionately, opening her mouth, feeling the warmth of him, the smoothness, the youth!

And then she pushed him away. "Silly boy!" she said. "I'm old enough to be your mother. What's all this about?"

But he wouldn't be defeated. "I'll tell you what it's about, Grace O'Malley. This is a young man with little experience of women, clutching to his bosom a woman who's slightly older—by twelve or so years—and hoping that this slightly older lady will oblige him in the ways of making love."

"So you're a virgin?"

"No. I've had a few ladies in my time, but more in drunken lust than in seduction. What I need is for a lady who has your experience of the world to show me what it is that I've been missing all these years. I've suffered at the hands of the Church and my mother and father for long enough. Now's the time I should be living for myself."

She looked into his eyes. There was no dissembling there. He was opening his heart and body to her. Grace smiled and looked down at Hugh, pleased when she saw that he was growing in manhood and stature before her very eyes.

She started to unbutton her jerkin. "Start learning, Hugh darling, for I'm here to teach you."

His eyes widened as she swiftly removed her clothes. She lay beside him on the bed and began to kiss him, whispering in his ear that if at any moment he wanted to stop, if ever he decided that for any reason he didn't want to go further with her, then it was too late, for if he didn't hold her and kiss her and fondle her and fill her with his manhood, then she'd take him deep into the Atlantic and feed him to the sharks.

Hugh looked at her delightful face, her bright green eyes, her still-vermilion hair, and burst out laughing. She never failed to amaze him with her boldness and her bravery, yet she was feminine too. It was true that he had little experience with women; frankly, he had hoped that putting to sea, out of the clutches of his overweening family, he would find opportunity aplenty in foreign ports to gain the experience that the timid ladies of Wexford and Dublin had failed to afford him.

But not two days out of Scotland, having picked up his cargo of weaponry which he was taking to Portugal, he'd foundered trying to find safe harbor to avoid the storm, and instead of lying dead on the seabed, he was abed with a luscious and lascivious woman, a woman who was passionate and gentle and wise beyond her years and who had experienced more of the world than most men twice her age.

As he held her and kissed her warm mouth and breasts, he realized that he was in love. No, it wasn't lust, for that was what he knew he'd feel in the foreign bawdy houses where wenches bared their breasts and buttocks. No! This was a feeling which suffused his entire being, a yearning to be with her, to possess her, to share himself with her, now and in the future.

It was love! Hugh de Lacy was in love with a pirate woman.

Now how was he going to explain that to his mother and father?

Chapter Fourteen

Westminster Palace, 1568

"She is the bane of my life," Elizabeth hissed as Sir William Cecil related his latest intelligence about Mary Queen of Scots.

"She will be the ruin of me. She is so flighty, so demented of the mind, so amoral of the body and dishonorable and unscrupulous of the spirit, so uncaring of her people and her society, that she will be the ruin of me and of England. And now she is the mother of James, she is even more pleased to ridicule the heirless throne of England.

"I tell you, Sir William, this Scottish harridan, this strumpet, will take from me what is mine by rights, what I have fought for and am succeeding in, and she will become Queen of England and Scotland and, knowing her, of France and Spain as well. She will trample on everything that stands between herself and the very heavens themselves. Jesus Christ and all the Saints, this woman is beyond belief!" Elizabeth's voice rose so that the others in the presence room could hear what she was saying.

Sir William Cecil begged her to keep her voice down, but he should have known better, for any mention of Mary of Scotland turned the Queen of England from a sensible and mature woman into a fiery fishwife.

"First she has an unseemly dalliance with some Italian secretary called Davy Rizzio, whom my English cousin Darnley and the Scottish lords had to remove from public view for the probity of the realm. Then she's complicit with some Scottish lords, especially Lord Bothwell, in the murder of her husband."

The Queen was becoming agitated, and attracting the attention of ambassadors. Cecil wanted her to retire to the privy chamber, but she was in full flight now and her anger could barely be contained.

"Then," she continued, her voice now loud enough for all those in the hushed room to hear, "as a widow of just a short year or so, she marries this rapacious, murderous and arrogant wretch Bothwell, a man responsible for the death of Darnley, and then she takes poor Darnley's clothes and has them altered for her Bothwell, her lover and now her husband. Jesus God, how many fuchking husbands will this woman have? Will she bed the whole of Scotland, and then continue with the men of England?"

"Majesty," said Cecil, trying to refocus the Queen's mind on the issue at hand. "What will happen if Mary escapes from the custody of the Scottish lords? Since she was forced to abdicate her Crown in favor of her son James, she's been like a madwoman, plotting and scheming and—"

"I know!" Elizabeth shouted, surprising Cecil, who jumped backward in shock at her vehemence. "She writes me these mewling and pleading letters, one moment asserting her queenship, next moment demanding my assistance in fighting the Scottish lords and their supposed usurpation of the throne, and the next begging my understanding as a woman. What am I to do?"

"We fear that if she does escape, she will come to England, Highness. We worry that she will seek your protection. Your council knows that she is aware of the intention of the Scottish lords who wish to see her dead. But if she comes here, then Spain and France will demand that we support her in her quest to return as Queen of Scotland. It is a perilous situation, Highness. A perilous situation indeed."

"My God, but this is an evil and impetuous woman," Elizabeth cried in fury. But then she looked at Sir William, and then at her court, full of ambassadors and cousins and hangers-on. Cecil's face told her to moderate her tone, that this latest matter must not become the common tittle-tattle of the courts of Europe. And so, wordlessly, she took his advice and nodded. This wasn't the time to deal with such matters of state but to show that England was above the petty squabbles of another land. "Enough of this," she smiled.

"Let not the clouds which darken the reign of Scotland be cause to rain upon our pretty land. Cousins all, let us retire to the gardens, where the reign of England waters the green and pleasant land which is our Scepter'd Isle."

The court applauded her pun, and when the Queen moved from her throne, they made an aisle for her to retire outside into the gardens.

The Queen's day, however, didn't improve with the walk, nor did it brighten as the night drew on. Although her attention was diverted by a masque which was put on by the Queen's men, and later a ball, and although she danced with a dozen gallants, she was still gravely distracted by the continuing threat from Scottish Mary.

Elizabeth was frightened about the consequences of Mary seeking refuge in England; if she did, how would Elizabeth deal with her? To arrest her was out of the question, for even though she'd been implicated in the death of her own husband, she was a queen, and a queen's body was inviolate. And no doubt, the Parliament would demand her death, and that was more than unthinkable, it was impossible. Nobody, not Parliament nor even Elizabeth herself had the right to kill Mary; only Almighty God could ordain such a thing—and in His good time, no doubt He would exact retribution for the terrible life this silly strumpet had led. If by some hideous crime against the divine right of kings, Mary was executed, would this not send a signal to any recalcitrant faction in the land that any king, or queen, might suffer the same fate?

But Mary was not the only thing preying on Elizabeth's mind. She was worried that her council were still pressing her to find a suitable husband and secure the succession. Their importunities would become even more strident as Mary journeyed nearer and nearer to England.

Other problems beset her. The anger of the Pope in Rome hadn't abated since her father Henry had caused the schism; Spain was gaining wealth and power at an alarming rate and was looking to expand its empire, not just in the

New World but west toward Portugal, north toward the Dutch, and elsewhere as far as she knew; Mary of Guise, once mother-in-law to Mary of Scotland, was rustling her skirts at the way in which her former daughter-in-law was treated by the Protestant Scottish lords. . . . So many problems, and all on Elizabeth's shoulders.

The next morning's business of state started no better. As though the news of Scottish Mary wasn't enough to put her into evil spirits, Lord Connors, her Governor of Ireland, who had the previous day returned from Dublin to present reports to the secretary of state, told the Queen of the increasing and disconcerting influence of the woman pirate Grace O'Malley.

"Your Majesty, she is the very personification of evil. She is a devil woman who has gathered together under her banner an army of over seven hundred men—ruffians and ne'er-do-wells—and they roam the countryside robbing and thieving."

The Queen felt her exasperation getting the better of her. "But I fail to understand, my Lord Governor. Where is her power? Is she a brigand, a highwayman, a common bandit? You have informed me that she is chief of her clan and that she owns large estates in the northwest of that isle. Yet now you tell me that she is a common ruffian. And why has this been allowed? I have appointed you to rule over her lands. Are you not capable? There are many in England who are."

Lord Connors blanched with the threat, and struggled to appease his queen. "Irish custom is very hard to understand, Majesty. Some years ago, a young ruffian called Murrough of the Battle Axes who was a chieftain in the Barony of Moycullen went on a rampage against nearby chieftains and soundly defeated them. Because his territory of conquest was so remote from England, you issued him a pardon and appointed him lord of all Iar Connacht. Your Majesty's decision overturned the ancient Brehon Laws of Ireland and caused some concern—"

"Yes, yes, my lord, but what has this to do with O'Malley?"

He toyed with his ruff in consternation. "She still feels angered that her dead husband's power was so diminished by England, Your Highness. She does not accept the Brehon Laws, and she does not believe that the laws of England are an adequate replacement. She feels powerless, and she has gone on a rampage to win back that power."

"A woman? But how can this be, Master Governor? Surely the English Council in Dublin or the Galway Council will never countenance an Irish woman in command of a county!" Elizabeth looked at her court, who were amazed by such a statement coming from the second queen to rule England in a decade. "After all," she said loudly, "not all nations are as modern in their thinking as ours. Which is why King Henry visited their land, to bring Ireland into the modern world, and allow the light of our sun to shine on her dark meadows."

The audience hall erupted in applause. The Lord Governor of Ireland breathed a sigh of relief.

"Tell my cousins in my court and my lords ambassador what else this piratical subject of mine has done, my Lord Connors."

"Her latest exploit, ma'am, was to do with a ship which foundered in a terrible storm on the western coast of Ireland, not two months back. She and her vicious band of cutthroats went down to the shore and stole the cargo, and then left the innocents to fend for themselves—men, women and children who had been washed up onto the shore praying to Almighty God for help in their moment of adversity. But instead of God's grace, this Pirate O'Malley refused them help. She left many in the water to drown, and it's said of some to whom she took a dislike that she slit their throats as though they were cattle."

Behind him, he could hear the entire court gasp in horror. He knew the whole assembly was listening with rapt attention as he told of the seduction and murder of Sir Hugh de Lacy.

"This young gallant, Majesty, was the very scion of Ireland. He was the son of Baron Francis de Lacy, who traces his ancestry to Norman times. Baron Francis, ma'am, was one of the first Irishmen to be titled by your late and illustrious father."

"They say, Majesty, that this pirate woman had her evil way with Hugh de Lacy night after night, until the poor boy was spent. In that state of deflation, when he was of no more use to her in the arts of manhood, and when no doubt another had happened by and fallen into her evil clutches, she determined to be rid of him. Majesty, she invited him to go hunting for deer on Achill Bay, the sight of his near drowning. Oh, Your Highness, what a perfect irony that was . . . She had plucked the boy from the water when he was in a state close to death so that he could service her lascivious needs, and then when she had drained the boy of his life's fluids, she took him back to where the Almighty nearly claimed him for His very own, and there as a sacrifice she offered the boy up in the name of sin and evil."

Enraged by his prevarication, Elizabeth shouted, "My Lord Governor, I have poets and playwrights aplenty to create drama. What I need from you are clear and unsullied reports. How did the boy die?"

"In the most devious manner possible . . ." he began, but altered his rhetorical flourish when he looked up and saw the Queen beginning to scowl again. "The woman O'Malley, not wanting her people to know that she had rid herself of a failing lover, organized for a nearby clan, the MacMahons of Donna Castle, evil cutthroats all, to murder the poor boy surreptitiously while he was chasing a stag. His body was returned to the woman O'Malley on a litter, and it's said that when she saw the youth's face, she retired laughing to her room, well satisfied with her part in the deed."

None of her maids dared to force the door. Neither did her castellan. Eventually, it was her elderly mother Margaret who stood outside the locked and bolted oaken door, knocking tentatively, saying, "This is your mother. Grace? Grace, are you inside? If you are, then come out now. For a week we've been preparing food and you've eaten none of it. Darling girl, come out and talk to me."

But there was no response.

On the day that Hugh de Lacy's body was brought back to Clair Castle, Grace O'Malley had been a model of restraint. Dressed in black, as she'd dressed when Donal had caused her to be a widow, she had left the castle and come down the hill to greet the burial party. His face was uncovered. It looked as though he was asleep, he was so peaceful.

She bit her lip, determined not to wail in front of her bond- and kinsmen.

But when she looked at his pallid face, it reminded her of the first time she'd seen him those two months earlier, washed up like a child's doll on the seashore, not far from where the MacMahons had come upon him hunting, while they were traveling on pilgrimage to Clair Island. The report she'd received was that they'd played games with him, sent him into the thick forests without weapons and hunted him down as though he was a stag.

And they'd killed him! Killed her lovely Hugh. Killed the gentlest and sweetest and most beautiful boy she'd ever known. A boy who had grown in stature as she'd taught him to be a man, who had learned and then taught her the pleasures of loving.

Killed! No, not just killed, but tortured. First an arrow to the leg, then when he was lying in pain on the ground, they'd stood around and fired arrows into his poor and defenseless body until one had pierced his lovely heart, and he'd died. Dead! Her Hugh! Dead!

She'd refused to bury him in the Clair Island cemetery, but had returned him to his rightful place in his parents' home of Wexford. She'd sent a letter to them, explaining the circumstances, and promising them terrible retribution on the MacMahons. And as she'd said farewell to his cold and joyless body, she'd retired to her room and hadn't been seen for seven days.

Not even the behest of her mother could drag her from her mourning chamber. They knew that she was alive, because from time to time one of the trays of food was lighter after than before; and the maids often heard her crying out in pain and grief. As to how or when she would come out, nobody knew. Nobody dared ask.

But events turned out surprisingly, for the day after her mother's plea, the castellan knocked loudly on her door and announced, "Ma'am, there is a party of pilgrims who have begged your permission to land and visit the monastery on top of the Isle of Caher. It's the MacMahons, ma'am. Shall I—"

"WHAT!" she screamed, making the hapless castellan jump back from the door. "The fuchking MacMahons are here?"

He heard footsteps running to the door, which was unbolted and flung open. Grace O'Malley stood there looking gaunt and untidy. Her hair was uncombed, her dress untended, her face thin and pale. But her eyes sparkled.

"The fuchking MacMahons dare to visit my lands!" she screamed at him.

"Madam, they're not on Clair, but want to visit the Isle of Caher. They don't know that Master Hugh was your friend. They wouldn't even connect him to you. Why, they'd—"

"Get me my sword and fifty fighting men. I shall be avenged for Hugh."

It took only half a day for the fifty men to be rounded up. But it gave Grace time to plan her revenge more carefully.

Having sent her permission during the afternoon for them to land on the nearby holy island, she watched them hitching their boats to the jetty on Caher Island, just spitting distance from her own Clair Island. Caher had been in her family's possession for two hundred years or more, and never had an O'Malley refused permission for any pilgrims to land and worship there.

Grace stood on the rampart and used her opticometer to watch the family MacMahon as they landed their boats, one after the other, and tethered them together by the wooden jetty which ran deep into the sea.

When the last rowing boat had landed and disgorged more of the evil monsters who had killed her Hugh, Grace signaled for her own ship to set sail for the island. In the rowboats the MacMahons had struggled against the tide, but it took her captain only a matter of minutes under sail to cover the distance from shore to the jetty. There he ordered the rowing boats to be removed and towed behind his ship away from the island.

Grace smiled with satisfaction. She had cut off the MacMahons' only route of escape, and they were now stranded on the uninhabited and desolate holy island.

Then she waited. And waited. And finally she saw the MacMahon clan, twenty or so of them, men and women, walking down the path which led from the deserted and ruined monastery down to the sea. She watched in satisfaction as they neared the shore and saw that there were no rowing boats tied up to the jetty. She imagined their surprise, and then the fear and concern on their faces as they realized that they'd been left without food or drink and would probably have to spend the night on the island in the open. And she took even greater pleasure in the fact that the women were no doubt blaming their men loudly for being so foolish in failing to tether the boats properly, and were now demanding their men to do something to prevent such a catastrophe as having to spend the night in the open.

But God knew, thought Grace, that they had no idea what a catastrophe lay before them.

It took her captain just a few moments to sail around the north point of the island and sight the MacMahons. The MacMahons began to wave their hands frantically and shout for assistance.

It took her captain just a few moments more to load, aim and fire the cannon. The balls sped through the air and landed north and west of where the family was standing in a group. At first they didn't move, too stunned at being fired upon by cannon. Then they shouted in their fear that they were Irishmen. But after another round of shot, some of them screamed and fell. Huge mounds of earth were dug up by the exploding balls, and suddenly the entire murdering MacMahon family was sprinting off in all directions like terrified rabbits.

Grace gave a grim laugh as she saw cannonballs fired again and more villainous MacMahons fall down in silent agony and not get up again.

And then she went down to the water's edge and into a rowboat so that she and her men could land on the island and hunt down the rest of the MacMahons like rabbit or deer, as they'd hunted down her poor Hugh.

Westminster Palace, January 1569

The Queen of England looked at the elderly Cecil and shook her head in fear and sorrow. Knowing what news he would bring did nothing to lessen its impact. Mary, troublesome, willful, silly, sluttish Mary of Scotland had been imprisoned. To imprison a queen was monstrous! A princess, perhaps. Elizabeth had been a princess imprisoned, and she remembered vividly how it had felt. Still to this day she shuddered whenever she thought of the damp walls and the dank stench of the Tower.

But to imprison a queen! It had all begun with the conference of York during which letters had been produced to prove that Mary was guilty of complicity in the murder of Lord Darnley. But although the Lords of Westminster were unhappy with the weight of the evidence, they had decided to remand her in custody and now Mary was imprisoned. Yes, to imprison a queen, even one implicated in the murder of her husband, and place her infant son onto the throne as king, and then to put such a man as Moray as regent to the child. Well, these were matters of the greatest possible urgency to Elizabeth.

And so she had sent Sir Nicholas Throckmorton to Scotland with a plan. While he was not allowed to visit Mary in prison at Loch Leven, he was to get messages to her. He was to inform her that her son James, Elizabeth's ward, must be brought to England to be raised as an English gentleman. Throckmorton also carried with him Elizabeth's most earnest plea that Mary denounce Bothwell, her husband, as a murderer, divorce him immediately, and then Elizabeth would work to restore Mary to the Scottish throne.

Yet when Throckmorton had arrived in Scotland, he'd found that the silly woman was pregnant to Bothwell, had managed to escape to her liberty and was out raising an army to overthrow the lords of Scotland, to remove her son from the throne, and to imprison and execute Lord Moray and many other Scottish lords for treason.

The situation was so complicated. Now that she was pregnant, if Mary divorced Bothwell, the child she bore would be a bastard. In a sudden rush of sympathy for her pathetic cousin's plight, Elizabeth had written and declared herself willing to go to war on Mary's behalf. She had only just been stopped from entering on this course by Cecil, who'd informed her that if she did attempt to send an army into Scotland, the lords would certainly behead Mary without thought to a trial. And worse, for all Europe would then say that Elizabeth had deliberately embarked upon this entire hazardous expedition for that very reason, being too terrified to execute Mary herself.

Sighing, Elizabeth read Cecil's report, gathered from his intelligence agents in the north of England.

"Where is she now?" she asked.

"Ma'am, Mary's army was soundly defeated at Langside. She has fled the border and crossed into England. She crossed the Solway River in a fishing boat. She escaped the ire of the lords with barely any luggage, and was forced to borrow clothes from local crofters. She was almost bereft of staff and household, and only managed to take with her some loyal followers.

"When he heard of her escape, Master Richard Lowther, the deputy to the Governor of Carlisle, set out with four hundred men to escort Mary to the governor's castle, and then sent word to ask what course of action he should now take."

"So she is finally in England," said Elizabeth.

Cecil nodded.

"And if I don't help her, she will appeal to the French."

"And worse, Majesty, for now that she is on our soil, all English Catholics will rally to her defense, and will in their hearts anoint her as their Catholic queen."

"But isn't it more likely that Mary will appeal to Spain to help her?"

"And if that is the case, ma'am, then the Scottish lords will appeal to the French, and together they will take arms against Mary's return. It is not a pretty picture, Majesty."

Elizabeth remained silent. Cecil was loath to interrupt her thoughts. He was surprised when she finally said, "And her clothes?"

"Her clothes?"

"Yes, my Lord Cecil. You said she arrived in borrowed clothes. Yet she is a queen, and for all her sins deserves a retinue and a household and a wardrobe. What of her clothes?"

Sir William looked through his sheets of intelligence, and finally found a line which enabled him to answer the Queen's question.

"She appears to have been given a length of black velvet by the Governor of the Castle of Carlisle, with which to make herself a gown, Majesty."

The Queen of England sat thoughtfully on her throne, surrounded by the enormous wealth of her court. She thought about how she would feel if she was suddenly usurped and forced into exile, of how she would react if overthrown. Who would come to her aid in such perilous circumstances? After a few moments, she said to Cecil, "Sir William, instruct my ladies of the wardrobe to send to the Queen of Scotland a trunk of my clothes for all occasions."

"All occasions, Majesty?"

"All occasions, Sir William!"

"Even that occasion when her head shall be removed from her body?"

Elizabeth looked at him in sudden fear.

"No, cousin. No! Never for that occasion."

CHAPTER FIFTEEN

The Western Coast of Spain, May 1569

She'd sensed the growing disquiet of her crew even before the English ship had disappeared out of sight over the horizon. She'd been hard on the men this past year, demanding more of them than ever before. They'd sailed further, through more isolated waters, taking on board heavier cargoes and chasing fat merchant ships even when their own holds were full to bursting. But what happened yesterday was different. It was a matter of right and wrong.

During the year since Hugh's murder and her revenge on the MacMahons, Grace had thought much about life and death. She was almost forty, and by rights she should be resting in front of a fire at home. Yet her short time with dear Hugh had reawakened her body to its full flower of womanhood and her mind to the joys of inquiry and knowledge. Since he'd been so cruelly taken from her, she'd spent night after night reflecting on what life held in store, compared to what she had the right to expect.

She was still angry with Almighty God and the entirety of mankind for killing such a sweet and gentle youth. In her anger, she'd put herself through torments which would crush most men, yet she smiled at the end of each day and waited eagerly for the next day so that she could test her body and her mind even further.

She'd arranged her estates in Ireland so that they could be run by her castellans and seneschals, and although she checked their accounts in the most minute detail, she was pleased that things seemed to be running smoothly, smoothly enough for her to spend most of her life at sea. Her two sons, young though they were, were captaining ships of her line; and Margaret, dear Margaret, was with her often, sailing and enjoying the feeling of wind and sea spray in her hair. She didn't see her sons as often as she'd like, for they were busy captaining their own vessels and making a reputation for themselves. Thank God they'd turned out to be O'Malleys, and not like their father. They were gentle lads, yet firm in resolve when commanding their crews, and by all accounts were liked and respected by their men.

Things were not going so well for Grace at the moment, for yesterday an English merchantman, full of wind and not an oar to its name, had lowered its sail as it approached her and asked for a midsea parley. The lowering of sail was a clear indication from her captain that he carried no cargo and was offering to open his ship's holds to the Pirate Queen in order to avoid a confrontation.

At first Grace had been tempted to blow the English bastard out of the water to show the Queen of England precisely what Grace O'Malley, the Queen of the Seas, thought of her. But when the Englishman had lowered his sail and offered to be boarded without a fight, sense had calmed her anger and she'd ordered her galley to be rowed over to the becalmed merchantman.

The captain of the merchant ship stood on the poop deck and doffed his cap. "It's an honor to tie up next to you, ma'am," he shouted across the narrowing gap. "I assume from your flag that you're the famous Grace O'Malley of Ireland."

"And to what do I owe this peculiar honor, Captain?" she shouted back. "Are you in trouble? If you're devoid of cargo and riding high on the waves, why are you of interest to me?"

The captain didn't answer, but waited until the two ships had tied up together, the waves funnelling in the narrow gap between the hulls. Grace ordered her men not to board the merchantman, fearing that it might be a trap. She knew that the English Queen had ordered her navy to blast unauthorized pirate ships out of the water, and for the past year, Grace had been in the habit of shooting first and determining the consequences afterward. She'd also heard that the English had given orders that she was to be arrested if ever she ventured onto English soil, so Grace was particularly careful about approaching unless her guns were firing.

Sometimes merchant ships were genuine, carrying minimum firepower and trading under the protection of navies. At other times the merchantmen were also pirates which the English Queen would allow to sail under her flag, and acted as pirate privateers when there was a fat Spanish or French or Dutch prize to be taken. Of course Elizabeth feigned no knowledge of the assaults, but secretly shared in a tenth of the profits.

So Grace had no reason to trust an English merchantman asking for a parley in the middle of the Spanish Atlantic.

Warily she called across, "So, Captain? What is it that you need?"

"So, madam," he replied. He turned to his first mate and whispered an instruction. The mate disappeared down into the bowels of the ship. Grace also turned, not to her first mate but to her gunnery officer. "Arms ready!"

He nodded to his men, who picked up their muskets and aimed it at the crew of the merchantman standing on deck. The captain said, "Easy, men!" to warn his crew against panicking.

Then she heard the sound of chains rattling. It came from the hold. Grace saw the first mate appear at the top of the galley, a grin all over his face. Climbing out of the ship's bowels behind him was a blackbird, coal-black eyes squinting in the harsh sun. The man lifted his hand to shield his eyes, and Grace saw that he was manacled. Following this man was another blackbird, who also squinted and tried to hide from the glare of the sun. And then another walked tentatively up the galley steps, and another, until fifty black men and women, all naked or wearing torn rags, were up on deck, all having arrived without any words of protest, all without the means or the strength to fight, and all looked upon by the captain and the crew of the merchantman with contempt.

Grace was joined on deck by Margaret. The girl looked at the slaves and gasped, "Oh dear God!"

Grace called over to the other ship, "What is this, Captain? You lowered your sail, inviting us to come on board peacefully. It seemed to me that you had no cargo. Yet you're carrying a fortune in slaves. Why show them to me now?"

"Because, ma'am, thanks to Captain John Hawkins, the most dangerous thing to do in these Spanish waters is to carry slaves. We found out the dangers only after they'd boarded my boat in Black Africa. We were setting sail for Hispaniola, when we were told by another Englishman that to travel there would incur the vicious wrath of the Spaniards. So we decided to set sail to England, with the intention of trading the cargo on the docks of London, so that someone with more guns and powder could transport these black heathen to the New World. Unfortunately, a gale three days back has blown us hundreds of miles off course, and if my calculations are right, we now find that we're deep in Spanish waters. If a Spaniard naval ship comes upon us, as is likely, then without proper guns or the speed to outrun him, our ship will be impounded as a slaver, and we'll be arrested and imprisoned. As you have a hundred oarsmen as well as sail, and as you're loaded up to the gunnels with cannon and shot, we were wondering . . ."

"You were wondering if I'd buy the cargo from you, and take the risk of running slaves to the Indies?"

"Correct, ma'am," said the captain, doffing his hat.

"Sorry, Captain, but I don't deal in human cargo. They cost too much to feed, and they cause problems—"

"But," interrupted the captain, "you don't hardly need to feed the bastards. A couple of square meals between here and the Indies, and they'll be happy. And some of the men will fetch a good price . . . a very good price. The women are much in demand as servants, and to satisfy the wants of white men, and—"

Margaret began to protest, but a look from Grace told her to be quiet.

"I said I don't deal in human cargo," Grace told him firmly.

She could feel her men murmur in the background. A cargo of slaves could set them up for months, even years. It was worth a fortune, and they didn't have to spend time on a festering, plague-ridden shore rounding them up and paying off the tribal elders. The blackbirds were here, ready for the taking, chained and manacled. This was straight profit. It was a simple job of transferring them to their ship, altering course for the New World and offloading them on one of the Caribbean islands.

"Ma'am, these aren't humans. They're Negroids, savages, just cargo; no less valuable as commodities than gold or jewels or carpets or grain."

Again, she heard the men mutter.

"We'll have none of them on my ship, sir," she called across, both for his benefit and for that of her own men. "I can't abide slavery in any of its forms, Captain, and I will have no commerce with it."

"But the Queen of England herself invests in slavers. She financed John Hawkins's last voyage, and—"

"Fuchk the Queen of England! It's John Hawkins himself that's caused all these problems we're having with the Spanish and the Portuguese; Captain Hawkins who has made trading along these shores so dangerous."

"Ma'am," the captain shouted back in astonishment, "where's your sense of duty? Captain John Hawkins is as fine an Englishman as ever breathed. You treat me like an enemy, while the enemy is Spain!"

"Oh you think so, do you? So Spain is Ireland's enemy, is it? Well listen to me carefully, Captain. The Irish are currently being enslaved to the English in our own land. We'll soon be servants to Elizabeth, every man jack of us. I object to that, just as I object to tethering a man, woman or child by manacles and indenturing them to a life of utter misery. These people—"

The merchant captain burst out laughing. "People? Oh, for the sake of sweet Jesus Christ, ma'am, these aren't people, they're no more than animals. Savages. They're black as coal, they're Negroids. Their own people sell them to us. They're born to a life of slavery, as the Good Lord determined at the time of the creation of Adam and Eve. Have you seen the way these creatures live, ma'am? They live in mud huts and burrow in the ground for their food like animals. They stink and have no manners. They're not—"

But he could see by the look of anger on her face that this was getting him nowhere. In frustration, he changed tack. "How much do you think you'll get for a cargo of Negroid slaves when you offload them on some dock in the New World? A fortune! A veritable fortune, that's how much."

Again the murmuring from her crew. This man was dangerous, for he was saying things which could make her crew mutiny against her, especially as they felt she had been working them so hard they were fit to drop.

"Now listen to me, Captain, and listen well," Grace said, raising her voice. "I'm an Irish woman, born free and unindentured. I am beholden to nobody but my own people. But little by little, Ireland is being sold out into the slavery of the English.

"How long do you think it'll be before the garrisons of English soldiers are so strong that all Irishmen will be enslaved to England's will? Now tell me, Captain, how will the Irish enjoy the prospect of being manacled and tethered and made to work till they drop at the behest of some English lord who owns the land that the good God gave us?"

"I keep my nose out of the matters of politics, ma'am. I know nothing of such things. I'm merely a humble seafarer, sailing the waves, trying to make an honest living."

"Honest? Taking slaves and clapping them in irons, and making them suffer in the stinking hold while you transport them from their homes to some plantation somewhere to be worked to death?"

The merchant captain remained silent.

"How many have died since you left Africa, Captain?"

He continued to remain silent.

"Ten, twenty maybe?" she said contemptuously. "No thank you, Captain. I'll have none of your blood money. My cargoes don't die on me. Not even the animals I carry, unless I slaughter them to feed my crew. Good day to you, Captain. May your cargo arrive in good condition."

She ordered the two ships to be untethered.

In desperation, the captain called out, "Their deaths will be on your head, Grace O'Malley."

She stopped short, and asked, "What do you mean by that?"

He smiled like a cornered rat. "It's simple. If we spy a ship flying Spanish colors on the horizon, you don't think I'll be caught with fifty slaves on board, do you? I'll have them over the side and drowned in a thousand fathoms before any Spaniard claps me in iron. And as they go down to their watery graves, the last thing they'll be saying is, 'Why didn't that white-skinned lady save us while she could?'"

Margaret, standing beside her mother, called out, "How dare you shift your crimes onto the head of my mother."

Grace shook her head. "Pray then, Captain, that you don't encounter any other ships, Spanish or otherwise. Good day to you."

She ordered her crew to push the ship away with landing poles until the starboard side oars could be dipped into the water and put distance between them.

"I'm proud of you, Mother," said Margaret. "Any other sea captain would have taken the cargo."

She looked at Margaret and gave her a wry smile. "Darling girl, if you'd known as many races as I've known, you'd soon realize that a man's skin color has nothing to do with his nature or character. Those poor bastards will surely perish, either as slaves on a plantation or by drowning, but at least you and I'll have no part in their demise."

That had been yesterday. And today there were still rumblings from her men.

She'd spent a restless night, thinking about Margaret. Looking every day at her lovely dusky-skinned daughter made Grace think about the glorious sea captain who was Margaret's father, who had called himself the Man of Men, and my God, but hadn't he proven that to her. When she thought of Osman, she became even more furious with the slave trade, because under different circumstances, her lover could have been shackled and treated as though he was an animal.

She knew that slavery was a growing source of commerce, and that she could make a fortune out of the risks it required, but she was determined to have none of it. She'd heard stories of slavers failing to outrun Spanish galleons and being sunk, then allowing their black slave cargo to drown in the holds while the white crew took to the boats and threw themselves on the mercy of the

Spaniards. It was outright murder. Was there no morality in the world? Was there no value placed on the lives of men, women and children?

She rose from her bunk, wondering whether an irate party of mutineers awaited her on deck. What she found was a crew split; some concerned with the idea of their own slavery, as raised by Grace yesterday; some stewing over the loss of the valuable cargo.

The first to speak was Iain O'Brien. "You let a fortune go sailing away yesterday, ma'am. We could have made good money from trading the niggers."

"Oh could we?" Grace said. "And have you any idea, Mr. O'Brien, of the current state of play on the high seas? Do you know what the Spanish do to a ship caught with slaves?"

"We have guns, ma'am. We could take care of ourselves."

"And how many of you are prepared to die unnecessarily? Why risk a fight with the Spanish when they leave us alone while we're trading grain and carpets and spices?"

She looked at her crew, and it dawned on her that they had no knowledge of why the Spanish were becoming so vicious to French and English ships in open waters.

"Gentlemen, we're in danger of being caught up in a war which isn't ours to fight. We're traders in foreign lands, and pirates when we come across a fat and slow merchantman. But we have no quarrel with the Spaniards or the Portuguese. It's the English who have the quarrel, and let the Spanish blow the fuchking English out of the water as far as I'm concerned. This trading war was started by a gentleman of the name Hawkins, as fine an Englishman as you'll find . . . if you'll ever find a good Englishman. Now, Mr. Hawkins decided to thumb the Queen of England's nose at the Portuguese and the Spaniards by trespassing onto areas of trade which they considered their own by God's good grace. The Portuguese were making a fortune out of trading African slaves into the Caribbean, and the Spaniards considered the New World as their God-given right. Well, Madam Elizabeth, seated in velvet comfort on her throne in London, thought to herself, I know, I'll pull the King of Spain's whiskers. I'll become a slave trader.

"And that, gentlemen, is precisely what she did. Captain Hawkins had made a lot of money beating the Portuguese at their own game, and the Queen of England was so avaricious that she decided to invest in his next trip to try to make some money for herself. She financed Hawkins into his next ship, the *Jesus of Lubeck*, and he made her fuchking fortune. But just last year, at San Juan de Ulua in Mexico, he and his ships were attacked by the Spaniards and he was soundly beaten, and now the Spaniards are keen to prevent any other pirate bastard from stealing their trade.

"Which is why, gentlemen, I rejected the merchantman's offer yesterday. If we're intercepted by a Spaniard naval vessel, or one out of Lisbon, then God help us."

The men nodded and began to talk among themselves. Caution had always been the captain's watchword, which is why they'd been pirating for so long and with such success.

Just then Grace noticed that Margaret had appeared on deck, and said in a voice loud with self-righteousness so there would be no misunderstandings, "And anyway, it's wrong for us to trade in slaves. It's a life of misery for the poor bastards. I'll have none of it. Yes, we could have earned a lot of money, but we can still do so by other means, and I'll not be accused of being a slaver. If any of you want to run the risk, I'll put you off at a Spanish port and you can join the King of Spain's crew."

The men shuffled their feet.

Then Connor MacFaile, the first mate, asked, "And are we to become slaves to the English, Captain?"

"You mean like those poor niggers yonder," she said, nodding toward the distant horizon. "We may, Connor. We may indeed. Once the English are in control of the whole of Ireland, what's to stop them putting Irishmen in manacles and chaining them to their place of work? What's to prevent them taking your women and making them into indentured servants working all hours of God's day for nothing? And what's to prevent them from gathering up your children playing innocently in the fields, and forcing them into lives lived in cellars or pantries, fetching and carrying?"

The men began to shout and protest, but Grace raised her hand to silence them. "What? You didn't know all this? What do you think the MacWilliam and the O'Malley and the O'Flaherty and the other leaders of the west coast have been doing these last dozens of years, if not trying to protect all Ireland from the English? We've been resisting the onslaught of the English ever since it began. But we're fighting with a hand tied behind our backs. We're so much involved in quarrelling and squabbling and petty jealousies that we've almost forgotten that the enemy isn't our neighbor, but the Queen, over the seas, her fat cunny on a throne.

"Seeing those poor niggers manacled in the grip of that smug and self-satisfied English bastard, I've come to the conclusion that I can no longer shirk my responsibility to prevent Ireland from being taken over by the Queen. I have a mind and a body just as able to run the country as does any of those woody-headed shite-arses, the noble lords of Ireland.

"But it's your help I'll need if I'm to have any hope of knocking any sense into the wooden heads at home and making them see what's happening before it's too late."

The Tower of London, June

Seated in the banqueting hall, surrounded by the comfort of her many councillors and admirers, Elizabeth still felt a profound sense of ill ease. She hated the Tower. It reminded her of those occasions she had been imprisoned there, fearful for her life.

Elizabeth looked around the banqueting room and realized that all eyes were upon her. There wasn't a moment in her day when she could retire from the public gaze, even for the blinking of an eye. When she was asleep, the ladies of the bedchamber slept in her bedroom so that she could be attended at every moment. When she awoke, ladies-in-waiting brought her warmed and perfumed flannels to wash her eyes, and a drink of honey and essence of almonds in warm milk before she arose from her bed.

Her pisspot was given to her by another lady, and she sat upon it while her maids talked to her of the events of the day. Then that good lady would carry the filled vessel out of the bedchamber to a guard for disposal. Another lady, whom Elizabeth had facetiously dubbed "My lady of the teeth," brought her a sea sponge soaked in salt water, or in sulfur oil, which the Queen used to rub her teeth. Still another brought her hose made for her by Master Henry Herne, which she slipped on over her legs, then she put on her silk stockings, her satin shift, her dress, her bodices, buskins if she was going out riding that morning, or pantofles if she was merely walking around the palace, and each and every action watched by the ladies in her chamber.

Her lack of privacy didn't stop there, for the moment she stepped out of her privy chamber, she was surrounded by cousins and councillors and eagers who were desperate to catch her ear.

Even at this tiresome banquet, created by the Lord Governor of the Tower to celebrate the five-hundredth anniversary of the laying of the first foundation stone by William the Conqueror, who had begun building the palace on the same location as the Roman Emperor Claudius had built his fortress at the head of the river, was a battlefield of wits gathered against her.

Eyes were everywhere watching her every move. Spanish eyes to report on England's weaknesses to an eager king who wanted to establish his own rule as her husband or that of Scottish Mary; the eyes of the French, who sought an alliance to secure them against the might of Spain; the eyes of the Dutch, who wanted an alliance to ensure the continuation of Protestantism and a defense against the King of Spain who wanted the whole world to be Catholic; the eyes of the English, who sought her approval and favor to ensure their own fortune. Eyes everywhere, and all looking at her.

Yet all was not lost in the evening, for the food, prepared by her own cooks from Whitehall, was delicious. For her first course, she had eaten tiny pastries filled with cods' livers; for her second, hulled wheat boiled in milk with sugar to sweeten it; for her third course, a concoction of venison, lamprey and bream, all served in individual pastries created as her royal tudor coat of arms, which had caused her to laugh and clap as they were brought to table. There were six further courses, but by the end of her third she was already replete and merely drank some mulled wine and ate morsels of blancmange, jellies and wafers.

She loved and hated these banquets. If the truth was told, she preferred to retire to her private outer apartments and talk to one of her young bucks who had permission to enter the Queen's privy area. But Elizabeth had to be the epitome of correctness and rectitude. Not a word, not a hint of scandal could stain her, for her reputation had only a few years ago begun to recover from the disgrace surrounding the death of poor Amy Robsart, Robert's wife.

Scandal. It took only a few evil moments for a pure woman to be accused of scandal, yet it took years for that same pure woman to be released from the stain of guilt.

Her attention was distracted by the appearance of a messenger at the door. He bowed to the nobles in the room, and walked across to Sir William Cecil. The man whispered in Cecil's ear, and then retreated, bowing deferentially as he walked backward.

Cecil appeared to be in a state of consternation as he stood and walked over to Elizabeth. He bent down and said quietly, "Majesty, when you've finished dining, I will ride back with you on the river to Whitehall, if I may. We have a state of trouble in that most troublesome of states."

She turned to him. "Ireland?"

He nodded, though seemed reluctant to discuss it with so many pricked ears.

"What's happened in Ireland? What's happened in that dark and damnable land? Rebellion? Again?"

The councillor shook his head.

"It is a rebellion, isn't it, William? I thought we had finished with rebellions when that traitor, Shane O'Neill, met his death."

"No, Majesty, not rebellion exactly, although there is new talk of trouble from the Fitzgeralds of Desmond, but I have your new governor in Dublin, Sir Edward Fitton, ensuring that they cause your Crown no danger."

"Then what is it? Come now, sweet cousin William, tell me all."

"The Lords of Mayo and Munster and Connaught have banded together and are led by that woman O'Malley. She has declined to accept your nomination of Sir Edward as the governor of the province. The woman has threatened to slaughter every English soldier and nobleman in all of Ireland unless your governor is removed."

"She has declined to accept my governor!" the Queen shouted furiously, pushing her chair back on the plinth, banging her hands on the table. All voices in the room were immediately stilled. "She has declined! She declines what the Queen of England commands!"

"Perhaps, Majesty," whispered Cecil, "if we could discuss these matters on the river transport, rather than before the ambassadors."

Elizabeth turned for a moment and saw that the banqueters were listening carefully, some of them likely taking note so they could report everything to whomever it was that was paying them for information. Loudly, she said, "My lords and cousins, I have soldiers in Ireland to support my governor. He will ensure that these rulers of the Irish bogs, these people who walk the earth in sackcloth and linen, will obey the dictates of their English queen.

"Well now, cousin William," Elizabeth added, her voice of authority designed to be heard by the crowned heads of Europe, "I think it's time that this Queen of England taught this queen of Irish pirates what it means to be a fit and proper queen by divine right!"

The Border of Mayo and Galway, September

In the few months since she'd landed, Grace had visited those chieftains she knew well, especially Mayo and Munster and Connaught, and convinced them that a stand had to be made against the encroachment of the English and the fancy new governor they had had foisted upon them. Some of the chiefs she knew well and had anticipated their immediate acceptance; others she'd never met but had heard much about, and had been pleased that they were readily inclined to do as she suggested.

When the newly appointed governor of Ireland and a party of two hundred English archers and musketeers were on an expedition to punish a group of villagers from the lands of the O'Kelly to the northeast of Galway for refusing to pay taxes for using a road, Grace had the excuse she needed to teach the English a lesson. The message would soon be conveyed to Elizabeth that the Irish weren't merely there for the taking, but would cause the English a bloodied nose while ever they sniffed Irish air.

The battle began in the early morning, and the stench was still in the air well into the afternoon. The ground was a sodden bog of blood and guts and stinking water.

The troops of Governor Fitton had suffered greater losses than they had anticipated when they had entered the fray, all swagger and wind and piss, wearing their uniforms of burnished armor and laces and broad hats with huge plumes. They'd thought that, allied with the troops of the Earl of Clanrickard, they would quickly overpower the rough and ready clansmen of the MacWilliam of Mayo, the O'Flaherty, the O'Malley and the landsmen of Richard Bourke, the chieftain of the sept of Ulick of Burrishowle.

But what had begun shortly after sunrise as Sir Edward Fitton had put it, "a gentle perambulation through the Irish countryside to put down some crazed dogs" had turned into a series of routs. During the first hour of the battle, the Irish had swept over hills with bloody cries and turned the opposing army's blood cold, making them turn and run. If it hadn't been for threats and strong command, they'd have spread themselves all the way to Dublin.

The next hour, regrouped and threatened with execution if they turned their backs on the enemy, the English and their Irish turncoat allies had rallied and were pushing back the rebels hard and murderously, causing the men of Richard Bourke and Grace O'Malley to leave their defensive positions and enter the fray in support.

Subsequent hours had seen cannon in action, some English horse cavalry used effectively, and the Irish under Richard Bourke forced to mount an urgent pincer movement on the advancing English to prevent their back defensive lines being split in two.

Richard Bourke was just deciding that his pincer tactic had worked, when he looked up to see bearing down on him a warhorse spurred on by some young English buck trying to make a name and fortune for himself. He'd ridden through two lines of Irish musket-men, somehow avoiding injury, with the intention of skewering Richard with his lance. There was nothing between him high on his war charger and Richard Bourke's death.

Grace saw the young English cavalryman riding directly for Richard. She knew that she had no chance of downing him with her pistol, which might hurt him through his armor but wouldn't prevent the headlong thrust of his horse; so she aimed at the horse's head and shot the beast through the eye, sending the animal's skull and brains exploding all over the cavalryman.

The horse collapsed beneath the rider, pitching him forward and over the top, and he lay sprawled in the mud, moaning in agony.

When he saw his assassin on the ground, Richard Bourke realized he had two options. Irish war custom gave him the right to kill the man, but there was also another custom, a gentleman's custom, which gave that right to the person who had saved his life.

He smiled at Grace, doffed his cap, and shouted over the noise, "Yours, I believe, ma'am."

Impressed by his gallantry, Grace bowed and took another pistol from her belt. She walked over to the Englishman, lifted the visor from his face and saw that he was little more than a boy, probably the second or third son of an English nobleman intent on making his fortune out of Irish sweat.

The boy, eyes dulled from the fall, sweat matting his hair, looked up and saw that the Irish warrior who'd brought him down was a woman. His lips curled in disgust.

For a fleeting moment Grace had thought she might save the life of the boy and imprison him for ransom—even the second or third son of a lord was worth something—but when she saw his English arrogance, his snide supercilious contempt for someone who wasn't from the Scepter'd Isle, and a woman at that, she shot him dead.

She straightened up and noticed that Richard Bourke was now standing beside her.

"So," he said, closing the knight's visor with his foot to give the man privacy in death, "I owe you my life, Mistress O'Malley."

She shrugged. "He's English. He would probably have stumbled before he reached you. I merely assisted him in his fall."

"Is everything they say about you true, ma'am? That you're stronger than two men and lustier than a bawd?"

She burst out laughing. "Mr. Bourke, if you try to find out about the second, then I'll quickly enough show you whether the first is true!"

"Then the rumors aren't true?"

"God's teeth, Mr. Bourke, we have a battle to fight. The English are not yet won, and you're asking me questions about my chastity."

"Only because our paths have crossed many times these past ten years, but we've never truly met. Not until your late and much unlamented husband lay rotting in his grave. When you first became a widow, I thought I'd ride across and present my compliments, but you took to the seas and I missed yet another opportunity to see the legendary Grace O'Malley."

"Legendary?"

"Oh yes! There are enough rumors about yourself to fill another Book of Kells. They say you're—"

But before he could finish, a rousing cheer erupted from the battlefield. Grace and Richard tried to see what was happening, and realized that their Irishmen had turned and were running back toward the defensive lines.

"Shite!" shouted Grace. "Don't those bog-living bastards know how to fight?"

Eventually their men rallied, but as the day wore on, and both sides became increasingly tired and despondent, the certainty of victory was replaced by the reality of protraction. Ammunition was running short, cannon were lying smoking and spent, muskets and pistols were abandoned for want of powder and shot; wounds were in urgent need of attention, and the dead needed carrying from the field.

The men of the Clanrickard, fighting with the English, had been assured by their leader that this battle would last only an hour or so and then they could retire back to their farms with purses of victor's gold. They realized now the foolishness of this promise and began to drift away, back to their homes. Sir Edward Fitton shouted and threatened, but they ignored him and he was left with half the available men.

But the Irish fighters also began leaving the battlefield, and eventually the leaders themselves simply turned and walked away from the bloodied earth, the sulfurous tussocks of grass, the polluted rivers, and the day ended neither in victory nor defeat.

Grace was the last to leave the battlefield. She surveyed the dead and wounded and gave instructions that her dead men were to be placed on litters and carried up to the supply wagons waiting on the distant road. When this was done and the wounded had been given triage to enable them to return to their homes, she walked with two hundred and fifty of her men to the high road, which would eventually lead them back to Connaught. It would be two days before she saw her home again. But she was lucky, for she'd only lost twenty-two of her tenants in the battle, far fewer than other clan leaders.

But as she walked at the head of the column, her mind wasn't on the dead, nor on the implications of the outcome of the fight, but was on the tall and engaging figure of Richard Bourke. He was indeed a handsome man. Gallant, appealing, rich and, most especially, the owner of lands which had access to a hundred or more sheltered harbors.

Yes, she thought. I'll pay my respects to Master Richard Bourke and see how the land lies.

CHAPTER SIXTEEN

Castle Rockfleet, Clew Bay, Mayo, 1569

It was a very fine castle indeed, a square tower keep of four levels which was as solidly impregnable as it was impressive to look at. From a distance it looked to be at least seventy-five feet high, and the entryway was protected by a barbican. When she glanced upward at the top of the tower castle, Grace could see a walkway and ramparts. It had been cleverly constructed, for any attacking force would be punished by rocks and boiling oil plummeting vertically from the heights.

On closer examination, Grace noticed an unusual structure on the side of the castle, a sort of pipe or stone tube which led from one of the windows down to the sea. She smiled when she realized that it was a connection from the privy to the sea. What modern wonders, she thought. This master knew how to live well in his domain.

The castle stood on a rise from the water's edge, a promontory which gave it a commanding view of the entire expanse of Clew Bay, yet which, because of the peculiar lie of the land, made it difficult to spy from the sea. As Grace stood at its portico, she wondered whether she was mad or whether this was the sanest move of her life.

She tethered her horse to the hitching post, picked up the wooden hammer and rapped it solidly three times against the iron-banded oaken door. Then she stepped back so that she could be seen clearly from the ramparts.

Moments later, a young man's head appeared at the top of the castle wall.

"Yes?" the lad shouted.

"Yes, madam!" she shouted back.

"Yes? What is your business?"

"None of yours, boy! I wish to see your master, Richard Bourke."

"My master doesn't see strangers who arrive without warning."

"Tell him Mistress O'Malley is here."

The boy's attitude changed immediately. Without further word, he withdrew, and Grace could hear shouting within the castle walls and feet running on wooden and stone steps. She smiled to herself. Maybe Richard Bourke was right. Maybe she was legendary, though she'd spent so long at sea, she wouldn't know what stories were told about her.

Shortly, she heard the bolts being withdrawn from the door and the large wooden crossbeam being removed. Then the door swung open, and an older man, gray-haired, efficient and full of self-importance, stepped from the castle threshold and walked forward to greet her. He was followed by two younger men.

"Mistress Grace O'Malley, it's an honor to greet you. I knew your father Dubhdara, whom we called Black Oak. A fine man. A true Irishman and a patriot, unlike some Irish lords I could mention."

"Indeed," Grace said.

The castellan turned to one of the guards and said, "Untether Mistress O'Malley's horse, and bring it inside. Ma'am, will you honor me by entering my master's castle." He led the way. "The master has only just returned from a great battle, a victory which will be sung about by balladeers for all of history, in which he single-handedly beat the English and their overwhelming forces."

Grace fought back a smile. "Yes, I was there myself, though being only a woman, I sat on the hilltop and watched your gallant master fight a hundred men on his own."

The castellan nodded and said, "I believe that God Almighty Himself was looking down on the master. He might be called Iron Dick, but sure his iron armor alone can't protect him, he must have help from God Himself."

They walked up a flight of stone steps until they reached the first landing, which was devoted to the kitchens, food storage, cold rooms, bedchambers and places where the guests and retainers slept. On the next landing were corridors which, Grace assumed, led to where the master and his family slept. It was a cold place with few wall hangings to keep away the draft and break up the bleakness of the stone walls. A woman's touch is needed, Grace mused as she followed the castellan up the last flight of stone stairs.

Here the castle opened, not to a series of corridors or rooms, but to a huge open area with a roaring log and peat fire at the end, and a massive banqueting table in the center. Two wolfhounds, which had been lying by the fire, stood the moment the castellan's head appeared at the top of the steps, and bounded down the room toward him, barking in their low, guttural howls.

Grace saw that the hounds were huge but still young, and they greeted the castellan like babes. He fussed over them, scratched their heads, necks and backs, and told them to get out of the way. They both looked at Grace, sniffed her, and loped back to the warmth of the fire.

She surveyed the room and saw that it, like the rest of the castle, required the sensitivity of a woman. The rushes on the floor hadn't been changed in a week; the room stank of vomit and stale ale, as well as rotting food scraps; and it was obvious that nobody had emptied the pisspots, either that or some drunken visitor had pissed into a corner somewhere.

She followed the castellan across the floor, and as she walked, eddies of dust and the debris from the straw rushes rose in the air. She shook her head in disgust.

And then she saw Master Richard Iron Dick Bourke. He was sitting in a chair whose arms were the horns of stags. On his lap were parchments and scrolls. Grace wondered why he hadn't stood, but as she neared, she realized that he was fast asleep before the roaring fire.

The castellan coughed respectfully, and Richard Bourke shuffled in the chair. He turned, and when he lazily opened his eyes, he saw Grace O'Malley standing close to him.

In surprise he stood, the papers and scrolls cascading onto the matting before the fire. "Good God! Mistress O'Malley! What in God's name are you doing at Rockfleet?"

"I've come to pay homage to the hero of the Battle of Mayo, the man who fought off a hundred Englishmen single-handed."

"Ah . . ."

"And I've come because we're neighbors. I know that your stepbrother, William Fada Bourke, was murdered by my late husband, and I had assumed that there was bad blood between us; but since the battle, where I watched in awe as you so bravely led the troops and killed a hundred—or was it a thousand—Englishmen single-handed, well, Master Bourke, I realized I had to come as a humble woman to pay regard to so noble a leader."

Richard cringed under her sarcasm. He looked at his castellan and then back at Grace. "You mustn't believe half the stories that go around, ma'am. Liam, go get the Mistress O'Flaherty some ale, or would you prefer wine?"

When the castellan had retreated to bring refreshments, they seated themselves before the fire, and Richard, in some discomfort, said, "Ma'am, the story of my bravery in the battle, words to impress my people, I'm afraid."

"Why exaggerate when you were brave enough for any balladeer to sing of your exploits? I watched you on the battlefield, Richard, and you were brave enough to impress me."

"I thank you, but you didn't come here to sit at my feet and listen to my tales of the battle. What's the real reason you're visiting here, ma'am? Be straight with me, for I don't deal in pretty words nor double-dealing."

She smiled to cover her own discomfort. How could she come straight out and tell him? It was so preposterous.

"I'm here to make a bargain with you, Richard. You're a widower and I'm a widow. We're neighbors."

She swallowed. He was looking at her quizzically, wondering what this was about.

"I want us to be married, Richard," she blurted, "husband and wife. As I said, I noticed you on the field of battle, and notwithstanding the stories you spun like golden threads to your menservants here, you were brave and manly and I was truly impressed by you. I'm not an unhandsome woman myself. I have good bones, good teeth, a strong skin from a lifetime of sailing; I've borne three children and my womb hasn't dried up should you want another. I'm as comfortable in the kitchen as I am in the bed, and neither my husband, nor a Turk, nor a young Irishman whom I bedded not a year back, had any cause for complaint about my womanly skills. In lovemaking I use my hands and my mouth as well as my female parts. I'm not a bawd, but I am certainly lusty and enjoy fuchking as much as any man, drunk or sober.

"My breath doesn't smell, and when I'm of a mood, I use oriental perfumed spices on my body which pleases both me and those around me. I speak Latin and Greek and French and Spanish. I know the mathematics of the Arabs and so I can always tell when I've been robbed by a castellan who double-deals. I have almost two dozen ships at anchor and am known throughout Ireland, Scotland and the nations of the south as a hard but honest trader."

She paused to allow Richard to respond, but he looked as though he'd just been hit in his privates by cannon shot, and so she continued speaking.

"The advantages of our marriage are manifest. I will gain from you the protection I need from the northern side of Clew Bay; you will gain my protection from the south. I will bring you a dowry of a thousand head of cattle and horses, though if we divorce, I shall demand their return. But we can be far stronger together than separately, and with the English advancing so rapidly throughout Ireland, this is more urgent now than ever. Together we can field three thousand men, which makes us mightier than most of the lords of Ireland." She paused. "Well, what do you think?"

He continued to look at her. She was beginning to feel she had made a fool of herself.

"Well?" she demanded.

"Well?" he asked, his voice dry and soft.

"Are you willing to marry me?"

"Yes," he said.

She breathed a sigh of relief. "Good. But it's a trial. Under Brehon Laws, we each have the right to nullify the marriage without penalty after a year if either of us is dissatisfied. Do you agree?"

"Yes," he said again, though this time his voice was less audible.

She felt relaxed for the first time since the idea had imposed itself on her mind. It was a good union, a sound marriage. And if it did nothing else, it would keep her warm on winter nights.

Richard was attempting to formulate a thought. "Mistress O'Malley . . . Grace . . . I . . . Could you just repeat again what this Black Turk and the young Irishman said about you, the part when you and they were, I mean, I don't wish to . . . What I'm trying to say, without wishing to sound too indelicate, is that I'd like to hear more of that part concerning your ability in the bedroom."

It took a week for the arrangements to be made, the experts in Brehon Laws to travel from Galway to ensure that the interests of both families were maintained, the contracts to be signed and exchanged, the priests to be marshalled in order to ensure that the service accorded strictly to Catholic rite, and for the relations on both sides to be informed and invited.

The ceremony was held in the church on Rockfleet Castle's estate, and it took a mere quarter of an hour for them to enter the church as widow and widower and leave as married couple.

As soon as the priest had uttered the final words, Richard shouted out, "Right, now let's to the feast, and then the new Mistress Bourke and I are off to bed."

The feast consisted of twenty courses, but by the time the fifth course, a huge peat-smoked Irish salmon weighing as much as a small pig, was being served, nobody noticed that Grace and Richard had slipped away to their bedchamber.

Grace had spent the days before their wedding hanging carpets and tapestries on the walls, changing the rushes on the floor, cleaning out the soil trays and filling bowls with fresh herb waters to infuse the room with some freshness, and having the rugs and bolsters from the bed beaten to clear out years of dust which had accumulated.

Richard entered and burst out laughing. "I've been in bawdy houses which don't look as fancy as this," he said as he clutched Grace by the waist and drew her to him.

"You impertinent guts-griping hedge-pig, you," she said, punching him lightly in the stomach. "I've spent days trying to get a woman's touch into this room. You'll not insult me or my work, thank you very much, my husband and soon-to-be-lover."

"I'll be your lover, Grace, and make it sore for you to walk in the morning," he grinned.

"Then you'd better have a considerable amount of meat in your codpiece, Richard, for some years ago I was entertained by a gentleman Turk, and not only was it sore to walk, but for a week I felt like I'd given birth."

"Oh, Grace, trust me when I tell you that an Irishman's meat is not only more ample but far sweeter than any Turk's."

She moved closer to him so that her breasts were pressing against his chest, and her hands wandered over his back, his buttocks and around to where his codpiece was straining under the press of his excitement.

"Enough with words, husband. It's longer than a year since I've felt a man warming my insides. So if you'd be so kind as to take your clothes off, you might remind me just what it is that an Irishman's made of."

Hampton Court Palace, 10 September 1573

Her skin prickled beneath the dense white make-up which she applied thickly to emulate the virginal look of Mary, Mother of the Christ. She wore white linen gloves to cover the scars on her hands left by the attack of smallpox eleven years earlier. Every morning, she thanked the Lord God in Heaven that there were no pox scars on her face or neck, unlike her poor friend and Mistress of the Bedchamber, Lady Mary Sidney, who was so hideously scarred by the pox she'd caught while attending her, that she had retired to her home in Kent and refused to return to the palace.

In Elizabeth's hand was a fan which she opened and began fanning herself so furiously that she nearly knocked over the pomander which she kept close to her on a footstool so that if a visiting ambassador smelled badly, she could pick it up and refresh herself. Her blue bejewelled dress and high ruff collar suddenly felt heavy and uncomfortable, one weighing her down and the other threatening to strangle her.

She gripped the sides of her throne, wanting to scream out her anger; but she'd already shouted once that morning, and the wife of Sir Thomas Quincey had been forced to withdraw from her presence in order to recover from an attack of the vapors.

She breathed deeply and hawked a globule of phlegm into the spittoon beside her throne. The court watched in silence, used to their queen's manly manners.

Why? Why did the Almighty send bad news straight after good? Just when she'd had word from Plymouth of dear Francis Drake's theft of such a large fortune from under the nose of the Spanish king, just when her treasury was beginning to swell and give her the comfort in the event of any foreign adventures into her lands, why did everything have to be compromised? Why did her life have to be so consistently ruined by the Irish? When first she became queen, it had been the French, then the Spanish; and now this damnable Irish woman, this washerwoman in men's breeches. This . . . this harridan witch of a pirate woman had nearly scuttled three of her merchantmen who had put into some harbor to shelter from the storms of the Irish coast, capturing them and claiming their cargo as her booty.

Despite her fury, Elizabeth had to be so very careful of her public reaction. There were ears listening throughout the palace, and in this audience hall there were ambassadors from many different countries, standing close to men and women who were supposed to be loyal to the Crown of England, yet who would hang and quarter their own mothers for a new title or land or grant of trade. And wouldn't cousin Mary love to hear all about Elizabeth's woes?

So when she responded to the messenger's news, she had to be measured in her response.

"Where?" she demanded of the still-kneeling messenger whose terror at her reaction to his news had quietened his voice to the extent that she had to demand he speak up. "Where was this attack against our property?"

"In a harbor bay called Mullaghmore, Your Majesty. It's a large harbor in the county which is called Sligo in the northwest of Ireland. The area is known as Donegal Bay, Great Queen."

The messenger looked up to see whether the Queen needed further explanation, but immediately looked down again when he saw the displeasure that the meeting of their eyes gave her.

"How much were the cargoes of my ships worth?" she asked.

"Together, Majesty?" he whispered.

"Of course together, you fool! Do I look like some dealer in accounts? Am I a clerk who scribbles numbers on parchment?"

He deferred answering for a moment. He knew how much she'd lost, but he didn't dare tell her. It was a queen's ransom.

"Well," she hissed.

"Ten thousand pounds, Majesty."

There was an audible gasp from the assembly. Elizabeth ignored it.

The messenger remained silent, knowing for sure that with the wrong word, a sword would suddenly descend upon him and cleave his head from his shoulders.

But it didn't. Instead, he heard her sigh.

"Ten thousand pounds! So this Irish woman, this pirate, has cost me ten thousand pounds! Money not from my treasury, but from my own purse, cargo which I would have traded and made a profit of double that amount, money I would then have spent upon my people."

Turning in the direction of her Privy Council, she said, "And how much was the value of the silver which my dear Francis Drake captured on his way from the Americas to the coffers of King Philip of Spain?" She already knew the answer, but wanted the court to hear how little trouble the Irish pirate had caused her. Only she and some of her advisors would understand the full enormity of the disaster.

She looked directly at her friend and advisor, the man who had already built up a network of spies which made him the best-informed man in the court. "Well, Sir Francis?"

Sir Francis Walsingham stepped forward and bowed slightly. In his position as principal secretary of state, the most powerful of all Elizabeth's servants, Walsingham had earned the right to make a mere deferential nod before his queen, rather than a full bow.

"Your Majesty's captain, Sir Francis Drake, this month has relieved our esteemed brother king in Spain of silver worth twenty times that value, my Queen. And in this year, he has stolen from Philip gold and pearls and spices worth five times twenty the value."

Elizabeth nodded. "Let it be understood by all present that while we take it as a grievous offense that our person was assaulted and robbed by this witch of the waters, her attack on our innocent merchant ships has been but a fleabite in a dog's ear. We have felt her puny fangs, but we scratch the bite as no more than a moment's irritation."

The entire court burst out into laughter and applause. Elizabeth joined them in laughter, even though she could only just contain her fury. Under the layers of lead make-up on her face, she could feel her skin tighten and sweat in her anger.

Her entire performance had been for the benefit of the Ambassador of the King of France, who would report the attack against the English merchantmen to His Majesty. And from the French king's court, the news would quickly find its way to the court of Spain, where they would spend days laughing at Elizabeth's expense.

She rose from her throne and, with a swish of brocade, walked toward a door which was hastily opened by two sergeants-at-arms who swiftly uncrossed their halberds. Behind her followed Walsingham, Burghley and Cobham, as well as Edward Fiennes whom she had only recently ennobled as Lord Clinton. These were men on whose shoulders she rested much of the weight of her kingdom, though she was always in command.

She refrained from speaking until she was further down the oak-paneled corridor of the palace, out of hearing of the audience chamber.

And then she turned and spat out in fury, "Well?"

Lord Burghley was first to answer. "She must be stopped. The price on her head must be doubled."

"Why?" asked the Queen. "Why double the already heavy weight of money I've put on her head, when she laughs at every move my captains make? This woman will not be meshed by the net of money."

The Queen stopped in her tracks and turned, the breadth of the folds of her gown brushing against the walls of the corridor. "How dare she attack ships flying my own personal flag? How dare this mistress of the high seas attack my merchantmen?" Elizabeth screamed, stamping her foot. "How dare she flaunt my seas? By God, I'll cut her breasts off when I've captured her, and make her like the man she masquerades as being!"

Elizabeth turned to Henry Cobham. "Sir Henry, you're Lord Warden of the Cinque Ports. Isn't there a ship or a crew or a captain in my navy which can find and stop this cursed woman?"

"Majesty, it isn't the woman but the waters in which she sails. The west coast of Ireland is a maze of a thousand bays, all of which hide a thousand inlets. One bay alone, Majesty, is said to contain over three hundred islands, and she can hide in any one of them. She appears and we give chase, but then she rounds a headland and disappears. We search and search, but by the time we've explored all the narrows and isthmuses and coves and harbors, she's fifty leagues down the coast. She can hole up in a bay hidden from our gaze until our crews run out of food and water; she's supplied by her people on her own land, whereas we're run a merry chase by the Irish when we commandeer food and wine. Were she but to put into Galway or—"

"No buts, Cobham! This woman sails the high seas at will. Despite my navy, my merchant ships, my privateers and those English buccaneers who sail the waters, she appears and commits mayhem and then disappears as though she was the very Devil himself. Is there nobody who can stop her? This woman will be found and dragged before me ere the year is out, or there'll be another warden in my Cinque Ports and a fresh widow in England."

Cobham blanched as his queen turned with a swirl of skirts and walked into her private apartments. He had no answer to the Irish pirate queen, but not for lack of trying.

Part
the Second

Chapter Seventeen

Mullaghmore Harbour, Northwest Coast of Ireland, 1577

It was a life worth leading. At her age, women were either gray-haired grandmothers, shawled up and sitting beside a fireplace contemplating death, or they were slow-moving mistresses of their husband's domain, nodding and smiling when he made a joke or reaching over to pass him some fresh slices of ham for his dinner, waiting, always waiting for the men in her life to do something.

But for Grace O'Malley life was never that dull. Grace had rough-hewn her own life, had sculpted a reputation in Ireland and France and Spain and throughout the Mediterranean, and from what she was told of Elizabeth's hatred of her, was both feared and hated by the English.

And she certainly wasn't a gray-haired and toothless crone. There were still violent steaks of red in her hair which gave the lie to her aging. It wasn't the vermilion with which she'd been born, of course, but a duller red, the red of rocks which bleed with ironstone or the claret of blood which congeals around an old wound.

Neither was her face lined with the cares of those who lived in constant fear of the approach of the lords of the manor, or the priests of the parish; she controlled her own life. Her face was ruddy and fair and beaten into the glow of a morning sunrise by the fresh winds and the spume of salt spray.

It was the sea that kept her young, that fed her and her men, that brought her riches beyond those dreamed about by either of her husbands, that made fools of her enemies. Some viewed the sea as their enemy; but all her life, since she was a child in her father's arms, the sea had been her friend.

Yet there were times when she walked the decks that she hardly knew who she was. They called her the Pirate Queen, the Devil's Spawn, a woman in man's trousers; yet to those who knew her she was Granuaile, daughter of Owen Dub-hdara O'Malley, chieftain of Umhall Uachtarach, the Baron of Murrisk. And now the Mistress Bourke.

She was a curiosity to many who knew nothing about Ireland; yet had she not been a pirate, had she not robbed the Queen of England herself, had she gone along with the English as so many other lords and ladies of Ireland had done, then Grace would have been recognized by Elizabeth as being able to gather the clans and give England true sovereignty over the hearts and minds of the men and women of Eire.

Not now, of course. Now there was a price on her head and every English man-o'-war had its guns set to blast her out of the seas. Now she would never meet the Queen of England, or stand as equal before her. Ah well, a minor opportunity lost. But the world was replete with grand opportunities, and she still had many years left to benefit from them, years which she'd now enjoy in the company of her marvelous and virile husband, Richard.

She had been married to Richard Bourke for nearly eight years, a time which had seen great affection, frequent passion, the birth of a son and the further takeover of Ireland by the English. Grace and Richard's own property hadn't yet been touched by the English, but they realized that it was just a matter of time. The English had ennobled increasing numbers of chieftains, had sent over more local governors and more and more troops, and were engaged in endless double-dealing to convince the Irish that their path to happiness led to London.

No matter how Grace shouted and argued at the gatherings of chieftains, she, Richard and a handful of others were the only voices which seemed to be raised against the English.

But in all other matters—her family, her increasing wealth, her husband and his gentle yet manly ways—all were greatly pleasing to her. And especially the son she'd borne to Richard, Theobold, now a lusty lad of eight. Nobody, however, called him Theobold. He was known far and wide as Tibbot-ne-Long, Toby of the Ships, for he loved to sail with his mother and father when they went voyaging and trading. Every one of her children, God bless them, was drawn to the sea like it was their second home.

Grace constantly surprised, and often delighted, her husband. They were both intelligent and strong-willed, and they suited each other well.

Richard had been forced very early on in their marriage to come to terms with just how single-minded his new wife could be. On the very last day of the first year of their marriage, Grace had awoken early and asked her husband to travel to Newport to acquire some medicine from an apothecary.

"Can't I send the castellan?" asked Richard, surprised that she insisted he go out on such a menial task.

"No, love, for it's important that you fetch it yourself. It's a secret remedy and the apothecary won't give it to anyone other than you or me."

And so out of love and respect, Richard Bourke, known far and wide as Iron Dick for his strength in battle, had his horse saddled and rode out. The moment he was out of sight, she rushed up to the fourth floor of the tower and signaled for a hundred of her own O'Malley men to enter, along with a Galway lawyer and the local priest as witnesses.

When she opened the castle door, the castellan was overcome by the mob and locked in his room, unharmed by the incursion but huffing and puffing in wounded pride. The few guards who were in the castle were quickly disarmed and they, too, were locked up.

Then they waited for Richard's return. It took him an hour to reach Newport, a few moments with the apothecary to realize that he'd been sent on a goose chase, and less than an hour to return, for he rode quickly, knowing that something was amiss.

He slowed his horse as he approached his castle. Normally a guard on duty would shout down to the guard on the door that the master was approaching, and the door would open to admit him. But the door remained firmly closed. So he dismounted and tethered his horse at the hitching rail, walked to the hammer and knocked loudly.

Before the noise of the hammer blows had died down, he heard his wife shouting to him.

"Richard," she yelled from the top of the castle.

He stepped back so he could look upward.

"Grace, would you please get that damned man Liam to open the damned door for me."

"No."

"What?"

"I said no."

Looking upward, he saw that Grace had been joined by a dozen other heads on the battlement. He recognized some as senior members of the O'Malley clan.

"Grace," he said quietly, as though trying to speak to her privately, "what's going on?"

"Richard Bourke, when I married you a year back today, I told you that under Brehon Laws I had the right to divorce you within the year if the marriage wasn't satisfactory for either one of us. Well, husband, have you returned with my medicine from the apothecary?"

"Grace, you know there was no medicine. It was all an excuse to get me to leave the castle. Now what's going on?"

"As you have failed me in fetching my medicine, I cite Brehon Laws, and before God and these witnesses, I now dismiss you, Richard Bourke, as my husband. We are no longer married. And there is a priest and a lawyer here to verify that all this accords with the ancient laws of our land by which we were married."

"You're divorcing me?" he said in astonishment. "Haven't I been a good husband to you?"

"Oh darling, you've been the very best of husbands. Kind and gentle and considerate and wonderfully lusty in bed. But I have to prevent myself from becoming your widow. When my first husband died, my inheritance as his wife was taken away and I was left with nothing that was his and should have been mine by rights. I'm determined never to be in that position again. So I've taken possession of your castle and I'm claiming it as my own. And because I'm in possession at our divorce, it's mine by rights. And there are a hundred of my men inside should you—"

But Richard didn't hear what else she said, for he burst out laughing, and nearly convulsed on the ground with the comedy of the situation. Grace looked at him in amazement. She hadn't been able to predict how he'd react to having his castle taken from him, but she hadn't expected him to burst into paroxysms of laughter.

When he'd managed to control himself, he shouted up, "You silly woman. Don't you realize that I'd have given you everything I have? I love you, Grace. What am I going to do now that we're divorced? Will I have to leave Rockfleet and go and live in another of my castles? Without you?"

"God forbid that you'd do that. Although we're no longer married, I'll open the door and we can go to bed right away to celebrate our divorce. My body aches for you when you're not here, and I couldn't bear the thought of you not being by my side when I fall asleep at night and wake up in the morning. But before I let you in, I have to know something. Do you agree to the divorce?"

"Yes," he shouted up, starting to laugh again.

"Be serious, damn you, Richard. This is important to me. And do you agree that this castle is mine by possession and that you'll return to me my thousand head of cattle and horses?"

"Thousand? But at least twenty have died during the year. And we slaughtered ten when we hosted the entire MacWilliam clan not three months back. A thousand? No, I'll return you nine hundred."

"A thousand, damn you, you surly heavy-handed remnant, you. We've had heifers and colts during the year which more than make up the numbers. A thousand, or you can go to Hell."

"Nine hundred and fifty, and that's my final offer, you damned meat-headed fishwife, you."

"Nine hundred and seventy-five, bastard of a former husband," she shouted back, trying hard not to laugh.

"It's a deal. Nine hundred and seventy-five. Not one more nor less. They're yours. And you can have my fuchking castle as well. Now, my dearest divorced wife, for the love of God, will you let me into my own home?"

"My home, divorced husband. No longer your home, but mine."

"Your home then, damn you. But open the fuchking doors and let me in. I have a fierce passion for you, Grace, and I want to satisfy it now."

She turned to the lawyer and the priest, and asked if his agreement signified acceptance under Brehon Laws. They conferred, beginning the discussion of moot points of the articles of the law. After a few moments Grace lost patience and said, "Oh for God's sake, gentlemen. Am I the owner and in command of the castle or am I not?"

They agreed that she was.

"Good. Then I'm off downstairs to be with the gentleman waiting at the door," she said, and called for the servants to open the door to the former master of Rockfleet, and for her guest to be admitted to her castle. She heard a man's raucous laughter, and rushed from the ramparts, through the upper living chamber to the head of the stairs to her bedroom. As she descended, she shouted out instructions for her bed to be made ready for her first act of sexual immorality in many years.

The priest, the lawyer and her kinsmen listened to the shouted instructions and smiled as they saw her run down the stairs to greet the man who had once been her husband.

Grace told Sir Philip Sidney the story of what she'd done to her former husband Richard in the early days of their marriage to ensure that she was never poor again, and the young and very attractive man roared with laughter. He had a lovely smile and an all-encompassing laugh; she'd been mistrustful of him at first, but his winning ways had disarmed her.

The young man, nephew to Robert Dudley, was visiting Ireland to accompany the Earl of Essex who had been made Earl Marshal by Elizabeth. Sir Philip's first unofficial engagement had been to write the most charming and poetical of notes to Grace, begging her to agree to see him during his visit to the north and west of the island, or to come to where he would reside for two weeks in Galway in order to meet his father, Sir Henry.

Fascinated by the charm and warmth of his correspondence, Grace had told her ex-husband, Richard Bourke, that she would visit Galway and make the acquaintance of the young courtier. Richard, who couldn't tolerate the fancies and folderol of England's perfumed lackeys, was surprised. Grace would never normally be eager to meet an Englishman, but it seemed this young man had set the hearts and minds of the womanhood of Ireland aflame.

Grace wrote back, saying that she would meet with him in the governor's Galway office, in private.

What Sir Philip didn't know was how irritating the meeting would be to the gentlemen of Galway, from whom she had stolen so much money and cargo. She smiled to herself as she imagined dismounting her horse and giving the reins to the governor to hold, while she met with a man who sat on the right hand of the Queen of England and hence was protected from any local irritation.

When she finally met Sir Philip, she was quite bowled over by his charm and wit and good looks. He was already gaining a reputation as a poet of the English language, and a man of intellect and wit. He was about the age of her son, yet he had none of Murrough's crudeness of manner. But this man was no pampered and mannered fop, but was strong and masculine, not at all the popinjay Richard had predicted.

At the beginning of their interview, Sir Philip greeted her warmly in English, but she steadfastly refused to answer.

Somewhat disarmed by her silence, he asked whether her hearing was in order, shouting the words close to her ear. She smiled, and replied in soft and delicate Latin, "My hearing is very good, thank you, Sir Philip. It's not the ears which are the problem, but the tongue; you see, young man, you're using a tongue which I refuse to speak."

Sir Philip changed to Latin. "Your Ladyship has a difficulty with speaking English. It's a complicated language, made more so because it is the language of poetry and of the theater."

"Oh no, Sir Philip," she said, correcting him in her fluent Latin and then changing seamlessly to Greek, "I understand the language well enough; I just refuse to speak the tongue of a nation which is intent on conquering my people and denuding me of my inheritance."

Also switching to Greek, he said, "We English steal nothing, m'lady, which isn't ours by right or by conquest, and we haven't conquered this green isle. Your lords are giving over their rights voluntarily in return for the grandeur and glory of English titles which enable them to sit at the table of any high-born Englishman and look him in the eye as his equal. These, surely, are the hallmarks of a compact written in Heaven."

"Written in Hell, more like. Silly fellow, Sir Philip, if you believe that an English title has value to an Irishman. How many sheep equal a knight? How many cattle a duke? How many bulls an earl?"

He burst out laughing, and offered her a goblet of mulled port wine. He looked at her with new appreciation. She was motherly and thickened around the neck and waist; and her hair, once red, was now streaked with gray and white; and unlike the noblewomen of England whose faces were painted white to follow the fashion of the Queen, this matron's face was dark and leathery from years at sea. Yet there was a look of raw strength about her, an unbridled and honest lustiness, a knowledge of life, and an enjoyment of the body and all the pleasures it brought, and all swaddled in a wrap of intellect and native cunning. This was a woman not to be trifled with, a woman who would defer to no man. Here, for sure, was a woman who would stand up to the Queen of England and give as good as she received.

Although he wouldn't tell her, he had been instructed by Elizabeth herself to meet with Grace O'Malley, to talk with her, find out her strengths and weaknesses. After only moments of being in her company, Sir Philip knew that, along with the King of Spain and the King of Portugal, and all the other royalty of Europe who were England's enemies, this queen of pirates was as much a formidable enemy of England as any monarch ordained by God Himself to rule.

"Tell me, Grace, these adventures I've heard told about you, these amazing things you've done these past many years—are they all true? Or is there a touch of Irish whiskey in them all which makes the stories headier than the facts?"

She was flattered that this clever and pretty young man was interested in her, but she was not naïve. "And how much of our conversation will stay between us, Sir Philip, and how much will be measured by your ruler?"

He smiled and refused to answer.

But there was no real reason why she shouldn't throw him a tidbit or two, so she told him about the way in which she'd captured her husband's castle without a blow being struck.

After he'd finished laughing, he said, "So you and Master Richard Bourke are . . . How can I put this discreetly?"

"Living in sin? Living without the grace of God? Fuchking all night long without the goodly angels in Heaven blessing our union? Put it any way you like, Sir Philip, for it's of no earthly concern to me. My friend and partner and one-time husband is as fine and decent and strong a man as any I've met. Now you tell me any man who would lose a castle to trickery and laugh about it."

The young man shrugged, and admitted that most of the English aristocrats would kill their mothers for a castle or two.

"Will I be permitted to meet with Master Richard Bourke?" he asked.

"No, you won't. He has no interest in meeting with you, nor the new marshal of these parts, the Earl of Essex. Richard believes that if he ignores you, you'll go away."

"And you don't believe that?"

"I believe that you're intent on taking our lands, and that we'll have to fight you to retain what's ours."

He was about to argue, but decided that it would be of no use. So he determined to find another way to get her trust.

"What other adventures have you had, ma'am, during this extraordinary life you've led? Delight me with your stories."

And she did! For over an hour, Sir Philip sat as still as an ocean rock while the maelstrom of her tales swirled around him.

"By God, Grace," he said when she'd finished, "if you were in England, I'd put you on a London stage and we could charge a shilling a head to hear your tales— we'd make a fortune. Who but Grace O'Malley could have lived such a life?"

"Elizabeth of England," Grace replied without pause for thought.

He looked at her in surprise. He'd deliberately not mentioned her arch enemy for fear of driving a wedge into their conversation.

"You're surprised? Don't be, Sir Philip. I respect Elizabeth as much as I dislike her, for she's a woman of my own type, and had she not been born to the throne, she would have fought her way to it. She's a strong and inspiring woman, and although we're bitter enemies and I detest what it is she stands for, I respect her for what she's achieved. She rules the nation with the will of a king while she wears the prettiest of dresses; she bares her arse to the Pope, yet won't allow the wholesale persecution of Catholics even though they're conniving and plotting to supplant her with Scots Mary; she imprisons Mary, yet won't execute her—for reasons which I don't understand—even though the Scottish whore has openly said that her greatest wish is to take the throne of England and hand it over to Rome or Spain. She's restored the value of the English pound and now her sailors and merchants trade with all the world, yet she will have nothing to do with the might of Philip's Spain. She is an enigma, for there is much more to her as a queen than there would be were she a king.

"You, Sir Philip, could not possibly understand what it's like to be a woman in the world of men. We not only have to perform the same feats as men if we're to be successful in our own right, but we have to overcome the curse of being born a woman."

He shook his head; this was a surprising woman indeed.

"I admire Elizabeth greatly," Grace went on, "but she has failed on one score—as a woman and a wife."

"Our Gloriana is more concerned with securing the kingdom than securing her succession," the young man defended.

"She has had time to do both. If I'd sat on my cunny waiting for my first husband to build up our family fortune, we'd be begging on the streets today. As it is, because of the evil laws of inheritance of this country, a woman who's widowed has no status. I intend to write to Elizabeth and point this out to her, and say that if she intends to be queen both of England and of Ireland, she should correct this monstrosity immediately."

Sir Philip looked at her in amazement. "You're intending to write to the Queen? While you're fighting her army?"

"Of course I shall write to her! If she dares to assume me as her subject, regardless of my feelings in the matter, then surely I have a right to petition her and make her aware of the injustices we are suffering? I might fight her until my dying day, Sir Philip, but if she wears the title of Queen of Ireland, with or without my consent, then she might as well earn it by righting the wrongs done to the womenfolk of this country."

"You amaze me, ma'am, but I can't fault your logic. Tell me, how did the women of your country come to be so poorly served by its laws?"

Grace looked at Sir Philip with narrowed eyes. If the boy wanted a history lesson, she'd give him one. "Before Ireland was conquered by Saint Patrick who brought us the dubious benefits of Christianity and our allegiance to the Pope in Rome, we women of Ireland were respected and held equal rank with the men. But a thousand years ago, all that changed. It's said that Saint Patrick drove all the snakes from this land and into the sea, but he also did the women great wrong. Yes, he did far more than rid us of snakes, the old fuchker. We'd obeyed Brehon Laws long before Patrick, indeed since time began, which gave good account for women and saw them equal; then Patrick introduced the Salic Laws of the old Franks with their prohibition on women inheriting land, and suddenly there was an almighty clash of interests between the menfolk of Ireland, who saw their chance to grab for power, and the womenfolk, who saw in these old laws their downfall.

"The men won out because the fuchking priests and monks who followed Patrick joined up the two laws and incorporated the woman-hating laws of the Franks into the Brehon Laws. Now do you call that fair, Sir Philip?"

He shook his head, and said, "Manifestly not, ma'am."

"And how would your Queen of England like to live under those rules?"

Sir Philip Sidney could think of nothing more to say, so he remained silent.

"Perhaps I should present the petition to Her Majesty personally, Sir Philip. How do you think the Queen of England would react if a pirate queen were to present herself?"

He smiled. "It's a prospect joyously to be imagined, my lady. A delightful prospect indeed!"

The following afternoon, Grace returned to her Rockfleet, and was greeted by Richard. She told him of her interview with Sir Philip, and the conclusion she had come to. Yes, he was a fine young man, honest and intelligent, open and witty; but he was also a scion of England and within him contained all that was worst about England—the arrogance of their assumption that the world belonged to them; the zeal with which they were defending the Church Henry had created against the ancient authorities of Rome; the pride with which the English navy sailed in Irish waters, as though the God of England was also the God of all the seas and had given the English the right to sail wherever they wanted.

Richard laughed and kissed Grace on the lips. "I'm glad you weren't seduced by the lad, as half the women in Ireland seem to have been." Then he added, "And did you meet just Sir Philip?"

"I met his father, the deputy governor. Sir Henry is his name, and he's as sly and slippery a one as England ever produced."

Then she told him that Sir Henry had begged her to provide him with two galleys and two hundred men should Galway need to be defended. The enemy, he said, might very well be Spain, for Queen Elizabeth was afraid that King Philip would use Ireland as a back door to an attack on England. She agreed to his request at a price, which he reluctantly said he would meet.

"You're a shrewd businesswoman, Grace, and that's for sure. And talking of business, word has come from some of our friends in the south that the Earl of Desmond in Munster is expecting four fat and lovely ships from the Mediterranean to decorate the new additions to his castle at Askeaton. Now to me, it would seem a pity for this silly and arrogant man to rob you and me of the pleasure of his possessions, wouldn't you agree? So why not rob the old bastard first?"

She smiled. It was many months since she'd been pirating on her ships, and she sorely missed the sea. These days she spent her time with Richard in land raids on distant parts of Ireland's north and east, in fighting land claims, and in the many things necessary in increasing their territory before the English came and tried to take it all. She longed to be back sailing the crests of waves, watching the shoreline disappear, and then slowly finding herself and her ship alone in a vast sea. So the moment Richard suggested that she captain one of her ships to the vast southern lands of Munster owned by the effete Earl of Desmond, a traitor to Ireland who had been one of the very first to queue up for a title from the Queen, she was overjoyed.

She walked over and threw her arms around her ex-husband, kissing him tenderly and lovingly. "You're a good man, Richard. A truly and honestly good man. It was the best thing I ever did that day I turned up on your doorstep and demanded you marry me."

"Then it seems such a pity that you divorced me," he whispered into her ear. "I could have made you a fine husband."

She lay off Cobh on the entry of the huge inlet which led to the harbor city of Cork. It was far from the eyes of the city, at the outlet for the River Lee that she was provided with the most secrecy so that she could hide her ship while anchored deep in the vast harbor.

She chose a spot behind Great Island which was far enough from the sea and the city to make her invisible. After testing several suitable locations, she chose to drop anchor and wait behind a small clump of rocks which constituted a tiny island. To ensure that she was not visible from Cobh, she took her wondrous opticometer, clambered up the rock and spied out the scene. From the crow's nest, her lookout could see clear into the deepwater harbor, which led to the heads and then into the sea. This would give her half a day's warning that the four ships of the earl were sailing toward Cork.

It was an ideal position, because the moment she spotted the four merchant galleys, she would order her oarsmen to row the galley to the southern end of the harbor, and there she'd lay in wait to relieve them of their cargoes, well before the vessels of Cork knew that she was there and could set sail to attack her. It was a neat and clever plan: she was hidden from the city of Cork, hidden from the sea, and yet her lookouts had good visibility.

And so she settled down to wait for the fat ships to appear. The following day, no ships were sighted, other than the usual fishing boats and coastal traders which entered and left the busy port. She and those of the crew not on watch duty spent their time telling stories, playing games of bones and die, and wrestling. In her younger days Grace could have wrestled a good number of the crew one on one, but nowadays she knew very well that even the cabin boy was allowing her to get the better of him. She was still strong as an ox, but her reflexes were nowhere near what they had once been.

The next day, life on board followed the same pattern, other than a scare when a fishing boat drifted too close to the small island which hid them from the city. They contemplated capturing the boat and imprisoning the crew until they had achieved their goals, but by good fortune the fishermen managed to find a school of fish and followed them to another part of the harbor.

On the morning of the third day, Grace looked through her opticometer and spotted the masts of one, then two, and then three ships sailing north into the harbor. They had traveled from far out to sea and used the morning wind to blow them into the harbor. Now they were only fifteen leagues from Cork, and by the time the fourth mast had appeared, Grace had already given orders to weigh anchor, set sail and man the oars to take them the mile and a half to the mouth of the harbor so they could attack.

"Let's lower sail and wait inside that hook of rock," she said, pointing to a small peninsula of rocky land which jutted out before the river mouth widened dramatically into the harbor.

The men rowed hard and fast, but suddenly they heard the fiercest scraping noise from deep in the bowels of the ship. It was a noise which made the guts of every sailing man knot in horror. As the noise grew sharply in volume, the ship came to a sudden stop and skewed hard to starboard. Everyone on and below deck was pitched forward, sprawling on all fours, hitting heads and arms and shoulders as they slid around the ship which started to list dramatically.

"Jesus Christ and the fuchking Saints preserve us, what was that?" Grace screamed out. She struggled to her feet, rubbing her head. Her hair was matted with blood from a deep gash she'd received. She looked around, and the rest of the crew were pulling themselves up, all hurt but no one badly injured.

Grace steadied herself against the angle of the ship and clawed her way up the deck which was now listing steeply. Then she suddenly realized the full and awful enormity of what had happened. Grasping the ship's railings, she hauled herself upright and looked down at the water. The ship's hull was half out of the sea, and a massive beam had appeared out of the water, like a harpoon thrown by some ancient and powerful sea god. The beam, covered with barnacles and seaweed, had punctured her ship and forced it to starboard, where it was held fast on the same submerged rocks which had sunk the drowned ship in the first place. The superstructure and rigging of the sunken ship was holding fast her hull, anchoring it to the rock shelf which was covered by the tide.

"What is it, Captain?" asked the mate.

"There's a shipwreck down below, caught on submerged rocks, and we've just rowed over the top of the damnable thing. The mast and rigging has pierced us, and we're stuck fast. Damn and blast the fuchking luck. We've been skewered by a ghost, if you don't mind. Holed below the waterline. We'll sink for sure. Damn!"

And then, as though their current plight wasn't bad enough, one of the men on the other side of the ship called out, "Captain! Look!"

Grace turned and saw three naval vessels beginning to leave Cork Harbor. She had no doubt that they were headed for her, now that her position had been revealed. And she also had no doubt whatsoever that she and her men were headed for the Earl of Desmond's prison.

Chapter Eighteen

Askeaton Castle, Near Limerick, 1577

She winced as the light suddenly burst into the pitch dark of the dungeon, assaulting her senses which had grown dull since her incarceration. In pain, she turned her head away from the door, shielding her eyes from the flaming brand in the dungeon master's hand.

She had sat for who knew how long in the hellish black of the dungeon, feeling the deepest fear she had ever experienced. She was tethered to a wall, chained like a blackbird in the holds of a slave ship. For all she knew, she could have been in an abyss, somewhere in the middle of the earth, separated from happy and laughing men and women by a thousand miles.

Grace was a woman who lived almost her entire life in God's blessed sunshine, or the gentle light of His moon and stars. In the unfathomable time since she'd been cast rudely into this dungeon, she'd felt as though she was in the limbo of which the Italian poet Dante had written.

Unable to see a thing, unable to move because of her chains, it was a fate akin to death. Perhaps it was death, and the light from the jailer's torch was the fire of the Hell itself into which she'd been cast.

Since her ship had foundered close to Cork and she'd been arrested, her life had been one nightmare after another. When the naval vessels from Cork had first approached her and seen that she was stuck fast, they had surrounded her on all sides. She had fought back, naturally, but without maneuverability, she was like a wounded bird; so in order to save the lives of her crew, she hoisted the flag of submission, the first time in her life she'd ever done so.

The captain who boarded her was a young man, and frankly admitted to her that capturing Grace O'Malley was the finest thing to happen to him, and his career and reputation would benefit greatly. She asked the young man if he was in the English army, but he told her that he was a Cork man, in the army of the Earl of Desmond. Somehow it didn't make Grace feel any more secure.

She was separated from her crew who were all taken aboard another vessel, and she was sailed to Cork. First, she was hauled out of the ship and up onto the jetty, manacled like some rabid cur instead of being accorded her rights and station as a lady and a chieftain. Then she was dragged behind her captor's horse by her neck, like some prize heifer, northward for seven days until they came to the banks of the River Deel where Askeaton Castle, home of the Earl of Desmond, was situated a few miles from the confluence of the River Shannon and the city of Limerick.

She'd hoped that when she was presented to the earl, he would accord her the status she warranted, and use her for ransom from Richard. However, she was not presented before His Excellency but instead dragged down stone steps into the dungeons of the castle, thrown into the black and evil void of a cell, and left alone to ponder her fate.

Since then, the door hadn't even opened for food or water. She was left to starve and to sit in the stench of shite and piss left by others, and then by herself, God help her, for an inestimable time. She knew that she'd been imprisoned some time in the morning, but when the cell door was closed, and there were no noises except the scurrying of rats, she lost all communion with the passage of the sun and the moon, and had no idea whether it was day or night.

She slept, she woke, she prayed, she sang songs, she recited poetry in Gaelic, then Latin, then Spanish, then Greek; then she tried to stand up, but the chains were too short; she examined as best she could the area around her, but to no avail. When her hunger and thirst became near to unbearable, she imagined the meals she enjoyed with Richard—tender lamb and beef and a variety of the choicest vegetables; sweet jellies and the tangy innards of animals, hearts and kidneys and lungs in stews which were rich and made richer with port wine or sherry or herbs fresh from a summer rainshower. She thought of fruit, of apples and berries and pears and plums and all the other delicious things which grew wild in the forests of Ireland and which she had once taken for granted. Never more!

Eventually, she began to plan how to capture the rats which occasionally ran across her legs. Eating a raw rat wasn't something she savored, but it was better than starvation. She planned the capture of the rat with military precision. She would feel it run on top of her shoe, then it would explore the inside of her trews, and if it ventured higher into the open legging, she'd trap its exit and bring her other leg down hard, breaking its spine. As to how she'd eat it, well that was something she hadn't fully contemplated, but her stomach was so empty and her hunger so gnawing that no doubt she'd work out a way.

But then, without any warning, the door to her dungeon suddenly opened, and the light flooded in like a shipboard explosion at night, and she screamed in fear and pain.

The jailer walked down the stone steps carrying the flaming brand, and said, "God's truth, you bitch, you've made the place stink worse than before. Who'd have thought it possible?"

He unlocked her chains and hauled her to her feet. But in her weakness, and still shielding her eyes from the brilliance of the flaming brand, she nearly collapsed.

"Come, woman, stand up. I have to clean you and take you to the captain of the guard. The earl himself wishes to see you."

He dragged Grace up the steps and out of the cell. Grace stumbled and fell, only stopped from falling by the jailer's rough hand underneath her armpit.

Up another flight of stairs and the air smelled better up here. Indeed, it was almost pleasant with its aroma of candles and food from the nearby kitchen.

The smell of whatever the kitchen was preparing for the earl's mealtime suddenly made Grace feel weak and sickly for lack of nourishment.

"Jailer, I have had nothing to eat since I was brought in here, and—"

"Eat? Don't be stupid, woman. You'll get nothing to eat or drink until I'm given orders by the captain of the guard. And my orders now are to wash the shite and piss off you and present you within the hour to the captain."

He pushed her into a large room in which there was a high wooden tub. "Take off all your clothes and step into the water. I'm sure your ladyship is used to perfumes from the Spice Islands, but all we've got is potash soap, so use it."

He stood there and waited.

"You can leave me," she said, too weak for it to have an impact.

"I stay. Take off your clothes," he ordered.

Slowly and painfully she unbuttoned her jerkin and bodice, and then her trews, leggings and slid off her stained and putrid underthings until she stood before him, naked and filthy. He stared at her breasts, her thighs, her womanhood, and she felt dirtier than when she'd fouled herself during her three days of incarceration. Ignoring him, she turned and climbed the step into the tub. The water was freezing, but it was clean and very refreshing. She reached over and picked up the lump of potash soap. By its smell, it had been made from rendered horse fat and bones, and she used the gritty ash to rub the congealed excrement from her thighs, legs and buttocks. She felt revolted, but determined not to allow the jailer to see her embarrassment or discomfort. And as she was scrubbing herself, she began to fantasize about what she would do when Richard Bourke rode down to Limerick with a thousand men and raided the castle to release her. First to die at her sword, painfully and slowly, would be her jailer; then the captain of the guard, and finally the earl himself.

She dressed in the clothes of a serving woman. She was taken up to the family apartments, where, in the long hall with its wooden roof and oaken beams, emblazoned with the swords and shields and rondels of victory, the earl sat at the head of a dining table laden with dozens of dishes.

She felt heady and ill as she looked at the mountains of food, and her stomach grumbled. But worst of all was her vicious thirst for, except for the water of the bath which was putrid with her own shite, she'd drunk nothing since she'd been thrown into the dungeon.

If the earl knew anything of her agony, he took pains to ignore it. He continued to eat, reading a document, while the guards on either side of her forced her to walk over to the table, and to stand to attention while His Lordship continued to dine on mutton, spatchcock, eel, vegetables and sweetmeats.

She stood there for a long period—she had no idea of how long—until she nearly fainted from lack of food, lack of water, and exhaustion. And still, despite the commands of the guards for her to stand straight when her legs gave way beneath her, the earl continued to ignore her and eat his repast and read his reports.

Grace decided to speak. "Desmond. How dare you treat—"

But one of the guards thumped her hard in the ribs, and she collapsed on the floor. She was rudely hauled back up to her feet by the guards, who supported her underneath her armpits.

And still the earl continued to ignore her. Grace's hatred of him grew by the minute.

Eventually he put down his spoon, wiped his mouth with a napkin, took another sip of wine and looked up at her for the first time.

"So, Mistress Grace Bourke, you're in a fine state, and no mistake. What have you got to say for yourself?"

"I say, Lord Desmond, that this is no way to treat a leader of an Irish clan. I am the leader of the O'Malley and the O'Flaherty and the Bourke. You've imprisoned me falsely, treated me cruelly, and all to your great disservice, for when my Richard comes riding down with his thousand men and his thousand Gallowglass, you'll be splintered from arse to elbow and will rue the day that your eyes ever graced themselves on me."

The Earl of Desmond smiled and nodded. He turned to the guards and nodded to them. "You hear that, men. Richard Bourke is going to ride down here and murder me. Now isn't that interesting. For you see, if he loves you, if he truly loves you, he'll do no such thing. I've already written a letter to him, you see. The moment you were imprisoned in my dungeon, I wrote to him, advising him that you were my captive."

Grace frowned. Suddenly her gnawing hunger was less pressing, for something in his manner told her that things were going to get even more grim.

"I told him that you were in a dungeon of mine. I said to him that I expected him to ride south and release you. After all, he has a fearsome reputation for gallantry, and as a man of arms, your Richard is second to none in all of Ireland. But I also told him one more little thing which might just dissuade him from trying to rescue you."

Grace stopped breathing. She couldn't imagine what would prevent Richard from jumping on his horse the moment he heard she was a prisoner; but from the look of this earl, she felt sure that she was in for bad news.

"I told him that I have a strong castle, able to withstand a siege for ten years. And I also told him that if I saw even one of his horsemen or one of his Gallowglass on my land, I would drag you up from the dungeons, and I would hang you by the neck from the castle battlements for him and all his men to see. I said that your dead carcass would be swinging in the breeze while he was trying to break down my doors.

"I tell you, madam, I'd be most surprised if he comes to rescue you. Most surprised indeed."

He burst out laughing and continued to sip his wine, reveling in the simplicity, yet the totality, of his victory. With the merest of nods to the captain of his command, Grace was pulled violently from the earl's presence and out of the room.

But things changed for the better after the interview. To her surprise and delight, Grace wasn't returned to the dungeon. Instead, she was taken to the prison cells and placed within a cell with clean straw and a window high in the wall. Nor was she placed in manacles, but was allowed free rein to roam over her new, though confining, domain.

The cell was little bigger than one of the minor bedrooms of her Castle Rockfleet, but after the dungeon, it felt like a palace. And she had a pissing pot which was emptied every morning, as well as a basin with fresh water brought once a day. She was given towels to wash and dry herself with, and in her second month of confinement, she was brought fresh clothes to wear, though still the clothes of a washerwoman.

The food in the cell was passably good, consisting of bread and beer in the morning, some watery gruel in the midday, and in the evening she was brought a stew containing the bones and flesh of some animal, accompanied by a lump of barley or wheat bread, which on some days was quite soft and newly baked.

As the days of her incarceration blurred one into another and she became increasingly convinced that she would live and not be murdered, she began to build up a defense against her plight in order to protect herself from a fury against her jailers, and especially the earl, which might otherwise have destroyed her. She imagined that she was the mistress of the world, and that her cell was the globe itself.

Over there in the northern corner was the New World which had recently been visited by English adventurers. It had strange and discomforting animals and peoples, men and women whose skin was the color of clay and who lived in conical cloth huts and wore animal feathers in their heads and prayed to strange gods.

Over here, in the southwestern corner, was France and Italy and the German principalities and Spain and Portugal. She spoke the languages of each country when she visited them, and created conversations with the Pope in Latin, with the various royal members of each country in French or Spanish or Italian, and with commanders of armies, with whom she planned exploits and campaigns.

There, in the east of her cell, was the empire of the Ottoman Caliphs, with their dark skins and their mysterious black eyes, their rich attires and sparkling jewels. She thought of the harems in which the Sultan of Constantinople lived, with all his slaves and women and janissary guards. And she fantasized that she was a member of the sultan's harem, sitting around the private apartments, dressed in exquisite robes and smelling of the sweetest of perfumes, with jewels in her hair and adorning her body. It was a silly, girlish fantasy, but it took her away from the bleakness of her cell and made her feel better.

Another month went by, and then another, and still no news from any source. The window was high up on the walls, but she managed to use the sparse furniture in the room—the wooden bed and the table—to build a small ramp so that she could spend part of each day making her way up to the window, and then, grasping the bars, look out of the castle walls at the River Deel and the commerce of the waterways.

And during the months of her incarceration, not once did the earl ask to see her again, nor was she interrogated, nor told what would happen to her.

She lapsed into a state of quiescence, and by the end of the fourth month of isolation, with only the guards to interrupt her loneliness three times a day— and then for just a moment to deliver food or remove night soil or once a week to throw in a new bale of hay which she'd spread on the floor—she was in a state of abject depression. The games of traveling the world in her cell no longer held any interest for her, and instead of using her imagination, she confined her- self to staring out of the window for long periods of the day. She looked at the passage of the world far below her and fantasized that the bars would disappear and she would grow wings and fly out of the castle window down onto the river, where suddenly she'd become a brilliant silver fish, flashing in the water, and swim down the Deel, into the Shannon, and then into the welcoming embrace of the huge Atlantic, to be lost in the vastness of the great unexplored and un- knowable depths.

At the beginning of the fifth month, the door suddenly flew open. It was so sudden and unexpected that Grace shouted in fright.

A guard stood at the doorway. "Gather your possessions, ma'am. You're to see the earl."

Silently, for she knew that this youth knew nothing and would be unable to reveal her destiny, she picked up her meager things and followed him out of the cell into the corridor. She looked around, not having seen this area of the cas- tle for five long months.

The captain of the guard, whom she barely remembered, walked from his chamber and said curtly, "Follow me."

Silently, she did, and he led her through the kitchens, up the stairs to the buttery, and then into the official and family apartments. They crossed a large and imposing hall and were escorted into the family salon.

The Earl of Desmond was standing before his roaring fire, two hounds lying inert and disinterested before him. He looked up and appeared to acknowledge her presence. She stood before him, but unlike the previous time, on this occasion she didn't need support, for she was rested and passably nourished and did regular exercises in the confines of her cell.

"Well, Mistress O'Malley. You seem to have friends in high places. Very high places indeed. You're free to go. I've made a horse available to you. I'm sure you can remember your way home."

He turned and stared at the fire. But she didn't move. She was too shocked, too stunned at the sudden reversal in her fortunes.

"Free?"

"Yes, you're free to go."

"But I don't understand. Why?"

"You'll find out soon enough. Now leave my castle and return to your home. And remember that my patience is worn ragged, and if you're still on my lands tomorrow, I'll have you thrown back in my cells, friends or not."

The captain of the guard pulled her arm roughly and spun her around, pushing her toward the door. Suddenly she was close to bursting into tears, but she bit her lip hard so that she showed no weakness before the earl, who was obviously in some way restraining the fury he felt at being forced to release her.

She remembered little of the journey home. Her horse headed northward as though riderless, finding paths, testing the ground, recognizing landscapes without any help from her. Yet slowly she began to encounter sights and smells increasingly familiar and each one came as a little jolt of shock, as though she was a winter bud suddenly awakening to the warmth of a spring sun.

She was sufficiently aware to sense the erotic, overwhelming perfumes of the land, the smell of new-cut hay, the dampness of the forests, the salty tang of the sea when she was high on a cliff. Grace had never before appreciated her country as much, never truly understood its breathtaking beauty or freshness or verdancy. As she traveled she woke more and more from that waking slumber which her incarceration had forced upon her.

It was when she was two days' journey from her prison that something within her said that she was free, that she was going home, that she was safe. And suddenly her senses came properly alive. She felt impelled to ride faster than safety or the weakness of her body should allow, for she knew she was getting closer and closer to her home in Castle Rockfleet, and her sons and daughter and her wondrous lover and best friend, Richard.

As she rounded a hilltop and the city of Galway came slowly into sight, she reined in her horse to take in the vista. For most of her life she'd hated the city and its men who kneeled toward England; for years she'd robbed the bastards blind. But now she looked at Galway with fresh eyes and saw how pretty it was, standing proud at the mouth of the huge bay, like a matronly woman whose arms were open to sailors returning home. She felt tears welling up inside her but she stifled them—plenty of time to cry when she was home, safe and sound.

And then she saw a man galloping fast toward her on the road. He was too far distant to see properly, yet from his haste and purpose, somehow she knew it was Richard.

Grace dismounted and held her horse, waiting for the rider to reach her. From a distance, she heard her name called faintly on the wind. "Grace! Grace!"

But that was all she heard, for she fainted dead to the world, right where she stood.

She came to, enveloped in Richard's welcoming arms. She felt him kissing her and stroking her hair, and gently trying to prize open her lips so that he could give her brandy from his flask. She opened her eyes and smiled.

"Hush now, darling, say nothing; just drink this brandy and it'll warm you," he told her. "You're safe now, my darling girl. Safe in my arms."

"Richard," she whispered softly. "I'm going to kill him with my bare hands. When I'm strong, I'm going to return and take his castle down, stone by stone. I'm going to make him regret he ever was born."

"Sure you are, my precious darling. Sure you are. But for now, rest and we'll take you home and feed you up, get some meat on your bones, some vitality back into your body. Plenty of time for revenge, once you're stronger."

She closed her eyes again, the brandy making her feel muzzy-headed. And she drifted off to sleep.

By the time she awoke, there was a roaring fire and she felt warm and comforted. What woke her was the divine smell of rabbit, roasting on a spit. Richard was slowly turning it and basting it with its own juices.

He noticed her movement. "Jesus Christ and all the Saints, darling, but you've been asleep for the whole damn day. I thought you'd died and gone to the Good Lord in Heaven, except that you were breathing so gently. Are you strong enough for some food? I've got fresh bread and some milk from the town. How's about you sit up and take some nourishment."

She did as she was told, eating the delicious flesh of the rabbit, sipping the milk and tearing off lumps of the freshest bread she'd ever tasted.

Grace looked at Richard. He was the epitome of concern, fussing over her like a mother hen, and deliberately not asking her a single thing about her incarceration. He was obviously waiting for her to broach the subject and knew instinctively that she'd tell him when she was ready.

Suddenly the entire weight of the past months pressed down upon her. She was so happy, so at peace to be with Richard and beside a warm fire, eating tasty food in complete security, that those bonds which had held her together during her stay in prison, the way in which she'd withdrawn into herself for her own protection, were suddenly released, and her fears and grief and anger suddenly erupted in an anguished outburst.

Grace looked up at the vastness of the Irish sky with its myriad stars and began to wail. She howled like a tormented wolf, crying and choking, releasing the poisons which had built up inside her, shaking and sobbing even when Richard rushed over to her and held her tightly in his arms. She cried and cried until he laid her on the ground, covered her with a blanket, and she fell into the deepest sleep she'd ever known.

She began to tell him what had happened to her when they were ten miles north of Galway on the road to Maum Bridge. There was nothing chronological in her narration; rather she told him the least distressing parts first so that he didn't become too angry. But as the day progressed, she told him of her capture and the days she'd spent in the dungeon. She looked at him and saw his jaw clenched in restrained fury.

"My men—what did that bastard do to my crew?" she asked.

"I had to ransom them back. Two were killed and I've paid their widows compensation, but the earl sold me back the rest. That's another thing I'll never forgive him for."

Grace's face was red with anger. She spurred her horse onward.

By the time they had ridden to the foothills of the Maumturk Mountains, it was already nightfall, and they made camp. Again, Richard quickly shot and plucked their evening meal, this time a wild moorhen. He also managed to find a nest and used the griddle to make her some fried eggs which she downed quickly, delighting in the yolky taste, something she hadn't experienced in more than half a year.

During their meal, Richard informed her of what had been happening to their castles during her incarceration. He had managed their affairs well, although he had often been fearfully distracted and unable to concentrate on what was going on.

She pulled a leg from the carcass of the bird and ate the skin, almost gleefully, its warm and delicious fat running down the side of her mouth. She felt an overwhelming joy, but she didn't care, for she was in God's open air and was eating freshly caught food with her man, and she was safe.

"Tell me, Richard. Are you planning to raid the castle of Desmond soon? I have to be revenged."

He remained silent.

"What's happened?" she asked gently.

"When I learned that you might be released, it was on condition that I sign a blood oath with the Governor of Galway that I take no action whatsoever against the Earl of Desmond." He breathed a sigh of regret. "I'm sorry, Grace, but it was more important that you be released than that I have vengeance for us both. If I attack him, I become liable to the council for all our lands and properties."

Grace nodded; she'd suspected as much, for the prospect of their mounting a vengeance raid on Desmond's castle was just too obvious.

When they'd eaten, she asked him another question. "Earl Desmond told me that he was releasing me because I have friends in high places. What did he mean? And why didn't he have me killed straightaway? Why not try me, or ransom me? Why imprison me without trial?"

Richard remained silent.

"I think I know," she said softly. "He's a servant of England. Perhaps he was waiting for Elizabeth to make a determination. Or perhaps the Lords of Westminster. But if so, who are my friends in high places who had me released? It doesn't make sense."

Richard picked up another branch, prodded the fire, sending sparks up to the heavens, and finally placed it on top of the embers so that it began to crackle and blaze.

"To be honest, I have no idea, but in my guts, I think it has to do with your friend, Sir Philip Sidney."

She remained silent.

"See, darling, you must have impressed the young man very greatly, for a couple of days after your departure, a letter arrived from him, brought by one of his servants. I didn't open it, naturally. But shortly afterward, I received another letter, this one from Earl Desmond saying that he'd captured you and would string you up by the neck outside the castle wall if I was to attempt to rescue you. Imagine how frantic I was and what a furious rage I flew into. I had to be restrained by my own manservant Liam, for God's sake, who stopped me from racing out the door and ordered four of my own men to hold me back and prevent me from mounting a horse. It was fortunate he did so. Liam knew that

I was going to thunder down to Askeaton and tear the earl's body apart limb from limb, but that would have resulted in your death. The good man saved your life from my impetuousness, and I'm eternally grateful to him.

"Anyway, I was like a caged animal, pacing the walls of the castle, not knowing what to do. A day, a week, two weeks went by, during which I wrote to the Council of Ireland and to the Lord Governor in Dublin, and to everybody else I could think of. But that had no effect for they're all churlish dog-hearts and lovers of the English and wouldn't lift a finger to help a true Irish woman. And then I saw the letter Sir Philip had written to you, and I determined to open it, without your permission. It was a charming letter, Grace, full of pretty phrases and nice words. But what he said made me see another way. He said that he'd thought deeply about your plight as a widow of the O'Flaherty, and that he would suggest he petition the Queen Elizabeth on your behalf, suggesting that she examine your complaint and to beg her to relieve the distress of the widows of Ireland. He sent his respects and offered to assist you in any way he could.

"So I took him at his word, my darling. I wrote to him immediately. I told him what had happened to you. I begged him for help, or for advice as to what I should do. But there was nothing in response. Not a single thing. Not a word of reply, no letter, message, nothing . . .

"Frankly, with all my fears for your safety, I forgot all about it. But then suddenly, a week ago, the amanuensis of the Council of Galway arrived at Rockfleet with a contract, which I had to sign for you to be released. It was signed in my blood. That was when I promised not to attack the castle in reprisal, or we'd lose everything. Then, two days ago, a messenger appears at the castle gate, sent from the Governor of Galway, saying that the earl had been instructed to release you, and you were to be freed immediately. I jumped on a horse, and the rest you know. As to whether Sir Philip was able to do anything, I just don't have an idea, except for my guts telling me it's too much of a coincidence . . ."

"But Elizabeth wants my head," said Grace, still astonished at the revelations.

"I know, love, but maybe Elizabeth never got to hear of your imprisonment. Maybe Sir Philip is well connected at court and took the initiative himself. Either way, you are free, and that's all there is to it."

He covered her with a blanket and kissed her on the forehead. He had been shocked by her appearance. Her hair was grayer than when she'd left to go on her pirating mission; her skin was sallow and sickly, with pustules formed where she'd been bitten by lice and other vermin, and she'd lost a lot of weight. She thought about Sir Philip too. Richard wasn't certain whether the young English nobleman had intervened or not. But she was.

Had it not been for Richard and her son Tibbot, and her other children, especially Margaret, Grace knew she would have gone mad. Her release from prison hadn't assuaged the fury she felt at the indignities that had been heaped upon her by the Earl of Desmond and his jailers. Yet how could she wreak revenge without risking everything and spending the rest of her life impoverished?

It took Grace two full months of walking over the hills and through the valleys of her home to regain her strength. Two months of eating the very best of food, as much fat and meat as she could manage, and swimming in the cold waters of Clew Bay every morning.

Once she was fully restored, she called her man into the castle hall and said to him, "Richard. You can't attack Askeaton, but I can. I made no such bargain with Desmond, nor the Council of Galway, nor the Crown of England, nor anyone. I am the aggrieved party, and it's my right to revenge myself. And revenge myself I will!"

He nodded. "It was just a matter of time. Are you well enough? Has your strength returned?"

"I'm fine, darling. I have strength both of body and of purpose."

"Good. Then I'll hire a thousand Gallowglass and you'll take three hundred of our own men. I've been thinking more and more that he needs to be taught the lessons of retribution. What does it matter if we lose our castles? We're mighty enough to build other homes for ourselves and start again. The bastard should swing from a gallows for what he did to you, and I'll—"

She interrupted him. "No, I want no war, nor do I want any man of ours to die because of me. It's bad enough that Earl Desmond hung two of the sailors from my ship. Now I shall extract my revenge without further loss of Bourke or O'Malley life."

He began to argue, but she silenced him. "There are many ways of winning a battle. Yours is to pit one army against another. But the way I choose is guile. I want the Earl of Desmond to suffer bit by bit, hour by hour."

The hiding place she chose was far away on a hilltop, yet still within sight of the Castle Askeaton; it was sufficiently well hidden from the roads and local farmhouses that she was, to all intents, invisible. She even built a shelter for her nighttime fire, so that no flame could be seen from the nearby countryside, and the smoke would be invisible in the dark of the evening.

With her opticometer, she could see well into the castle, and knew the movements of the guards and the comings and goings of the staff. But she was waiting for several people in particular.

The first man against whom she would avenge the indignity of her incarceration appeared suddenly out of the castle gate almost at the very beginning of her secret encampment. It was the jailer who had cast her into the dungeon and watched her undressing before she had her bath. She watched him as he trudged up the long hill from the shores of the River Deel to the crest of the hill which then led down to the village of Ardagh.

The fat and ugly bastard stopped halfway up the hill to pull a flask out of his sack and refresh himself. He tore at a piece of loaf and chewed it as he trudged upward. Grace waited until he was just beyond the crest of the hill, not far from her encampment in the woods, and out of the sight of the guards on the ramparts of the castle. Then, in the quiet and still of the countryside, she began to sing a gentle Irish song, a ballad about a young girl who falls in love with a soldier who dies in battle. The jailer immediately heard the singing, and stopped. He looked around and stared into the thicket of trees, but could see nobody. "Who's there?" he called out aggressively.

But Grace simply continued singing, clutching a knife in case he should take fright and bolt back to the castle. She'd overtake him before he got twenty steps and skewer him.

"Who's that singing?" he said, this time a little more pleasantly, thinking that if his luck held, there might be an afternoon's dalliance with a local maiden. Grace simply continued to sing.

The jailer tentatively entered the copse of trees where Grace had hidden herself. He pushed his way through the bracken and foliage and over the fallen logs. He stopped and listened for the direction of Grace's voice. Then he continued, with greater keenness of step, walking deeper and deeper into the woods.

She could almost smell him from where she was lying, covered by undergrowth; he smelled of the dungeons, and her mind reeled from the horror of it. But she stopped herself from descending into the nightmare, for she was the hunter, and her prey was close at hand.

"Come on, girl, show yourself," he said, his voice attempting romance. He looked around, puzzled by the sudden silence, by the fact that he had clearly heard a girl's singing but she was nowhere to be seen.

In that instant Grace threw off the covering of undergrowth and sprinted the twenty paces to where he was standing, his back to her. He heard the cracking of twigs and the rustling of leaves, perceived the noise of someone running, turned, and reacted in horror as he saw a shape charging toward him like some demented animal.

He yelled out in shock and surprise, but it was too late, for Grace leaped upon him with a nightmare howl which froze his blood. Despite his size, she knew that the force of her body against his stationary frame would overwhelm him. He fell backward onto the ground, immobilized by the sudden ferocity and her weight which pinned him to the undergrowth. Grace raised her knee and thumped him aggressively in his most private parts. He yelled in pain, and began to double up. It was what she'd anticipated, for it enabled her to clutch both his legs and turn him over onto his front, just as though he was an animal she was wrestling to the ground. He was gasping for breath and began to scream with the pain.

After swift movements wrestling him so that his fat stomach, rather than his back, was toward the ground, she slashed her knife across the ligaments at the back of his legs and those at his ankles.

The jailer roared in pain, screaming his head off. Prepared for the commotion and concerned about drawing attention to where she was, Grace stuffed a kerchief in his mouth, and used rope to bind his hands behind his back. The man was only trussed by the arms, for his feet and legs were now useless.

Feeling strangely cold and distant, she watched him as he writhed on the earth, making muffled moaning noises, his eyes wide and white with fear, the pain from his groin and his legs and ankles threatening to overwhelm him. Grace then walked behind him and put her arms underneath his armpits, using all her strength to haul him to the nearby tree. She tied a rope around the tree, and then around his neck, so tightly that he was one step away from garrotting; but she didn't tie the rope so tightly as to kill him. That would come later.

Before she took the kerchief from his mouth, she whispered into his ear, "Remain silent, jailer, or I'll pull the rope more tightly around your neck, and kill you where you lie."

He looked at her, silent now, his eyes wide in fear at what this mad-woman would do next.

Slowly, she took the kerchief from his mouth. He remained silent, spittle dribbling from his lips, his eyes red with the stress of the pain.

"Do you recognize me, jailer?" she asked.

He was about to curse and threaten this evil harridan with all manner of deaths, but then he looked at her closely and as recognition dawned, what little blood was left in his face drained away.

She smiled. "That's right. I'm the woman you forced to shit and piss into her own clothes; I'm the woman you starved, the woman you watched lasciviously and forced into the indignity of undressing in front of you, so that you could ogle her body and think of what you'd like to do to her; the woman you treated worse than an animal. Well, jailer, my name is Grace O'Malley, and while you were thinking of all the things you'd like to do to me, I secretly promised myself that one day I'd return and wreak my revenge on you."

He started to shout, and she stuffed the kerchief back into his mouth. Then she opened his legs, and with her knife, cut his trews from his body, pulling them down so that she exposed his manhood. It was a puny manhood, a silly thing, all wrinkled and gnarled like a tiny old tree stump and half buried in an undergrowth of gray.

Then, with staves she'd found in the undergrowth and rope she'd brought with her, she staked his legs into the ground, secured them and poured fresh and sweet honey over his penis and scrotum.

Immediately he knew that he was in for the greatest agony a man could suffer.

"The ants are vicious around these parts, I understand. And the beetles, and the ravens, and no doubt there are nasty little animals in the undergrowth who'd just love a meal of honey mixed with your blood and guts. Anyway, I'm away to kill myself another member of the Earl of Desmond's household. I wish you a very unpleasant death," she said, and walked from him. All she heard was the sound of his muffled pleading.

It took her another day to capture and kill the captain of the guard. But she made his death swift and clean, for she'd satisfied her blood lust with the jailer and wanted to see no more of a man's agony. All she wanted was for him to know that his life was about to end, and that it was Grace O'Malley who was ending it. It was important to her that he knew who had killed him so that when he went up to God, he would give the Lord her name as his assailant and explain to Himself why she'd killed him. On the following day she captured two other guards who had been merciless to her. Both were killed. She had fantasized about killing the earl, but the implications for herself and for Richard were too horrible, and she had a better idea of how to destroy the man, in many ways more painful than killing him.

She hid the bodies of her victims in the undergrowth and concealed the evidence of her presence. Then she waited until two hours before nightfall and walked to the nearby village, where she surreptitiously stole a horse and cart. Grace returned to her secret encampment in the woods and hauled the four bodies onto the tray of the cart.

She looked at her handiwork. The jailer's face was a mask of shock and agony, the bloodless mouth gaping in pain and misery. His privates had been eaten away totally and the blood had drained from his body and out of his nether regions. Good! He deserved no better. His guts, too, had been pecked by animals or birds. The others had died swifter and cleaner, but they looked no less surprised.

She looked down at the castle. She could only surmise what was happening there as it was realized that four of its loyal servants, one after another, had disappeared. She wondered if the Earl of Desmond had been informed. She hoped so. But what she was about to do would tell the whole district of the sort of man he was, and from this moment on, he would be hated by everyone who knew him.

As best she could, Grace covered the dead bodies with a large horse blanket and led the horse and cart out of the woods and back onto the road. Then she walked it down the hill and toward the village. By now it was dark and she entered the village unseen by the villagers, who were either asleep in their beds, or drinking themselves into a stupor.

She left the horse hitched to a post in the middle of the village, threw off the blanket and put it over the animal so it wouldn't be cold during the night. And then she walked back to the woods, where she'd left her own horse. She would wait till sunrise and then ride swiftly back home. Her revenge was now complete.

When the villagers awoke in the early morning and left their homes to go to the well to draw water, they saw the smith's horse and cart, attached to a post just beyond the church. On it were four bodies. Curious, the early risers looked, and felt ill at the sight. The priest was called for, who made the sign of the cross before the gathering crowd but instructed nobody to touch the bodies of the murdered men.

Although he was loath to do it, for fear of his patron and master, the priest was forced to bow to the wishes of the infuriated population, who were demanding to know what message was written on the note which was attached to the body of one of the men.

None of them could read, and certainly not the Latin language in which the note was written.

It said, "*These men tortured an Irish woman by order of the Earl of Desmond. This is the revenge of all Irish women against such as the earl and his minions. From this day forth, any who serve the ends of the evil and ungodly Earl of Desmond shall meet a similar fate. Be warned!"*

Grace would have been gratified by the howls of fury and disgust with which the villagers greeted the note. Yes, she thought as she rode toward Galway, the Earl of Desmond would regret he had ever heard the name Grace O'Malley.

CHAPTER NINETEEN

Rockfleet Castle, 1586

Now, she felt old and alone. Now, she felt every one of her fifty-six years. She was tired and knew that soon God would allow her to rest forever; and her only sadness then would be that she wouldn't see her children any more. For after a lifetime of pirating and fighting and building up her treasury, for the first time in her life she realized, when it was too late to do anything about it, that she barely knew her children, although she loved them all with a passion. Owen and Murrough were captaining their own vessels, and she only saw them when they were in port. Margaret was married to a lovely man, the younger son of the O'Mulrians in the middle of the south of Ireland. She came to visit often, especially when her husband Fergal O'Mulrian was away in Dublin protecting his family inheritance from the rapacious English. Grace's one consolation was the son she bore with Richard. He had been named Tibbot of the Ships, because since his birth, he'd loved her fleet of vessels as much as she'd loved her father's ships when she was a girl. He was a lovely boy, growing to look just like his wonderful father, God rest his precious soul.

In these days of the winter of her life, Grace only just managed to confine her tears to the beginning and the end of the day, those times when she retired for the night and lay awake between her cold sheets, or when she awoke stroking his pillow and found it to be nothing more than a cold empty space; when she rose from her friendless bed and had to somehow garner the energy to begin the day. She would look at the portrait of Richard, a man to whom she'd been married for only a year, but with whom she'd lived for sixteen wonderful years, and her courage and strength would fail her, and she'd weep for the loss of such a good and generous man. He'd been dead for some years now, and she felt his loss as acutely as on the day he'd died.

In their last years together, when they'd fought the English incursions into Connaught and Richard had gained the MacWilliamship, making him the second most powerful leader in all of Ireland, he'd said to her oftentimes that when Jesus Christ determined that his brief existence on earth was over, he'd just love to die on the battlefield, riding a charger, surrounded by English mercenaries, slashing at all and sundry with his sword, and then suddenly, just at the moment when he was about to be pierced through the heart, he'd be plucked up by an angel like some Norse warrior and fly upward to his God, watched by all in the midst of the battle.

But it wasn't to be. One day they'd been at rest in a field on the shores of Clew Bay, watching the birds skimming across the water and talking about the mysteries of the hundred islands, when suddenly he'd clutched his heart and been unable to breathe. By the time she'd stood to call for help from the castle, he'd been thrashing about like a landed fish. He'd died in her arms, his face contorted in agony.

She'd clutched his dead body to her breast all morning and all afternoon, stroking his matted and thin hair with as much tenderness as if he'd been a newborn. Eventually she had roused herself and trudged the lonely way up the shore to the castle and instructed her menservants to retrieve the master's body and bring it back for burial.

So many years! And each day she'd kissed his portrait and brushed her cheek with the lock of hair she'd taken before he was inhumed, praying directly to him to watch over her and their lovely son, and to ensure that she maintained his strength of purpose and courage in the face of the coming adversity with the English.

Their success as a couple, as a team and as leaders of the Irish clans who opposed the English, had come close to leading to their downfall, because they had so denuded the Galway merchants of their income that the city nearly went into penury and had to borrow vast amounts from the Jews of Germany to pay its wages. So the lords of Galway had appealed to Elizabeth in London, and she'd sent over a force of her army to settle Mistress O'Malley and her lover Master Richard Iron Dick Bourke.

They'd laid siege to Rockfleet Castle, surrounding the place with hundreds of men; but Richard and she had long been made aware of their arrival and had mounted a sterling defense, assisted by hundreds of O'Malley men from over the bay. They'd sent the English packing with their guns between their legs and their courage left floundering in the gentle waters of Clew Bay.

That victory had raised the Bourke status no end, but my God, it had alienated the English. So furious were the lords of England and advisors to the Queen, that they determined to do something about Grace and the rebellious lords of northern Ireland.

Grace felt so old and tired, but she dried her eyes with a kerchief and stood to face the day. The first of the evil bastards sent to control the rebels was the newly appointed governor, Sir John Perrot. He was Queen Elizabeth's bastard half-brother, the illegitimate son of Henry VIII and a slut called Mary Berkley.

In the beginning Sir John had tried conciliation and reason with those Irish lords who would not bend their knees to the Crown of England, but when this policy failed, he went on a rampage throughout Ireland, warring against castles and causing mayhem. He had managed to confiscate vast tracts of lands in the area of Munster, and now these were rapidly being filled up with the sons of English gentlemen, eager to make their fortunes on the fertile soil of Ireland and by the sweat of Irish labor.

No better was the new Governor of Connaught, Sir Richard Bingham, who had no interest in conciliation but only in making the lords of the recalcitrant region bend to the will of his sword. And he had Grace O'Malley firmly placed in his sights. So evil was Sir Richard turning out to be, that he was eclipsing all previous governors and administrators in his lack of empathy with the Irish right to live on their own lands.

Grace had first been introduced to the awful Sir Richard Bingham two years earlier, just a year into her widowhood. They had hated one another on the spot.

An invitation had been sent to Grace by the Clanrickard to attend a reception in honor of Sir Richard. For some obscure reason, the Clanrickard had thought he could win over the man with pleasing company and good manners. The Clanrickard seemed to think that if Sir Richard walked into a house with a typically genteel English dining-room atmosphere, then he would feel well disposed and side with the estate of the Irish. How naïve that was.

Grace had accepted because of her interest in the man Elizabeth had chosen as her new overlord; stupidly she believed that he could be no worse than those who had gone before. How wrong she was!

When she arrived at the reception, she overheard a loud conversation conducted by a knot of men standing by the fireplace. One of them, in a very broad accent, which her experience with sailors from around England allowed her to identify as coming from Dorset, was saying, "No people was ever tamed with words, but only with swords. Those Irish who still defy Her Majesty will learn this to their regret."

She heard the commotion the speaker's remarks created and walked over to him. As she approached, the knot of men opened, and she saw a diminutive puffed-up little man standing before the fire, looking more like a portrait by Holbein, or some fancy courtier to the Queen of France, than a real person. He was more fox than person, shorter than her by a head and a half, dressed in the finest ruffs and laces, feathers and leathers she'd ever seen. Compared to Sir Richard, Grace felt as though she was a huge fisherwoman, crude and ill-mannered, unrefined and badly kept.

Sir Richard Bingham looked up at her and appeared to be scrutinizing her as the Clanrickard introduced her.

With a malevolent smile, he said, "So you're Grace O'Malley. Well, ma'am, I have to say honestly that from the exploits I've heard tell of you, both in England and here in Ireland, I expected an altogether younger woman. You're a lot older than I'd been led to believe. If all they say about you is true, I had expected to meet a woman half your age, not a gray-haired grand-matron."

She prickled at the insult. "I'm sorry to disappoint you, Sir Richard. I must say that I, too, am surprised at meeting you. It seems that Her Majesty has made a strange appointment, to give such a mighty office to a man of your underwhelming stature. I wonder if you have the size of boot to fill the station to which you've been appointed."

All present felt him bridle in fury. "I may have a small stature, ma'am, but I have the courage of a lion and the determination of a hound. Perhaps, madam, a man of my stature needs to deal with your husband, rather than with someone who should be at home, making the evening meal."

"Then, Sir Richard, your intelligence is very poor, because you'll either have a long or a very short wait, for my husband, both of my husbands, indeed, are dead and buried and in God's Heaven. Treat Ireland with this sort of typical English arrogance and scorn, and we Irish will take great pleasure in facilitating your meeting with both my husbands in the very near future."

Bingham was an educated man and had never been spoken to in this way, especially in polite company and by a woman. While he was fighting for the words to respond, Grace examined his features carefully. He had a fox's eyes, sharp and burrowing, and a mean and nasty snout for a nose, which gave him pinched and discomforting features. She shuddered involuntarily as he peered at her, trying to get her measure.

"I'm told, Mistress O'Malley, that you lead a force of many men, and that you employ Scottish mercenaries to do your bidding. I'm not certain whether or not you're aware of my past military record, but I have fought much in Scotland defending the name and honor of Her Majesty, as well as fighting in France and the Netherlands. I have met these men you employ as Gallowglass, and I find them greatly overrated as fighting men. Indeed, I have fought against many armies, and I must tell you that the Scottish are the least manly of them all."

Before she had a chance to reply, he continued, his voice gaining in volume to ensure that all in the room heard. "I am also called the hero of the Battle of Lepanto for my courage in that great battle where the Church of Christ was defending itself from the onslaught of the heathen Ottoman Turk. Thank God and Christ that because of men of my stature, we defeated them and left many thousands of black godless Turks floating in the waters off Greece."

She looked at him in disgust, thinking him like an animal marking its territory. Grace responded slowly, "I don't doubt your military prowess, nor your bravery, and neither do I doubt your martial skills, Sir Richard. I only doubt your ability to comprehend the mind of Ireland and your skill in understanding its people."

"Understanding its people, ma'am? Now why on earth should Her Majesty's chief commissioner want to understand the people? I'm here to administer English law, English might and English custom. To bring the light of God's Queen on earth shining into the Pope-darkened corners of this bogland. My job is to impose the dictates of Her Majesty upon her subject Irish, regardless of their mind or their will, and by sword if necessary."

She was about to damn him to Hell when both he, and she, were saved from further discussion by the Lord MacDonagh whose lands were to the northeast, who immediately realized that if the new chief commissioner was to begin his rule in a state of hostility with the lords of this area of Ireland, there'd be no end to his fury. In pacification, he said, "Tell me, Sir Richard, now that the Queen's one-time intended husband, the Duke Francis of Anjou, has just died, is there another suitor on the horizon to sit beside Her Majesty?"

The little fox turned slowly, his eyes still staring at Grace until he decided to ignore her and address the MacDonagh. "Her Majesty is the Virgin Mary of England. The Catholics who were once the scourge of England, especially under the evil Mary Tudor, are in disrepute and in full disrepair. They are an isolated rabble, and have lost their own Virgin, the mother of the Lord Jesus, who has been shown to be a false idol. But Elizabeth is the embodiment of the Mother of Christ, virginal, pristine, faultless. So to answer your question, my lord, I must tell you that to think of our queen knowing a man in a carnal sense is simply unconscionable. No, my lord, there will be a queen alone on the throne of England until God takes Her Majesty."

MacDonagh sensed that Grace was about to say something treasonous, and he impolitely kicked her in the ankle. She winced, but held her peace.

It became obvious from the first few weeks of Bingham's arrival that his intention, maybe even his instructions from London, was to make the lords of Connaught kneel to the weight of the English boot, and if he had to use excessive and deadly force to achieve the aims of the Crown of England, then so be it.

One of his first acts as chief commissioner was the theft of the Castle Ballymote, fifteen miles to the south of Sligo, the ancestral home of both the O'Connors and the MacDonaghs, depending on which family was in the ascendancy at the time. For some time it had been in the possession of the O'Connors, who had beaten off the MacDonaghs in a fierce fight from which they were only just recovering. But the English Crown decided to claim the strategically placed castle for itself, and Sir Richard Bingham was given the task of securing it.

With the passion of an evangelist, Sir Richard took seven hundred English troops, and marched south, through Ulster and Connaught to Sligo, where he laid siege to the castle. By force of arms, as well as the systematic murder of local villagers before the castle gatepost in an attempt to demoralize the defenders within, it took him a mere two weeks to force his entry. He murdered most of the defenders, women as well as men, and immediately installed his brother, George Bingham, as custodian and occupant.

Word of Sir Richard's assault spread like a brushfire of anger and consternation throughout all Ireland. Even the Lord Governor of Ireland, Sir John Perrot, wrote to him asking him to desist from killing so many innocents. Yet despite the criticism of what the man had done and the deaths he'd caused, he was anything but repentant.

Indeed, nothing deterred him from shaking the ferocious sword of England at the Irish people, and Sir Richard wrote to all the lords of Connaught and Sligo, the MacSweeny and the O'Dogherty, the O'Connor and the O'Ruairc, and all the other chieftains in the north of Ireland.

Noble Lords of Ireland. Resist the command and rule of Elizabeth, by the Grace of God Queen and Supreme Monarch of England, and destruction will be your re-

ward, your lands will be made barren, your fields salted and useless for ten gener-
ations, your people slaughtered and your treasuries ruined. Accept the command and
rule of Elizabeth, and you will prosper and find your place among the mighty of the
world. God Save the Queen.

When the letter was delivered to the door of Rockfleet Castle, Grace O'Malley read it several times, trying to contain her fury before composing a reply.

The messenger took it from her and rode swiftly back to his master, knowing that Sir Richard was particularly keen to read Grace's response. Despite his mound of correspondence, Bingham immediately broke the seal of her letter and read what the Queen of Pirates and chief mischief-maker of Ireland had written. Then he cursed an oath to God about what he'd do to the shrewish hobgoblin of a woman, screwed up the letter and threw it over his shoulder toward the open fire. It missed, and bounced harmlessly onto the floor, near to his dog which was lying inert close to the inglenook.

Sir Richard's secretary picked it up, intent on carrying out his master's wishes, but curiosity forced him surreptitiously to open it, and what he read nearly made him cough with convulsions. The harridan fishwife of Connaught had written in Latin:

> *Sir Richard. It's often said that the larger a man's mind, the smaller his manhood.*
> *I suspect that you have a very large manhood, for you undoubtedly have a very small*
> *mind. If you continue on your present course of depriving my fellow countrymen*
> *of their property and their lives, then one day soon it will be my pleasure to display*
> *your manhood above my fireplace for the lords and ladies of Ireland to laugh at.*
> *Grace O'Malley.*

All the indications throughout that first year of Sir Richard's suzerainty were that he had in mind an assault on Rockfleet Castle. Twice he'd ridden his army close to the borders of Grace's land. And twice she'd been forced to call together her men in order to mount a defense, only to be told that Sir Richard's army had decamped and moved on.

He'd ridden through the nearby towns and villages requisitioning cattle and sheep to feed his men, robbing fields of the food the peasants needed to survive, and administering summary justice to any who dared to cross his path. On occasion, Grace had reports that men had been dragged from their homes on some minor pretext, and hung from some nearby tree, until they were almost, though not quite, dead. Then, while gasping for breath and pleading for mercy, they were drawn by a sharp sword from the top to the bottom of their stomachs and their innards cut out and burned before their eyes; then they were beheaded and their bodies quartered and delivered back into the village as a warning to the local inhabitants not to even consider an uprising.

Hundreds of villagers appeared at Grace's door each month to beg for her protection. She sent them all away with the assurance that she would cause all the other lords of Ireland to rise up and to overthrow this bastard messenger from Hell if it was the last thing she did.

But she hadn't counted on just how cunning and evil Sir Richard could be. The news came to her early one morning, when she had dressed and left the bedroom, drying her eyes from her mourning of Richard, and straightening her trews and clothes to present herself to her family and the castle staff.

She kissed her daughter Margaret good morning, and was just sitting down at the table to eat her oatmeal and bread, when there was a fearful racket at the door; someone was banging for admission. Her heart dropped. It would almost certainly be another claimant reporting some injustice, or yet another tale of what Sir Richard had done. She heard scurrying in the bowels of the castle, and tried to enjoy her food while the sounds of footsteps on the stone stairs grew louder and more insistent.

Margaret began to talk to her about ending her visit and returning to her home in the south, when the castellan coughed and begged for admission. Grace waved him over.

"An urgent message, ma'am. Will you see the bearer?"

Grace nodded, and the rider came walking diffidently forward. She'd seen him before, when Sir Richard Bingham had first arrived in Connaught; in sudden shock and consternation, Grace recognized him as Sir Richard's amanuensis.

She didn't ask him to sit down, nor offer him refreshments, for she saw by the look on the man's face that he was grievously troubled. She prepared herself for bad news.

"My name is Master Dawson. I am secretary to Sir Richard Bingham, Governor of Connaught. I am sent on an urgent dispatch by Sir Richard, though it troubles me greatly to be the bearer of such news."

Closed-lipped, she said, "It's your duty, Master Dawson, to tell me as quickly as you can what is the purpose of your visit."

"It concerns your son, Tibbot."

Grace froze. She heard Margaret gasp. Tibbot had been gone these past three days to Sligo, visiting his cousin, Edmond, who had promised to take the lad hunting.

"My son? What of my son?" she asked.

The Englishman coughed, patently uncomfortable. "He was returning from Sligo when he was found by a party sent out by Sir Richard to ensure the good peace of the land. He was taken to Sir Richard . . ." And then he appeared to break down, as though the terrible news had been building up inside him. In a quivering voice he said, "I hate to be the bearer of such news of your son, ma'am. Forgive me, Mistress O'Malley, but I am a father myself, and I know what this awful news would do to me."

"Tell me of my son, damn you."

"The lad was walking back from Sligo . . ."

She fought to remain calm. Tibbot was little more than a lad, yet he'd insisted that he was old enough to visit Edmond, accompanied by only one servant. Why had she allowed him to go? She held her breath as she waited for the rest of the news.

"He's been taken, ma'am. Little more than a boy and he's been kidnapped by Sir Richard. I tell you, ma'am, I can't abide any more of the violence. I was raised to a life of prayer and should have been a man of the cloth, but my family couldn't afford . . ."

He coughed and tried to contain his anxiety. "Your son has been taken by Sir Richard. Sent to the castle of his brother Sir George. And I've been sent with a message to you, ma'am, which is that you are to attempt no rescue, for if you do, the boy will be killed immediately. If you trespass near to the castle, the boy will surely die. Sir Richard wants you to be in no doubt."

Margaret gripped her mother's arm, but Grace was sufficiently calm to ask, "Did Sir Richard say anything else?"

"That the boy would be brought up as an English gentleman, ma'am, sent to London and be taught how to read and write, and that he'd have the stench of the bog and the insolence of the Irish beaten out of him. That's all, ma'am."

Grace turned slowly to Margaret, and said with a terrible sorrow, "I don't know what's worse, him being killed by Sir Richard or brought up as an Englishman."

Grace hadn't seen Sir Richard for some time, but she remembered his eyes as she entered his library. They were the eyes of an animal, a nighttime predator stalking its prey.

"Mistress O'Malley, thank you for accepting my invitation and joining me," he said, his sincerity patently artificial.

"You have my son, Sir Richard. I want him back."

The secretary escorted her to a chair before Sir Richard's escritoire. The little governor remained silent, arranging the papers on his desk, looking at her.

"I assume there is a price to be paid. What price my lovely boy, Sir Richard? What do I have to pay for the return of the son of Richard Bourke, my most precious memory of a great man?"

"Such an ugly thing, to haggle over price. Like fisherwomen arguing over the penny worth of a catch. Please, ma'am, have some port wine. It's very good."

From the decanter, he poured her a glass and one for himself.

They remained silent, Sir Richard sipping his port, Grace waiting to know what price a mother had to pay for her children in an Ireland ruled by the English.

"What crime has my son committed?"

"The crime of being Irish."

"Is it a crime to be born as a free citizen of a country?"

"Yes, if that country refuses to bow to the wishes of its masters from over the seas."

"I will not argue with you, Sir Richard, for that is not the point of my being here. I want to know how to release my son from your custody."

He sipped his wine, savoring both the drink and the moment. "Hand over title of your castles and land to the Crown of England. Your son will be returned. You will be given a title of lady to the English court. You will pay taxes to the Crown, and allow your land and its animals to be used by the English army and navy at our will. You will defend Connaught against the enemies of the Queen. You will not allow any Spaniard to use Ireland as a means of attacking England. You will swear a blood oath of loyalty to Elizabeth Regina. You will become a member of the Church of England and renounce Catholicism forever for yourself and all your kin. You will swear to fight by England's side should she be attacked by any enemy. Then, and only then, ma'am, will Tibbot be returned to you."

Grace knew as much already, for these were similar bargains made with other lords of Ireland.

"And if I refuse?" she asked tentatively.

He smiled. "The death of your son would be a swift and sudden way of causing you great pain . . . and great resentment. And I fear that he would make a martyr for the whole of this area of Ireland. To kill a village full of peasants is something that people forget in a matter of days, but to kill the son of a chieftain is something which will be written in the annals of Irish history forever.

"No, I think for Grace O'Malley, the slow and painful death of her son is nowhere near as attractive to Gloriana as is his slow and painful life. He will be taken to England where he will be imprisoned and indentured to the household of a great and noble lord. He will become an English gentleman. He will return to Ireland in a few years and will reject his family and his homeland for he will look upon you for the peasants that you are. You see, Mistress O'Malley, your son will have been shown a life which someone of your position couldn't even begin to imagine. A life of such riches and opulence, of such culture and prosperity, that he will be dazed as though he has looked upon the sun. Give in now, Grace O'Malley, or lose your son to us forever. The choice is yours."

Grace stood and walked from the room. She didn't want this hideous little cunny of a man to see the tears beginning to well up in her eyes.

Although Grace knew that Tibbot was being held at Castle Ballymote, she also knew that any attempt to rescue him would lead to his death. So she had to rely on subterfuge. At first, she managed to persuade one of the grooms to carry her notes into the castle, notes designed to help her son maintain his courage; but a sergeant-at-arms found the note when he undertook a search of the groom's possessions. Tibbot was moved that very night to the east coast of Ireland.

It was only two weeks later that a messenger was sent by Sir Richard to inform her, curtly and arrogantly, that Tibbot was now in London, where he would be instructed in the wherewithal of the great houses. The note explained that because she had communicated with him, and "enthused him with the disease of being Irish", the process of making him English would be accelerated.

"Nial!" Grace screamed when she'd read the note. "Nial Morrigan. Come here immediately."

She screwed up Sir Richard's note and threw the hateful thing into the fire, where it briefly flared.

She heard the sound of scuffling feet from three floors below, and screamed again, "Nial Morrigan! Where are you, you blasted godforsaken rude-growing bum-bailey? Come here when your mistress calls."

She walked closer to the fire, glad of its warmth on her body. She was still solidly built, but now that she was elderly and her blotched skin didn't quite fit her muscles, she felt the cold something fierce, and then there were the aches in her knee which often kept her awake at night.

At last her estate manager appeared, flush-faced from running up the stairs. "God Almighty, but what's the matter, mistress?"

"The matter is that the fuchking cunny-faced little urchin-snouted snipe of a governor of ours has been true to his word; not only has he abducted my son, but he's done what he said he'd do and taken him to England. And I intend to get him back!"

Still puffed from running, the manager said, "I'll get quill and paper and we'll write a—"

"Writing be damned. I'll not write and beg. Get me my ship ready. I'll take *The Maid of Roscommon*. She's the best and fastest galleon I've got. Get a crew together. Experienced sailors and fighters. Good rowers, too, for when there's no wind. I want a quick trip to England."

Nial Morrigan's eyes widened in shock. "You're not thinking—"

"I am. I'm going to England, to demand the return of my son from the Queen herself. She was once the child of a loving parent. She'll understand . . ."

"Are you stupid, woman?" he said, forgetting the difference in their ranks. "She's a virgin with no children. She'll never understand what a mother feels. She's the Queen of England and she's forcing all the sons and daughters of Ireland into slavery. Why should she release the child of her enemy?"

"She'll understand right enough when I talk to her. And talk to her I shall, Nial. Nobody stands between Grace O'Malley and one of her children!"

"And what makes you think she'll see you, mistress? Do you think that she has time to discuss the son of one of her minor enemies, when Philip of Spain is plotting to invade England? You've heard tell the stories. Every sailor knows what's happening, so you can be sure as God made Ireland that Elizabeth knows it too. They say he's putting together the greatest flotilla of all time, bigger than the Persians took against the Greeks in ancient time. With all that to occupy her mind, what in God's name makes you think she'll devote even the blinking of an eye to worrying about some sprat caught in the Irish Sea, Tibbot or not?"

Grace remained silent. She knew that England was beset by difficulties, but that was the whole point. For the last thing that Elizabeth needed was another problem to appear over the horizon in the west when she had storm clouds billowing in the south.

Softly, she said, "Just get the ship ready, Nial. I want to sail on the morning tide."

•   •   •

She sailed south from Mullaghmore Harbor, skirting Galway by many leagues to avoid any confrontation with the city authorities, some of whom still hated her sufficiently to dally with the idea of impaling her head on a seawall pike to warn off other pirates.

She made south, past the Earldom of Desmond, where she spat into the waters in hatred of the man who had once imprisoned her. Further south, past the Knight of Kerry and the O'Sullivan and the MacCarthy Mor and then east past Kinsale and Cork, sea with which she was familiar, sea where she had spent decades waylaying ships and stealing their cargoes and then running for cover when the naval boats appeared over the horizon.

But before she headed southeast to sail into the channel which divided England from France, she was forced to make a quick trip to Dublin, and to put in at the port of Howth. She had left Connaught so quickly that the quartermaster hadn't had time to fit out the ship properly, and sailing into the waters off the English coast would possibly demand more shot and powder than he had been able to put on board in the short time he'd been given. Even the local providor needed another day to re-stock the ship adequately.

Tired from lack of sleep and not enough rest while preparing for the sea voyage around the coast, they sailed north until at last they sighted the turrets and keeps of Dublin's port. Howth was a bustling and friendless place, one she preferred not to tarry in too long. She knew it of old; it was dirty and disease was rampant and the men of Howth were a surly and incommodious bunch of dogs and footpads and cutthroats.

The following day, Grace sailed south to the southern coast of Ireland until she was hidden within the deep water which was common sea to the Irish, English and French nations; but instead of heading further south as she so often had done in the past when sailing to the warmth and riches of France or Spain or Portugal, she ordered course to be set for the waters of England, seas which were mysterious and worrisome to her.

She and her crew had rarely sailed this close to the southern coast of England. They'd traded with the northwestern ports of England and also with all the major ports of Scotland, but England was the enemy, the nation from which she and her ships fled when chased by some hubristic admiral.

Grace had fought against the English navy, against English merchantmen, against English traders for most of her life; she'd resisted the encroachment of England into Ireland, and stood square beside her husband Richard when they'd fought off the English army. But now she was no longer on Irish soil. Now she was entering the realm of England, and would be standing head to head with a woman whose power was truly awesome, who wore jewels and dresses which alone were valued at more than the worth of a thousand sheep, who had the power to decapitate the Scottish Queen with the stroke of a pen, who could change the course of her nation's history at her whim.

And Grace was nothing more than a minor chieftain of some minor clans in a minor country which was now a minor part of the growing English empire.

Right at this very moment, England was beset with more problems than she'd ever known. What if Philip of Spain became more than merely a threat, if his huge armada, being made ready in the ports of Spain, set sail to put right the Catholic world? Then Queen Elizabeth would be forced to go to war, and all her other problems would be swept aside and would count for nothing.

This was either a propitious time, or it was the worst time imaginable to pursue her hopes of releasing Tibbot. But Grace had to do something, for she had to save the soul of her son from being contaminated by England. And so she found herself sailing above a deep and dangerous ocean into unknown waters, intent on doing battle with the mightiest woman, not just in England but in all of the world.

CHAPTER TWENTY

Westminster Palace, 1586

Queen Elizabeth watched in irritation as the foreign doctor cautiously pried the leech off her knee, slowly and carefully goading its suckers from her skin so that the leech came away intact and nothing of its tiny teeth were left behind. Once, when he was a very young doctor studying contagion in Verona under the maestro, Hieronymus Fracastorius, Piet van Leewen had been too inexperienced and presumptuous in pulling the leech out of the arm of an elderly woman whose humors were out of balance and who showed the symptoms of melancholia. The whole of the leech's mouth had stayed in the skin of the woman, and within days she was swollen and black, and not even Fracastorius himself could restore the woman's humors and prolong her life. Ever since, van Leewen had been slow and painstaking in his application and removal of leeches.

Elizabeth was glad he was taking his time, for although she had been leeched many times before, she still felt a revulsion when she saw the evil tiny beast growing ever larger, filling up on her blood, and she would have been utterly horrified if any part of the nasty thing had been left in her skin.

The aches in her legs and her hips were now crippling, and although the leech had been placed on the soft part of her knee by this Dutch doctor for an hour each morning and an hour each night during the past twenty days, the damnable and painful swellings still continued, making sitting uncomfortable and walking an agony.

She demanded to know whether the treatment had worked this time. The Dutch physician had been sent over from the Netherlands by Robert Dudley to treat her, with the assurances that van Leewen had been of great benefit in helping to relieve the pains from his stomach which were so troubling to him.

The doctor looked at the Queen's still-swollen knee and smiled in apology. He began to explain that this sort of treatment often took time, and that Her Majesty must have patience.

"Patience!" Elizabeth shouted. "Patience? Be damned to patience, sir. What good is this leech, Master Doctor, when I still can't walk without the pains of childbirth in my knee and hip? Are you a fraudster, despite all your leeches and your bleedings and your proddings? Where is poor John Caius when I need him—dead and gone to his Maker! And now I have you and other quacksalvers who prod me and prick me and bleed me and leech me, and still I feel no better."

In sudden fury—more the result of the news from Spain than the poor physician's attempts to heal her pains—she lifted her foot and pushed him rudely away. The physician sprawled backward onto the floor, and his robes and cap went flying. All arms and legs, he looked like a deer that had just been brought down by an arrow.

Amused by the sight, Elizabeth started to laugh, as did her court. The doctor stood and tried to reorder his gowns and regain some semblance of dignity.

He began to speak, but the Queen talked over him, saying, "Go away from us, Doctor, and return to Holland. Go and practice your knavery on your own countrymen. England needs no help from such as you. We have our own and finest doctors in our court, each quite able to bend his own knee to his queen, as well as helping us to bend ours."

The man turned, red-faced and insulted, and walked away. The Queen watched him go, and turned to Sir Philip Sidney, who was standing beside her.

"What do you think, young Sir Philip?"

"About the physician, Highness? I think he served you better bent at your feet than bending your knee."

She nodded, but she was saddened, for tomorrow Sir Philip would go to Holland and fight the Spaniards beside Lord Dudley. Now two of her favorite men, one young and bursting with ambition, the other ambitious but by now too old to fulfill his dreams and too sick to last out the year, would be lost to her. True, Robert had been lost to her when he married Lettice Knollys, that silly and pretty woman, but she had forgiven him, though she would never look kindly upon Lettice again.

She loved Sir Philip with all her heart. Such a clever, witty boy. So young and handsome and virile. Such an excellent horseman, so good at the joust and the tilts and the tourneys. And so good with words. His energetic and passionate and, in parts, very naughty *Astrophel and Stella* was a work which she often read in bed, at night, alone.

She shuddered when she looked at Sir Philip and thought of all the many pleasures she had denied herself because she was the Virgin Queen. She didn't want Sir Philip to be away from court; she needed him here, beside her, to comfort and guide her. For England was now facing her greatest ever threat. That traitorous Scottish whore, Mary, had named Philip of Spain successor to the English and Scottish crowns when eventually she became Queen of England . . . treasonous, villainous, traitorous harlot.

For what would happen to England if Elizabeth was to order the beheading of Mary? Philip would surely sail to England with the huge fleet he was building, and fight to claim his ownership. And the Pope would no doubt collude and pontificate about the rightness of Philip's cause to overthrow the Protestant rule of Elizabeth and make all England Catholic.

If Mary was freed—or executed—there would be nothing to stop Philip from attacking. The succession of Mary, the fact that England was Protestant and not Catholic, and the continuous attacks against his treasury and trade from English pirates and merchantmen had driven Philip to desperation. Soon, Elizabeth knew, he would unleash his fury and he would attack with everything in his power. The only thing stopping him was the safety of Scottish Mary, and if Elizabeth allowed her to be beheaded, then God help England.

The threats which Philip was making were so sharp and evil that if he did launch this fleet, how would she ever be able to defend her people? They had not the ships, nor the crews, nor the defenses to protect the whole of the English coastline. Where would they defend? Portsmouth, Dover, Plymouth, Liverpool, the Port of London? Would he attack from the south via France, from the west in Ireland or from the east, via Holland, aided by the Duke of Palma who was causing such havoc in the Netherlands? Elizabeth knew that the duke had tens of thousands of battle-hardened men who would set sail if accompanied by Philip's armada of ships, and they would land in the east coast and hack and kill and pillage their way through the nation until they reached the seat of her government in London. Then they would conquer the palaces and kill all her good cousins and friends, her noble courtiers and landsmen, and most likely herself too, and then the Catholics would again be in control of England, and the lights of joy and laughter would be extinguished.

She was distracted from her worries by a gentle cough from Sir Philip, who indicated that her court was awaiting her pleasure, and that her dress was still pulled up above her knees from the leeching.

Elizabeth straightened her dress and glanced around the court. So many young people, so vibrant and happy. Painters and poets; singers and sculptors; mathematicians and astrologers and philosophers from throughout the world had come to her court, some by invitation, most because they'd heard that Elizabeth's palaces were alive with gaiety and inquiry and a pleasing mixture of serious thought and good-hearted banter.

She restrained her smile, for there was still much about her court which she despised—the backstabbing and favoritism and nepotism, though God knew she was the worst offender, but she was the Queen, and it was both her kingdom and her right to promote those on whom she could count.

Elizabeth took a deep breath and indicated that it was time for her to begin her official audiences. These would last till lunchtime, when she would retire to her privy chambers and eat a meal in the company of a book or state papers.

The afternoon would be taken up with horseriding, for even though she was fifty-three years old, she still liked to ride at least a few hours every day for the feeling of good country air on her cheeks; then she would return to more state duties, or preside at her council; an entertainment in the evening—a dance or a masque or, better, a banquet—and then to bed at one or two of the clock. And to sleep. She yawned and scratched her neck.

"Well, Secretary Walsingham," she said to the man whose extensive and very costly—costly to him, that was—spy network had detected all plots against her, and who was the most strident in calling for Mary's execution. "What business attends us this morning?"

Sir Francis unfurled his order of precedence, read briefly, and said, "Your Majesty, Sir George Bingham, brother of Your Highness's chief commissioner in the county of Sligo in Ireland, has recently come to London, and craves an audience. He brings with him one Tibbot of the Ships, a young Irishman whom he wishes to place in the custodianship of a peer of the English realm, for reasons of educating the boy and breeding out of him his Irishness."

"Tibbot of the Ships? An unusual name."

Walsingham nodded. "Indeed, Majesty. The boy's real name is Tibbot, son of Richard Bourke and Grace O'Malley, female chieftain—if there is such a position in Ireland—of Connaught."

Elizabeth thought for a moment. Grace O'Malley? Now where had she heard that name before? She had been queen for these nearly thirty years, and she must have met with thousands of people who had come to pay homage. And then she remembered. A pirate woman. Grace O'Malley. She'd robbed Elizabeth of a fortune in cargo destined for the English treasury. And since then, every few years, word had come to her of this damnable woman, who led a navy of cutthroat Irishmen in flagrant violation of Elizabeth's right to the free passage of her navies around Scotland and Ireland. This pirate woman was also active in Spain and Portugal, carrying large quantities of sherry and port wine and selling it in the north of England, offending those to whom Elizabeth had sold the sole and exclusive rights to trade in the wines. Yes, thought Elizabeth, now she well remembered Mistress Grace O'Malley and her interference in the good governance of England.

She looked at Walsingham and nodded formally. "Very well, Master Secretary. Command Sir George Bingham to attend upon me. We are interested to see the son of Mistress O'Malley and determine what shall be done with him."

Sir Francis looked up from his list and nodded to his servant at the back of the room. There was a scurry of feet in the audience hall, and the sound of doors opening. Halberds were banged upon the floor and commands shouted through echoing corridors for Sir George Bingham to attend upon Her Royal Majesty. Then the crowd of courtiers parted as a fat man, wrapped in a blue cloak, walked imperiously through them. He stopped halfway and bowed low to the feet, taking off his hat and sweeping the floor with it. It was a studied action, thought Elizabeth, no doubt practiced a dozen times in the antechamber while he was waiting for admittance. She was amused, but kingship forbade her to show her disdain for country bumpkins putting on courtly manners.

But of more interest to Elizabeth was the youth who walked in the wake of the self-important man. He was a tall, gangly boy of indeterminate age, maybe twelve, maybe sixteen, who didn't bow before Her Majesty, but instead stood there in the middle of the aisle, looking in curiosity and scorn at the royalty of the English court and its throne.

In her twenty-eight years as a monarch, Elizabeth had observed the many emotions and feelings experienced by the people who came before her; those unused to the pomp and circumstance of the court were often cowed before its magnificence. But not this boy! No, he was anything but cowed . . . or bowed!

Here was a boy who looked at Elizabeth with . . . with what, she wondered? Contempt? No, there wasn't contempt in his face. Hatred? Nor hatred. No, in this boy's face was sadness. She could have commanded him to bow. But what price such a minor victory?

Sir George straightened up and rejoined his cap to his head, the feather in it having suffered from its brush with the floor. He walked majestically toward the throne, the boy from Ireland following in his wake. When he came to the plinth, he stood still and began his practiced words.

"Great and most majestic Queen, Gloriana, Royal Majesty and glory of the world, regal virgin and mother to your beloved people, Magnificat and—"

"Yes, thank you, Sir George. I am aware of my titles and my magnificence. You are returned from Ireland? How are things in that unhappy land?"

"Majesty, the people of Ireland fall to their knees before your munificence and thank the Lord God in Heaven that He has sent them a true and much-beloved queen to save them from the servitude which—"

"Then why is there still such opposition to my rule, Sir George? Why is it that your brother, Sir Richard Bingham, continues to put fear into the hearts of the people by killing them and murdering them and purloining their property? Why are you living in the Castle Ballymote, which was stolen from the Lords O'Connor and MacDonagh, and causing the people to hate you? Why has Sir Richard set upon a policy of murder and mayhem instead of winning the people over with firmness, yet with understanding?"

Like a fish just landed in a boat, Sir George stood there, his mouth agape, then closed, then agape once more. How did she know so much? Did she have spies in Connaught? He'd come prepared with a story, but her intelligence would make him out to be a liar.

"Majesty . . ." he spluttered.

"Understand this, Sir George. There is nothing I do not know about my lands, my territories and my possessions. If a man steals a trinket from another in a hamlet in the remotest part of the county of Cornwall, Elizabeth will know of it. If a priest dallies with a member of his flock in a village in Northumber-landshire, Elizabeth will know of it. And if one of my commissioners and governors, even in the furthest part of my realm, even in remote Connaught in Ireland, acts as if the crown was on his head and not on mine, then Elizabeth knows of it."

She looked coldly at him. She repeated the words, "Elizabeth knows of it."

The fat and ungainly man stood still, but he could hear the titters of amusement throughout the hall. From confidently entering the audience chamber as brother to the Queen's master of a foreign land, he was suddenly a figure of ridicule, a man completely out of place and ill-at-ease.

He turned and saw that the boy he'd brought with him, Tibbot, was still standing instead of kneeling as he'd commanded in the antechamber.

"Kneel before the Queen of England," he shouted to Tibbot. But the boy merely stood there and looked at Sir George.

"Kneel!" he commanded.

"Sir George," said Queen Elizabeth, "this is my court and I decide who shall stand and who shall kneel. Come here, boy. While Sir George tries to find the answers to my questions, come closer that I might see you better. These eyes aren't as sharp as once they were."

The boy refused to move, and so Sir Francis Walsingham stepped forward and took him by the elbow, gently encouraging him to stand close to the base of the Queen's thronal plinth.

"You are the son of the pirate Grace O'Malley?" said Elizabeth.

At the mention of his mother's name, Tibbot's eyes widened. He nodded. "My mother is Grace O'Malley, Chieftain of Connaught," he said, loudly and with pride.

"Why is your mother a pirate? This seems a most disagreeable occupation for a woman."

"No more disagreeable than being a queen who steals other people's lands," he said, his voice maintaining its confidence despite being shrill with youth.

The court gasped. Even Sir Francis Walsingham was taken aback by the boy's deadly treason. He was about to cuff him around the ears, when Elizabeth said, "How much you say, boy, yet how little you know. We are not in the habit of punishing puppies; rather we shall punish the bitch who gave birth to you."

The court roared in laughter, and applauded. Tibbot turned in confusion, not understanding what had been said, nor why it was funny.

"I ask you again, sir. Why is Grace O'Malley a pirate instead of owning land submitted to me and regranted to herself?"

"She is a pirate because you English are robbing us in Ireland of what is ours by right," he said.

Elizabeth listened carefully. She had to deal with the child, for the court was listening for her response. What right did Elizabeth have to plunder Ireland? The right of a king, she thought.

"By what right?" replied the Queen. "My father Henry gave your chieftains and ruling lords in Ireland the God-ordained right to be English! And as though that was not enough, he gave them English titles and the rights to their land in return for tithes and taxes. Ireland is a part of a great and growing empire, the English Empire, which one day will rival and exceed that of Spain. Yet your mother and many like her fight against me, causing much bloodshed and death and unhappiness. Is this what your mother wants for Ireland?"

"No," replied the lad. "We just want to be left in peace."

Sir Francis could bear it no longer. Such lack of respect from a child toward a monarch would become the stuff of legends in the courts of Spain and France and Holland.

"How dare you speak in this way to Her Majesty?" he shouted, and moved forward with surprising speed, boxing the boy's ears. Tibbot sprang back in shock. "Stand down, boy. Kneel before the greatest monarch on earth."

He pushed the boy's head down, and Tibbot fell to his knees. At the same moment, the still-terrified and quivering Sir George Bingham collapsed, and he too fell to the floor, groveling before Elizabeth. A hush fell over the entire audience hall, as courtiers looked on in bemusement.

Queen Elizabeth looked at both figures before her. "So, the lamb of Ireland and its wolf are prostrate before the bare of England," she said, noticing that one of her legs was still partially uncovered from her time with the Dutch doctor. She straightened her dress, her knees continuing to ache from the pains she suffered.

Again, the court laughed and applauded. Elizabeth acknowledged their appreciation.

"However, King Henry sent no great army over to Ireland to conquer and subdue the inhabitants, but rather encouraged them to join us in a commonweal, allowing them to be English in return for their tributes."

Irritated at talking to two kneeling heads, she said, "Arise, Sir George, and face your queen."

Bingham rose stiffly to his feet.

"Well, Sir George? Or are you Saint George and do you treat Ireland as a dragon which you're intent on slaying? You seem to have murdered and pillaged

your way into the hatred of the Irish people, whereas my father Henry conquered an entire nation with guile and subtlety. Surely this is a better way of
dealing with an intransigent and stiff-necked people. Look at the love which exists today between England and Scotland now that bloody and Catholic Mary
is incarcerated and no longer a tyrant to her people. Today we enjoy a close and
peaceful harmony between our two nations, and we greatly love our nephew
King James of Scotland."

She looked at the little fat man before her. "Well, Sir George? How often
do I have to repeat myself? Tell me why your brother, our commissioner, is
killing so many Irishmen and women . . . and children?"

Sir George felt as if his legs had turned to liquid.

"You, sir!" she said to Tibbot, who was still kneeling. A guard stepped
forward and pulled him up onto his feet. The boy looked at the Queen. "Before our good Saint George informs us of the future of your dragon-like
country as seen through his eyes, you, sir, need the nourishment of education
so that you learn far more about England than the sour and curdled milk
which came from that perverted breast from which Mistress Grace O'Malley
has fed you. Sir George, young Tibbot of the Ships will be sent to the house
of the Earl of Ashby, where he will be a servant to his lordship, and from
him he will learn what it means to be given access to the might and privilege
of the English peerage. And perhaps with this knowledge he will return to
Ireland and tell all those who oppose us of the benefits of bowing their knee
to our will."

With a nod, the Queen told her guards to take the boy away. She was happy
with her decision. The Earl of Ashby was a gentle and learned man, and Tibbot
would go to him with a note from her instructing him to teach the boy the benefits of being an English gentleman. Then all would benefit.

The River Thames at Greenwich

Captain Rory Donnaghue looked at the closeness of the banks in fear and consternation. He glanced over toward the royal shipyards at Deptford and saw the skeletons of galleys and galleons which would soon be ready for launching, and which might one day be sent by the Queen against his own ship and his own men. And he knew that just upriver was the other newly constructed shipyard at Woolwich, both now busy in preparation for what everyone knew was the coming war against Spain.

Grace O'Malley, seeing her captain's concern, walked across the deck and stood beside him. Climbing up to the fo'c'sle was particularly easy for, being on a river rather than the open sea, the deck was pleasantly calm and not rolling in an ocean's swell.

"A problem, Captain Donnaghue?"

He shook his head.

"Not used to sailing up a river, are you?"

"I've sailed up rivers before, ma'am, but not an English river. The rivers of Spain and Portugal and Italy present me with no such concerns. But this is English water within English soil, and the land of the enemy is so close I can touch it. If we have to turn and run for our lives, God help every man jack of the crew."

"What!" she scoffed. "It's a fine river, this Thames. It's wide and swift, and if the bastards fire upon us, we'll keep them busy firing back, spin round like a fly in a bottle, and be out into the North Sea, round past Dover and out into the Channel before they've had time to reload their cannon."

"It's no joke, ma'am. Not only do I feel discomforted, but so do the men."

She looked down toward the deck and agreed that most of her crew wasn't engaged in the normal commerce aboard a ship at sea, but were staring sullenly at England on the banks of the river, looking at the buildings and speaking quietly among themselves. She had noticed that since turning into the Thames estuary at the hamlet of Margate, her men had become somehow darker and more worried; for they were entering into the waters of the nation that Grace had been telling them was their ultimate enemy and would enslave them within their lifetimes.

"Would you rather turn back, Captain Donnaghue?"

He looked at her in surprise. "You know I wouldn't, ma'am. But I still maintain, as I did two nights ago when we were at sea, that it would have been better if we'd moored further down the river toward the coast, say at Tilbury, and come here on foot. Then we wouldn't present such a target."

"Rory, understand this. I'm here as a woman to demand the release of my son from another woman. If we'd landed with the entire army of Ireland, the English forces would still have blown us to pieces. In this land resides a huge army, as well as a fair-sized navy. We've neither the cannon nor the men to surprise the English or to fight them. This is a time for talk, not action."

"But there's a vast price on your head, Mistress O'Malley. A queen's ransom, for God's sake. Surely you don't expect to simply march in there," he said, pointing to the enormous Greenwich Palace built like a vast red boil on top of the hill of Greenwich, "and ask for your son to be returned? Do you?"

"I don't know, Rory. But what I do know is that my incarceration affected me badly. And I have no intention of allowing Tibbot to be so treated, if I can possibly prevent it."

Her captain shrugged his shoulders, and turned to face their goal, the home of the Queen of England at Greenwich.

Softly, so none of the rest of the crew would hear, she said, "Rory, what if you put me ashore here, and you take the crew and ship to deeper waters closer to the coast? I'll be fine. No need to worry on my account. I'll have done with my business here, and when I'm finished I'll join you again. Or find my own way back to Ireland."

Rory Donnaghue turned to her in astonishment. "Are you mad? D'you think I or any of the men would allow you to go in there on your own?" he said, pointing to the palace.

Grace smiled and said, "No, but I wanted to give you the option. Now, Captain, I suggest that we row against the current and put in at the dock yonder. I need to have a strong word with the woman who lives in the big house over there."

Rory Donnaghue looked up at the vast palace. "Ma'am, how do you know where she is? From what they say, she has many palaces."

Grace smiled. "Unlike her father and the rulers who went before her, the great Queen Elizabeth has built no palaces of her own. She's too tardy with her money. She lives in the homes built by others. And she follows a routine, Rory. A routine which I've known about ever since I knew that we'd be enemies for life. There's little I don't know about yonder Elizabeth of England."

The captain gave the order and within minutes the large sailing ship had docked and moored at the Greenwich Palace pier. Immediately after they had tied up, three palace guards came hustling down to see which unauthorized vessel was docking at Her Majesty's private landing area.

Grace O'Malley climbed down from the railings, followed by her captain and five of her crew. The palace guards looked at the newcomers with some consternation. From their dress, they weren't English sailors, yet they couldn't remember any sea-going sailing vessel which had ever moored here without the express permission of the queen.

"And who might you be?" huffed the sergeant-at-arms.

Grace replied in Gaelic. "My name, sir, is Grace O'Malley. I am here to see the Queen of England."

"What?" said the sergeant-at-arms, not understanding this foreign language.

Grace repeated what she'd just said, still in Gaelic, but adding for the benefit of her crew, "And don't expect me to speak in English, for it's the language of my enemy, and I won't sully my lips by speaking it."

Her crew, listening to the exchange from the ship's deck, burst out laughing and began to cheer. The three Englishmen realized that they were the stuff of ridicule, and became angry.

"Now listen to me, madam. You sound like some foreigner whore! Nobody lands on the queen's—"

But he failed to finish the sentence, because Grace immediately strode past him, leaving the three Englishmen in her wake.

The sergeant shouted after her, but she was already far beyond him by the time he and his companions had collected their wits and decided to follow her.

However, they were held loosely in check by Captain Donnaghue, who invited them, in perfect English, to board his ship for a noggin of port wine. It delayed the guards long enough for Grace to have strode halfway up Greenwich Hill before they set after her, shouting for her to return immediately or they would arrest her for trespass. In fear that this lone woman, followed by her sailors, would breach the security of the palace, the sergeant took out his pistol and fired it into the air. Grace turned in shock, thinking she'd been fired upon, but when she saw what he was doing, she continued up the hill.

She reached the walls of the palace and marched straight through a gate as men began running toward her. But they expected to see a raiding party, not a lone woman, and didn't know what to do. Some stared at her, but none seemed ready to stop her. She was dressed in jerkin, trews, a scarf around her neck and on her head, and was wearing a silken shirt in the manner of a captain on the high seas; yet despite her dramatically different appearance from the elegant and painted women of the court who dressed in velvets and ruffs and were bedecked with magnificent jewels, none of the guards for one moment thought that this matronly lady was any sort of security breach. Instead, they looked around, swords and pistols ready, for a gang of armed men. And so no one attempted to stop this weather-beaten middle-aged woman who strode purposefully toward the entryway of the palace.

Because it was so safe a location, situated far upriver from the pestilential center of London, and because the spies had brought no reports of danger to Her Majesty, the guard posted on the doors was minimal, and so Grace was already just within the building before she was prevented from further entry by a small detachment of the Queen's bodyguard and yeomen who had been alerted to her presence.

"Halt!" commanded the captain of the Queen's yeomen. "Stay, madam! Put up! Hand me your sword and dagger immediately. Go no further or I'll run you through with my weapon for trespass on royal property."

Grace turned to face him as he rushed down the corridor toward her. She could see that he was followed by ten men, all running, their swords and capes askew and flying in their wake. She had come far, but now was to be frustrated in her attempt to see the Queen. Well, she thought, she'd give as good as she got.

"Stand!" she shouted in Gaelic, putting up her hand.

Unsure, the captain of the yeomen stopped, and the men behind him clustered in a disorderly rabble, nearly tripping over themselves in disarray. The captain found it hard to understand what was happening. This woman was of a grandmother's age, gray-haired and dressed like a sailor. Yet she was alone.

"Who are you?" he demanded. "What business do you have in Greenwich?"

"How dare you assault me with your evil English words," she shouted, again in Gaelic.

"What?" said the captain.

Again, Grace repeated what she'd just said, only this time louder and with more menace.

"What words are these you speak?" he asked uncertainly.

"You are too much of a peasant to understand good honest Gaelic," she said.

"Ye Gods, ma'am, but you sound like a dog barking. I don't comprehend a single thing you're saying. Who are you? What's your name? What business do you have here?"

"Perhaps you'd like me to speak in Latin," she said in the language of the ancient Caesars.

He shook his head, though suddenly he was more cautious, for in his experience, this language was spoken in church.

"Or Greek," she said in the tongue of the blind poet Homer.

The captain turned to his men, but they shrugged.

"Do you not speak English?" he asked, this time more quietly.

"I speak Gaelic, Latin and Greek," she replied in Latin, "and I'm also capable of speaking French and Spanish and its sister tongue Portuguese. I was also taught some Arabic by an Ottoman lover, but that was a long time ago."

The captain had heard some of these words before, used by his priest and by officials in the court. Now he knew for certain that he wasn't dealing with some ignoramus, for he'd recognized that this woman—for she was certainly no lady, dressed like a rude sea-farer—was educated and on her own was no threat to the safety of the realm. He'd already ordered the grounds to be secured and the ship to be impounded, so there was no threat there either.

"Ma'am, I beg you, do you speak English?"

Again, Grace shouted in Latin for all to hear, "I will speak to your queen. I will speak to Elizabeth. I am Grace O'Malley, Chieftain of the O'Malley and the O'Flaherty and the Bourke clans of Ireland. Tell Elizabeth that I am come to speak with her."

The meeting of the Privy Council had been going on for more than three hours, and they had reached an impasse about the perennial difficulties of what to do with the Netherlands, and what action should be taken against Spain.

She looked around the table, determining to bring the discussion to an end, and was about to make a pronouncement when a noise from outside the antechamber of the audience hall intruded. Elizabeth listened carefully, for the words were insisting themselves on her mind. They were guttural and foreign. And spoken by a woman! But then the words changed to what sounded like Latin, and then Greek, and then Latin again. It was strange. And interesting. And Elizabeth was bored and was sorely in need of a distraction.

To the surprise of Sir Francis Walsingham and the others intimately involved in matters of state, Elizabeth suddenly stood and, without dismissing the council, strode to the door. It surprised her household yeomen too, who, though standing as guardians at the doors, were almost asleep at their stations. When they saw their queen striding purposefully toward them, they sprang to attention and opened the doors.

The doors to the audience hall were opened, and Elizabeth strode out into the vast reception hall. What greeted Elizabeth there was one of the most extraordinary sights she'd seen. A tall, gray-haired woman, dowdy and of middle age, aping the dress of a common sailor, was standing in the outer chamber, arguing with the captain of the yeomen.

When the guard saw the Queen, he immediately bowed low, raking the floor with his feathered hat. She strode toward the frozen tableau, bemused and interested.

"Majesty," he said.

"Mr. Long? What's this?"

The captain straightened and said, "Highness, this woman . . . I've been trying to have words with her, but she speaks in a language which is alien to my ears."

The Queen of England turned to the woman and asked, "And you, madam. What have you to say for yourself? What business do you have in Greenwich?"

Both women were as tall as each other, both possessed straight backs and firm flesh and were strong-boned. And both had pre-eminent confidence in themselves. Only Grace suddenly felt distinctly ill-at-ease in the company of a woman she'd never met yet knew well by legend. And what surprised her most was Elizabeth's white face, which looked as though it had been painted. Suddenly Grace felt . . . gross.

In Gaelic, Grace said, "I bow in respect before the Queen of England."

And she bowed.

Surprised, Elizabeth said, "Speak in the tongue of this nation, for your words are strange to me, madam, though your bow is pleasing enough. In England, women of the court usually curtsy."

"In Ireland, Majesty, the women are too busy to bother with such courtly manners," Grace said in Latin.

Hiding her shock that this ruffian who smelled of the sea was speaking in Latin, the tongue of the Church and of learning, Elizabeth responded, also in Latin, "Ah, so you're from Ireland. Then it was the tongue of the Irish you were speaking just now. It is called Gaelic, or so I'm told. Am I correct?"

Grace smiled and nodded.

"Then why are you here, madam? What is your business in the court of Greenwich? Why have you appeared without my permission? And why do you not speak in the English tongue to your queen?"

"I chose not to speak English, Majesty, for it is the language of the conquerors of my nation. I chose to speak in the tongue of Cicero and Pliny and Julius Caesar himself."

Affronted, the Queen snapped, "You dare to speak to your Queen in that manner?"

As the Queen's tone changed, the yeomen began to reach for their swords. The members of her court who had left the audience hall and gathered to listen to the extraordinary interview, though there were few who understood the interchange, were shocked by the Queen's sudden anger.

"Ma'am," said Grace, "if my manner offends you, it's because your servants in my land are offensive to me. And also because your language offends me."

"Then get used to it, madam, for your nation is England. Now and forever."

Suddenly feeling uncomfortable and worried about the reception she was getting, Grace realized that she had to be more guarded before the most powerful woman in the world.

"Majesty, I am not here to argue with you, but to claim back something which was stolen from me. One of your lords, Bingham by name, has stolen that which has no value whatsoever to you, but which is of inestimable value to me."

Elizabeth was puzzled but curious. It was so pleasant to be distracted from the overwhelming affairs of state. And truth to tell, despite herself, Elizabeth was beginning to warm to this strange woman who wore trousers and a leather jerkin and had the audacity to answer her back in a way in which no man nor woman had dared to do these last thirty years.

And suddenly Elizabeth's eyes widened in shock. The mention of the name Bingham immediately made things clear. Elizabeth realized that she was standing not two feet from a woman she'd vowed to hang from a scaffold, and whose head she had promised to impale on a spike at Traitors Gate in the Tower of London.

Softly, Elizabeth said, "You're the Irish pirate woman, Grace O'Malley."

Grace nodded.

"You dare to enter my palace?"

"I would enter Hell itself to reclaim my lovely boy."

Elizabeth turned to the captain of her guard. "Arrest this woman."

Immediately Mr. Long and his retinue jumped forward and pinioned

Grace's arms behind her. When she was fully secured, Elizabeth came forward and stood close to her.

"Mistress O'Malley, you have robbed me of what's mine. You and your navy have embarrassed me before the eyes of the world, and for that, I have determined that you will be tried and when found guilty of piracy and treason, you will be hanged and drawn and quartered."

Grace began to struggle as Mr. Long relieved her of her weapons.

"Majesty," she said, "I came without firing a shot. I came not as your enemy, but as a woman bound to implore another woman to release her captive son. I mean no harm to you. Please!"

The stupidity, or bravery, of this woman left Elizabeth breathless.

"No harm, when you steal from my merchant ships?" she said.

"I take from you what you have taken from the King of Spain."

"Have a care, madam, or you'll lose your tongue," Elizabeth told her.

"Then, Your Majesty, you will truly disarm me, for my tongue is the only weapon I have to beg you to return my lovely son to me."

Elizabeth looked at Grace closely. She decided she was a woman of outstanding bravery to have done what she had done. Slowly, the Queen turned to the captain of her guard. "How many men at arms has this woman brought with her?" she asked.

"Ma'am, she came with a single ship, and all her men are still in the dock. She ascended to the palace alone."

"You come into Greenwich alone?" said Elizabeth, stunned.

"I am a mother, Queen Elizabeth. I would give my life for my children; just as you would give your life for all your children of England."

Taken aback by her frankness, Elizabeth looked at Mr. Long and the other guards. She turned and saw that the entire Council of England was now in the doorway, crowding around to be witness to the extraordinary sight of a queen talking to a ruffian woman of the streets . . . in Latin!

But Elizabeth realized that this Grace O'Malley was neither ruffian, nor of the piratical classes. She was educated, sensitive, intelligent, worldly . . . and, despite herself, Elizabeth was enjoying this exchange far more than any she'd had in years. And speaking Latin conversationally took her back to her days as a young woman in the home of Catherine Parr, Henry's last wife, who had insisted on her husband's reconciliation with his daughters. It was then that Henry had delighted in Elizabeth's education, and she had been able to spend many hours conversing with him in the ancient tongues.

But there was greater importance to this exchange than a woman who had come to retrieve her son. With the Spanish about to set sail for England, Elizabeth knew that she must marshal all her forces for the coming battle. And she couldn't afford any dilution of her manpower fighting an unnecessary war in Ireland. Perhaps she could trade with Grace—her son in exchange for peace on England's western flanks?

"Mr. Long, release the prisoner. Keep her sword and dagger and any other weaponry well away from her. Ensure that her crew is properly restrained and that her ship is impounded."

In gratitude, Grace bowed to Elizabeth, a calculated act of deference.

"Your Majesty is a disarming woman," she said.

Elizabeth smiled. "Well, Mistress O'Malley! What's to do? Come with me and we'll dine in my privy chambers. I think we have much to discuss. But remember, Grace O'Malley, that one shout from me and a dozen English stalwarts will burst into my chambers and tear you to pieces like a pack of wild dogs."

The Queen turned to her captain. "Put up your sword, Mr. Long. This lady is of no danger to me. She is only of danger to England."

And, leaving the entire court stunned, Elizabeth led Grace all the way to her private chambers.

CHAPTER TWENTY-ONE

The Corridors of Greenwich Palace

As the Queen of England and the Queen of Irish Pirates walked down the long oak-paneled corridor, tall mullioned windows casting shafts of afternoon light onto the dark wood, a sudden draft of cold air blew up, and the change of temperature made Grace sneeze.

Not carrying a kerchief, she was at a loss as to what to do. Sir Walter Raleigh, who had been asked by the Queen to accompany them to the door of her privy chambers, pulled out a silken kerchief, newly acquired from a haberdasher in Cheapside, and offered it gallantly to Grace, who took it gratefully and blew her nose.

But to the Queen's amusement, she did not put the kerchief in her pocket, but rather carried it in her hand until the corridor led to an antechamber where there was a lighted fire. Grace walked over to the fire and threw in the kerchief; the fire burst into a momentary incandescence as it scorched and melted the burning cloth.

Stupefied, the ladies of Elizabeth's court gasped at the rudeness of the action, and looked to the Queen to reprimand the boorish and discourteous Irish woman.

Surprised by their reaction, Grace asked the Queen, though this time in English, for she was beginning to warm to her enemy and wanted the court to understand the exchange, "Have I done something wrong, Your Highness?"

"Yes, Mistress O'Malley. That handkerchief you threw away in so inconsiderate a manner cost my cousin Raleigh a pretty penny. Silk is expensive, and that was a particularly fine silk. In England, madam, we don't throw kerchiefs away, but put them in our pockets and at the end of the week have them washed by the servants."

Grace frowned in amazement. "You put a dirty kerchief in your pocket? In Ireland, we don't blow our noses on silk, but on cloth made from hemp, and though it's rough, it costs not a farthing and we dispose of it in the fire without thought. What you do is stupid, for if I did as you've told me, my pockets would become as dirty as the kerchief."

A lady-in-waiting came close to fainting at the rudeness. The entire company was utterly silent and breathless with incredulity at this woman's crudeness, and waited for the Queen to reprimand her severely, perhaps even order her to be put in the stocks.

But instead, the Queen of England looked at her for a long moment. Then her brow furrowed. And then she smiled. And then she laughed. All the court looked on in amazement as Elizabeth roared a laugh to the ceiling. Then the entire court joined in, the antechamber echoing with their laughter. Only Grace was silent and apprehensive.

"Of course," said the Queen when she'd begun to calm down. "You're quite right. Your crude Irish manners have pointed to our English errors; if we put a dirty kerchief in our pockets, we make our pockets dirty."

She continued to giggle, and turned to Raleigh. "What say you, Sir Walter? Eh? Do you have dirty pockets? And you, my cousin Walsingham?"

Then she continued to walk down the corridor, chuckling to herself, Grace and the rest of the court following in her wake.

When they arrived at the Queen's privy chamber, Sir Walter and Sir Francis bowed, and the ladies-in-waiting opened the door to admit Her Majesty. She walked inside, followed by Grace O'Malley, but when the other ladies of the chamber attempted to enter, the Queen turned and smiled. "Ladies all, good cousins, I would prefer to be alone with this Irish woman. I shall be quite safe. Leave us, and attend to your duties elsewhere."

Then, quite deliberately, she closed the door behind Grace, and suddenly, for the first time in . . . in how long she couldn't remember, Queen Elizabeth was almost alone. It brought her a frisson of excitement.

The two women entered the outer privy chamber, three rooms joined by open doors. The dark oak ceilings were ornately carved and decorated, the walls paneled in oak lightened with carvings made from ash, and chairs and escritoires were placed throughout the room. Grace looked at the paintings which adorned the walls. She recognized paintings by King Henry's court painter, Hans Holbein, as well as others by Albrecht Dürer, Matthias Grünewald, and Lucas Cranach, whose work she'd seen in merchants' houses when she'd traded with the Dutch and the Germans. She also recognized the work of the Italians Andrea del Sarto and Raphael, and some by painters whose style she didn't recognize. One which looked familiar caught her eye. Elizabeth saw her staring at it. Unlike the others which were painted in oils, this was a drawing.

Elizabeth came over and stood beside her Irish enemy. They looked at the drawing together.

"I hardly knew her," said Elizabeth softly.

"Queen Anne Boleyn?" Grace guessed.

Elizabeth nodded. "The drawing was done by Maestro Holbein. I'm told it is a fair likeness."

"It must have been terrible not to have known your mother. You were, what, two when she was beheaded?"

"Three."

Elizabeth turned and walked deeper into the room. Grace followed her.

"While ever my father was alive, my mother was always referred to as 'that whore and witch'. Only when he died and my half-brother was on the throne could I refer to my mother in company as 'Queen'. Then Mary became queen, and again, my mother was excoriated as the evil bewitcher who had seduced my father from his true and proper Catholic wife. And then by God's grace, I was queen, and . . ."

Elizabeth lapsed into silence.

"That's why I took pity on you just now. For I know what it's like to be a child deprived of a mother. God knows what it must be like for a mother to be deprived of her child."

As they walked further into the apartments, something else caught Grace's eye. It was a magnificent rug which had been laid over the oaken floor.

Grace smiled and said in Latin, "Majesty, you have a carpet from Constantinople. It is a very fine carpet, beautifully woven of silk and colored in the style and patterns of the people who live in the western lands of the Ottomans, close to the border of the land of Persia."

Elizabeth listened to her with interest, just as she did when one of her captains or admirals returned from a voyage to the New World, or the great Southern Lands of the warm oceans which were south of the New World, and told of impenetrable jungles, and of snakes which were longer than a ship's rope and thicker than a man's body, and of strange peoples who wore capes made from the skin of large and hairy beasts and wore birds' feathers in their hair.

But the Irish woman had made a mistake. "I'm sorry, Mistress O'Malley, but while I admire your experience, you are wrong about this carpet. It was given to me by an ambassador of King Albert V of Bavaria, who informed me that this carpet was made in the Indies, in a place called Kashmir which is in the northwest of the land of East India."

Grace looked at the carpet, and said, "Forgive me, Your Majesty, but that rug is not from the Indies—it was made in the land of the Ottoman Turks. See here," she said, walking to the rug and pointing out its particulars, "this is a flat-woven carpet which they call a kilim."

She pointed to the swirls and geometric patterns that were repeated throughout the carpet. She told Elizabeth that every carpet-making district of Persia and the Ottoman Empire had its own distinctive style and color as identifiable as a mother's face to a child. It was an impressive lesson.

"And pray, Mistress O'Malley, how did you learn so much about carpet-making?"

Without any sense of embarrassment or hesitation, she said, "I once had a lover. A big black Turk. The most beautiful man in all of the world. His name was Osman Abdul Mehmet, and he called himself the Man of Men, and also the Beylebey. This man, Your Majesty, was formerly a captain in the Imperial Navy of Süleymân I, and when I met him he was a captain in the merchant fleet of Grand Vizier Kemalpasazade. He's been dead these fifteen years, drowned in a ferocious storm, but it was he who told me all about the making of these carpets. After I first stopped his ship from entering Galway Harbor, he and I spent time together, talking about Turkey and his native land. Since then, I saw him several times, and each time, as a gift, he gave me a carpet. My castle in Connaught has four of his carpets, for each of his carpets represents to me a time when he and I enjoyed each other's—"

"Yes!" said the Queen curtly. "I can imagine what it represents."

There was an icy silence. And suddenly the Queen burst out laughing. "You are a terrible woman, Grace O'Malley, and I stand in mortal danger of being corrupted by your lifetime of sins."

Unable to resist smiling, Grace responded, "I thought that the body of a monarch of England was incorruptible."

"Ha! Don't you believe it! England has been blessed with a monarch for every season. We've had monarchs who were lovers of boy children; we've had monarchs who chased every woman in the court, from the scullery maid to the wives of the earldom; we've had monarchs who were of the most virtuous persuasion and were as loving of their people as any father and as any chaste virgin in a nunnery; we've had monarchs who were wise and those who were fools, those who were brave and those who were cowards. Truly, Grace O'Malley, choose a color in that rug, and there's been a monarch on the throne of England to match it."

After a long pause, Grace asked, "Why did you stop your guards from sending me to the dungeon and clapping me in irons? I understand what you said about a mother's pain, but that wasn't the only reason, was it, Your Majesty?"

Elizabeth thought for a moment. "Every day, every hour of every day, I am surrounded by men who connive and scheme behind my back, who measure every word I say for what it might mean to them. Only two—dear Robert Cecil, son to our loyal servant William, and cousin Francis Walsingham—act for and on behalf of England, risking my fury and disapprobation for the greater good. Every other thinks only of himself.

"And every lady-in-waiting too, or every wife of some gallant who stalks the corridors of my court. But for just the briefest of moments, a woman who is like me, yet not like me, crosses my path and looks me in the eye; and I know deep within me that this woman will speak to me from her heart, telling me what I must hear, rather than what she thinks I want to hear."

Grace nodded. "But I am your enemy. You've captured my son. I came here to grasp him back from you. Yet you invite me for a meal, you give me an audience alone, which not even an ambassador might have. Yet I am your enemy and you wish me hanged."

"What is an enemy, Grace O'Malley? One moment we are at war with a nation; we swear to kill them and ruin their land, salt their fields, take their women and children as our slaves, destroy their buildings, plunder their wealth. And the next moment we are their closest and most beloved allies because we must join with them to defeat a new enemy. So what is an enemy? And what is a friend?"

"In Ireland, Your Majesty, the English are the enemy. Of that, we have no doubts."

Elizabeth sat in her favorite chair, the one in the window which looked out over the vast emerald swathe of grasslands which led down to the water at Greenwich dock. She ushered Grace to a seat opposite. She looked at her closely in the strong light which came through the window. Grace was a tall and heavy woman, but there was a strength and handsomeness, indeed a comeliness, about her which the Queen found appealing. Her skin, especially that on her face, was remarkable. This was a woman who, by her gray hair, must be in her middle fifties, an old woman of the same age as herself, yet her skin was firm and clear and devoid of marks. It wasn't sallow like Elizabeth's underneath all the white paints and powders; nor was it as lined and creased as Elizabeth's. Oh, certainly

Grace's face was weather-beaten, as was every sailing man's she'd ever seen; but unlike Elizabeth's skin, Grace's was shining with health and vitality and strength.

As she was being scrutinized, Grace was looking just as closely at the Queen of England. Elizabeth's hair was vermilion, the brightest red she'd ever seen. Yet it was thin and wispy like high clouds in a morning sky. And despite the fact that her face was painted with a thick white coat, which Grace assumed to be a mixture of the powder of rice and the white of eggs, at the edges of her hair, where the paint hadn't been applied, her skin was gray and mottled, aged and flaked. Because her skin had shrunk over the bones of her face, it had accentuated her nose, which was now as hooked as that of a bird of prey. Those teeth remaining to her were yellow with age, and some were even brown. But it was her eyes which held Grace's attention. Her eyes were as hard and penetrating as a gimlet, and they seemed to bore through to Grace's very soul. These eyes told her that she must not prevaricate, nor must she lie before the Queen, for if she did, she and her boy Tibbot would surely die.

On the low buffet between them was a salver of sweetmeats and Elizabeth delicately picked one of them up, indicating to Grace that she too should partake.

"You're not the least what I expected," said the Queen between bites. "I assumed from all the reports I've had about you these last twenty years, that you were some foul and misbegotten harridan. A witch in men's breeches, a murderess and seducer."

"Well, I do wear breeches, for a dress at sea would be an encumbrance; and as to being a murderer . . . again, Majesty, I've killed men, but never with joy or happiness. And yes, in the last matter, ma'am, you're right, for I am indeed a seducer. I've never considered it wrong to enjoy the body which God gave me. Faith, I've seen enough good women who should have enjoyed themselves live their entire lives in a state of anxiety for the want of a man . . ."

Grace suddenly flushed in horror in the realization of what she'd said. Elizabeth smiled, and willed her to continue. But Grace was suddenly tongue-tied.

"Mistress O'Malley. I am a virgin. I was born a virgin and shall die a virgin. My lover is England and all the people in it. Throughout my life, I have been importuned to be married, but although I've toyed with many men, none has entered my body, and none will. That is my decision, despite all the pressure placed upon me by my council. I am married—to England. So suffer no hesitation when you speak to me of the pleasures of the flesh, for I have known greater pleasures than you will ever enjoy . . . not of the flesh, but of being the most beloved woman in all the world."

Grace smiled, and continued, "Then I shall be very bold with you, Majesty, for I will tell you how my body responds to the freedom which I am able to enjoy. I love the freedom the sea gives me. It allows me to distance myself from the restrictions of Ireland and family and community, to sail into unknown waters, where I can be myself. And yes, there I am a seductress; there I do enjoy dark-skinned men; they pleasure me, be they from France or Spain or Portugal or Egypt."

She again pulled herself back, realizing that despite Elizabeth's invitation to be frank, she might be speaking too freely in front of a monarch who was known for her piety to the Church and her anger at any untoward immorality in her nation.

Elizabeth again noticed her reluctance and said, "Please continue. I find your honesty so refreshing after the behavior of some of the ladies of my court. They behave in a disreputable fashion and then use elaborate lies and schemes to cover their paths . . . as if I don't know what they've been up to."

"Do you really want me to continue?"

"Yes, Grace O'Malley. I want to hear about your adventures, your loves, your life aboard ship. Understand that I am locked in a cell every moment of my life. I take my court on progresses around the country, stay at stately mansions with lords and ladies, see much of England, but never have I been free to experience the life which you have led, and of which my admirals and captains tell me so much. And you being a woman—a woman of my years—makes me even more curious. Tell me, how did you begin your life at sea?"

They waited. And waited. And continued to wait. They waited all morning, and by the time of the midday meal, they were beside themselves with anticipation.

Occasionally they would hear laughter, but most of the time there was only an unnerving silence.

Some were breathless, having to expend their pent-up nervous energies by walking outside in the gardens to overcome their insatiable curiosity. Others were so overwhelmed by their inquisitiveness that they paid gold coins to the ladies of the outer chamber for permission to be within two rooms of the interchange between the Queen and the pirate. Others still announced that they would take the air, and walked around the palace to where the Queen's chambers were situated, and tried to peer through the windows, or to stand on the earth beneath her windows and listen to any snippets of conversation which might escape.

But to no avail, for the Queen's chambers were virtually invisible from the grounds in order to afford her the greatest possible privacy, and Grace and Elizabeth were speaking in normal conversational tones, and so their words were impossible to hear from without. Only the occasional and infuriating guffaw of laughter from either woman, and occasionally from both.

Sir Walter Raleigh, a man of action, could stand the wait no more, and said to Sir Francis Walsingham, "Damn it. I'm going in there to see what's ado. Surely the Queen's been murdered by a *muttucashlass* which this damnable woman brought into the palace under her armpit."

"A what?" asked Walsingham.

"A *muttucashlass* . . . It's a small and deadly double-edged dagger used by the warriors of Scotland. They conceal it beneath their jerkins, under their armpits, and when—"

"The woman was secured by the guards before she was admitted to the Queen's company," said Walsingham, annoyed at being distracted from his lists by Sir Walter who was always making up fantasies to please the court.

"Anyway," Walsingham continued, "this woman is Irish, and wouldn't be carrying a concealed Scottish weapon."

"Ah! But that's where you're wrong," insisted Raleigh. "The Irish lords are using Scottish mercenaries called Gallowglass to help them in their—"

"I know what Gallowglass are, Sir Walter. And I assure you that Her Majesty is perfectly safe."

"How do you know?" Raleigh shouted. "How can you be so sure that this mad Irish woman pirate isn't standing over our Queen's dead body right now, drinking her blood and gloating over her foul deed?"

Sir Francis Walsingham sighed and handed his lists to his amanuensis. "Very well," he said in exasperation. "I shall enter the Queen's presence, and God help me and you if you're wrong."

In dudgeon, he walked out of the audience chamber, followed closely by Sir Walter Raleigh, and down the corridors which connected the official part of the palace to the privy rooms occupied by the Queen and her most senior ministers.

At his approach, the guards opened the doors to admit him. All others were excluded from this part of the palace except the ladies, certain favorites, and most certainly Sir Francis Walsingham, who had direct access at almost any hour of the day to the Queen.

He walked swiftly through two more sets of doors, until he came to the Queen's inner court. There, he was met by a surprised Lady Amelia Rouche.

"My Lord?" she asked, standing up from her escretoire.

"I wish to see Her Majesty."

"I have the most strict instructions to admit nobody. Not even you, my lord."

"I have reason to believe that the Queen might be in some personal danger."

Lady Rouche blanched at the news. In a quandary, she shook her head. "Not even . . ."

"Out of my way, woman," insisted Sir Francis. He walked past her, and stood before the double doors which opened upon the Queen's antechambers.

Cautiously he grasped the handles and opened the doors a fraction. He peered through the tiny fissure between the doors and looked into the room. And what he saw amazed him.

The two elderly women were seated by the window, talking to each other in animated and lively terms, nodding and interrupting each other as though they were lifelong friends . . . or sisters.

Sir Francis continued to stare, open-mouthed. Nobody was permitted to sit in the presence of the Queen; not he, nor her ministers, nor her ladies-in-waiting. Only when the Queen was on her throne and in council was it permissible for her ministers to sit to discuss matters of state. Just then the Queen glanced toward the door. Sir Francis closed the door immediately, and turned to walk away. He saw the irate Lady Rouche looking at him in fury.

"My intelligence was incorrect. You may continue . . ."

And he walked back to berate Sir Walter.

From the far side of the room, the Queen thought she noticed a disturbance and turned her head to look for its origin. Grace also turned to the door, but if it had been opened, it was now closed, and the two women were left undisturbed. She had been with Elizabeth now for most of the morning, and her occasional glances through the window showed her that it was well past noon.

"And then you lost your inheritance?"

"Yes, Majesty. My husband Donal died and two-thirds of his estate were given to his blood family, rather than to me and my children. I thought I was going to receive the remaining third which, while not as much as I deserved, bearing in mind that I had earned virtually all the money from my trading and piracy, was at least enough to keep me and my children in food and lodgings. Of course, what nobody knew was that I'd retained much of my income for myself, against the eventuality of finding myself in such distressed conditions. That's between us, though, Your Highness."

Elizabeth nodded in collusion.

Grace continued, as though this was a conversation she might be having with another elderly Irish widow, sharing their secrets. "But then his younger brother Liam, who became the *Tanaist*—that means successor to the chieftain in our Gaelic language—became evil toward me and my children and so I was forced to deal with him. I then returned to the castle of my parents, and the anger of it almost overwhelmed me."

Elizabeth frowned. "Many years ago, someone told me of this. It was Sir Philip Sidney, dear boy. He begged me to do something about the inequity in the treatment of widows in Ireland. I instructed my governors to look into the matter, but they told me that it was the will of the Irish and that its retention was at the request of the Irish lords. I took no further action."

Grace nodded. It didn't surprise her that her hopes had been dashed by the other Irish chieftains, nor that Sir Philip had passed on her request. Now she had something else to thank him for.

Grace continued with her story, and when she told Elizabeth how she'd acquired Richard's castle, so that she wouldn't be left an impoverished widow for a second time, the Queen burst out laughing, roaring her amusement to the ceiling.

In surprise, a guard burst in, halberd aimed at Grace's heart. But the Queen waved him away, saying, "I'm in danger only of dying from laughter."

The door remained open, and Elizabeth saw her ladies-in-waiting staring at them in incomprehension.

"My Lady Rouche, perhaps you will send to the kitchens for some food for us."

Lady Rouche entered the room and curtsied. "Certainly, Your Majesty. I shall order your tables to be set up here for your ladies-in-waiting to dine. Will I order tables to be set for any members of the council?"

"No, Mistress Rouche. Just a buffet for Mistress Grace and myself. You and the ladies-in-waiting may dine with the Privy Council in the common banquet hall with the other ladies and gentlemen of the court."

Lady Rouche's face turned white in shock. "Majesty? You will dine alone?"

"No, I shall dine with this dreadful and immoral Irish pirate. You are excused, Lady Rouche."

"Majesty, I hardly feel it's—"

"Lady Rouche, I shall determine what shall and shall not be. Leave us please."

Stiffly, Lady Rouche curtsied again and walked backward toward the door and out of the room, much to the amusement of Grace.

"Why do they walk backward, Majesty?"

"Because it is respectful. Don't seek to question English manners, Mistress Grace. You have already succeeded where all others have failed. Allow me, please, the measure of my own court. Now, you were telling me about your nuptials with Master Richard Bourke."

•   •   •

Sir Francis Walsingham looked disdainfully at those eating at his table. Their silly talk was disturbing him as he read his reports and the intelligence from his spies. He looked at the other tables in the banqueting hall and saw that all those dining were holding hushed conversations, heads close together, lips whispering into ears. Even on his own table, Lady Rouche was in urgent conversation with other ladies of the royal household, keeping her voice soft and cautious but he could still hear the occasional snippet: *Queen . . . Irish woman . . . alone . . .*

It infuriated him. There was much urgent business which should attach to the court, yet all they were interested in was gossip. He could, perhaps, understand this at the lower tables, but not at his own. His, naturally, was the table of primacy in the banqueting hall, the table where the earls, lords, the most senior knights and all members of the Privy Council, as well as the ladies of the ennobled, sat. On other tables were lower knights, ambassadors, visitors, foreigners and observers, as well as their ladies. On peripheral tables, closer to the doors or the kitchens, sat important personages from Greenwich, and subsequently others of lower status who had been invited to court as a privilege or because they had donated some gift or money or superior service to the Queen.

But the talk on all seven of the tables seemed exclusively to be about the Irish woman who had importuned, monopolized and immobilized the entire morning of the Queen of England, as well as the luncheon hour. Who was she? What did she want of the Queen? And why was the Queen allowing her such unprecedented liberties?

All knew that she was the Irish pirate, the chieftain of Connaught, Grace O'Malley, the woman about whom horrific stories of murder, piracy and brigandry on the high seas were told. For the Queen to speak with her, let alone restrain those who would throw her in prison, was extraordinary. And for Her Majesty to spend time alone with her . . . well, that had set tongues wagging throughout the palace, and soon throughout all the land.

Sir Francis concentrated on his mutton stew with barley bread, silently sipping at a goblet of wine, and wondered when the conversation would turn to loftier matters. He would have maintained his silence, had he not clearly overheard an esquire of the Earl of Bath, seated at a lowly status table near to the door, say in a youthful voice suffused with the effects of wine, "Why's she so long in there? Maybe they're planning to be pirates together, her and the Queen—"

"Enough!" Sir Francis shouted, banging his fist on the oak table.

The room was instantly silenced.

"Enough of this tittle-tattle and gossip! Enough of this girlish whimsy, these ridiculous and unfounded remarks about our Queen. She is Elizabeth, by the Grace of God, Monarch of all England, not some scullery maid caught in a secret assignation. There will be no further discussion of our Queen at these tables, nor her decision to grant audience to Mistress O'Malley, nor what she and the Irish woman may be speaking of. Is that understood?"

He waited for heads to nod, for the murmuring to cease. Lady Rouche looked at him with hostility; it was the second time that morning that he'd directly contravened her activities. But because he was secretary of state to the Queen, she held her tongue.

"Good," he said, and went back to eating his meal.

But despite the heavy silence, Sir Francis could have sworn he heard two youths on a far table whispering to each other, "Still, it would be wondrous interesting to know what they were talking about."

They finished their meal and Grace sat back, tempted to burp from the effects of the delicious spicy food, but holding back because of her respect for the Queen.

But then the Queen burped, shocking Grace.

Elizabeth saw the surprise in her eyes and said, "They say that my manners would be unacceptable to the courts of France and Spain. They say that because I pick my teeth and scratch myself when I'm itching, and hawk my spit into a bowl, that I am not as ladylike as the women of those foreign courts. I care nothing for these manners. It's not the outward symbols which are the exemplars of gentility, but how a person is within. Tell me, how are women in Ireland, Mistress Grace?"

"As women anywhere, Majesty. They are true to their menfolk, they are loving mothers and are sturdy in their work. They pick the crops when it's harvest time, and change the rushes in the house every fortnight. They are normal women."

Elizabeth shook her head. "That's not what I mean. Are they lusty like common English women? Do they rule the household, or are they subservient to their men?"

"As to lusty, well, perhaps we've suffered the Church less than in England, for rarely do Irish women wail to the moon in desire of a man's body. Yes, they're lusty and honest with it. No airs and graces about wanting a man's body. When Irish girls' buds begin to grow into breasts and they begin to feel warm and welcoming between their legs, we parents or lords and ladies of the land don't forbid them their pleasures, or lock them in their rooms to prevent them seeing the boys of the land. Many an Irish lass goes to the altar several months with child. And only the priests are upset by this."

Grace took another sip of malmsey, which she'd never previously tasted even though she'd traded with Portugal for many years; it was a very sweet and delicious wine.

"The question of the ruling of the household, Majesty, is another matter. For while ever our husbands are alive, we are as much queen of our domain as he is king. But when he dies, then the ancient laws of our land take away from us two-thirds of our inheritance, and that is something which is both wrong and immoral. It robs widowed women of the money they need to ensure a peaceful old age; it denies the children their rights and property and security. It's wrong, Your Majesty, and you should do something about it."

"Me?" Elizabeth said in surprise. "Me? But you are fighting my ownership of all Ireland. You resist me every step of the way; you deny the authority of Sir Richard Bingham, my governor; you fight my soldiers, offend my sailors, steal from my merchants; yet you want me, your enemy, to offer you the protection of our English laws? How now, Grace?"

"As to Bingham, ma'am, you must do something against that murderous and malevolent little devil. He's not there to represent you, Majesty, but to rob the land of whatever he can grab. But as to the other matter, yes, you are my enemy, but while you rule in Ireland, then your laws must apply to us as much as to your English people.

"Majesty, I speak to you as a woman asking to be understood by another woman. You know more than most what it's like to be endangered of your inheritance. Before you became the Queen of England, were you not sent to the Tower of London for conspiring to marry Thomas Seymour? And aren't you still restraining Mary of Scotland in a prison because you wish to prevent her from taking your throne? Surely you can understand why it is imperative that we women of Ireland are protected when we are at our most vulnerable; otherwise what use are you to us as our queen? We might as well overthrow the men who govern us and establish a world like the kingdom of the Amazons, or become like the women of the Isle of Lesbos."

Elizabeth was furious, but fascinated, too, by Grace's boldness. In the other world Elizabeth inhabited, the world just beyond the doors of her bedchamber, the world of courtiers and ambassadors and councillors, not a single man or woman would have survived the night had they been so bold and offensive. An inclination of her high and arched regal eyebrow would have sent the offender straight to the dungeons. And the court would have expected nothing less, or it would have shown Elizabeth to be a weak queen, one unworthy of the throne on which she sat.

Yet for reasons which she might not understand until the interview was over and she had time to reflect, the privacy of their interview was allowing Grace impudences far greater than any which might be enjoyed by those who came before her.

Why was Elizabeth according her such privileges? Was it because she was a brave and forthright woman who had sailed around the world and seen and done things of which Elizabeth could only dream? Was it because, like Elizabeth herself, Grace was a strong and determined woman living in a world made for men? Was it because both had risen to command whole legions of men and were respected for who they were, and not just for their position at birth? Perhaps it was all these things.

Elizabeth, who had met the most brilliant, important and illustrious people in the world, pondered for a moment why she was so fascinated by a drab Irish woman who looked and dressed like a bog dweller.

Softly, Elizabeth answered, "One day, Grace, when you are in Ireland and at peace with all the world, you will understand why it is in your best interests to be subject to the might of England."

Grace sighed, and wondered whether she should dare raise again the subject of her imprisoned son.

Before she could frame her question, the Queen surprised her by saying, "I have drunk too much mead, and I'm sure that after all your malmsey you'll also need to relieve yourself. Please follow me. I have two privys installed and we can continue our conversation there."

Without waiting for a response, Elizabeth rose and crossed the floor to a door which opened onto another dark and wood-paneled room. In the center was a large tub for bathing and against the wall were two wooden privies, seats built above holes which, Grace assumed, descended down into the bowels of the palace.

Elizabeth entered the chamber and hitched up her voluminous gowns. She struggled for a few moments, swearing beneath her breath.

"May I help Your Majesty?" asked Grace.

"If you would be so kind. Normally my ladies of the privy chamber undo my laces and bows so that my garments fall from my body. But my dresses are so large and cumbersome that . . ."

Grace fell to her knees and saw that the Queen's undergarments were firmly tied and knotted. She undid all the knots and the laces and silks fell to the floor. But there was still the problem of the massive dress, which was almost as wide as it was long. Grace could feel the weight and stiffness of it. It must have required great strength to wear, let alone walk around in all day.

Grace unhooked the skirts and allowed them to fall in a heap on the floor. Elizabeth was left with the most elegant and beautifully dressed upper half, and an utterly naked lower half. Grace helped the Queen to sit on the privy. Then, when the Queen was settled, Grace removed her own trews and underdraws and sat on the other seat.

Both women looked at each other without embarrassment. Grace burst out laughing. "Forgive me, but it's not often that I do my shite in front of the Queen of England."

"How do you void your wastes when you're on a ship, and before all the men of your crew? Do you have a privy?" Elizabeth asked.

"My cabin is at the rear of the ship, ma'am. There is a window casement, built with a wooden seat. When I need to shite, I open the window, swing the seat out over the sea, and sit down, grasping the rails. Then I void into the sea far below. To wipe myself, there's a rope which hangs down from the stern of the ship and which is always dangling into the water. The end is finely frayed and sodden with sea water. It does me very well. And because it rides in the waves behind my ship, it's always clean and pleasant."

Elizabeth nodded. They sat for several moments in strained silence, until Elizabeth asked, "It is time, Mistress Grace, for me to be direct with you, as you have been direct with me. We've spent much of the day in pleasantries. I've learned more from you about the conditions of Ireland than from the hundreds of dispatches sent to me by my governors. For that I thank you. But you've come over here to free your son."

"Tibbot of the Ships."

"From what you deem to be his imprisonment. You have been straight and generous with me, unafraid of me, somewhat presumptive, occasionally impertinent, but always honest. For my part, I shall be honest with you. Tibbot was sent to me by Sir Richard Bingham. He was brought here by Bingham's brother, a man who is weak and silly and vainglorious.

"I have placed the boy in safekeeping with the Earl of Ashby. I shall release your son, and return him to you, for now that I've met you, I can see as much value in him learning the ways of his ancestors as in him learning how to be an English gentleman."

Grace looked at the Queen in amazement and gratitude, but before she could say anything, Elizabeth said, "But there is still the problem of Grace O'Malley, Queen of the Irish Pirates. I have orders extant for your capture and execution should you set foot on English soil, which you patently have done. I would like to grant you a royal pardon, and do the same to all your crew. But you continue to render me grave disservice. You continue to attack my soldiers, my sailors and my dignity. What am I to do with the mother of Tibbot of the Ships?"

Grace remained silent.

"Am I to set her and her son free, and then as they leave England feeling they have gained so much, shall I then silently and surreptitiously attack them on the high seas? And if I don't, what then, Grace? You and your son are free, and I have no restraints over you. Surely I would not be a good commander of men if I simply assumed, with no assurance, that my act of generosity would encourage Grace O'Malley to lay down her arms forever and not to attack me again?"

Grace turned to answer, but before she could, Elizabeth said, "Or am I to discuss with Mistress Grace O'Malley another matter altogether, something which will greatly appeal to her sense of excitement as a merchant, and as a pirate and woman of adventure? And if Mistress O'Malley says yes to my proposition, then I shall pardon her and all her crews and ships of her line, and she shall sail into the pages of England's heritage as a woman of valor and substance and worth."

Elizabeth became quiet, and turned to Grace.

Still taken aback by the incongruity of talking of such matters alone in a privy with the Queen of England, Grace thought for a moment, and then said, "I wish to be the friend of Elizabeth of England. In my heart, I wish to be your friend and not your enemy. But you are attacking my land, my country, my people. How can I kiss my enemy's feet?"

The Queen struggled off the seat of the privy and muttered, "Kissing your enemy's feet is far more pleasant than wiping your enemy's arse."

When the two women reentered the Queen's chambers, Grace noticed in amazement that the plates and cutlery had been cleared, and fresh glasses of mead and malmsey had been poured. Yet the doors of the chamber were firmly closed, and neither movement nor conversation could possibly have been heard outside. So how had the maids known that the Queen was vacating the room and there was time for them to tidy? It was a mystery.

Instead of returning to their seats, the Queen stood before the opened window. "Why don't we discuss these great matters of state outside in the air, while the sun still shines on our gardens and lawns?"

Again, without waiting for Grace's agreement, the Queen swung her voluminous skirts and walked toward the door. As she suddenly pulled open the door, a half-dozen or so ladies, who were keenly pressed against the door in the hope of catching any snippet of conversation, almost fell against the Queen.

"Ladies," she said without acknowledging their eavesdropping, "Mistress Grace O'Malley and I are going for a walk. You will remain here."

And they flounced past, leaving Lady Rouche in an ugly state of distemper.

As they walked down the corridor, Grace asked, "What is it that you wish to ask of me, Your Highness?"

Elizabeth whispered, "We will speak of it outside, where the walls have no ears. My court, like all the courts of Europe, is full of ambassadors sent by other monarchs to importune me, or to find out what's going on in the English court; these ambassadors have my own courtiers in their pockets, paying them vast amounts of money just to deliver to them my innermost thoughts, or those of my chief advisors. The Spanish ambassador, for instance, would love to listen to our conversation, as would the ambassador of the court of France. It pains me to tell you that in my court, matters of great confidentiality must be dealt with in the open air."

The two elderly women descended the steps of Greenwich Palace and walked through the green swathes of grasslands. They walked beyond majestical oaks and beeches and firs, through beds replete with a profusion of the most colorful flowers, past apiaries buzzing with excitement, and aviaries in which birds from all over the world—peacocks and peahens, pheasants, ptarmigans, owls, bluebirds, finches and even a nest of nightingales—sang and trilled and fluttered in exhilaration.

They passed the bearpit where Grace saw two huge black bears chained by the neck, kept for the sport of bear-baiting. They walked past the kitchens and outhouses where the food for the thousand or so ladies and gentlemen of the court was prepared three and sometimes four times each day. In shock, the maids and servants and kitchen hands looked up and saw their queen walking by. They didn't know what to do, and so they merely stood to attention until Elizabeth and her strangely dressed companion had passed by.

The Queen walked on into the Greenwich woods, Grace in tow.

"Grace," she said, seeing that there was no living soul within hearing. "Soon King Philip of Spain will send his armada against us. There is great pressure on me from many quarters, and persistent calls by my ministers of state, and also by the people themselves, for me to put an end to the life of Queen Mary of Scotland. She still believes that she is rightful Queen of England and her backside should be on the throne. Indeed, she has made King Philip her heir and successor should I execute her."

"And will you?"

"Not while ever God grants me breath. For although she is an adulterous and whorish sloven, a murderer and treasoner and conspirer, she is nonetheless an anointed queen, anointed by God Himself. Yet . . ."

"Yet you must, for if you don't, you'll be seen as weak and it will encourage your enemies to attack you."

The Queen remained silent.

"And if I do," she said eventually, "there will be nothing to prevent Spain from sailing its armada to England to claim the crown which Mary has placed upon its head."

"Is there an answer?" Grace asked.

"No! There is no right answer. Nor is there a wrong answer, for whatever I do, Spain will eventually attack us. This year, next year. And while we are attacking Philip's treasure ships which sail from the New World, we are a constant source of hatred to him. Every day, some of my ministers beg me to attack him even more, and others beg me to desist from causing him greater irritation."

"What does Sir Francis Walsingham believe?"

"He says to attack. He and Raleigh beg me to allow Sir Francis Drake to burn the Spanish ships in Cadiz Harbor. But Philip is no fool—yes, he's painfully slow to act and indecisive, but he will eventually complete the building of his vast naval flotilla and send it against us. I have neither the time nor the wit nor the money to build a navy as large as his."

Suddenly Grace saw what it was that the Queen of England wanted of her.

"I will not give you my ships to fight the Spaniards. Not while you are fighting against my people," she said vehemently.

In anger, Elizabeth turned and shouted, "Do not presume to tell me what you can and cannot do, what you will and will not do. Madam, I hold your life in my hands."

Stung and surprised by the sudden change of mood, Grace withdrew. Elizabeth walked on in silence.

"Understand this, Mistress Grace O'Malley. Your life and that of your son are nothing to me when I am considering the safety of my realm. I am shortly to be in a state of war. I have avoided war while ever I have been able throughout my reign. Because I have not been involved in any great and horrible battles on foreign soils, my people love me, my treasury is regaining its stability after it was denuded by my own father and his daughter Mary Tudor, and England is at peace. But I am soon to be attacked, and for the love of my people I must defend myself. I can compel you to give me your ships. I can impound them and then requisition them and oblige you to my service. But if I did that, I would be in danger of your men turning and fighting my own sailors. This I know. So there is another way; and it is this of which I wish to speak."

Still reeling from the Queen's sudden attack upon her, Grace felt herself flush with fear, and she listened silently as Elizabeth said, "The current leader of King Philip's naval armed forces is the Marquess of Santa Cruz, Don Alvaro de Bazan, who, though elderly and infirm, is still the best naval commander in the Spanish fleet. Now, Mistress O'Malley, there are two ways for the marquess to attack England. One is from the east, by landing in Holland and there being joined by the Duke of Parma and his troops. The other is to use Ireland as a staging post, to re-equip himself there, and then to attack from the west while Parma attacks from the east, so splitting my forces into two.

"Should he decide on the latter course, I want you and those other Irish lords who do not hold submit and regrant titles, those lords in the west of Ireland especially, to combine with those loyal to me in a force of might, and deny him landing, food, sustenance and all else. I want you and the lords of Ireland to fight him on behalf of England; to damage him and wound him so that when he comes after England, he is a broken man with a broken force. Then my sturdy English acorns will smash his Spanish olives."

The Queen looked at Grace and continued softly, "Understand this. You will be defending a Spanish invasion of Ireland as much as defending England from the Spanish. If England falls to Spain, Ireland will soon after speak Spanish. It is as much in your interests to resist as it is in ours."

She looked at Grace, waiting for a response.

After a long while, Grace replied, "If Philip lands his navy on Irish soil, we will repel him. If he attacks us, we will attack him. That I can promise."

The Queen of England sighed. "Good," she said. "Very good, Mistress Grace."

They walked on for another ten minutes, passing only occasional observations one to the other. And then Elizabeth stopped suddenly.

"Well, I think we've accomplished all we came for. You have your son back, and I have the security of knowing that Ireland will not side with Philip." She turned and began to head back to the palace, now almost hidden by the thickness of the trees.

Once again, Grace dared to be bold. "Ma'am, we're completely alone, and nobody can hear our conversation—"

"Almighty God, Mistress Grace, can hear everything."

"Nobody apart from the Almighty. I have something to ask of you. Earlier I told to you how evilly the women of Ireland are treated when they become widows. Surely you can help us to fight this injustice."

"Yes, I can help you. I shall write to Sir Richard Bingham and tell him that he is to be more sensitive to your needs and those of the other chieftains in his governorship. And now that we are joined in the common enemy of Spain, I will help you with your laws. I shall write to all of my governors of Ireland and command them to institute English law."

Grace looked at the Queen in consternation. She worried that replacing the Brehon Laws with English law might make matters worse for the people of Ireland. But having come so far in her quest to release her son, now was neither the time nor the place to show her disquiet.

"Thank you, Majesty," Grace said, meanwhile intoning a silent prayer for all to be well for Ireland.

They stepped over a dead log, covered with lichens and mushrooms, Grace assisting Elizabeth who found movement cumbersome in her fabulous dress.

"But in time, Grace, you may not thank me. For now that my army is in Ireland, and now that you and the other chieftains who have so far disobeyed my government will accept English law, English rule follows quickly behind for you all. I fear, cousin, that you are the last of your breed. That in you lives much of Old Ireland, and with your death, a new and different Ireland will arise, one governed from London. Perhaps it's time for you and those who fight me to accept the responsibility of being English. Why, I shall even grant you a title . . . a dukedom. And the title will suit you. Her Grace, the Duchess of Connaught."

And the Queen of England burst out laughing.

"Grace is now held in good grace . . . do you see?"

Grace O'Malley saw but, unlike the sycophants of the English court, could find no reason to laugh.

When they had cleared the woods, and Greenwich Palace stood large and dominant in front of them, separated only by the beauty of the green lawns, the Queen suddenly stopped. She gestured toward the aviary, a smile on her face.

"In our short time together, Grace, we have discussed much. I know that you still look upon me as a great and potent monarch, but in some ways I am like these birds. I am caged by the court and those who guard my interests.

"There are times when I just want to fly free of the constraints. To be myself, and not what people want me to be."

And then she smiled again. "Grace O'Malley, I have a request for you, which you may not grant if you don't wish to, but I will be eternally grateful to you if you do."

Grace was mystified. Elizabeth whispered the request into her ear. Grace almost stepped backward in shock.

"Are you certain, Majesty?"

"If you will do it, then I am certain."

"But—"

"But what, cousin? But the danger? I am confident in your presence. But the propriety? I am England, and for me there is no impropriety. But my ministers? Ah, there you have me, so it must remain our secret.

"So what say you, cousin Grace O'Malley? Will one elderly lady grant such a wish to another elderly lady?"

"Of course I will, Majesty. Of course I will."

The Queen of England beamed a smile, and walked briskly back to Greenwich Palace, her step lighter than when she had set out.

Chapter Twenty-two

Nonesuch Palace, Midsummer, 1588

Even Sir Francis Walsingham, despite having ignored most of Elizabeth's mood swings during the nearly fifteen years in which he had faithfully served her, was worried about the state of health engendered by her fury.

Indeed, several ladies had left the presence chamber in fear of their sanity, afraid that the Queen's melancholic wrath and furies would transfer by some agency from her mind into theirs, or somehow spread through the ether to infect the room, like the stories they'd heard of mass hysteria developing from evil humors emanating from a devil in a depraved mind.

Several councillors had attempted to mollify the Queen's distress, but to no avail. Indeed, any interruption to her vehemence seemed to stoke the fires which were flaming within her.

It was all the fault of the book. She flung it to the ground in disgust; her whole court reeled back from the venomous thing as though it was a snake let loose.

"Majesty," Walsingham tried, "this cardinal is a traitor to all England. His words are a mockery of the truth and a travesty of God's own reason, but—"

"His words are the stuff of the Devil!" she screamed. "His words are infamy and they offend our eyes and ears. At the beginning of my reign, Walsingham, I was assaulted by such diatribes. But I've proven myself worthy to be called England's greatest monarch, greater than my father and all who went before him. Did they call my father's reign 'the Age of Henry'? No! Yet poets and scribes call this the Age of Elizabeth. And despite what I have done for England, despite the sacrifices I have made for this great land, sacrificing my very own body and womanhood for my country, yet still I am attacked by this damnable Church of Rome.

"This cardinal should be burned at the stake for his perversion of the truth. He is no Englishman; he is a turncoat Italian, a Papal lapdog, a sniveling hound who licks the shite from his master's slippers. And to think that England bred him, nurtured him, educated him, made him canon at York, and now he sits in the pocket of the Pope and writes these . . . these foul and pestilential evils about me, diatribes which are so scurrilous as to make the Angels of God weep for their infamy. And at a time when our nation is under such dire threats from Catholic Philip."

Walsingham again tried to speak, but Elizabeth shouted over him, opening Cardinal William Allen's latest treatise against the Protestant Queen. "Listen to this," she hissed, flicking through the pages until she came to the particular piece. "This bastard Englishman, this Catholic, this priest calls me the supposed daughter of my supposed father Henry. He calls me an incestuous bastard, begotten and born in sin of an infamous courtesan.

"What, Walsingham? Am I supposed to ignore this? Am I supposed to remain silent in the face of this blasphemous heresy? Surely you of all people want me to stand on the rooftops of all my palaces and shout to all my subjects who might read this heresy, that I am not born of a courtesan, but of a beloved queen whose only crime was in being unable to bear my father a son? Surely you—"

"Enough, Majesty! Enough, I say!" Walsingham shouted. "These are unworthy words for you to read and we have neither the time nor the wit to consider them when our very nation is at risk. We have great matters of state to deploy. Enough of this Willam Allen and his nonsense! We cannot waste precious moments dealing with the tittle-tattle of Rome's priesthood, while Philip of Spain sharpens his fangs and digs his claws into our throat."

Even the Queen was taken aback by being shouted at. Nobody had ever shouted at her, not since she was a little girl.

Walsingham had been driven beyond the bounds of frustration by the petty matters which were currently torturing Elizabeth and which might eventually distract her altogether and overshadow the vital task of discussing grave matters of state, such as the preparations for the imminent invasion. But by the sudden silence in the room, and when he saw Elizabeth staring at him in shock, Walsingham immediately realized what he'd done, and felt the executioner's sword against his neck. He paled at his own lack of subtlety.

"Forgive me, Your Highness," he whispered. The court had become so silent that nobody dared breathe. "I forgot, I . . . Majesty, I . . ."

Yet by a miracle, his shouting seemed to have brought some rationality back to Elizabeth. For she looked at him, put the book aside and nodded.

"No, dear cousin Walsingham. You have nothing for which to be forgiven. You are right. There are matters far weightier than these empty words. Today Mr. Allen has his day, but come tomorrow, a queen shall still rule England while he tries to look at the sun from beneath the Pope's vestments."

The Queen picked up a goblet of malmsey, drank deeply to refresh her spirits, and looked at her court. "Cousins," she said loudly, "my Lord Walsingham reminds us that Philip of Spain is the enemy and not the Pope in Rome. Our duty is to protect England from the rapacious Spaniards, and Mr. Allen will have to wait for another day. Now, how are the preparations for our coming war?"

The elderly and gaunt Earl of Leicester stepped painfully and slowly to the front of the throng. He looked and felt exhausted, knowing that he had only been saved from the ignominy of his recent failed leadership of the Dutch army against the Spanish Duke of Parma by the slender thread of love which Elizabeth still felt for him. The knot in his stomach seemed to be growing every day, and the ailment had weakened him greatly, yet there was still, deeply buried within the jowls and weight of his gluttonous life, a vestige of the Robert Dudley whom the Queen had once loved so dearly. He was ending his days, and had been given the task of preparing England for the invasion, despite his debacle leading the troops of the Netherlands.

"Majesty," he said, his voice slow and deep with age, "England is as well prepared for the coming invasion of Spain as she possibly can be. As Your Majesty knows, the major harbors of England have been braced and strengthened against an attack. Artillery and other cannon have been placed in strategic positions so that any Spanish adventurer who dares to enter our sacred waters will be blown into the very firmament itself. Land defenses have also been fortified, and clifftops on the southern coast have been armed with batteries of cannon. Furthermore, eleven new and powerful ships of the line have been built and are bulging with cannon to smite our foe. We have built a chain of beacons on all the clifftops to signal the arrival of the invasion and inform our English gallants to prepare themselves to defend their homeland.

"By your command, Your Royal Highness, twelve other older ships have been brought back into service. In addition we have requisitioned stores for a protracted sea battle, and recruited additional soldiers and sailors."

He bowed, and retreated backward to the periphery of the chamber, where a seat had been prepared for him. He hoped that the crowd would prevent the Queen from seeing that he could barely stand on his feet for more than a few minutes at a time. At moments like these, when the pains in his stomach were very great, he felt as though the Devil himself was inside him. The potions which the doctors had given him to balance his humors seemed to produce large amounts of stinking wind but no relief from the pain.

"I thank my dear and eternal friend and councillor, the Earl of Leicester. Yes, we are well prepared for the impertinent adventure of King Philip."

The Queen turned to her other favorite. "Cousin Walsingham, what of the parley between Dr. Valentine Dale and the Duke of Parma?"

Walsingham stepped forward and said, "It has come to nothing, Majesty. Your former ambassador to Paris met with the Duke of Parma, and although both parties expressed the great desire that no further action should be taken in the king's adventure, the discussion was held on the very day that the Spanish fleet set sail. Majesty, thirty thousand men under the command of the Duke of

Medina-Sidonia put to sea in one hundred and thirty vast galleons. They sailed from Lisbon for England. We have placed your fleet at Plymouth on battle-station preparedness. These Spanish galleons carry much armament as well as vast hoards of treasure. Naturally, they are laden with the trappings of Catholicism, as well as—"

He fell silent. The Queen knew that he was holding something back from her, and said, "Well, Master Secretary?"

"It is of no consequence, ma'am."

"Walsingham. I shall decide what is and is not of consequence."

"Ma'am, it is a trifling matter which will insult your ears as greatly as the monstrous book by—"

"Walsingham! What is it that you hold from me?"

"Just some petty leaflets."

He looked at her and still hesitated. His spies in Lisbon had managed to purloin some of the leaflets as they were being loaded onto the ships. He knew that they would make the Queen of England furious beyond words.

"Leaflets?" she asked.

"The Papal Bull, reconfirming your excommunication and blessing the enterprise. It is King Philip's intention that the Duke of Medina-Sidonia should distribute these leaflets to all English Protestants when they reach our shores and he marches toward London. It calls upon all English subjects to depose you, and says that you will be tried for usurpation, treason and heresy when victory is theirs and the King of Spain becomes King of England."

He waited for the Queen's explosion. But he was surprised when she said, "Then we must rob him of his victory and deny the Pope's slippers their footfall on my green and pleasant land. I shall want a thousand sheets of the Bull delivered to my palaces throughout the land, so that I and all my ladies may wipe our arses on them."

The court applauded, this time not for reasons of sycophancy, but because of the bravery the Queen was showing in the face of such grave danger. When the applause had died down, she asked, "Tell me, I know nothing of this Duke of Medina-Sidonia. What of him? What is he like?"

Sir Francis Drake stepped forward at the invitation of Walsingham, and said, "He is of trifling consequence, ma'am. Had the enemy been led by the Marquess of Santa Cruz, I would be most fearful of our chance of victory. He was a canny sea dog, that Santa Cruz, and no mistake. Outwitted many a brave French or English captain, he did.

"But since God recalled the brave and excellent seaman to His side, the King of Spain has appointed Medina-Sidonia as his commander. And a more unlikely commander you will not find. He has been selected because of his exalted station among the Spanish nobility, presumably in the hope that the other Spanish nobles commanding ships will obey his instructions. Yet our spies in the court of Spain say that the duke has written to the king, telling him of his great displeasure at being recruited for this exalted station. The Duke of Medina-Sidonia, it seems, was brave enough to tell the King of Spain that he has no experience in commanding ships, or navies, and that he is better fitted to the life of a nobleman in a great castle than that of a sailor on the sea. Yet the king rejected his entreaties and commanded him to lead the invasion. The king, it appears, told the duke that he will give him exact and precise instructions as to how to sail, where to sail, and how to fight the battle to ensure success. And now, Your Majesty, the tragic bastard sails north, not knowing the difference between sail and rudder, port and starboard, nor his arse from his elbow."

Elizabeth burst out laughing. Drake's broad and irreverent Devonshire accent always amused her, and she loved his dismissive ways. But there was danger in his attitude.

"Dear Francis," she said to him, "while we may question the King of Spain's competence, it is dangerous to underestimate the size and might of the forces rallying against us. We in England have neither the time nor the treasury to compete with Philip's armed and massing forces. And his armada of ships imperils our island England."

"Rubbish, Your Majesty," interrupted Drake, who was renowned for not giving a damn about court protocol, "the very size of his navy is his disadvantage. And even with Philip's might, we have other advantages. His galleons are massive, slow to maneuver and turn. Our English ships are smaller and swifter;

with our ability to turn on a nun's tit, we can fire our volleys to starboard, and by the time the Spanish captains have looked at the damage, we can be round to port and firing off another round."

Elizabeth nodded. "Then put your faith in English ingenuity and seamanship, Captain Drake, for if it comes to might, we have a pretty battle on our hands."

The first sail of the armada was sighted by Tom the crofter, a crippled farmer who lived off the charity of his sons, having fallen halfway down a cliff as he was returning drunk one night from the Turk's Head Inn three miles from his home. Barely able to walk, even on his crutches, Tom had been given the task of watching in daylight hours for any sign of the Spaniards.

At first, he looked closely, for the tiny speck of white on the horizon could have been a gull or an albatross or even a cloud. But it didn't wheel in circles, nor float across the sky at the behest of the wind. It grew moment by moment, and was quickly joined by others which appeared like white rabbit ears out of their burrows. As he stood and stretched, and blinked and cleared his eyes and took another swig from the bottle of rum, the gulls or albatrosses or clouds became a vast panoply of sail which seemed to stretch halfway across the horizon.

Terrified by the enormity of the spectacle appearing before him, he remained inert, rooted like a tree to the spot. He had been commanded to run as quickly as his bent legs would carry him across to the brazier, where he would strike the flint, light the straw and alert the rest of England to the advancing Spanish navy. But instead of running, he stared with increasing apprehension, and then horror, at the incalculable might of arms sailing unimpeded toward him. He had heard rumors in the inn that Spanish Philip was sending the greatest number of ships the world had ever seen to destroy England, but the tales always seemed to grow with the consumption of ale. Now, however, he was the first man in all England to see for himself that the tales were true. How could England possibly defend herself against this host of evil angels sent from beyond the seas?

He couldn't move, he was so terror-struck. It was as though God had taken from him his legs and placed his trunk in the ground, for try as he might, he couldn't get his useless legs to work, not even to hobble to his crutches to alert his people. Instead, he called out, "They're here! The Spanish are here!"

But there was nobody to hear his words. The Lizard was a lonely windswept spot on the southernmost corner of England, fit only for cliff-side gannets and foxes and hares.

With courage born of a lifetime of struggling against the weather and the vicissitudes of the Almighty, Tom tried to count the number of ships, but his ignorance made him incapable of going beyond twelve. However, he knew from looking at the multitude of galleons looming over the horizon that his figure was far fewer than were approaching, and he cursed himself for his inability to read, write or count. But it impelled him to grab his crutches and shuffle quickly over to the brazier, where his was the first smoky beacon to alert England to its greatest peril since William of Normandy had crossed the Channel in 1066.

As guards further north and east saw the column of smoke rising into the air, they rushed to light their own. Within an hour, news had arrived in the coastal city of Plymouth, where Admiral Lord Howard of Effingham was lying in wait, assisted by Sir Francis Drake and the English fleet of one hundred and fifty ships flying the green and white colors of the Tudor monarchy from their masts.

The moment a scout returned from the high cliffs down to Raleigh's former vessel, the flagship *Ark Royal*, and told the admiral that the beacon had been sighted, Effingham turned to Drake, the much more experienced seafarer.

"Well?"

"Not yet, Admiral. We'll wait till they're upon us. I'd rather come at them from their portside as the sun is behind us, than meet them in open water where we'll be visible for five miles and allow them time to turn and engage us in their own spaces."

Effingham nodded. Although he was commander of the fleet, he'd made it very clear to Queen Elizabeth that he intended to bow to the greater experience of Sir Francis Drake in matters of guile and strategy.

· · ·

When the fleet was first sighted, Queen Elizabeth was walking in the grounds of the home of Sir Edward Parry in Portsmouth, two hundred and fifty miles away, thinking of the strategy which she and her ministers had developed. It was now well known from Walsingham's spies that the Spanish fleet was sailing along the French coast to meet with the Duke of Parma's 16,000 troops stationed at Dunkirk, waiting for the escort to attack England and enter through either the Thames or through Eastbourne or Hastings. The threat to England from the Spaniards massing in Ireland had been negated by direct order from the King of Spain to the Duke of Medina-Sidonia. Elizabeth, on the other hand, had given Effingham and Drake permission to act as they saw fit under the circumstances.

When the messenger came running to tell her, she reacted calmly, and whispered in his ear to run to the harbor and inform the captain of the ship called the *Richard Bourke* that it would soon be time for her to set sail. The Queen gave the messenger a gold piece and commanded him to tell no one of his mission.

As night was beginning to fall, the distant lights of the Spanish ships, like stars hung low in the sky, slowly appeared as the armada sailed across the water. It appeared as though an entire evening city had miraculously come into being on the horizon.

On the dockside the crews of the English fleet stood staring, not out to sea, but upward toward the distant hill. The lookout stationed there, high above the city, suddenly waved his lantern three times to the right, three times to the left. The sailors suddenly burst into cheers—the time had come.

Captain Drake turned to Effingham and said tersely above the hurrahs of the mob, "Now, Admiral."

It wasn't a question, rather it was a statement that Drake's ship would be the first out of port, and all others would follow him.

The admiral ordered lanterns to be lit, to signal the English fleet to move out past the Eddystone rocks and engage with the enemy.

The messenger bowed low as he handed the Queen of England the slip of paper which he had brought from Plymouth. He was the last of twenty dispatch riders, and the message had taken a mere fifteen hours to travel the distance. Elizabeth tore it open and scanned its contents. Only Walsingham knew what it would say, for his own service had brought him the information half an hour before that of her Majesty's. Diplomatically, though, he had decided to allow her to break the news, though he allowed himself a slight smile.

She was seated on a high chair in the banqueting hall of Parry House in Portsmouth. She cleared her throat, and began reading.

> *By the Grace of God, to Elizabeth, beloved Monarch and Queen of England from her loyal and devoted subject, Lord Howard of Effingham, Admiral and Commander of Your Majesty's Fleet at Portsmouth, this 20th day of July, Anno Domini 1588. Be pleased to Know, Highness, by these presents, that your loyal shipmen engaged with the Spanish Enemy sent to our shores by Philip of Spain, accursed in the Eyes of the Almighty, and there we did battle. It was not a mighty battle, Majesty, for it was our intention to strafe the enemy and determine his strengths and weaknesses and count his fire-power.*
>
> *But know you and all England that your Majesty's sailors all acquitted themselves most gallantly and although the skirmish yesterday was brief, we have bloodied the cur and he now sails, bested, to Calais in France.*
>
> *Majesty, Your fleet is following the dogs of Spain and we will engage him once again near Portland, off the Dorset Coast.*
>
> *God Save the Queen. God Bless England.*

The court cheered. Elizabeth smiled, and nodded in satisfaction. When the noise had died down, she said, "The first blood is ours. It appears that we have lost no sailors or ships, and that the Spaniards have felt the sting of the English wasp."

Walsingham walked forward and bowed, a mischievous smile on his face. "Unfortunately, Majesty, the first blood is not ours, but that of the Almighty. One of your sailors, with too much ale in his body, was so anxious to engage with the Spaniards that even before Drake and the fleet had left the harbor of Plymouth, this gallant man drew his pistol and fired in the general direction of the sea. Yet because his eyes were dimmed by the drink, his shot went askew, and he accidentally shot the captain's dog, a favorite of the crew. The man was relieved of his pistol and his station and spent the first engagement with the enemy sound asleep in the ship's hold."

Elizabeth and the court burst out laughing.

"Kindly send one of my dogs to the captain of the ship in question, and wish him well."

"On a somewhat more serious matter, Majesty, now that the armada from Spain is here, we must take precautions with your person. It is not wise for you to be in Portsmouth, Your Highness. As the Spaniards move closer and closer to the Duke of Parma at Dunkirk, it has become imperative that we leave the south coast and travel back to London. The Earl of Leicester has assembled four thousand troops at Tilbury in the estuary of the River Thames in order to guard the approaches to London should, Heaven forefend, Parma manage somehow to break our shire levies and musters. Leicester has built a blockage of ships across the river's width, so no Spaniard can reach England by water.

"I shall make the arrangements for Your Majesty to decamp immediately, and the remainder of the court will follow—"

"No, Walsingham."

The secretary was surprised and silenced.

"No! I will not leave. The fleet is some time away. It is, according to my best advice, being followed by Drake and Effingham and they will act as shadows to the Spaniards all the way along the Channel. They inform me that they will engage the fleet from the rear, periodically, both as a way of damaging Spanish morale and damaging Spanish ships. They will sail rapidly into the fleet, fire off volleys and do much damage, but before the mighty galleons can turn and engage, they will sail out of range. It will be like gnats infuriating a dog.

"By Drake's reckoning, and this is confirmed in the message from Effingham, the engagements will begin at Portland, and continue through toward Portsmouth. My mind is firm on this, cousins, for I do not want my people, England, to think that at the first sight of the Spaniards, their mother turned and ran for the protection afforded by my palaces. No, Walsingham, a king's place is with his troops."

The court began to shout in disagreement, for many were afraid that the battle in the Channel could go either way and if the Spaniards, who vastly out-manned and outgunned the English, were to triumph, then the Queen's person must be secured behind lines which could be fortified.

But she held up her hand to silence opposition, and then climbed down from her chair.

Chapter Twenty-three

Elizabeth rode her horse gently down to the docks, attended only by Lady Rouche, who disliked riding at the best of times, and especially alone with the Queen in a rough port city, in the early hours of the morning.

It was two days after the Queen had received the rapturous news of the battle against the Spaniards off Portland. Unlike the first engagement, which had been more to establish the presence of the English forces and to test the Spanish mettle than to do real damage, this battle went badly for the Spanish.

It was in part the fault of the orders given by the King of Spain which instructed the Duke of Medina-Sidonia to sail without any delay and not to engage in any battles whatsoever before he had met with the Duke of Parma in Dunkirk. But that was only part of the reason, because much of the fault lay with the almost total inexperience of the hapless Spanish duke himself. While a competent administrator of his estates and treasuries, his understanding of maritime war was nil. So when Drake and the English fleet suddenly appeared fast and furious out of the morning sun off Portland Bill, and sailed directly toward them, intent, it seemed, on ramming them, Medina-Sidonia ordered evasive action to be taken. To Drake's amazement, the Spanish ships turned their rears to the English instead of engaging them portside with a fusillade of cannon. Several of the Spanish galleons were severely injured in the first half hour of the skirmish. Drake's men sailed so close to the galleons that the massive super-structures towered over them and the Englishmen feared that the Spaniards would throw cannonballs down onto their decks by hand. Certainly the Spanish cannon couldn't be moved, remounted or aimed to fire downward.

In disgust at not having a worthy enemy to fight, Drake ordered his men to withdraw. He'd sunk three ships, and that had showed him that the Spaniards were like gigantic whales, wallowing in the water. As soon as the fleet sailed into the narrows between France and England, he'd have them. This he promised his queen. By her judgment and best advice, Elizabeth thought the Spaniards would now be off the Isle of Wight, ready to turn south toward Calais where they would meet the Duke of Parma's men, and then from there to England for the invasion.

This was where the English fleet would properly engage with the Spaniards. This was where Drake and Effingham would attack. At midnight they would let loose the hell-burners, fire-ships packed to the gunnels with wood and pitch. The fire-ships would sail unmanned toward the Spaniards, either at sea or moored in Calais Harbor. They would be unstoppable. They would set fire to the sails of the galleons, which would then ignite the ropes which would drop and set aflame the wooden decks and the railings, and ignite the gunpowder and create an incandescence which would be Hell on earth, impossible to put out, and spread quickly from vessel to vessel.

And as the Spaniards were distracted, vainly trying to stop the flames from spreading to their other ships, Drake would pound them with cannon fire.

Elizabeth imagined the scene, and suddenly felt pity for the Spanish men and their womenfolk waiting at home, and the children who would always wonder why their fathers hadn't returned.

Soon they arrived at the harbor, and in the dull light of the early dawn Elizabeth looked for the red lantern-light on the masthead. She identified the *Richard Bourke* and stepped off her horse.

"You may return, madam. And remember, whoever asks for me, tell them that I am confined to bed with a malady. I shall be better in the morning."

"Highness," Lady Rouche protested, "I cannot leave the Queen of England unattended."

"As the Queen of England, I say you will. Now, madam, be off, and do as I command."

Without waiting for a reply, Elizabeth turned and walked along the pier. She was greeted at the *Richard Bourke* by a woman she hadn't seen for some time.

"Mistress O'Malley. How do you do?"

Grace curtsied. "See, I've learned how to do this since our last meeting."

Elizabeth smiled. "You've learned to do it well, Mistress Grace. And may I thank you for remembering our bargain."

"How could I forget it, Majesty? Walking in the woods with the Queen of England, and being importuned to assist her in hiding away like some guilty Papist and sailing out to see a sea battle. I've been waiting every day these two years for this adventure."

The Queen walked toward the gangplank, but because the ship was high in the water, it was pitched at a steep angle.

"I wonder if you would ask your men to assist an old lady. My bones are stiffer than yours."

Two men from Grace's crew jumped over the side of the ship and assisted the Queen of England to board.

When the two women faced each other, taking measure of how the other had aged during the past two years, Grace asked, "Tell me, Majesty, do I have to be formal?"

"No. I want no formality here. There is enough at court. No, here I want the freedom of which I've dreamed since I was a girl of twenty, running about the fields of England. The freedom of the wind in my hair, of the smell of the sea, of seeing my navy victorious."

"Then, ma'am, would you like to be one of the lads and help me with the ropes and the rigging?"

The Queen laughed. "No, that I will not do. God forbid that the Queen of England does anything akin to laboring. No, Mistress Grace, this is your domain. When we are at sea, you are the ship's master."

Grace curtsied once more, mainly because she'd spent a month practicing to get it right, and then began to give instructions to her crew for sailing. "Let go f'ward; let go aft; push away. Mr. O'Farrell, lower the mizzen topsail; push off aft."

Queen Elizabeth watched as thirty or more men jumped to action at the behest of this remarkable woman. Old enough to be a grandmother, white-haired, yet strong and straight with a noble and weather-beaten face, Grace was queen of her domain, strutting around the deck, checking with measured determination, ordering and cajoling and sometimes demanding, yet always with some degree of respect for those around her. Elizabeth smiled to herself.

Yes, she thought, this could indeed have been a Queen of Ireland if her birth or luck had had it.

It wasn't until late in the afternoon, when the sun was almost at the point of disappearing into the distant Atlantic Sea, that Grace put down the opticometer and said, "There they are."

She handed the device, which she had been told was now called a telescope, over to the Queen, and pointed in the direction of the setting sun. Elizabeth held the device to her eyes and squinted, looking through it until she was able to focus on a distant point. She reacted in shock, for once-distant clouds were suddenly near to her face, and birds, which were mere specks on the horizon, were now close enough for her to see clearly. She took away the instrument from her eye, and looked again at the distance to check that nothing had altered. Then she put the remarkable instrument to her eye again, delighted at being able to see clearer and further than she'd ever seen before.

"This is a handsome and devilish device, Grace."

"It has enabled me to see further than other captains, and so prepare myself for piracy long before the fat and slow merchant ships knew I was upon them."

"And did you invent it?"

"No, ma'am. Spectacle-makers from Holland have known of the properties of such lenses for many years. But by putting two special lenses into a tube, it enables us to see much further than with the eye the Almighty gave us."

"So, where are the Spaniards?" the Queen asked.

Grace pointed out the white sails which were growing on the horizon as they neared moment by moment.

"Dear God in Heaven," the Queen exclaimed in horror. "There are hundreds of ships."

She put down the telescope and turned to Grace. Her white and lined face somehow seemed to blanch even whiter, her thin frame appeared to sink into her dress and cloak. Grace realized that she was looking at an elderly and frightened woman, not a Queen of England, regal, resplendent and omnipotent.

"How in God's name are we supposed to triumph?" she whispered to Grace.

The Irish woman stepped close to her and put her hand on Elizabeth's arm. "Don't worry. You have good and fast ships against these lumbering dull-witted tardy-gaits. These," she said, contemptuously spitting over the side in the general direction of the Spaniards, "are like old fat lords of the manor who have just eaten a large meal. They're dull-wits, slow to move, slow to turn, slow to react. Over the horizon, out of sight, you have a hoard of buzzing insects with vicious stings, set to pounce and send these frothy malignancies down to the bottom of the Channel."

Elizabeth smiled. "I pray to God you're correct. For if you aren't, then England is lost forever."

As she spoke the words, the first mate, Mr. O'Farrell, came toward them with two mugs of mulled wine. Without any of the ceremony due to the Queen, he said, "Thought you ladies might like some refreshment. Evening's turning a bit chill."

Gratefully, the Queen and Grace reached for the hot drinks. Grace said, "Well, Mr. O'Farrell, what do you think of the Spanish armada?"

He looked over the bow toward the west. The sails of the fleet, now lit by the descending sun, looked as though they were flames in the water. There were over one hundred vessels visible, and growing in number all the time . . . and there was no sign yet of the English fleet following them.

O'Farrell shrugged, and said laconically, "It's a big enough fleet, but I'd hate to be its commander."

"Why?" asked the Queen.

"Ships of that ilk? Cost a fortune to make and a fortune to replace. They make a lot of sound and fury, but they don't respond quickly to the turn of the wheel or the breath of the wind. Too big, you see. Good for carrying vast amounts of cargo, but useless in a battle. Mind, if they were in a harbor, anchored, and sending fusillades against an on-shore battery, well, they'd be very dangerous. But at sea, having to respond to the pull of the tide or the change of a wind to get the best advantage . . . why, they'll be like great dead weights. If they needed to change sail, it'd take them too long and they'd lose their advantage. No, Your Majesty, a good five dozen Irish pirate vessels could send that lot down to the bottom in half a day."

He turned and walked away without being excused, leaving the Queen to pray, for once in her life, that the English were as competent at sea as the Irish.

Four days after returning to land from her very private adventure on the sea with Grace O'Malley, and having seen the flames of the fire-ships and heard the screaming of the Spaniards as havoc was wreaked off Calais Harbor, the Queen of England was waiting anxiously for news.

When it came, it brought a smile to her face and unbounded joy to her heart. The news was delivered by her favorite, Robert Dudley.

He walked painfully into the presence chamber, carrying a piece of paper which he waved in the air, shouting out from the back of the room, "Ma'am, Your Majesty, Highness . . . great and glorious news. We are won. The English have prevailed."

Without waiting for permission, he pushed past other courtiers and began relating the contents of the letter. "Your admiral tells you that many Spanish ships have been destroyed off France. The hell-burners with their burning pitch and wood were helped on their way by strong winds which blew up in the evening sky. The winds caused the fire to spread more rapidly than we had dared hope, and the panic and distress caused chaos among the grandees and their crews, who didn't know how to deal with such a situation."

He paused, and said, "Great and wonderful news, Your Majesty."

"Please, cousin, continue."

He cleared his throat and continued. "Following the evening engagement, the morale of the Spaniards was at its lowest ebb, and our spies tell us that a number of grandees determined that the adventure was already lost, and petitioned to return to Spain. The Duke of Medina-Sidonia refused, and again pointed to the explicit orders of King Philip.

"But when the light of day dawned, there was still a formidable armada left to face your English navy. The Duke of Medina-Sidonia regrouped what remained of the assembly off Gravelines, near the mouth of the River Aa, close to Dunkirk."

Leicester smiled. "It is a pretty enough town, Majesty, but minstrels will sing not of its beauty nor its sandy beaches, but of the great victory which God gave this day to your island England.

"The Spaniards were waiting for the Duke of Parma to embark, but the duke insisted that he and his men were not yet ready. Concerned about the delay, the Duke of Medina-Sidonia watched in growing fear as the large number of English ships, led by your gallant Captain Drake, sailed rapidly south and began to strafe and attack, again sending in fire-ships. But because of the loss of so many ships, the Spaniards were out-numbered.

"We can only imagine the horror, Your Majesty, as the Duke of Medina-Sidonia saw dozens of his ships being holed and irreparably damaged. In panic, after a long and vicious battle in which few English casualties were reported, the captains of the Spanish ships broke what was left of their ranks and sailed north between Holland and England to escape our wrath. By our estimates, and by the intelligence which has come to us from our spies following the Spanish fleet, the losses are two thousand men and eleven ships. Victory was ours. But even greater joy visited us, Majesty, for as the Spaniards were fleeing from our English sea dogs in disarray, a great wind blew up, a Protestant wind, and sent the Spaniards flying in all directions. Your captain, Sir Francis Drake, said that he has never been as pleased as seeing the enemy flying with a southerly wind northward. He then ordered his ships to go after them, but unfortunately, Majesty, he could do little, for he had expended all his ammunition in the battles of the past three days. Then terrible storms blew up and the enemy was rendered helpless, floating like great lumps of useless detritus in the water, blown hither and thither.

"Captain Drake and Admiral Lord Howard of Effingham continued to chase the retreating Spaniards northward toward Scotland. God save the Queen and our holy enterprise."

The court cheered. Elizabeth looked and saw Grace O'Malley standing in the presence chamber, smiling and nodding. All were ecstatic. Their eyes were wild in the frenzy of victory. Yet none seemed to remember that although the armada was damaged and beyond repair, and being scattered by God's Protestant wind toward Scotland, there was still a vast army under the control of the Duke of Parma waiting in Dunkirk and poised to attack England!

Tilbury, East of London, 9 August 1588

She was not afraid. She was well guarded. The Spaniards were just over the water in France and her ministers had begged her not to go to Tilbury, but she had insisted. Not for herself, but she was most concerned for the safety of England.

Word now reached London from the shores of Scotland that Spanish galleons were beaching in narrows and shallows, and others were sighted off to sea, a pathetic and struggling navy. Effingham had long given up the chase and returned to England in triumph. News came of hundreds of bodies of Spanish sailors being washed up on shore; those unlucky enough to have landed were quickly murdered on the beaches by furious locals, or died in hideous isolation from wounds or starvation.

Yet the second foe, the great army of the Duke of Parma, was preparing to invade, and this was even more deadly, for the 16,000 battle-hardened men had already wreaked their havoc over Europe, expanding the empire of Spain far northward.

Elizabeth, dressed as an armed Pallas in silver breastplate with a small silver and gold truncheon in her hand, rode to the encampment of her army atop a white gelding, led by the Earl of Leicester who walked before her in humility, holding the horse's bridle.

A woman walked behind the Queen. An unknown woman, dressed not in the finery of the court, but rather as a simple yet elegant woman of substance. Occasionally the Queen of England turned to this elderly woman and asked a question. Grace O'Malley answered. She told the Queen of England once again of her adventures as a young woman pirate, how she'd roused her men to heights of courage by telling them that although she was only a feeble woman, she had the heart and mind of any man good and gallant enough to be a sea captain. In this way they passed the time until they arrived at the encampment.

The troops of England were ready for the visit of their queen. They put on a mock battle to show that they were fully prepared and ready for any assault by the Duke of Parma and the Spaniards. Afterward, the Queen rode into the very midst of the men so that she could be heard.

"My loving people," she shouted, "let tyrants fear! I am come among you at this time being resolved in the midst and heat of the battle to live or die among you all, to lay down for my God and for my kingdom, and for my people, my honor and my blood, even in the dust.

"I know I have the body of a weak and feeble woman, but I have the heart and stomach of a king, and a king of England too, and think it foul scorn that Parma and Spain, or any prince of Europe, should dare invade the borders of my realm; to which, rather than any dishonor shall grow by me, I myself will take up arms, I myself will be your general, judge, and rewarder of every one of your virtues."

The men cheered, drowning out the remainder of her speech. Grace O'Malley beamed a smile, thinking back over half a century to the time when she'd been in Tangier.

When the Queen rode out of the crowd, all of whom were kneeling or bowing, she spied the Irish pirate woman and asked her to walk beside, rather than behind her, back to the great house which temporarily quartered her household.

When the noise of the army was a distant rumble in the background, Grace said, "That was a fine speech, ma'am."

"Thank you, Grace."

They rode on, one woman majestic on her horse, the other majestically walking by her side.

Softly, Elizabeth asked, "Grace, if we are victorious and beat off the Duke of Parma, and all settles back to the way it was, what will you do?"

"Do? I shall return from where I came. To Ireland."

"And what will you do there?"

"I still have battles to fight with your governor, Sir Richard Bingham. I have to save my family and my people from his avarice and brutality."

"I told you that I have written to him . . ." the Queen said softly.

Grace held her breath. Should she tell the Queen, in her moment of glory, that despite her letter, Bingham was still merciless?

Elizabeth knew from Grace's silence that the letter had achieved nothing. "I shall write to him again, and command him to desist from his practices of destroying the love which the people of Ireland should enjoy of their English cousins."

They progressed through the woods which lined the banks of the entryway to the River Thames until they came to within sight of the house where the Queen's servants were waiting.

Elizabeth reined in her horse and looked down at Grace. Old now, she must have looked very wonderful when she was young—tall and straight, with vivid red hair, strands of which still grew among the white. Elizabeth wondered if they would have been friends had they been girls growing up together. And quickly realized that they would, indeed, have been true and firm companions, girls who loved each other and shared secrets and went on daring adventures together.

If only circumstances had been otherwise.

"Even if I write to all of my governors in Ireland, Grace," Elizabeth said, "even if I remove the impediments to your future happiness, there is still a great obstacle which we have to discuss. That, madam, is the life of crime you have led, the assaults against my ships, my merchants, my treasure."

Grace turned in anger, and began to speak, but Elizabeth lifted her hand to command silence. "It is my intention to forgive you your piracy, and your men too. I shall award you a stipend, an annuity so that you may live in comfort with your children and grandchildren."

Grace realized that she had stopped breathing.

"Yet all this is on one condition," continued the Queen, "which is that when you have your beloved grandchildren on your knee and you are relating to them the stories of your voyages and adventures, you'll tell them that your greatest adventure was to welcome aboard your boat the greatest queen in all of Christendom. The Virgin Queen, Elizabeth Gloriana. Tell them of my bravery in the face of the Spanish foe, of how this little island fought and won against the greatest navy in the history of all the world. That, Grace O'Malley, I command you."

Grace smiled, and said, "And that, Majesty, I shall do willingly. You truly are a great queen. In these last weeks I've seen how you have managed to command the love and fear and respect of your people. If only we had a queen such as you in Ireland, we wouldn't be in these difficulties."

Elizabeth smiled. "But you do have such a queen, Grace."

The Irish woman looked up in surprise.

Elizabeth could barely contain her amusement. "Me," she said.

Grace O'Malley burst out laughing.

As did the Queen of England. For Elizabeth realized that whatever happened, the Duke of Parma would never win on English soil while ever she was queen, while ever she commanded such a fine army, and while ever she had such loyal and loving subjects as Grace O'Malley, Queen of the Irish Pirates.

Author's Note

Grace O'Malley should by rights be as well known to us as any extraordinary woman in history. Her astonishing life as a pirate in the era of Elizabeth I, her role as a leader of men and a dominant force in Irish politics, has largely been ignored. Indeed, she has effectively been written out of history.

Grace is a fascinating character whose influence is still felt in Ireland to this day. At Howth Castle, a place is permanently set at the dinner table for unexpected visitors because of the row Grace caused when she turned up one day and was not afforded the hospitality due to her as an Irish chieftain. It is even rumored that, through marriage, Grace was an ancestor of the late Lord Louis Mountbatten, and hence a distant relative of Queen Elizabeth II.

Writing about Grace has been a privilege and a pleasure. When creating a fictional work based on a real character, a novelist is often torn between real-life events and the needs of the narrative. In the case of Grace O'Malley, so little is known of her that liberties could be taken without too much risk of offense. Nonetheless, this is a work of fiction and so I have altered and omitted certain minor details of Grace's life for the sake of the plot, and ask any scholar with knowledge of Grace and her circumstances to please forgive me.

My thanks go to Eva, Georgina, Jonathan and Raffe, my long-suffering family, for their good grace while I was wrestling with the complexities of this woman.

Thanks, as always, to the wonderful people at HarperCollins for their patience, insight and imagination: Brian Murray, Shona Martyn, Linda Funnell, Nicola O'Shea, Christine Farmer, Jim Demetriou, Darian Causby, and Karen-Maree Griffiths; and particular thanks to my eagle-eyed and visionary freelance editor, Julia Stiles.

My sincerest thanks go to the wonderful people in Penguin and NAL who have supported me in every measure, especially Laura Cifelli, Rose Hilliard, Julie Samara, Francesca Belanger, Phil Wilentz, and Sally Franklin. While I was looking backwards toward the time of Queen Elizabeth, they were taking care of the present and the future.

I am represented throughout the world by the best literary agency there is, and my special thanks go to Tara Wynne of Curtis Brown who surely deserves the title of the agent's agent.

Alan Gold
Sydney, Australia
agold@bigpond.net.au

The Pirate Queen

The Story of Grace O'Malley, Irish Pirate

ALAN GOLD

A CONVERSATION WITH
ALAN GOLD

Q. *To what extent do you move between fact and fiction when you are writing about an historical character?*

A. Whenever an author writes about historical events, there's always the element of supposition. We know dates and places and who fought and who lost, but contemporary historians rarely record the conversations which took place in times of momentous events. And don't forget that historians usually record the success of victors, and don't often tell us what happened to history's losers. So when fiction writers take as their subject a real person about whom little is known, provided they stay faithful to the genuine events and the actual outcomes, we're free to roam palaces and ancient streets and to enter rooms and record details and wander about as observers, and then use our imaginations to recreate what might have happened. As to Grace . . . well . . . she was such a towering and impressive woman that you can believe almost anything about her. I certainly do.

Q. *So did what you've portrayed as happening in* The Pirate Queen *between Elizabeth I and Grace O'Malley actually happen?*

A. Grace certainly wrote letters to Elizabeth about the behavior of Sir Richard Bingham which, surprisingly, were answered by her in full. Sir Richard also arrested Grace's brother and son. Grace sailed to England to beg for her family's release; amazingly—and remember that Grace was a pirate—she gained an audience with the Queen, and it is understood that they spent a long time together and became firm friends. Grace left England with a pardon and an order to Sir Richard to give her a lifetime pension. Her son was released soon afterward,

READERS GUIDE

and Sir Richard was replaced in Ireland. As to what was said between the two women, history doesn't tell us . . . but it's fun to imagine what these two extraordinary women spoke about.

Q. *Were there other female pirates apart from Grace O'Malley?*

A. There were three or four female pirates of whom we know something. We know about the exploits of Anne Bonney and Mary Reade who were active as pirates about a century after Grace. But there was also Ching Shih, a Cantonese lady who infested the South China Sea in the early 1800's, and who commanded an astounding 1800 ships and 80,000 pirates. And there were also other women throughout the centuries who took up pirating, though often they were forced to hide their womanhood by dressing and behaving as men. And don't forget that in the time of Elizabeth, non-Military sea-farers also acted as privateers, often sponsored by the aristocracy, who went out to plunder treasure and other ships. While pirates gained a terrible reputation in the 18th and 19th centuries, in the time of Elizabeth, it wasn't quite as bad an occupation as it later became.

Q. *What first drew you to write about Grace O'Malley?*

A. I've always been fascinated by women who have been largely written out of history. I've written about Jezebel (who was given a terrible reputation by the Prophet Elijah in the Book of Kings, but who was probably nothing more than a nature-worshipping Phoenician priestess) and about Gertrude Bell, the Englishwoman who was responsible for inventing modern-day Iraq. When I came across Grace O'Malley, and started to research her, I was appalled that we knew so little about her. She's a larger-than-life genuine heroine who has been buried by the overwhelming reputation of Queen Elizabeth.

And when you think about it, almost all of the women we know about who lived before the 19th century are known to us because they were somebody's daughter or wife or mother or lover. You can count on one hand women in history who have become famous in their own right . . . Hypatia and Artemisia come to mind but very few others. So I've set myself to the task of finding great women who have been written out of history, and recreating their lives.

READERS GUIDE

QUESTIONS FOR DISCUSSION

1. It would have been so easy for Grace O'Malley to settle down to a life of luxury and do what all her friends would have done . . . become a good wife and a good mother. Yet something within her yearned to be free and unconstrained. What qualities does Grace exhibit which were uncommon to her era, and to what extent does the freedom of the sea instill in her the desire for adventure?

2. Henry VIII began the full-scale conquest of Ireland, both of its land and its religion. Elizabeth continued this conquest. How much of a role did Grace's nationalism play in her choice of a career as a sea pirate?

3. The Courts of Elizabeth and Grace were very different. What do you consider the major differences, and what were the similarities?

4. What similarities and differences are there in Elizabeth's relationship with Robert, Earl of Leicester, and Grace's relationship with her second husband, Richard Bourke?

5. Elizabeth was called "The Virgin Queen" of England. Grace, on the other hand, is portrayed in *The Pirate Queen* as a lusty woman of the world. How different would England have been if Grace O'Malley had been Queen of England instead of Elizabeth?

6. What are the similarities and differences between Donal O'Flaherty and Richard Bourke as the husbands of Grace? What is the difference in Grace's attitude to the two men, and how did this influence their treatment of her as a wife? Would her Ottoman lover, the Man of Men, have made a good husband? And would Grace have made a good wife to him if she was forced to live in a harem?